DEAD TEMPTED

BOOK ONE

Pomegranate Seeds

R.M.RAYNE

R. M. Rayne

To the Mincham family, for their undying support.

PROLOGUE

Donovan stumbled on the virgin frost of his manor house garden. It did not matter what he looked at in the shadows, he could not escape the horror he had just witnessed; the inhumanity he had arrived too late to stop.

How had so much blood come from something so small? How had so much evil come from something so beautiful?

He slipped on the icy, cobbled path and his knee hit the floor, the impact jarred his joint and shuddered up his leg, making it slightly numb, but it didn't stop him from protecting the little bundle in his arms.

He had a brief flicker of concern that the child might catch a chill in the mid-winter air, then blood dripped crimson roses onto the frost and he remembered.

The man yelled at the night sky and the moon with its congregation of stars; cursing God and his cruelty.

"He is not here to listen to you, Donovan," a voice hissed behind him. "Nor does he care."

Donovan started and turned around, still on his knees and gripping his precious bundle too tightly.

Firelight leaked from the open doors of his large home, casting shadows on the stones and creating stars in the snowflakes that had begun to fall. The light did not reach the cloak of the midnight figure and it cast no shadow but itself. The thing was tall and wide with strength and somehow also gaunt and deathly, as if a breeze might knock him down but the weight of the world was no burden.

Donovan tried to focus his eyes on the creature. His vision was blurring through the water of his tears and it was easier to stare at the ground than upon the black hollow of the cloak where its face should have been.

"You are him? The one they call master?"

"And you are he who denied me and refused my invitation to join my followers, Baron Wintre."

"You offered me money and power I already have. I will not serve you."

"Is that so? And what if I offered you something you no longer have. A life perhaps?"

Donovan looked down at the baby in his arms; lifeless and cold.

"What do you want?"

"What is it *you* want?" The demon's voice held a thousand souls in one. He stepped closer to Donovan and his bundle, bringing with him the darkness of shadow and a cold to rival the surrounding ice.

Donovan reluctantly loosened his grip so the creature could see into the bundle. He held out a long, black clawed nail and used it to pull out a silver crucifix from within the cloth. The cross skittered down the chain away from the hand that had revealed it.

"Please, help us," Donovan pleaded as the faceless creature looked down at him. "I will serve you, if you bring back my daughter."

"Is the soul of one worth that of many others?"

Donovan's mind hesitated where his heart hadn't. He looked down at the white and red cloth in his arms and his heart won his mind over.

"I will find a way to make it so."

The creature laughed, making Donovan cringe. "We shall

see."

Flurries of snow followed the demon's path into the Under-realm. White flakes hovered in the air around him as he strolled through the emptiness of the void towards a wriggling bundle on the floor.

The creature had returned to his natural human form; finding fingers and thumbs easier to pick up babies than talons and claws. He carefully gathered the bundle from the misty floor, perturbed to find it was not in the ordinary confinements of the Halfpoint.

The baby gurgled and sighed and kicked its legs and arms out, as babies do. The creature grimaced at the display but still found himself staring down at the tiny face of the child. It was a pretty little thing. Most newborns were discoloured and oddly shaped, but this one had eyes that captured him.

He wondered if those eyes would change as time went on. Evil did not discriminate when spreading its corruption; turning optimists to pessimist.

"What are you?" He asked the baby and poked a finger at it. The little thing grabbed the accusing finger and he could *feel* it do so. Not as he usually felt souls - as a human would another's touch - he felt this child like a breeze on rosy cheeks. Real, but impossible to capture.

"Unusual," the creature said and suddenly found it difficult to part with the child. What would this tiny thing be if left to grow to adulthood? He had no use for babies but the possessive sensation that was rising within him made him struggle to part with this soul. It was not an unpleasant emotion, only unfamiliar.

The demon decided then that he would uphold his bargain to Donovan and return his daughter's soul, but only so that she might develop into something more. Something like him. And something he would later come to desire.

He returned them both to the living world.

Donovan was sobbing quietly when the creature blocked

8

his light again.

The man looked from the black mass to the bundle hopefully. The little girl opened her blue eyes and stared up at the stars, then scrunched up her face and opened her mouth in a silent cry, her pink lips wrinkling.

"What's wrong?" Donovan asked, suddenly panicked. "She can't breathe!"

"Give her a moment," the creature said, his voice distant.

Finally, the small thing took a ragged breath and the tears broke over the rim of her pretty, optimistic eyes as she wailed loudly. It was the most precious thing Donovan had ever heard. He pulled his coat around her and his own tears joined hers.

"Thank you."

"Do not thank me yet," the creature said. "This can only be temporary. I need her back, Donovan."

"What?"

"I will gift her to you for twenty-five years then I want her returned to me."

Donovan felt his hopes falling away as he had just received them back. He himself was still several years shy of twenty-five.

"Do not look so concerned. There are worse things. Like what will happen to your wife after this."

Donovan shook his head. "No, not that."

"Return your daughter's soul to me and I will keep your wife's soul safe. In exchange, you will serve me in my Secuutus Letum."

Donovan looked down at the still wailing child. He had not grown to know her yet. Could he really repeat the events of the night, when the child was old enough to understand she was being murdered by her own father?

"Is there nothing else to be done?" Donovan asked quietly.

"No," the creature replied. "Your wife cannot return from this sin. Taking life from the innocent cannot be undone.

This is the choice."

Donovan knew what he wanted. He wanted his wife to be safe and his daughter to be alive. Wasn't all life only temporary anyway? Was twenty-five years enough? It was more than most people had, and less than others. In exchange for an eternity of safety for his wife, it was more than enough.

"I accept," Donovan hung his head in sorrow.

"I thought you might," the creature said, the hint of a smile in his voice.

"And the mark?" Donovan thought he heard a slight growl before a reply came.

"We all have our scars."

"Not like this one." Donovan sensed the wraths displeasure, but he had pulled back the blanket wrappings of the hiccupping babe and seen the slices in her stomach remained, healed but still there.

"There are worse things," the creature repeated. Then, it loomed over Donovan who tried not to flinch as it placed its palm over the man's heart.

Donovan felt something cold and foreign deep within himself and gasped as the demon pulled his hand back, dragging with it an elaborate blue dagger from Donovan's very soul.

Donovan gripped his chest, feeling for blood. There was nothing there but a strange emptiness he couldn't put words to.

The demon placed the dagger on top of the wrapped baby and it seemed to calm. The blue of the blade matched its eyes. The same shade as her mother's.

{For the return of a soul and salvation of another, the servitude of the husband and father}

Light from the still open doorway reached Donovan's face again and he knew the creature had gone. Donovan pulled his weary and stiff body off the cold floor, his pale brown hair damp from the falling snow and his hazel eyes ringed with fatigue and sorrow.

"She has been blessed, we are grateful, Dominus."

Donovan turned to see his wife stood behind him. She was wearing a white night gown, so covered in blood it stuck to her form tightly. Her nipples puckered from the cold and she still had a small stomach left from her pregnancy.

Donovan strode up to her then he struck his wife hard across the face with a closed fist. Her head whipped back and her lip split. Blood from the wound joined the blood from their daughter on her gown.

The baby started wailing again and Donovan pulled his wife to him and hugged her desperately. The bundle crushed between their bodies and the blood that covered the three of them already starting to taint the dagger which was destined to take his daughter's life away from him once more.

GENESIS

Et tenebrae erant super faciem abyssi...
[And darkness was upon the face of the deep]

I

{Good without evil is like light without darkness, which in turn is like righteousness without hope}

Lady Bronwen listened as the actors on the stage performed. Her father and future husband sat beside her in the theatre box, watching with disinterest. They were there for show only - to be seen, not to see others. Bronwen was the opposite. She deliberately sat in the shadows of the curtains, turned towards the stage as best she could be. It didn't matter what the play was, she just enjoyed the escapism.

For a time, Bronwen could forget she was the daughter of Baron Donovan Wintre, only heir to his expansive land and wealth and betrothed to Earl Kole Guild of county Surrey. Bronwen tried not to look at her future husband. He was only a little older than she was, something to be grateful for. Kole was attractive and courteous and intelligent, but she did not love him. Care for him, yes, sometimes deeply, but not love.

They had met at one of her father's many parties, as had been planned. Bronwen had spent most of the evening by herself. She was used to it. She had very few friends. Her father had always discouraged any form of relationship with other people, his intimidating disapproval and almost aggressive manner towards anyone who so much as smiled at Bronwen had eventually forced her into an exile from social interactions.

So, it had come as a shock to her when Lord Guild had strolled over and asked her to dance, neglecting introductions. She remembered glancing over at her father first and awaited his approving nod before she took Kole's hand and allowed him to lead her to the centre of the floor.

"Forgive my forward nature, my Lady," he had said to her as they spun together, Bronwen keeping one eye on her father for any sign she had read his nod incorrectly. He had looked tense, but approving. "I am Lord Kole Guild and I have been waiting a long time to meet you."

"*Earl* Kole Guild?" Bronwen had been surprised. She knew of him of course, but had been unaware that he would be attending the ball and how young he was. It had made sense to her then, why her father had been so agreeable. How could he refuse an Earl? But it was not a matter of refusal and she knew that. It was a matter of social climbing.

Donovan had reached the height of what money could get him, buying his way to a Baronage with the wealth he had earned through a dominant fabric empire. Now the only way to progress was to marry off his only daughter.

Yet, it had still been two more years before Kole had finally proposed to her, and another two before they were due to be wed. The date was set for spring the coming year, following their four-year courtship.

Bronwen stole a glance at Lord Guild, then blushed and looked away when she saw he had been watching her. Kole was reclined back in his chair, relaxed and confident, unlike Bronwen who was straight backed and uncomfortable in her own pale skin.

"I have seen better performances in London," Kole said, a little too loudly for Bronwen's liking. "How do you find it, my Lady?"

Bronwen glanced around the theatre. It was small and plain in decoration. The curtains were a new, bright red like the chair covers and the stone carvings of the pillars were simple. She preferred the intimacy and proximity of the stage compared with the rare shows she had seen in London. She opened her mouth to say as much but saw her father's stern gaze was upon her and stifled her reply.

"I agree, Lord Guild," she said and turned back to the stage. Bronwen could sense he was still looking at her but she refused to meet his gaze. Kole had a complexity to his dark blue eyes that overwhelmed her when she looked into them for longer than a moment. Her own were dull brown like her wavy hair, styled away from her face in a loose braided bun.

"And what are your thoughts, Lord Wintre?" Kole asked.

"It is fine," Donovan grunted.

Bronwen was used to her father's moods but Lord Wintre had been especially volatile the past year. He hadn't started this way, so gruff and distant, Bronwen remembered he was once a loving and attentive father. She only remembered small snippets from her youth; a kind stroke of her hair, a loving whisper goodnight, advice on her horsemanship, holding her hand as they walked. She had a sense that things had begun to change after her mother died. Donovan quickly became cold and harsh. He refused to spend any time with Bronwen and that was when he had started to force away any friend Bronwen had made or tried to make.

Instead of getting better as the grief of losing his wife faded, it became worse as each year passed until it was the norm for Bronwen to never be alone, but always lonely. She wished she had siblings at least but Donovan had never remarried, despite the numerous offers - Bronwen's good looks were not solely from her mother and many a young woman had tried to catch her father's attention only to be coldly turned away.

Bronwen felt someone staring at her. It wasn't Kole this time, it was someone the other side of her. She rearranged herself so she could see who it was, even though her suspicion was correct. Lord Guild's personal bodyguard was stood in the shadows of a pillar next to the box where they sat, watching Bronwen, not his employer. Mr Adam Whyms was a peculiar man, his long dark jacket and long dark hair made him blend nicely with the shadows. Bronwen perhaps would not have noticed him there if her skin hadn't prickled at his unnerving gaze.

Bronwen should have been used to Mr Whyms after four years of knowing Kole, but he still made her uncomfortable. His looks always seemed to linger on her longer than was polite and he hardly spoke. No one else seemed to notice him which she supposed was part of his job, as well as being proficient in whatever weapons he kept hidden under his long jacket that made him look greasy and smelt of metal.

Lady Bronwen shifted her body away again, not sure if she preferred Kole's stare to Adam's, and tried to concentrate on the play. There was not long left and she absorbed their words carefully.

She made a note to write to Josette about it later. She would have enjoyed the story.

Josette Emry was Kole's sister-by-law, or at least she was before her husband, Clarence, Kole's elder brother, had died. She was the only friend Bronwen had, despite Donovan's multiple attempts to keep them apart. Josette was tenacious and would not be dissuaded. They had met soon after she and Kole were introduced. Lord Guild had invited Bronwen and Donovan to his estate near Guildford and despite Josette's unconventional mannerisms, Bronwen had taken a liking to the older woman.

After Kole's brother had passed, he had allowed Josette to stay at the house she might have owned, had she borne children before Clarence died. She and Bronwen wrote to each other every month and tried to meet at least once a year. Donovan had once kept Josette's letters from Bronwen in an attempt to stop their friendship from growing, until Josette had turned up on their doorstep with a week's worth of luggage. Donovan had soon given in, deciding he would tolerate their correspondence as long as visits were kept to a minimum.

{All yet seems well; and if it end so meet, the bitter past, more welcome is the sweet}

Bronwen clapped her hands lightly as the players took their bows, feeling sad that it was over. The actors were very talented and the story interesting, despite what Lord Guild might have thought. She wished she could stand to show her pleasure as some of the other patrons were, but it would not be proper and her father would not like it.

Kole applauded lazily. Donovan did not, and stood to leave as soon as the curtain closed.

Bronwen lingered in the seat for as long as she could, savouring the smell of the stage lamps and velvet of the chairs, the dimness of the theatre and the ambience of the audience, before following the gentlemen into the hallway.

An attendant helped her into her coat and she thanked him quietly. Lord Guild and her father had already started for the lobby and sent someone to fetch their coach without a second glance at her.

Bronwen hurried along behind them, not wanting to be left behind with Adam Whyms who had startled the attendant with his sudden appearance in the private hallway. He didn't question the bodyguard's presence after one daring look from the man.

At the bottom of the lobby stairs, Kole paused and finally looked back at Bronwen. Lord Guild was a tall, slim man and the way he walked demanded attention. He held himself high, shoulders back and lean arms keeping time with the pontifical gliding of his movements. His dark brown hair was always neatly combed to one side, a slight wave to it around his neck and his facial hair and side burns were always well kept. Lord Guild was always in control.

He smiled at her and held his arm out. Bronwen would have preferred for him to have done so at the top of the stairs when the heavy layers of her dress were most cumbersome and threatened to topple her with each careful step. She did not say so though and took Kole's arm with a weak smile of her own and allowed him to lead her out of the theatre and into the waiting carriage.

Donovan was already in the vehicle, sat in the centre of one seat so that Kole had to sit next to Bronwen. She tried to sit as close to the wall of the carriage as possible. There was plenty of space in the plush interior but Kole still felt too close to her and Bronwen was very aware of his arm brushing against hers as the carriage pulled away and bounced down the cobbled streets of Winchester.

"There is something so primitive about Shakespeare that I find almost unpalatable," Kole said as he pulled on his leather gloves, scrunching his hands to get his fingers in. The weather had turned in the last few weeks from summer to a brisk autumn and it was cold in the carriage.

"I find it rather endearing," Bronwen replied, her voice catching as they jolted on a particularly unforgiving part of road.

"Yes, I suppose the oblique nature of his words *would* appeal to a woman."

"Or perhaps only a woman can appreciate the subtle poetry of it," Bronwen murmured back then instantly wished she had not spoken. Lord Guild had not meant his comment unkindly but the implication of it nagged at Bronwen.

The sound of the horses' hooves were so loud on the stones that Bronwen didn't think either man had heard her comment. However, when they passed a gas street lamp it briefly bathed her father's face in a fiery orange glow and she knew he was displeased with her again.

"I did not mean to offend, my Lady," Kole said after an uncomfortable silence, ever the gentleman. His arm brushed Bronwen's again and she tried not to shift away. He was to be her husband but she was still unsettled by any form of contact between them.

"No, I apologise for being so brusque, Lord Guild," Bronwen said sincerely, before firmly setting her gaze to the dark world outside the carriage, hoping her father was placated.

The glass of the carriage window was moist and the world looked damp outside, the brickwork of the city shops glossy, their dark windows reflecting the carriage as it moved noisily through the streets. Bronwen was used to staring out of windows for hours. There was not much to do when one did not have many friends. She wrote her letters to Josette, went to the theatre whenever there was a new show and someone was available to chaperone, she had ridden as far as Owslebury parish in a single day, before her caretaker had made her turn back, had read over one hundred books and had sewn almost all the embroidered décor in her father's house.

Bronwen was used to being alone, but one never truly gets used to being lonely.

This was one of the few things she looked forward to when she wed. She would likely spend most of her time at home with Josette in Guildford and Bronwen looked forward to having as many children as God would give her to keep each other, and her, company. She had wondered how different her life would have been if her father had remarried and given her plenty of siblings. She wanted that for her children. She also never wanted them to feel like they were a burden to their parents.

Bronwen looked at her father at this thought and found

him staring at her with a mixture of sadness, anger and fear. It was only a fleeting expression before they moved away from the light of the street lamp and she knew he had turned away.

Bronwen opened her mouth to say - she wasn't sure what, and looked back out of the window.

The two men soon moved to discussing business and politics which Bronwen had little interest in. Thankfully, the journey was not long and Bronwen soon recognised the long pathway that led towards Metrom Hall, her home.

New gas lamps lined their path up to the house at intervals in halos of golden light. Passing through darkness to light. Bronwen could see her reflection in the glass in the dark intervals. She looked sombre and pale, eyes dull and square jaw giving an aristocratic mien. She studied her expression with disinterest each time it appeared and faded.

Dark-light. Dark-light. Dark - Bronwen let out a small squeal and jumped. She whipped her head around but found only Kole beside her, staring with concern.

"My Lady, are you quite well?" Kole asked.

Bronwen nodded, not trusting her voice while her heart was still trying to jump out of her mouth. She could have sworn she had seen something behind her shoulder. A dark shape. No, a face. One that did not belong to Kole, her father, or anyone or thing she had ever seen before. She was not even sure if it had been human, it was so... she couldn't even think of the words to describe it and struggled to keep the image of it in her mind, not that she wanted to. It had been so menacing and distorted and left her with such a feeling of dread that she worried she might be sick.

Kole was still staring at her with worry.

"Just a hiccup, Lord Guild," she explained, hoping her voice didn't betray how disturbed she felt. "Excuse me."

It must have been a trick of the light and mind, but Bronwen still refused to look back out of the window and was relieved when the carriage came to a halt.

A footman jumped down to open the door and Bronwen couldn't escape the box fast enough. She noticed her hand was shaking when she reached for Kole's, waiting to help her step out. She knew he had noticed too and he thankfully did not mention it.

They made their way up the few stone steps to the house and were bathed in light as the butler opened the door for them.

James Durward was tall and slim, progressed in years but with the strength and energy of a young man. He was a trusted member of the household and Bronwen was quite fond of him despite his interminable professionalism.

"Welcome home, Lord Wintre, Lord Guild and Lady Bronwen," he said, taking his master's coat and hat.

"We will have drinks in the drawing room before retiring," Donovan said gruffly before heading straight for the room. James was used to his employer's blunt form of address, seeming to prefer it and simply indicating to various other servants to do his bidding while he took Bronwen's coat.

"I must apologise, Lord Guild, but I have a wish to retire early this evening," Bronwen struggled with her words as her throat had become bone dry and she stifled a cough.

"Are you sure you are quite well?" Kole asked. He moved closer to her and she had to focus on not stepping away.

"Yes, I am well but fatigued, my Lord."

"Then I shall give you your rest," Kole said with a warm smile. Bronwen held out her hand to him which he took firmly and used it to pull her closer as he planted a swift kiss on her cheek.

Bronwen flushed.

"Lord Guild," she stammered, wishing Mr Durward was not stood in the hallway.

"Lady Bronwen," Kole smirked. "We are to be wed. Surely you will forgive me my trespass?"

Bronwen glanced at James but he was studiously arranging the coats and hats. Bronwen looked shyly back at her fiancé, retrieving her hand under the pretence of holding her skirt as she curtsied, trying not to focus on the warm prickling of her body at her embarrassment.

"It is not a trespass, when given honourably."

"Honourably indeed, Lady." His smile made her blush again. "Until tomorrow." He entered the drawing room, closing the door behind him. Bronwen breathed out and headed up the stairs, avoiding Mr Durward's eyes.

Bronwen turned the handle of her bedroom door and was greeted by the smell of jasmine and oak. A scent she always used. Bronwen's room was on the second floor to the far right of the manor. It was not the largest in the house but it was unique in the squared indent from where the building overhung the servant's entrance. Here it had been large enough to attach curtains to the flat of it, creating a private changing room and curtained window seat separate from the main space without the need of a changing screen. A cream armchair was even able to comfortably fit in the extension where Bronwen could put on shoes or simply relax by the window.

The four-poster bed was neatly made, a cream crocheted cover laid atop a burgundy quilt. A matching canopy loomed over part of the bed where the pillows were and a long foot stool in the same fabric was kept at the bed end, golden tassels fringed a seam, hiding that it could be opened and used as a secret storage.

Bronwen's mother was a lover of hidden places and had many such items around the house and Bronwen was confident that she had found almost all of them in her youth. Some of them were ordinary such as behind the face of the grandfather clock in the hallway and the safe behind a painting in the morning room. Then others had been more obscure, like the hinged section on the banister of the stairs and the removable box clipped beneath the coffee table in the drawing room.

Bronwen had never found anything of interest in them, despite hoping her mother had left her a secret note only for her to find, and she had never known why she needed so many secret places. But each time Bronwen stumbled across a new one, she felt as though her mother were still all around her and was comforted by the thought.

Bronwen's Lady's maid was waiting for her in her bedroom. Alda Keeper was an elderly woman, wizened and once Bronwen's childhood governess. She was easily past the age of retirement, her grandson worked in the gardens of the house and was only a few years older than Bronwen. Servants tended to stay long term in the Wintre household if they survived her father's ruthless trial period. Sometimes he would hire and dismiss a servant even before Bronwen had met them and he paid the ones he did keep very well indeed.

There were times in her youth when Bronwen had wished Donovan had sent Alda away, mostly when her overbearing nanny was scolding her for some obscure habit, or lecturing her on the importance of being proper. It was understated to say Alda was set in her ways. She had been the first to protest when Lord Wintre had had the entire house fitted with new gas lamps, even the servant's rooms.

"The smell is intolerable, milord and it leaves soot everywhere," Alda had told Donovan. She was one of the few people whom Bronwen's father allowed to speak to him this way. She gathered Alda had been an asset to him when his wife was sick and he was left with a young Bronwen to care for. Her protests went unheeded however. Donovan was a man of the industrial age; it was how he had made his fortune, mainly through textiles, much of which was used around Metrom Hall.

Then, at other times, Bronwen was grateful for the

woman's coddling. It was the closest thing she had to a mother.

"Did you enjoy the play, Lady Bronwen?" Alda asked in a voice that was both demanding and soothing.

"Yes, thank you." Bronwen turned so that Alda could begin undoing the multitude of hooks and threads on her dress.

Bronwen kept quiet as she did so, thinking deeply about the kiss from Kole. It was not completely brazened of the man but it had been unexpected and had reminded Bronwen of something she had since been pushing firmly to the back of her mind.

They were engaged and one day they would be man and wife, which meant one day they would have to...

Josette had once offered to explain to Bronwen the intricacies of being married but Bronwen had politely refused, which she later came to regret. She had no mother to explain such things and cringed at the thought of asking Alda. What little was obvious to Bronwen was that she would have to unclothe and this was more frightening to her than what came after.

Bronwen unconsciously laid a hand on her stomach, on the mark that surrounded her navel. It was a five-pointed star with each point connected to one another in a continuous pattern. She had had it since she was a baby and it terrified her to know that Kole would one day see it.

Alda knew it was there of course and had explained to her that it was a birthmark but Bronwen had always known this was a lie. Especially after an encounter with one of her maids when she was only seven years old.

Alda had become very sick one week and someone had had to replace her with looking after Bronwen. It had not occurred to them then how this new maid might react to the unusual mark, to those few who knew about it, it was the norm.

"What have you done, girl?" the maid had said as Bronwen removed her clothes ready for bed. Her undergarments were thin and the woman could see the irregularity in skin tone on Bronwen's stomach. With her young mind Bronwen had thought nothing of it and lifted her chemise to show the maid. The woman gasped in horror and staggered back before taking an unexpected turn on the young girl, shaking her shoulders and yelling.

"Why have you done it this way? With the horns of the Devil?!"

Her shrieks had become increasingly frantic and so loud that it had even gained the attention of Donovan. He had burst into the room to find his young daughter curled with her knees against her chest in fits of hiccupping tears and a raving woman yelling her damnation.

Her father had been swift to throw the woman out of the room, and not gently, telling a much younger James to see that she never set foot in the house again. Then he had come back to his crying daughter and without hesitation, wrapped her in a blanket and carried her to the bed, then held her until she stopped crying and eventually fell asleep. It was one of those rare moments of affection he had shown her. After that, Alda had been her only maid and on the rare occasion she was not available, Bronwen arranged her own hair and clothing.

Alda had tried to explain to Bronwen that the woman was not well.

"There is nothing of the Devil in you," she had said firmly and Bronwen had believed her, for a time.

The event had been so absurd that Bronwen had almost forgotten it. But the recoiling sensation she had at the idea of anyone but Alda seeing it had remained with her.

She had one day thought to look for the symbol in a book but decided against it. She had even gained enough courage to ask her father but his reaction to the question was always unpredictable. He would either dismiss her with irritation at her vanity or become despondent and disappear for a few hours or days.

After a while, she stopped caring what it was, the pink puckered skin in impossibly neat lines, its main point thrusting downwards towards her toes. Deep down she knew it had been put there and that was as far as she was willing to contemplate. At least until faced with the prospect of having to reveal it to her husband.

What would Kole think when he saw it? What questions would he ask her that she could not answer? Or could she find a way of hiding it?

She pushed the thoughts out of her mind and tried to engage in conversation with Alda. It wasn't difficult to start the woman talking and it was a welcome distraction.

"Mervyn has been courting a girl from a farm and I found out today that they have been meeting since last June!" Alda prattled on as she led Bronwen to the little dressing table next to the door. Her grandson was one of her favourite subjects.

Bronwen avoided looking in the mirror, afraid she might see the terrifying thing behind her again while Alda brushed her hair. She had forgotten about her fright in the carriage until then and pinched her arm hard. It was a habit she had picked up when she was a child. A girl at a party had pointed out a young boy in the crowd and giggled with the other girls in the group, telling them to pinch her.

"Pinch you?" Bronwen had asked. The girls were only slightly older than she was but were already thinking about who they would marry.

"It is how you know you are not dreaming. Dreams cannot hurt you so if a pinch does, then you know you are awake." The girl had pinched Bronwen hard with her nails. So hard her eyes had watered but she refused to cry, she even welcomed the pain of it. Bronwen had always felt as though she was dreaming and she needed to pinch herself regularly to remind her she was awake. It never worked for long but she could not break the habit, no matter how many times Alda scolded her for it.

"The girl is no good for him if she is willing to put herself in his path so shamelessly. It is not ladylike and is not good enough for my grandson," Alda huffed, pulling Bronwen's hair into a tight braid.

"Perhaps they really care for one another?"

"You think the Devil will lessen their punishment because they care for one another?"

"I think God might."

"Oh, and you a priest now, domina domus?" Alda scoffed, using her pet name for Bronwen since she was a child, 'Lady of the house' in Latin. She guided Bronwen's shoulders over to the bed and helped her under the thick blankets. Bronwen found the weight of them restricting but the air of the room was cold despite the fire in the hearth.

Alda tucked her into the huge four poster bed tightly. She knew Bronwen always untucked herself as soon as she left the room but it was her little ritual.

"Sleep well, Lady Bronwen."

"Good evening, Alda."

Bronwen stared at the canopy of the bed above her for a moment, listening to the familiar crackle of the fire and the rustle of the trees outside and remembering her favourite phrases from the play. The phantom from earlier was forgotten, even after she dimmed her bedside lantern and let the shadows of the room envelop her into sleep.

II

{A sound woke Bronwen. Or was it a feeling? Perhaps a smell? She leant up on her elbows and looked around. The floor of her room was obscured by a grey smoke. An odourless smoke that swirled in lazy circles. A mist so dense, the embers of the fire were a faint glow. There was something in the darkness. A creature. A person.

Bronwen was not afraid as it moved towards the end of her bed, wrath like and so dark she could not see its features – his features. She knew he was gazing at her, as she stared at him. "Will you not reveal yourself to me?" Bronwen asked, her voice quiet but sure. 'Soon,' he replied, then faded away, pulling the mist with him. Bronwen's eyes closed and she relaxed back onto her pillow. She had forgotten to pinch herself awake... She would forget she had woken at all.}

"Oh, my goodness!" Alda's exclamation woke Bronwen from a deep sleep. Was it morning already? "It is positively winter in here. Did that girl forget to close the windows again?"

Bronwen squinted as Alda opened the curtains and flooded the room with morning light, muttering to herself when she saw the windows were closed. Bronwen rolled onto her side, not wanting to leave her bed. She had the sense she had had a pleasant dream, but could not remember it.

"Oh, my goodness," Alda repeated, she was crouched by the fire now with a matchbox in hand. "The fire has frosted over. These logs will be far to damp to light. I will send for more. None of the other rooms are this cold."

Bronwen's mind finally caught up with what Alda was saying and she felt the chill in the air too. She rolled onto her back again and looked at her hands. They were horribly pale, almost blue at the fingertips. She stuffed them under the covers before Alda could see them. The elderly woman made her way to Bronwen's side and placed fretting hands on her Lady's brow. They felt like fire on Bronwen's skin and she almost pulled away.

"I don't know how you have not caught your death in this room."

"I am quite well," Bronwen said. It wasn't a lie. She was cold but it wasn't unpleasant. Besides, she didn't get ill. Not once had she shown any sign of fever or sickness in her young life. Alda always said it meant Bronwen would be affected worse with it when she was older.

"You will be once we have you dressed and the fire is lit."

Alda's breath came out in a small mist as she spoke and she left the room briefly to fetch a maid.

Bronwen breathed out hard to test the air but her breath was not visible like Alda's. It was odd, but she knew little about the science of it and forced herself to slide out of the bed onto the chilly carpet.

Her toes curled at the temperature as she tiptoed over to the dressing table. In the light of the morning she had no fear of looking into the mirror and seeing something behind her. It seemed silly to Bronwen how unnerved she had been by something she had only glimpsed in a reflection.

Studying herself, her cheeks were rosy but her lips were pale and cracked. Bronwen quickly dug out her lipstick and rubbed some of the clear pomade onto them. She absently unbraided and brushed her hair as she wondered what events had been planned for her in the coming day.

Lord Guild would be leaving in a couple of days and there was still business for him to attend to with Bronwen's father, or so she gathered. She hoped there would be time to spend with Kole to get to know him underneath the confines of propriety. His impromptu kiss the night before had reminded Bronwen that, as much as she might be nervous about the prospect, she was to be his wife soon and would have to get used to the idea. She wanted to feel comfortable around him and maybe even love him, one day at least.

They had spent very little time together, despite being engaged for so long. Kole was always busy with Donovan and their business dealings and Bronwen was always worried that one day her father would shun this person out of her life too.

Colour had returned to Bronwen's fingers by the time Alda returned with a very disgruntled looking maid carrying some firewood. The usual buzz of morning routine passed quickly and once Bronwen was brushed and presentable, she made her way downstairs to the drawing room where her father was waiting. She smiled at him as she walked in, not expecting a warm greeting in return but also not expecting the look he gave her. It was a haunted look, like he had not slept for weeks.

"Father are you well?"

He looked away from her and downed his glass of brandy. "Stop asking me so many questions," he barked, moving to pour another glass.

Bronwen was taken aback. Her father had always been stern, it showed in the lines on his face, his eyebrows in a permanent scowl. His dark eyes made darker by how his furrowed brow knitted over them. He was not unattractive for his age but he was an authority on looks alone. Bronwen got her strong square jawline and pale brown hair from Donavan, though his was rapidly turning grey.

Bronwen might not have forgotten there had ever been affection between them but it seemed Donovan had. He was indifferent to his daughter so long as she kept her mouth shut and did as she was told. He had grown colder towards her in the last few months and in the last week she had tried to avoid him as much as possible.

Bronwen had tried to seek out the reason for his gradual declining mood from visitors and house staff. She thought perhaps it was business trouble as he spent more and more time away from the house but he did not seem so crotchety with anyone but his daughter.

Bronwen kept quiet now, wishing she could return to her room but Lord Guild would be joining them for breakfast soon. He was staying at the house with them and was always up late in the mornings.

Bronwen went to sit by the far window on the cushioned seat in the alcove. It was not comfortable and it was colder away from the fire, especially with autumn claiming its time in the year, but it was out of the way and Bronwen could gaze out of the window.

The grounds of the house looked vastly different in the daytime, even under a grey blanket of cloud. It would rain later, she knew. The lawn was dewy in preparation and the border of trees were still and patient.

Thankfully, Lord Guild arrived soon, so Bronwen did not have to suffer the uncomfortable silence of the room for long. She could hear him on the stairs greeting Mr Durward happily. Bronwen checked her hair in the reflection of the glass and stood to straighten her dress just as Kole walked in.

He scanned the room quickly and beamed when he saw Bronwen stood waiting for him. It was another unexpected reaction. He looked almost giddy to see her where her father had been irked at her presence.

"Shall I serve breakfast now, milord?" James asked politely. He was directing the question at Donovan but Lord Guild answered.

"Yes, Mr Durward, that would be acceptable."

Bronwen looked from Kole to her father. He was still staring into the fire and appeared not to have heard. Kole moved to the back of the room to get a drink.

Bronwen waited until James had left and Kole was turned away before cautiously walking towards her father, like she was approaching a wild dog whom might bite her at any moment.

"Father?" she said quietly, her hands flat on the front of her dress. "Lord Guild has come for breakfast now. Would you prefer if I dine with him? You could retire for a rest if you wish. Lord Guild will understand." She was getting increasingly concerned for him and wondered whether it be prudent to have James call for a doctor.

Donovan turned his head slowly and stared at Bronwen with a blank expression before standing up so swiftly, Bronwen moved a step back from him. He straightened his waistcoat with a rough tug and strolled past her.

"I said, stop asking so many questions," Donovan said, but his tone had lost its previous bite.

Bronwen let out the breath she had been holding and joined Lord Guild at the breakfast table.

He gave her a brimming smile and Bronwen flushed. "Lord Guild, you are very cheerful this morning."

"Lady Bronwen," Kole replied with a smirk. "How could I not be? We are to be wed next spring and I am greatly looking forward to closing a long-awaited business arrangement later today."

Donovan spilt a few drops of brandy onto the carpet as he joined them at the table. He appeared not to notice and his glass was full almost to the brim of the strong liquid.

Bronwen looked at her father who was avoiding her eyes. He looked calmer however, more like himself again and she dared not question him in front of the Earl.

Her eyes soon drifted to the other side of the room where a man was inconspicuously stood. Adam Whyms, of course. She hadn't even noticed him enter.

His eyes were almost hawk like, a bright hazel colour that matched his coppery hair, long and tied in a loose knot at the back of his head. He had a chain coming from the pocket of his waistcoat but Bronwen had never once seen him check a watch and had caught glimpses of various implements hidden in the folds of his coat which he never removed.

He was staring at her again but let his eyes slide away smoothly when she caught him, as if he were merely checking the room and she had been in his view. Bronwen pinched herself under the table to stop herself from shuddering as the servants filled the table with breakfast.

"Does this suit you, my Lady?" Kole was asking her, bringing her back to the conversation. Bronwen had not heard a word that had been said but pretended otherwise. She doubted it would matter if it didn't suit her, whatever it was.

"Very well, my Lord."

"Is it?" Her father said, his eyes sliding away to his brandy glass, already half empty in such a short amount of time. Bronwen looked to Kole for support, wondering if he had noticed the strange mood her father was in. He just stared back at her, a sly glint in his eyes.

"I am sorry, Lord Guild, would you mind repeating what has been organised. For my own clarity," Bronwen said, helping herself to bread from the overfull plate. She would most likely not eat it. She did not eat much anyway, finding food had little taste to her. She ate because she had to, as was the nature of most of her life.

"Of course. I spoke to Mr Clare last night about having your dress finalised this evening. He was most glad to do it but insisted it must be done at his shop as he did not want to risk the dress by transporting it all the way to the manor at night."

"At night?"

Mr Clare was the dressmaker who was commissioned for her wedding dress. She had not used him before but both Lord Guild and her father had insisted upon it being him. He had previously come to the manor to discuss requirements with Bronwen and had seemed very polite, if not a little edgy.

"Yes, Mr Clare informed us that the time of year is very busy for him and in order for him to give you his full attention the appointment was made for ten o'clock this evening," Kole said. "I assure you; you will be perfectly safe."

Bronwen's father made a noise like a cough and Kole quickly continued. "I will send you with my personal guards whom I trust most utterly. They will take you to your appointment and be waiting to return you home when you are finished."

Bronwen's eyes slid to where Adam was still standing, for once not staring at her, and her stomach lurched at the thought of travelling the dark streets of Winchester with him.

"Will you be joining me also?" Bronwen asked Kole hopefully.

"I am sorry, my Lady, but your father and I have matters to attend to this evening that we really cannot delay any longer and it would be bad fortune to see you in your dress before the wedding."

Donovan downed the last dregs of his brandy and stood up unsteadily.

"Father? You are finished so soon?"

"The sooner to get this over with." His voice did not slur

but it was obvious he had been drinking and Bronwen was sure he had not eaten anything. They may not be close, but he was still her father and she was dreadfully worried about him. She didn't think she had ever seen him drink to such excess, even at parties.

"Yes, indeed," Lord Guild said calmly, placing his napkin down and pushing away from the table. "Sorry to leave you so suddenly, Lady Bronwen. Please, there is no need to get up. My carriage will be here to pick you up later this evening and I shall see you in the morning."

Donovan caught his foot on the table leg as he passed Bronwen and would have stumbled had she not caught hold of his arm gently. He looked upon her face again, as if seeing it for the first time, then his features darkened into a mask she knew well and he moved away, pulling his arm out of her grasp.

Bronwen watched them leave together, followed by Adam who glanced back at her as he closed the door, leaving her alone. She sat back down, picked up her tea cup, then returned it to the table again. It had been a strange few months and she hoped the obscurity would soon be over. She did not like the turn her father was taking and with any luck, the finalising of whatever business the men kept discussing would break his foul mood.

A ghost stared back at Bronwen with tired eyes and pale complexion. She had been left alone with the reflection, the dress she wore now completed and ready to be paraded.

It was silky and elegant, fitting the body tightly and adorned with lace. It was made from gold tinselled satin upon layers of net that gathered in bunches and clasped together with glass jewels.

Bronwen lifted her veil and the spirit of the dead was replaced by a saddened looking bride.

Lady Bronwen sighed at herself in the mirror, glad that Mr Clare had left her alone for a moment so that she could brood on her happiness for her future wedding, but all she could think about was how uncomfortable she felt in the garment. She had worn dresses all her life and yet this one was wrong for her; she was also uncertain of how right the wedding would be.

The material was heavy and uncomfortable and the bones of the corset restricted her. The sleeves were puffy and impractical where they fell at length from her elbows, though she was grateful that the fashion of trains had faded. The crinoline that held the skirt's structure gave the dress more bulk and she felt lost wearing it - as she felt lost in her life.

Bronwen had been correct in thinking it would rain, so she had spent most of her day reading and had started another letter to Josette which was sat on her desk half-finished.

Thankfully the rain had abated by the time she had left for the city centre. She had been accompanied by two armed men, as Kole had promised, to protect her against robbers and other malicious stalkers of the night and had been grateful to find Adam Whyms had not been one of the assigned guards.

Bronwen removed her veil and stepped down from the block she had been standing on. She grimaced at how tight the corset was. The tailor's assistant who had helped her into it had not been gentle. Bronwen had gasped as her whole body was tugged about by the woman. She almost thought the assistant would have put a knee to Bronwen's back and tightened the strings so much she would choke to death. Bronwen hadn't seen her face as she had not removed her bonnet and had kept it low over her eyes but vowed to have Alda with her next time instead.

Bronwen removed the crinoline and her heeled shoes and

placed them in a neat pile to give herself more freedom to breath and move. She was late to be married. She had turned twenty-five one month ago, and was much older than the other women of the city, some of which had children of their own, but she still didn't feel right about it. She had come to a sort of acceptance on the matter and even had a hope that Kole would make her happy, but seeing herself in a wedding gown had brought all her initial feelings of displacement back to her.

Her thoughts of woe were thankfully broken by the sound of Lowell entering the room behind her and she was glad she would soon have the dress removed and be back at home.

Bronwen did not turn to the tailor immediately, trying to compose herself in the small standing mirror on the desk she was stood by. Her features were too stern and were not softened by her smooth wavy hair. Her angled eyebrows and dark ringed eyes made her look stronger than she felt and hid her fragilities of will - she could not have protested about the marriage even if she wanted to.

Bronwen had a small ember of fierceness within her from her parents but without someone to fan it, the fire inside her had faded almost to nothing. She had the occasional outburst of passion, but her father was always quick to undermine it.

"The fitting is perfect, Mr Clare," Bronwen said when the tailor did not speak.

There came no reply.

Bronwen tipped the mirror upwards, tired of looking at herself and it had reminded her of the demonic vision she had seen in the carriage window the previous night. It had not been the first time she had seen such a thing.

Soon after Bronwen's mother had died she had been wandering aimlessly in the woods and came across a stream. She had laid down on her stomach and looked at her reflection in the water. A breeze had disturbed the surface of it and when the water settled again, it looked as though half of Bronwen's face had melted and her eye was red and bloodshot. It had only lasted a moment and her child's mind had not been afraid of it.

Then, at a party in Bronwen's youth, one of the favoured parlour games of young ladies was to divine whom their future husbands might be. This was done by entering a dark room with only a candle and standing in front of a mirror. The woman's future husband's image was supposed to appear in the mirror over their shoulder.

Bronwen had been coerced into participating and had waited in the dark room for ten minutes before a shadow with red eyes had appeared behind her. She had dropped the candle and run from the room screaming. The other guests had thought it very amusing that she had been so spooked and laughed off the incident.

Bronwen smiled at herself and how ridiculous she was being and tiled the mirror back down again, but this time, the thing over her shoulder was very real. A figure was behind her, wearing a black cloak and mask covering all but his eyes, dark with sinister purpose and holding a cloth in his hand.

The fumes from the cloth reached Bronwen's nose, momentarily waking her from her fear frozen state, surely having the opposite effect of what the chemical was intended for.

Bronwen took a breath in and opened her mouth to scream as the cloth was placed over her mouth and nose. Having a full lung of air, she had time to struggle with her attacker. He only had use of one arm around her waist while the other held onto her face. Bronwen was not strong enough to pull away from him.

Instead, she kicked out against the table and pushed as hard as she could backwards. Spools of thread fell onto the floor and made the man stumble. He let go of her mouth for a moment to steady himself. It was long enough for Bronwen to gather another lung full of air but she didn't waste it on a scream that might not be heard. She used her free mouth to clamp her teeth down into the man's hand.

Bronwen could not bring herself to bite hard enough to break the skin, despite the perilous situation she was in, but it had the desired effect and the man growled in pain as he let go completely, dropping a dark coloured bottle she had not noticed he had been holding.

Without conscious thought, Bronwen's instincts took over and she grabbed the bottle from the floor and flung it at her attacker. It missed his head but smashed against the wall behind him in an explosion of delicate glass and fumes that fell onto the man's shoulder. He stupidly tried to brush off the liquid but staggered from the fumes and fell back into the wall, hitting his head hard on a table. He slid to the floor, unconscious.

Bronwen placed a sleeve over her own mouth and left the room in a hurry. She rushed down the stairs of Lowell's shop and headed for a back door that would lead her to the alley behind the houses. She pulled the door open and prepared her lungs to scream for help, when her voice caught in her throat at the sight of two more cloaked figures, leaning in wait against the wall.

They were clearly not expecting her - conscious at least – so she was quicker to react and slammed the door closed, bolting it swiftly just in time before the two men were banging to get it open.

Bronwen ran back up the corridor and entered the front of the shop, more cautious to open the door this time. She looked into the street beyond the windows of the room. It was dim outside from the shadowy moonlight and her father's carriage was nowhere to be seen, it might have pulled out of view of the window but she did not want to risk yelling for help and alerting the cloaked people to her whereabouts until she was certain. There was no one in the street to help her so late, so she would have to run to the closest house and hope they would hear her calling in time.

Unbolting the door, Bronwen stepped out onto the vacant street, grabbing a pair of the tailor's scissors as an afterthought and - with the absence of the carriage - was just about to dash to the house opposite when she spotted three more cloaks stood by the entrance to the alley behind the shops.

Bronwen wondered how many there were but had little time to think, she could only do.

She ran in the opposite direction just as the men saw her and pursued, her bare feet slapped against the cobbles and she grimaced as the filth from animal and human alike squelched between her toes and soaked the hem of her dress, making it harder to run in the heavy fabric.

She ducked down the side of two houses, she had not enough time to bang on a door but hoped that it would slow her chasers down, having to follow single file through the narrow passage.

Bronwen exited the alley, just as the first cloak entered, then ran behind the houses, willing there to be a doorway left open she could hide behind, but all she found was brick and stone walls.

Her heart skipped a beat when a figure appeared at the exit in front of her; she could not turn back either, the first figure was free of the alley and blocked her in, a second close behind.

Bronwen swerved her head for an escape route, panting heavily from fear and exhaustion. She felt almost ready to collapse and give herself over but the feel of the scissors in her hand gave her strength and she ran back towards the barrels she had seen leaning up against the wall and used them to vault over it, kicking them out from under her.

She was just about to fall to the safety of the other side when a hand grabbed a fistful of fabric from her dress and held her there, dragging her back over the top, causing her to scratch off the skin on her arm.

With desperate venom Bronwen swung her hand behind herself and stabbed the scissors into the hand that suspended her, sinking blunt metal into flesh and lodging itself between two bones.

The figure yelled in pain, revealing it was a man who hunted her and she was released, falling heavily on her side. A squeal of pain escaped Bronwen and she dragged herself to her feet once more, tears in her eyes. The restriction of the corset helped steady the pain in her ribs and she ran down an alley again. It also made her feel faint from the lack of air and she regretted removing the crinoline as her free skirts clung to her legs, sabotaging her escape.

Out onto an open street once more, she was not sure how much longer she could flee, then recognised where she was from the building opposite; it was a beautifully decorated arched bridge that led from one house to the next on the upper level. A black faced clock in the centre told her it was almost quarter to eleven.

If her memory served her well, she was just one street from Winchester Cathedral. It was the safest place and she knew the back gate was always open.

Wasting too much time already, Bronwen ran under the clock, down the small side street there and seeing the spire of the church in the distance, turned blindly down a final alley that would lead to it, only to collide with a solidly build body. The force made her wince at a twinge in her side as strong hands clasped her arms, holding her firmly in place.

She looked up into the figure's face but his features were covered like the others and it was too dark to see clearly.

Frozen in fear once more and losing the will to fight further, Bronwen closed her eyes as one of the figure's hands clutched her throat and moved her so her back was against the wall. She opened her eyes again and, in the dimness and the shadows of the alley, where not even the moonlight could reach her, she could just make out the dark shade of a man's eyes.

An almost regretful expression crossed his brow, as if he had just thrown his best bit of meat to a dog to stop it attacking. Then the fabric of his mask twitched where he smiled cruelly beneath it and it was almost as if his eyes changed shape and colour. They were darker and sharper and full of vengeful hate and a hunger that was demonic beyond description. If she could have drawn breath, Bronwen would have screamed at this alone.

The half-man half-creature lifted a gloved hand and struck Lady Bronwen hard across the face.

She felt the throb on her cheekbone, the strain on her neck where her head turned violently, her head cracked against the wall behind her, her eyes blurred, and then the world became as black as the cloak her attacker wore and the evil eye of a demon.

III

The sharp scent of smelling salts clawed its way to Bronwen's senses, wrenching her from a refuge of blissful unconsciousness. There was no way of fighting the reaction to the chemical and she took a sharp involuntary breath which sent a flutter of pain shooting through her side. She suspected she may have broken a rib but that was not her primary concern once Bronwen saw where she was.

The spirit of harts-horn was removed from under her nose and Bronwen focused on her surroundings. She was bound by her wrists and ankles to a hard, cold rock that seemed to dig into every inch of her like thorns. Her arms were spread wide either side of her and her feet were together, forcing the bones in her ankles to grind together uncomfortably when she moved them.

It was clear from the stars above that Bronwen was outside, but there was no way of telling where. Dense trees enclosed the clearing in a rough circle of shadows and bowing branches that seemed made for the purpose of shadowy things. Bronwen turned her head to the side, though it pained her to do so where her cheek was bruised.

Flickering candles encircled her and she shuddered in terror when she saw a cloaked figure stood by each one.

Black shadowy wraiths of foreboding that did naught but stare at her venerable posture with callous expressions in their unconcealed eyes.

Bronwen let out a sob as she began to think of what they might do to her - she knew at least three of them were men. She frantically started pulling on her bonds, adding to the rope burns already beginning to rub her skin raw. They held fast, secured with metal rings embedded in the stone that refused to surrender her.

Her shuddering increased violently when one of the figures stepped forward and stood at her feet. Bronwen was too scared to speak or even make a noise, she couldn't think clearly, with hideous images of what was about to happen clawing at her mind from all the books she had read, all of Alda's stories about what happens to incautious women and her own imaginings she didn't know her mind could conjure.

The figure placed a hand on her lower leg. Bronwen froze, her eyes fixed on the figure's dark ones, the dim light making his eyes more menacing as they roamed her body hungrily. Someone cleared their throat behind him and he released her leg, the print of his touch still burning her skin.

He removed a silver dagger from the folds of his cloak and Bronwen's shuddering began anew. She shook her head from side to side, pulling at her restraints, not finding a breath of air to scream until she saw the blade come down and slice across her stomach.

She prepared herself for pain that did not come and struggled to pause in her screaming. The figure had cut away the material of her dress and corset in a neat cross, revealing her navel and the scar that surrounded it.

The group seemed unperturbed by her outburst and instead took a step into the circle of candles. The cloaked figure above her admired his work and ran a gloved hand down her exposed skin, orbiting her navel delicately before he ran a finger down the shaft of the knife, relishing its feel and deadly purpose. The light that danced off the ruby jewels on the handle shimmered across his face in a blood red frenzy and she recognised him as the man who had struck her in the alley. This frightened her more than anything. She didn't want to see that demonic face again that promised damnation.

"No. No, please God, no," Bronwen whimpered, her eyes shut tight.

The man was pulled from his distraction by her lamenting. Striding closer, he bent down towards her face. Bronwen sensed the proximity and unwillingly opened her eyes. She stopped struggling, tears rolling down her cheeks in silent sobs and she could do nothing but stare into his hidden face, praying for his eyes not to change again.

"He is not here to listen to you. Nor does he care," he whispered almost too low to hear and Bronwen shuddered.

Without pulling back from her, he placed the cold metal of the knife against Bronwen's bare skin, teasing her maliciously. Bronwen turned her head away and let out another scream, a high-pitched animalistic squeal she did not know she was capable of and barely registered it was her who made it.

The figure pressed his full weight into her body and placed a hand over Bronwen's mouth to dull her screams and turn her face back to him, their eyes locking again as he put the knife to his covered lips and hushed her quietly.

Bronwen gulped on each sob, her throat dry from screaming and eyes burning from her tears.

"*We begin.*" A sharp order came from one of the watchers in the circle, his voice sounding strangely strained.

The figure, still on her, twitched his head in agitation and kissed his gloved hand over her mouth before standing at her feet again.

The people in the cloaks began chanting in a low tone,

Bronwen was mildly aware it was Latin but could not make sense of it.

She twisted her head again, hoping to find a sympathetic face or some wish of survival, though it seemed futile now. If no one had come to the aid of her screams, she was far from any help. In a muddled thought, she worried how her father would judge her when he found out what happened. *If* he found out.

The warmth of her own blood was what Bronwen felt before the pain, she barely had time to register it before another cut was made across her stomach, splitting the skin in two, creating a channel for thick, dark red blood to pool and slither round the curves of her body, drenching her back in the hot liquid.

She cried out with each cut and wished she could pass out and have it done with. Why were they torturing her? Why would they not just kill her, if that is what they desired?

Finally, after five agonisingly slow carves, the man stepped away to admire his work.

Not a drop tainted him and he had made the incisions so expertly, that the blood flowing from each wound did not obscure the five-pointed star he had engraved. It followed the lines of the scar already there, reopening the hard skin.

Bronwen felt sick from the sight and smell of the blood, *her* blood. She wished for death to end it but whimpered even so when a second figure stepped forward, taking the knife carefully.

Bronwen could not force her eyes to close and could not compel herself to be unconscious and take herself from the pain and suffering and fear. Her senses were too cruel and adrenalin kept her alert.

She could only watch as the foreboding manifestation took his place at her feet. She was vaguely aware that the chanting had merged into one word and she hoped that meant it was coming to an end.

"Sacrificium, sacrificium, sacrificium..." {Sacrifice}

Bronwen could not think or speak or even feel. She barely saw what was going on around her, only begged for it to stop.

The new cloaked figure reached his full height, the knife raised above his head, poised and ready. His victim noticed a hesitation in his eyes, a pity, a desperation, a regret...

Do it...

The knife speared clean and precise into Bronwen's chest.

She barely felt it, dulled by her other injuries and pain and the taste of blood in her mouth, before the world she knew vanished for the final time and she prayed she would be united with her mother in the next life.

"I am pleased with your work, Dux Ducis."

The group of cloaked figures started as all the candles were extinguished and the voice of their master echoed through the trees. They each turned their heads around, looking for the source of the voice in the caliginous clearing.

Stood by the corpse of Lady Bronwen was the embodiment of a man. He wore the same black cloak as they did and stood a foot taller than an average human. They could not fully see his face but his red flecked eyes flashed under his hood as he studied them all in turn.

"Dominus," a cloaked man said, kneeling. The others followed suit. "You honour us with your presence."

"Perhaps I should not have," the master hissed, studying the wounds on the woman's body, now a simple vessel, empty of spirit and soul. "I ordered that she was not to be tainted."

"They did not touch her, Dominus." The man who the creature had called Dux Ducis replied, almost inaudibly. He was the only one still standing, staring at the knife that still protruded from the girl's chest. The knife that he had put there.

"She is whole, as promised," the first man who had

spoken added, aware that he had almost been the one to ruin her purity.

"Your thoughts may be dominated by the use of your cock, Servus, but I was not intending to find her body desecrated in such a manner." The creature put a long-fingered hand around the hilt of the knife and delicately pulled it from the pierced heart of the woman, as if extracting a splinter from a child's finger. "The knife sent her to me, not these petty symbols you so dearly cling to."

"We were honouring you, Dominus," another voice said, the human's head bowed in reparation.

"You do not need her body," a bitter voice added, this one sounded more feminine than the others and did not address him as master.

The creature was suddenly angered by this comment and stabbed the knife deep into the rock next to the dead woman's head.

"That is not your decision to make!" he yelled, seeming to become a foot taller. His eyes burned into each one of them as they winced and cowered from the ferocity of his outburst.

The Dux Ducis finally pulled his eyes from the woman's body and knelt as the others did.

"You need to learn where your loyalties lie. I may not be able to kill any of you, but never forget who has the power over your souls."

He swept his arm over the group as if to gather them all up and then crushed his hand into a fist. As he did, they all clutched their hearts in agony and shivered in fits, as if something froze them from the inside.

"You are Servos, *slaves*. Your insolence has not gone un-noted and when I give you instructions, I expect them to be followed."

Finally, he unclenched his fist and their hearts became free from the pain, though they all beat a little faster from it.

The creature snapped the hilt of the dagger from the rock and tossed it at the man who had carved the body in the first place. The man did not shy away from the thing and looked up to meet his master's dangerous eyes, panting heavily.

"*Pray*, if you think it best," the master said, calm once more. "Pray that her spirit is stronger than her body and you have not broken that also, or I will be returning on *my* promises."

They all bowed their heads to the ground at his feet and murmured their devotion in unison.

He dispersed in a mixture of blue flame and smoke, leaving his followers to ponder on his words and deal with the body of the woman.

Her soul was waiting elsewhere.

The next life started much the same as the first – violently pulled from peace and tranquillity, into a cruel place that binds.

Bronwen was chained by her wrists with metal shackles and dangled in an empty void, with nothing beneath or above. A misty cloud surrounded the intense tenebrosity that chilled her soul and she could not see where the chain binding her was attached.

The experience was quite unnerving but when she had awoken in the strange hollowness, Bronwen found that fear didn't grip her stomach as it would have in life. She knew that she was dead and accepted it without question.

For once, she did not have to pinch herself to know she was not dreaming, but Bronwen had not expected this to be her afterlife. Pearly gates and a warm loving embrace had not been her belief either. She had always privately thought that this was a fantasy, but still she had been anticipating some form of welcome and a lightness, not a deep foreboding nothing. Bronwen was sure she had not sinned to a degree that would send her to hell, nor did she see herself faultless enough to enter heaven.

Begrudgingly, Bronwen realised that she must be in purgatory. A place of atonement for sins committed in life. She would not be let into heaven until her faults were laid bare and she embraced her punishment for them.

With nothing to do but dangle and wait until a divine being decided her fate, Bronwen began thinking of all the bad things she had done in her life. Some of them were hazy, fleeting moments and others were vividly memorable so that she still felt twinges of guilt.

When she was a child she had stolen a sweet from a jar in a shop, she had once thrown one of her father's books into a pond because it gave her nightmares, she had called Alda a witch after she stopped her from visiting a friend at a farm a few miles from her home, she had hidden a bottle of brandy from her father after he forced her to continue piano lessons, she had pretended to put money in the alms box at church so that she could spend it on a new book, she had thought about kissing Lord Guild and what it would be like to see him without a shirt.

It seemed like another lifetime before Bronwen finally opened her eyes again, but found that she was in the same empty space she had been before.

There must have been something she had missed in her musings. Some part of her life she had forgotten to evaluate. She considered the commandments in turn, as the priest did in her confessionals, and found no sins other than the ones she had already thought about.

Instead, Bronwen considered how she had died. The memory was surprisingly clear to her - Mr Clare's shop, her kidnapping, the strange circle of candles, the chains that held her to the rock, the knife that split her soul from her body. It made her surprisingly angry.

She looked down at herself for confirmation of how death had befallen her, but she was intact. The dress she wore was plain and unadorned, clinging to her shape like undergarments in a way that did not hide her modesty. It was neither the dress she wore to the tailor, nor the one she was to be married in. The thin material of this one would cause offence and made her feel bare, though you could not see through it.

Bronwen wriggled her body to test the movement and found that the manacles around her wrists constricted the more she struggled. The bitter metal quelled her essence without forgiveness and sent a dull throbbing into the fibres of her being.

Wracked with despair that she could not think of what she had done to deserve her punishment and because someone had decided to remove her from life for no reason she could think of, Bronwen hung her head and sobbed quietly, despite there being no one to hear.

She had little time to dwell on her predicament before she saw a movement in the darkness. Mist was flowing away from her, summoned to the farthest point of her vision so the atmosphere around her began to clear.

Bronwen had barely the energy or the will to care what happened next and she let her head loll forwards again.

"Interesting," a voice murmured somewhere in the distance. "Perhaps you are not as welcome in the Halfpoint as I first assumed."

Bronwen fluttered her eyes open momentarily and found the abyss still as such. She began moving, though could not decipher if it was up or down until she saw a figure below her, his arms held out in waiting.

The closer Bronwen descended towards him, the clearer her surroundings became and she could see the ground, made of a stone which appeared to move fluidly and flow in a spiral towards the man beneath her, as if he were the centre of this universe and everything drifted towards and around him.

Her weak form comfortably folded into his arms and she was immediately filled with warmth and contentment, her own spirit gravitating towards this being.

"Do not be fearful," he whispered as he held Bronwen close, her head resting on his muscular chest.

It was warm and inviting - *too* warm and *too* inviting. She sensed the wrongness of the sensation and opened her eyes to look at her saviour.

He was a man, his features comelier than any she had seen before. His closely trimmed facial hair edged his characteristics and his angled eyebrows gave him an intense, smouldering expression that could cause any woman to blush from it. His hair was an organised mess of ebony, flecked with hues of crimson and a hint of azure. His eyes matched it perfectly; as if formed of the same elements and it were possible to burn from the fire within them.

It unnerved Bronwen. It was not human.

She wriggled out of his grasp and placed her feet on the floor, stepping back from him guardedly.

"I am fearful," Bronwen whispered, surprised to find she had her voice still.

"You need not be." He stepped towards her, a black cloak trailing the ground behind him. His feet were bare and his shirt was plain and as tight as her dress was, so she could see each muscle beneath his skin, moving with precision and power - an uncontrolled, elemental force.

Bronwen held her hands in front of her to shield herself, unsure if this was another punishment or substantiation of purgatory. Her wrists were still chained together and she felt them tighten as she moved away, the links grinding against one another.

"I apologise for how you have been treated."

The man's eyes flashed with an anger that caused even

Bronwen to cower and when he held his hand out to her, she took another step back.

This time the manacles tightened heavily and she grimaced and whimpered from the ache it left her with. It was like catching an elbow on something hard but she could feel it all over, incapacitating and painful.

"Move no further, please, they will not release you."

The man looked genuinely troubled by her pain and tried to move forwards again. Bronwen was too panicked and turned to flee, causing her bonds to constrict and send pain lancing through her being, so much so that she cried out in agony and fell to the floor. Just as her knees were about to hit the stone, she found herself wrapped in his arms again.

Before she could move away, the man touched a finger to the chains and they dissipated into a mist that followed the first cloud.

The discomfort subsided to a dull throbbing, one that still left Bronwen immobile and once again in this strange man's arms.

"Does it still hurt?" he asked, staring deep into her eyes, his voice low and appealing.

Bronwen nodded slowly and watched as he gently held her hand in his and lifted her wrists to his lips, then placed a tender and innocent kiss upon each one where black bruises had formed. His eyes never left hers.

Bronwen felt the pulsing twinge cease and she filled with warmth again.

He wiped away a tear that had taken pause on her cheek and she did not shy from the contact.

"Why am I here?" Bronwen choked, not knowing what was right.

"Come," he said quietly, as if seducing a lover. "Let us become acquainted."

He gathered her into his arms again and walked through the darkness. It seemed as if they had only taken a few paces when a warm light bathed them and Bronwen was in another room, still in the arms of the secure stranger.

The air was warm and the light was bright from golden flames in torches around the walls. They walked down the new hallway, with dark blue wallpaper and deep burgundy carpet, in silence. Doors of carved wood stood to attention down either side of the wide passage. The first one opened wide by an unseen force and the air became warmer still as they walked through. The new room was heated by four large fireplaces that burned brightly and gave the room a charred and homey scent of pine, baked bread, fruity wine and the spicy smell of frankincense.

In the centre was a long table dominating the space, a triangular tablecloth pointed towards the arched double doors to a balcony, the stained-glass panes too dark to see what was outside.

The man placed Bronwen down gently into one of the deep sofas opposite the first fireplace. The heat from the inferno sapped her energy and made her feel hazy and somnolent. She tried to stay focused but the walls flowed like water, the red fire was tipped with blue and the man sat on the sofa beside her was disarming. Bronwen forced herself to sit up, keeping her eyes on him, then he smiled and she panicked at the effect it had on her.

Bronwen got off the sofa and stood behind the arm of it, keeping it between them.

"Where am I?"

"This is one of the many rooms in my home," the man said, his voice silky and alluring.

"Where is your home?" Bronwen looked around again. The table was full of food but none of it looked normal to her. It was too vivid, like an anti-dream – too much like reality.

"It is wherever I wish it to be and at this moment I wish it to be with you."

Bronwen looked back at the stranger and he seemed closer without ever moving. She took a cautious step away and wrapped her arms around herself.

"Who are you?"

He stood and offered his hand to her. When she did not take it, he walked to the high-backed chair at the far end of the table before answering her question.

"I have been called many names among men and beast; Yama, Leviathan, Lucifer, Belial, Apollyon, Bumalin, Azrael, Eblis, but none which yet please me enough to keep. For now, you may call me Thanatos."

Anguish and fear filled Bronwen's soul. There were only two names of those he had mentioned that she recognised and she immediately comprehended who she was sat across from, and hence, where she was.

"I have been sent to hell?" Her voice was desolate as she tried to think of what she had done to deserve the punishment. She had led a good Christian life, gone to church on a Sunday and confession when she had wronged. She was even prepared to face purgatory, so why had she been damned?

"You are here because of me. And no, you are not in hell, at least, not the hell you have been taught to fear. This is the Under-realm, mine to rule and mine to share."

He picked up a piece of bread from the table and began eating it, a queer smile on his face.

"*You* sent me to hell?" Bronwen accused, ignoring the correction, much to Thanatos's distaste. Though she now realised she was in the presence of the Devil, he did not frighten her. The thought of spending her afterlife in the eternal fires of hell, alone and without her family who had passed to comfort her, terrified her far more than a solid being.

She moved to the table and the silver chair that matched Thanatos's, needing to sit. It was warm to the touch as she sat stiffly into it and took a closer look at the array of food before her. Despite it looking different and never having had much of an appetite, she wanted the food more than she had ever craved it in life. It was a conscious effort not to take a piece of even something small. Instead, Bronwen concentrated on the polished glass plate and glass cutlery in front her, distorting the delicate design of the blue table cloth underneath.

At least she felt her mind clear slightly, being further from the fire.

"Will you not eat with me?" Thanatos asked as he placed a pinkish looking berry in his mouth, still smiling with his unnerving gaze.

What Bronwen knew of the Lord of Demons was that he delighted in tempting mortals and was a master of tricks, which is why she had not eaten anything from his table, but it was difficult not to trust him when he was not the vile creature Bronwen had been expecting, with horns and forked tongue. Thanatos, as he called himself, was a handsome man who had rescued her from chains and who's piercing eyes made her blush as if he could see through her clothes. And, though she tried not to, she could not help admire his masculine body beneath his own thin attire. In every sense, he appeared as a man, and a man her female body responded to.

Bronwen briefly remembered something from a sermon at the city's cathedral, a passage from the bible, which she held onto in her mind, to keep herself in check.

{For even Satan disguises himself as an angel of light.}

"Why am I here?"

"So full of questions, my Lady."

"Of course I am," Bronwen snapped then looked down at her lap. It was a reflex action and she almost looked around for her father's disapproval. But, of course, she would never see him again, nor her mother.

"What must my father be thinking now?" She murmured.

Thanatos startled her with a short laugh. "You needn't worry about him anymore."

"He isn't..."

"No. Not dead yet."

Bronwen panicked. "What do you mean yet?"

Thanatos quirked an eyebrow at her in amusement and took a long sip of wine from a blue tinted glass.

"All things die, Bronwen," he replied slowly and with an air of nonchalance that irritated her.

"And are you aware of *how* these things have died?" Bronwen questioned with an edge to her voice. He looked up at her, grinning.

"I was intimately aware of how *you* died."

"And that amuses you!" Bronwen did yell at him this time before snapping her mouth shut and looking down at her lap again.

She felt the air shift around her and flinched as a gentle hand held her chin and lifted her face to look deep into Thanatos's eyes.

"Do not do that," he said softly, his expression suddenly serious. "You needn't bow your head anymore, especially to me. I will not harm you, even if I am displeased."

He was leaning in close, with one arm on the side of her chair. Bronwen's eyes darted away from the intensity of him. She noticed his shirt was looser than she first thought and she could see down it from where he was bent over. Most of his chest was in shadow but she saw enough to make her blush and look away and up into his eyes again.

Thanatos let go of her chin when he was sure she would not look away and seemed pleased by her blushing cheeks. He sat back on the table, giving her some space and room to ease her racing heart.

Bronwen was quiet for a long while, not knowing where to look as she tried to keep her emotions in check. She had to keep reminding herself that he was the Devil, but felt less sure with each moment that passed.

"I was murdered," Bronwen whispered, not really sure why she said it, she just needed to hear the words. "Who would do this to me?"

"Before I answer more of your questions, my Lady, it is time you answer one of mine." Thanatos turned and ran his hand along the tablecloth as he made his way back to his own chair. He didn't sit but took the glass goblet of wine from the table and fixed her with a serious gaze as he drank from it languidly.

"How would that information serve you? If I were to tell you who your murderers are?"

Bronwen thought about the question. Before, when she was hanging in the void, it had not been immediately important as to how or why she had died. But, when she had remembered it, the knowledge had filled her with a rage that was unfamiliar to her. If she did find out who had done this to her, how *would* the information serve her? She couldn't do anything about it, and yet, she found herself needing to know.

"It would put my mind at ease."

"Or exacerbate your hardships."

Bronwen stood and placed her hands on the table to keep steady and forced herself to look Thanatos in the eye.

"Why was this done to me?" Unexpectedly the demon looked uncomfortable by Bronwen's accusations. Perhaps it was the pleading look in her eyes, or he was trying to ruse her into thinking he cared.

"The people who killed you serve me. I wanted you, so I took you but your death is not on my hands. Not originally," he finally replied, not lowering his gaze, his demeanour once more commanding and puissant.

"*You* sent me here?"

Thanatos looked uncomfortable again. "Not precisely. I

cannot answer all of your questions, my Lady, but know that if I do, they will be honest."

Bronwen sat back down stiffly, confused that someone had killed her and for the Lord of hell no less. "For what purpose could you want me?"

"What purpose has any man for a woman? I desire your companionship."

"My companionship?"

"This Under-realm is mine and it is my wish to share it, if you accept." Thanatos fixed her with an intense stare. "I am not as heartless as your holy men portray and the wants of a man still ails me."

"What wants?" Bronwen felt her skin prickle at what he might mean. She had felt this fear before but could not remember when.

"Come now, you cannot be that much of a Lady that you do not know the ways of the world." Thanatos leaned across the table towards her and his eyes roamed her body. "The desires of men cannot be so unfamiliar to *you*, Lady Bronwen."

"You wish me to..." Bronwen tried to think of the words and decided upon the closest thing to what he was implying. "...be your wife?"

Thanatos laughed and relaxed back into his chair. "Marriage is a condition invented by men as a way to claim property over one another. What I want from you is a partnership. Be mine as I shall be yours and you can have all the freedoms the mortal world denied you."

"With you."

It was not a question this time and Bronwen put such a disgusted tone to the words that she saw a flash of anger and hurt in Thanatos's eyes. He dropped his glass to the table and before Bronwen could blink he had pulled her chair to the side and stood in front of her, both hands on the arms of the chair, encasing her so his conspicuous body dominated her vision.

The air caught in Bronwen's lungs, hot and painful.

"Yes, with me," Thanatos said bitterly, his breath was cool on her lips and his eyes were level with hers. She had the sudden fear that he might kiss her.

"I will not go willingly," Bronwen said quickly, shocked by her own fortitude - she was still not afraid of this creature, whose striking eyes bore into her soul.

"I will have you no other way." Thanatos straightened slightly so she felt less incarcerated by his presence. "You must give me your permission. I will not take it."

Bronwen looked at Thanatos quizzically but could not tell if he were lying. He seemed so genuine and why would he tell her this if he could simply force himself on her?

"You will not force me?" She asked slowly in an attempt to find any deceit in the master of lies.

"I *cannot* fuck you without your say so, but you are *mine* for eternity."

This notion clearly irritated Thanatos, who pulled himself away from the chair and turned his back on her.

In normal circumstances Bronwen would have been appalled by the way he spoke to her, but having it put so plainly, without the usual frills and dodged answers she was used to, put her at ease.

Bronwen had no desire to let him take her maidenhood, if it even existed in this forsaken place, but she was still confused as to why he summoned her here if he could not simply take such a thing from her.

"Then, for what other purpose could you want me if I refuse you this?"

Thanatos turned back to face her with an enraged expression that almost made her shy away from the hatred behind his eyes, even though it was not directed at her.

"I want your *companionship* and this is what I will have from you, with or without your permission."

Bronwen could not think of what to say so stayed quiet, their eyes locked on one another in a duel of wills. Bronwen yielded first, afraid that she might be taken in by his words and feel pity for him. She sensed a loneliness in Thanatos, one that was too similar to hers that it threatened to tempt her to him.

"So, what do you wish from me, my Lady?" Thanatos held his arms out and bowed in a submissive gesture that caught Bronwen off guard. "Ask but one thing from me and I shall grant it as a welcoming gift."

Bronwen looked back at him again, making her eyes as soft as she could in an attempt to disarm him, as his sincerity had momentarily done to her.

"I wish for you to release me, if you say you cannot force me to do... *that*, then you should surely let me free."

"You are bound here with me. I cannot send you where you will never be welcome."

Bronwen assumed he was talking about heaven. She realised then that she had clung to the hope that if she somehow resisted this evil being, she would be granted passage through the gates of heaven and find peace there. Now, with all hope dashed, she fought the desolation that threatened to overcome her.

"Then there is no hope for me and I wish never to see your face again. I wish for those who have condemned me to this fate to join me in this sorrowful pit and suffer a far greater loss."

"Now *that*, I can grant."

Bronwen looked at Thanatos doubtingly. The scowl on her face was still present as she wondered which part of her request he was referring to.

"I agreed to only one wish from you but perhaps I can sweeten this tribute. I have no desire to see you miserable. Eternity is a weight you must suffer and I will not have you associate it with me. I will send you back to the living, as a chance to enact revenge however you see fit on those who have wronged you." Bronwen's heart lifted. She would be able to see her family again, her home, her friends.

Thanatos stepped towards her again and lowered his voice conspiratorially.

"But," he said and Bronwen felt her heart sink back into despair. "I cannot have you thinking you will be returning to a normal life. You are dead, Lady Bronwen, any life I give you will be temporary, so, once you have found all of your killers, you will come back to me."

Bronwen nodded slowly, thinking carefully.

"And if I chose not to return to you? If I still refuse to give you what you want from me?" she said delicately, not wanting to make him angry again. He looked thoughtful and leant on the back of the sofa.

"*If* you can resist my advances through the duration of your revenge, then I shall grant your second request. You will not have to see me again. But, if you cannot resist and you give yourself to me," he smiled at the thought. "Well, you would already be mine by then and must remain with me for eternity."

The offer was tempting, but Bronwen still did not trust him. Everything she had been taught since she was old enough to understand was that this creature was evil and vindictive and took pleasure in other people's pain. He had power in the hearts of men weak enough to submit and was manipulative without mercy. It made no sense that he would be willing to barter with her and he was too confident in his ability to woo her.

"Why would you do this and not just hold me here?"

"The chase is far more thrilling." Thanatos smirked.

There was no doubt Bronwen could resist him. Despite his charm and handsome features, Bronwen was a woman of principle. Thanatos would not have her, he underestimated her strength of will and she would torment him with it, but she also had no way of knowing if he would keep his end of the bargain. Was this some form of artful chicanery? Would it be worth the risk to find out? What else could she do with herself here if not gamble an already uncertain freedom from the demon who took her?

"Life is a lonely thing, my Lady. You will come to know me and want what *companionship* I can offer you," Thanatos said as if he had been reading her thoughts. He studied her features carefully. "You must ask yourself, how it makes you feel knowing the ones who sent you here still roam free? How do you feel knowing that they may never be punished for this crime?"

It made her... angry. Instead of falling into a well of shame at her predicament, Bronwen clung to the one feeling that her mortal decorum had denied her. Rage - more than she had ever felt before. She had always restrained her feelings when something offended her, as her moral upbringing had taught her to do. Now that she was dead and chained to this place no matter her actions, she wanted revenge on the men who abandoned her there. And there were no repercussions for ill deeds when she was already in hell.

"You will keep your word?" She asked suspiciously, her decision made.

He pushed himself away from the sofa and held the armrests of her chair as he leaned towards her again.

"Every one."

IV

All sound was muffled and a strange pounding dominated Bronwen's hearing - the beating of her heart. Her lungs burned for air and she frantically pushed herself to the surface of the water she had awoken in.

Panic consumed Bronwen as she clawed at the liquid, following an instinct that guided her back to the air. It was a moment before she realised she had her head above water and took in a ragged breath. Her head dunked a few more times as she paddled awkwardly to the side of the river, struggling in the many layers of her dress.

The strong current swirled around her and she had to drag her nails into the mud of the bank to heave herself onto it before the river could pull her away again.

Bronwen lay face down and panting, coughing water out of her throat before she rolled onto her back and looked up at the stars.

The night was surprisingly clear for autumn and Bronwen briefly panicked at how long she had been dead for, then a chill wind brushed across her wet skin, bringing with it the crisp smell of winter to come.

Thanatos had warned Bronwen that returning to her body would not be a pleasant experience, especially if it was not entirely intact. She would momentarily feel the mortal pain of all that had occurred to her flesh since leaving it. The thought had not discouraged her from returning to the mortal world – a chance to see the sky again.

She was fortunate they had been rather delicate with her remains and had just started to think that her resurrection had not been as traumatic as the demon had said, when a violent pain lanced through her. Bronwen rolled back onto her side as her body convulsed and she vomited on the damp grass, the bile from her empty stomach burning her throat.

Bronwen gasped and clutched at her neck, feeling all the air escape her lungs. She arched her back and tried to cough out whatever was preventing her from breathing but nothing came. Her eyes watered and just as her vision began to darken she was allowed to breathe again, only to be incapacitated by a new pain. It felt as if every nerve in her body stung as it welded itself back with her spirit. Like putting freezing hands into hot water.

When it finished, Bronwen curled into a ball, clutching her knees as she waited for more, not caring if vomit caked her wet hair. She was not sure how long she lay there before she became aware of her surroundings again; the smell of the river and the contents of her stomach, the sound of the birds already calling the morning forth, despite the darkness.

Finally, she uncurled herself and looked around. She was sat on a gravelled and muddy bank next to a stone bridge. The water was fast flowing through it and there were a few trees looking like bare skeletons in the shadows.

Bronwen pushed herself up from the ground with difficulty and inspected her body. Her once creamy gown was now torn and filthy from the river and the dagger that had taken her life. She inspected each part of her that was supposed to have an ailment - a scrape on her arm and broken rib from falling off the wall, a bruised cheek and sore head from being struck in the alley, a deep gaping hole in her chest where she had been stabbed - none of these existed.

Other than being grotesquely dirty, her form was flawless. Or, at least as flawless as it had been. Bronwen moved the cut fabric aside from her stomach and saw that the scar surrounding her navel was still present. Despite it having been reopened, it was not completely gone like her other wounds, only healed. It was still puckered pink skin and was almost a welcome companion – at least she knew she was herself again.

Bronwen wondered, not for the first time, what the symbol meant. Perhaps that maid was right all those years ago, perhaps it had been the Devil's mark, considering someone had used it in a satanic ritual to take her life. Had someone tried to kill her before? Maybe now she had motivation enough to find out what it all meant. Was that not why she had come back?

A sound behind Bronwen startled her and she staggered in her sodden dress to hide under the bridge. She didn't want anyone to find her like that. A half-drowned, river rat in a tattered, bloodstained dress.

Horses hooves clapped through the stones on the road above and echoed into the ones that made the bridge. Bronwen could hear a murmur of voices and laughter but not what was said over the noise of the horse. She pressed herself to the slimy wall as they passed overhead, further covering herself in green moss where it painted the stone arch.

Once she was certain they were gone, Bronwen sighed heavily and stepped back onto the open bank. She started up the slight hill to get to the road. Her feet caught on her dress and she sprawled in the mud on her hands and knees.

A hand came into view in front of her eyes and she was more grateful than shocked at someone being there.

Bronwen looked up to thank the stranger and saw the Devil instead.

Thanatos looked impeccably clean compared to Bronwen. Even his black boots seemed untouched by the muck around him. Bronwen stared at him incredulously, then at his hand, like he was offering her a piece of rotten fruit thinking it a kind gesture.

"It is just a hand, my Lady," Thanatos said when she hesitated.

Bronwen tried to think of a clever retort but was too mentally exhausted and begrudgingly lifted her hand to accept his aid.

Thanatos easily, almost gracefully, pulled Bronwen to her feet, then held her about the waist as he assisted her up the steep bank, never stumbling or showing any sign of fatigue.

Once on the flat road, Bronwen was quick to pull away from him. A chill across her stomach reminded her that her dress was falling apart and she used her arms to hold the pieces together so he could not see her bare flesh.

Thanatos's eyes slid down to where she was hiding her scar and then away again, a flash of irritation in his eyes.

"So, my Lady, what doest thou here?"

Bronwen shivered in the cold. The first thing she needed was clothing and for that she needed a sense of direction.

"Which way is the city?" She asked, not expecting an answer.

"Just follow the sound of human suffering and the smell of rotting moral," Thanatos said and led the way across the bridge, the opposite way the horse had gone.

Bronwen hesitated before following him. She didn't know where she was but moving was better than standing in the cold.

A little way from the bridge, Thanatos turned off the path and started through the fields, keeping the Itchen river to the right. Bronwen hesitated again, deciding which path to follow. The one she was on was a rough track, with imprints of horse's hooves in the hardening mud, but it was darker than the one Thanatos was taking across the beaten fields and the ground was harder, full of stones that would cut her bare feet. She made up her mind and took the path she was less likely to be seen on.

Thanatos slowed down and allowed Bronwen to catch up with him and they walked alongside each other in the dim in a surprisingly comfortable silence.

As they walked between the trees to the sound of running water, Bronwen thought hard about her next steps. First, she needed clothing, then she needed to find her house and then, the difficult part began. What would she say to her father and Lord Guild? She couldn't tell them the truth, that she had been murdered, made a deal with the Devil and had come back to life again. But she needed to tell them something.

"How long have I been dead?" Bronwen asked Thanatos without looking at him.

"It is the evening after you were killed."

Bronwen was relieved. At least it would make her disappearance easier to explain. Perhaps she could say she just wanted a stroll or needed time to think.

"It felt like longer," she said quietly.

"Yes, it does," Thanatos replied, a wistful edge to his voice.

She looked up at him but it was difficult to see his face in the shadows and he didn't return her gaze.

Bronwen noticed she was pinching her arm. Apparently, the habit hadn't died with her. She still needed reminding that this was not a dream – she was in the present and all that had happened was true.

They fell into silence again, passing only one distant farmhouse through the fields of clustered animals, that kept warm by staying close to one another. Bronwen sniffed and tightened her arms around herself. As her mind became clearer, she was more aware of how her body was feeling. Her nose, ears, fingers and toes were almost numb in the cold. Her feet were still bare and she was glad they walked on soft soil rather than cobble stones despite the puddles of chilly mud that gave her squelching brown shoes.

A chill breeze touched each tree as it moved towards them and Bronwen sniffed again and felt her teeth chatter when the wind hit her soaked dress. She needed clothes soon, before she caught her death from cold - if that were possible. Bronwen looked at Thanatos again but he seemed unaffected by the weather, wearing nothing but loose shirt and trousers. At least he had boots for his feet.

"Is it not possible to just appear back at home?" Bronwen asked him. "I thought the Devil could appear anywhere?"

Thanatos seemed to bristle at the name but his tone was jovial when he replied. "*I* can be anywhere. You cannot. A human body cannot fall into the stream of the dead and come back up downriver like a soul can."

Bronwen thought to make a joke of how she had done just that but she kept quiet except for the chattering of her teeth. She thought Thanatos moved ever so slightly closer to her and a warmth seemed to radiate from his body, enveloping her against the breeze so she stopped shivering so much and began to relax her tense muscles. She supposed it was the equivalent of a gentleman wrapping his cloak around her shoulders. She could not remember Kole ever giving up his coat to her.

"I was not expecting to see you here," Bronwen said to fill the silence.

"I could not leave a Lady to walk alone at night. I am a gentleman after all."

Bronwen scoffed. "A gentleman would not have made such an indiscrete proposal to a Lady."

"No, they would rather wait until your wedding night when you cannot escape them and call it their husbandly rights. I, however, have given you a choice."

"I had no choice when my life was taken from me," Bronwen said bitterly, feeling sorrowful again.

"Incorrect. You could have chosen to inhale the sedative and die quicker. Instead, you fought for what chance to had and you chose to fight now."

Three deep thrums startled Bronwen and she looked up to see a tall shadow looming in the distance over the tops of the trees, blacker than the sky behind it. It was a church bell singing the hour, the gold letters on the face of the clock were small but clearly visible.

Bronwen almost ran towards it but stopped herself. It was an irrational impulse stemming from her upbringing, she had briefly thought that by barring herself in the church it would save her from the demon beside her, but no house of God would save her, now that she was Satan's whore. Instead, she treaded silently towards it, intending to find some clothing and thinking on Thanatos's words.

Perhaps by taking one small step at a time, she could rationalise what she had agreed to do and resist whatever sweet darkness he tempted her with.

The treeline soon ended and Bronwen could see the whole building. The main tower was squat and square with three more sections coming out of the base. Long brick walls came away from it which presumable hid a courtyard beyond. Bronwen suspected the main building to be in the shape of a cross and realised where she was - the Parish of St Faith.

It was next to the hospital of St Cross and Almshouse of Noble Poverty, a charity for the poor and men who could not work. It was maintained by the Brothers of St Cross. They were not monks, however, and Bronwen knew they would help her, but still she could not ask.

"Afraid you might be struck down?" Thanatos mocked when she stopped next to the high walls of the garden.

"No," Bronwen replied. "Just afraid." She finished more quietly.

Bronwen looked up at the wall in dismay. It was far too high to climb over and she wasn't comfortable breaking into a charity house.

"Assuming you do not live in a church, which could cause problems, why have you stopped to stare so intently at a stone wall?" Thanatos asked with a grin, folding his arms and leaning against the wall casually.

"I need to change my clothing before I go home. It raises too many questions." Bronwen looked down at her cut dress and tried to pull the tattered pieces over her stomach again.

"I do not think what you are wearing will be their main concern."

"I suppose you are right, but they will still ask questions I cannot answer."

"And why can you not answer them?" Bronwen looked at Thanatos, with his smirking smile too handsome to be human. Surely, he knew why she could not tell anyone of what had befallen her? It was too obvious to be voiced so she didn't answer him exactly.

"Perhaps because I do not know the answers." Bronwen turned away from him and looked around. They had been speaking at a casual volume and she worried they might wake someone.

"There are ways to find them." Thanatos's voice sounded like it came from above her and Bronwen turned to see him standing tall on the top of the wall. He extended his hand down towards her, bending his long legs so she might reach him. "You have but to ask."

Bronwen didn't pause this time in taking his hand. The sooner she got home, the better.

She let out a small surprised gasp as he lifted her in one smooth motion, without a hint of unbalancing, as if she weighed nothing. Bronwen, however, caught her feet wrong when he set her on the wall and would have fallen if he had not grabbed her waist and pulled her against his stable form.

She felt his warmth flow through her again and tried not to blush at how close they were.

"Would you prefer I let go?" Thanatos said as he released his hold on her waist. Bronwen unbalanced again, her dress still wet and heavy.

"No!" she cried and clung to him in panic. It was not far to fall, but it would hurt. Thanatos laughed softly.

"I will not let you fall," he murmured in Bronwen's ear making her open her eyes she had unconsciously closed. She loosened her hold on him and pulled her head back from his.

Thanatos loosened his grip then, in the same easy movement, began to lower her into the walled garden. "The fall of humankind was never *my* doing."

Bronwen's feet touched the soft ground. She let go of Thanatos's hand and stepped away as soon as she was balanced. She turned to view the garden but was not fortunate enough to find a line of drying clothing.

"But be sure to avoid the apples in this garden," Thanatos murmured close to her ear again, clearly amused by his own comment.

Bronwen took a moment to look around, hoping in vain to find a washing line that someone had forgotten to take in.

Unfortunately, the garden was empty of all but trees, flowers and a small green lake so she cautiously headed to the side of the building and a heavy wooden door.

She listened carefully but couldn't hear anyone on the other side.

"Do you intend to knock?" Thanatos said, making Bronwen jump. She had forgotten he was still following her.

"It is most likely locked," Bronwen whispered.

"Try it."

Bronwen was sure she heard the smallest of scrapes on wood before she twisted the handle. She cringed as the door creaked open just enough for her to slip inside.

The corridor was dark and silent and she waited for her eyes to adjust to the lack of light. There was a slight glow coming from under the doors and she avoided these rooms, heading to the one open door.

She was fortunate and found herself in a small kitchen with a basket of half folded laundry.

There was a fire smouldering in the hearth to see by and she grabbed shirt and trousers from the unfolded pile.

They smelt musty, like old books, despite being washed but it would have to do. It was better than turning up in a blood stained sliced open wedding gown. Men's clothing would be easier to explain.

Bronwen walked over to the fire and reached behind her to start pulling the laces of her bodice.

"Would you like some assistance?" came a silky voice behind her.

She turned on her heel to face Thanatos. She had forgotten he was there again; absorbed in her thoughts.

"I am hardly going to let you undress me," she said.

"I have no qualms with you undressing yourself," he replied with a smirk.

"You are despicable."

He shrugged one shoulder and grinned at her as he faded away. Bronwen blinked a few times and put her hand over the shadow where he had just been.

Once she was satisfied he was gone, she tried to remove her dress. It was a struggle and she had to rip the fabric even more to manage it. Luckily her inner corset was a modern one that allowed her to undo it from the front and the slashes across it helped.

The thick brown shirt scratched her skin and the dark trousers that farmers would wear had to be pulled tightly with the cord so they didn't fall down her slim waist. There were no shoes but there was a floppy woollen hat which Bronwen tucked all her matted damp hair into. She felt strange wearing men's clothing but she had little choice and doubted a brotherhood would have clothes suitable for a woman.

Once she was dressed, Bronwen picked up her wedding gown and considered throwing it to the fire, but it would cause too much smoke and perhaps the fabric might be salvageable. Instead, she folded it as best she could and left it on the lone chair next to the fire, hoping it was payment enough for stealing the clothes.

Bronwen went back out into the corridor and found another heavier door at the end of it with no light coming from behind it. She reasoned that it could be the exit and slid the bolt across as quietly as she could managed.

She was lucky again and found herself out the front of the almshouse.

She knew where she was now, her time exploring the city made it easy for her to navigate. Bronwen followed the outer wall until she came to an open arch and headed for the trees; into the night once more.

Bronwen stared up at the building that was her home. Metrom Hall. She had once disliked how it lorded over the grounds and stood away from the city, as if it was superior to rest. It was large with four floors, its white and grey stones free from foliage, its numerous windows tall with gold painted frames and the wide pillars at the entrance showed a strength that matched the Baron who owned it.

Bronwen just wanted to run to her room and cover herself in blankets.

It had taken her almost an hour to travel home; across empty fields, past quiet farm buildings, over the railway tracks that ran like a slash across the city, trying to avoid being seen and slicing her feet open any more than they already were. She had come across no one on her travels in the strange limbo of time after the wrongdoers and night walkers had gone to sleep and the workers of the day had yet to awaken.

Witching hour. Is that what she was now? Trading her soul to the Devil in exchange for powers beyond mortals? But she had no powers. Bronwen may have returned from the dead but she was still weak and female and human flesh.

She considered briefly if she could sneak up to her room without anyone noticing but the doors would have been locked. The curtains on the lower windows had been drawn but she could see firelight glowing around the gaps which was unusual for the early hour. She had been gone for a night and a day, perhaps they were still up looking for her. As she had awoken in the river, they had yet to pronounce her dead or recover her body. She expected Lord Guild would still be inside.

Bronwen took a steadying breath, holding onto one of the marble pillars on the porch. The stone was cold beneath her fingertips and bare feet as she stepped up to the door. Bronwen prepared herself, reaching her hand up to knock.

She paused, half expecting Thanatos to say something in her ear and reappear again but he had not returned since abandoning her at the Almshouse. She shook her head and lowered her hand to try the handle first. Bronwen gasped as it turned without her touching it and she shielded her eyes against the sudden brightness as the door opened.

"What the Devil...?" came the unmistakable voice of James Durward. Bronwen moved her hand away to see him looking affronted and disgusted at the dishevelled creature on the doorstep, no doubt thinking it would be a beggar calling at such an unwelcome hour. He had not been expecting to see anyone when he opened the door.

Bronwen looked up at him and found tears came easily. It took James a moment to recognise her beneath the brim of the hat she wore and in men's clothing but once he saw beneath the grime covering Bronwen's face a chaos ensued.

Bronwen was mildly aware of James shouting for help. A coat fell around her shoulders, a woman cried out and strong arms pulled her gently into the warmth of the house.

In the hallway, everything was so distinct and vivid it was almost heavenly, despite her only being away from it for a day.

Bronwen hadn't quite finished taking it all in before she was led to another room.

Through tears that now fell unbidden down her mud streaked cheeks, she could see her father at the far end of the room. There seemed to be a greater distance between them than ever before but despite this, and the tears blurring her vision, she could still make out his face clearly.

Donovan's face shuffled through a multitude of expressions to finally settle on the most dominant emotion - fear. Not the kind of terror that comes from seeing a ghost, but the kind of incapacitating horror from seeing every person you have ever wronged smiling back at you from behind a mirror.

Bronwen noticed a movement next to her and felt the arms that held her let go, then someone blocked her view of her father and she refocused her eyes, letting them settle on the face of Lord Guild.

"We have been so worried about you," he said, placing his hands on her shoulders, the weight of them felt like too much for Bronwen and her legs trembled and her body began to fall. Before she reached the floor, arms caught her and the familiar burnt oak smell of Lord Guild consumed all other senses. He gathered Bronwen into a bundle in his arms and placed her on the sofa next to the fire at the far end of the room.

"She needs water," Kole barked at one of the lingering servants before turning back to Bronwen. "When you did not return from your dress fitting, we feared the worst. Are you alright, my Lady?"

Bronwen was thankfully stalled in answering as Alda entered the room.

"Thank goodness!" She exclaimed, coming to her Lady's side and feeling her brow as she had when Bronwen was a child. "Where have you been? You are filthy. And what are you wearing? It is so unseemly. Ruth, hand me that blanket. I said you should not have gone alone. Where are your shoes?"

Alda continued her fretting and lecturing while placing a blanket over Bronwen and ordering some water, despite Kole already having done so. He crouched at Bronwen's side, a worried expression on his face. He had taken one of Bronwen's hands in his own without her noticing. It felt too tight and hot around her fingers so she freed herself gently so she could hold both hands out to accept the glass of water from James.

Bronwen put the glass to her lips and swallowed something that thankfully didn't taste like river waste. The pleasantness of it was short lived as she felt it burn her stomach and her body convulsed once before Lord Guild placed a hat under her chin, just as she vomited another bout of river and stomach into it.

"Sorry," Bronwen mumbled as the hat was removed. Her frizzy hair fell around her face and she realised it had been *her* hat which she had just thrown up into.

"The search for Lady Bronwen can be called off," Lord Guild addressed the room, uncoiling from his crouching position. "Fetch a doctor, immediately."

"No, please, no doctor," Bronwen murmured.

"She doesn't need a doctor," Donovan barked, as if Bronwen had not said anything.

Bronwen watched as Kole strode over to her father, who still had not moved from the fire. He remained staring at her, unnoticed in the disorder.

He started as Kole grabbed his arm and gripped it harder than was polite. Lord Guild leant towards Donovan and whispered something to him, snapping the man out of his state of shock - though the fear in his eyes remained. Donovan made a small movement of his head and finally moved to stand closer to Bronwen at her feet.

"Where have you been, milady? Why did you not come back with the carriage?" Alda was questioning her again but this time required an answer.

"It was not there," Bronwen said quietly, pulling her eyes away from her father. He had stopped staring at her and now avoided looking in her direction at all. "I was..."

"Hush," Kole interrupted, placing a hand on Bronwen's knee. "Rest now, Lady Bronwen, there will be time for questions later." He gave Alda a look that even she could not argue with.

Bronwen nodded slowly and closed her eyes. Someone pulled the blanket up to her shoulders.

"Kole," Bronwen heard her father say in a low and shaken voice.

"Not here," Kole snapped and Bronwen felt a shift in the air and the door to the room closed as they left.

She sensed Alda had remained and a few others so relaxed her newly gifted body and waited for the blissful void of sleep.

V

Despite her best efforts, natural sleep did not have the grace to visit Bronwen.

Instead she had spent the hours before dawn gathering her thoughts. The first hour she spent taking in the sounds and smells she had always known yet never fully appreciated before. How loud a crackling fire could be and the lingering smell of its smoke, how loudly Alda breathed and how she smelt mildly of damp soil, how Kole's authority in a room meant Bronwen could sense he was nearby, even before hearing him speak.

"I think it best we move her to a more comfortable room," Lord Guild said quietly to Alda when he came back into the drawing room. Bronwen's father was not with him, nor did he visit later.

Bronwen felt the air shift and Kole's distinct aroma dispelled all others - the light bouquet of lavender with a heavier scent of cedar, oakmoss and something else Bronwen couldn't place. It was almost like breathing in a cold frost on a summer's day.

"Milord, I hope you are not planning to..." Alda didn't finish her sentence and Bronwen had to stifled a startled gasp as Kole gathered her into his arms. He did so gently but it was unexpected and Bronwen felt uncomfortable so close to his chest, she wanted to wriggle free of him but kept still.

"Young man!" Alda scolded as Kole moved towards the door. He stopped suddenly and by the direction of her voice, Bronwen knew Alda had moved in Kole's way. "I hope you do not plan to whisk away my Lady like a barbarian gathering his spoil! I will not hear of it!"

Bronwen desperately wanted to peek. Alda was overstepping herself. She got away with speaking to her father this way just barely and only after a great many years of service, but Kole was an Earl.

"Mrs Keeper, if you are so concerned that I might take your Lady's virtue, in her father's home, whilst she is in this traumatised state and the whole household is listening, then you are gravely mistaken. If you are so concerned, then please do feel free to chaperone. Heaven forbid I get in the way of propriety."

Bronwen tried not to giggle. It appeared Alda had met her match. She made an indignant sound as Kole moved past her and began up the stairs. Bronwen imagined her expression and her mouth twitched at the corners.

"I would prefer to have my women conscious at least," Kole murmured to himself, his breath warming Bronwen's cheeks and lips. Suddenly his words were not so amusing and she felt the desperate need to be free of his arms again. Luckily it wasn't long before she was being settled into a deep bed in a room with scents and sounds that she knew to be her own.

A few more hours passed while Bronwen shuffled her thoughts and the grey autumn daylight established itself.

Lord Guild had remained in the room, as had Alda. Despite Kole's rebuff, Bronwen knew she would not have left her Lady alone with a man. Bronwen was irrationally grateful for not being left alone with Kole and the clacking of Alda's needlework had been a calming companion.

Just as Bronwen had decided to awaken, Alda had left the

room, she could only assume to fetch more yarn or to visit the washroom.

The room was silent for a long while but the atmosphere had a texture to it that told Bronwen Lord Guild was still present. It was strange that Alda had not said where she was going. Perhaps Kole was asleep, so Bronwen decided this would be a good time to wake, before Alda returned and overwhelmed her with questions.

Bronwen heard Kole move.

The shift in the air made her hair prickle and she struggled keeping her eyes closed as Kole moved closer to the bed.

More confused than alarmed, Bronwen wondered at his intention then felt his breath on her cheek.

Uncontrollably, her breathing quickened in response to his unnerving proximity. He remained staring down at her, his own breathing calm and measured in comparison. She desperately wanted Alda to return and the scar on her stomach started to prickle so Bronwen had to concentrate on not scratching it.

Why was he so close? Was he trying to wake her? Was it simply to check she was still breathing? Did he plan to kiss her?

A few moments later Alda's footsteps were audible outside the door and the stifling pressure that had been slowly closing around Bronwen abated. She heard a movement in the room as Kole returned to his seat in time for the door opening and Alda returned to her needles without comment.

Bronwen stayed how she was for a little while longer, unable to make sense of Lord Guild's strange behaviour. Finally, she had no further reason to keep up her façade, so fluttered her eyes open.

Kole's was the first face she settled upon. He was sat on the back wall, directly in Bronwen's view. An involuntary gulping noise escaped her at his almost menacing expression, adumbrated by the shadows of the burgundy curtains lining the window. His hands on either side of the arm chair dug into the cushions and his stare was unblinking.

Bronwen blinked once and Kole's whole demeanour changed, even his position. He was suddenly sat forwards, hands together almost in prayer and placed against his mouth, his eyes soft and full of worry.

The change had been so inhumanly quick that Bronwen wondered if she had imagined the first position. She had little time to dwell on it as Kole immediately noticed her awaken and gasped with relief, alerting Alda who dropped her needlework and hurried to her Lady's side.

"Milady, we have been worried half to death!" she exclaimed.

"I shall go and inform Lord Wintre," Lord Guild said; his voice full of relief.

"How long have I been asleep?" Bronwen asked meekly once Kole had left. She felt as if she were lying to Alda who had always cared for her beyond duty.

"Only a few hours. The whole household has been sleepless since your disappearance. Where have you been, domina domus?" Though her voice was stern, a waver in it and the use of the endearment betrayed Alda's worry.

Bronwen looked down at her hands, her fingernails had dirt underneath them and she hid them under the bedcovers.

"When I escaped Mr Clare's shop, I became disorientated and lost myself."

"Escaped?" Alda demanded. "What on Earth were you escaping from?"

Bronwen looked up at her with sorrowful eyes and Alda's expression softened. The woman glanced at the open door. The hallway was empty and she sat on the bed close to

Bronwen and leaned in.

"If you wish to escape from this marriage then, there are ways to," Alda said, startling Bronwen at her frankness. "I will help you, if that is what you wish."

"No!" Bronwen said in alarm. "I was not trying to run away from home."

Alda relaxed slightly and stood up again but Bronwen knew she had been serious. The notion was oddly comforting, though she could not guess at how Alda had planned to prevent her marriage to Lord Guild. Had she been planning for it the whole time, waiting for affirmation from her Lady?

Lord Guild returned then with Bronwen's father in tow.

Donovan stood at the end of his daughter's bed and nodded in approval. His entire character had changed dramatically from the previous day. He was stern and eminent once more, as Bronwen had always known him. The fear behind his eyes was still present, only now it was well masked. If Bronwen had not been looking for it, she would not have noticed at all.

"Father. Lord Guild," Bronwen breathed, well-rehearsed in her head while she had feigned sleep. "I am so relieved to be home."

"What happened to you?" Donovan demanded; his voice shaky. Kole moved ever so slightly between Bronwen and her father.

"Lady Bronwen, your father and I have been looking all over Winchester for you, I even sent word to Guildford to see if you had gone there. Mr Clare said you left his shop without your shoes or day clothes and the coachman and guards that brought you in the carriage claimed they never saw you come out and waited there all night before returning to Metrom."

Bronwen did not mention that the carriage and her guards had not been there, not wanting to get the men into trouble. She didn't blame them for getting bored while waiting for her and had most likely found the nearest public house.

It was interesting that Mr Clare claimed not to know anything. The ruckus that must have been made from the fight with her first attacker would surely have alerted him, as well as the mess that was made of his room, not to mention the unconscious body Bronwen had left there.

She cringed at the memory, at the feeling of being in blinding panic, mild relief and then back into terror again. She pulled her knees up to her chest and hugged them against herself. The movement reminded her that she was still in men's clothing and smelt like river muck. Bronwen blushed knowing that Kole had seen her like that - *was* seeing her like that.

"Might I wash and change first?" She asked in a small voice. Despite having decided upon what tale she would tell of her disappearance, actually doing so was harder than she thought and she preferred to be back in her own clothes and feeling herself again for it.

"Do not be so foolish."

Bronwen looked up as her father spoke, shocked by his tone. Donovan met her gaze for the briefest of moments before looking away. "We need to know exactly what you are going to say."

"I think what Lord Wintre means is," interrupted Lord Guild, fully putting his body between them. "The more information we have, the better we can help you and understand what happened."

"I am certain it can wait a few more hours, gentlemen." It was Alda's turn to step between them, though because of her height, both men could still see Bronwen over Alda's head.

The maid stood her ground, crossing her arms expectantly for them to leave. Bronwen's father opened his mouth to protest but Alda raised her eyebrows at him. On the matter of womanly ablutions, Alda was not to be contested with.

The men left swiftly and Alda wasted no time, ordering a bath to be drawn and Bronwen's bedsheets changed. Alda didn't pepper Bronwen with questions as she helped get her clean again in the methodical, matter-of-fact way she had.

Once she was bathed, clothed and brushed, Bronwen relaxed a little, feeling like a Lady once more. The bath water had been a murky brown when Bronwen got out and it had taken almost half an hour to brush the tangles out of her hair. Regretfully, she had not noticed when her borrowed clothes had been taken away.

When Alda deemed her presentable, she had sent Bronwen on her way. Bronwen breathed out heavily and made her way down the stairs. On the large landing of the first floor, Bronwen could see the door to the drawing room. It was closed and she paused to listen to raised voices coming from inside. She recognised her father's but could only make out Lord Guild's words.

"...think I give a shit about what this means to him?"

Bronwen frowned as she listened for her father's reply. It was too muffled to hear, even as she leaned over the banister. It was clear however, that he sounded just as aggravated as Kole. She had not heard the Earl speak such profanities before.

"If you do not get your fucking head together, you force us to do it for you."

Bronwen pulled back in surprise as James entered the hallway and tapped lightly on the door.

Her father barked for him to enter and as James opened it, Lord Guild glanced up and noticed Bronwen on the stairs.

He gave her a warm smile which she forced herself to return, then Kole entered the hallway to greet her, holding out a hand to assist the rest of the way down the stairs and into the room.

"Lady Bronwen," he said, bowing low and kissing her hand gently. "You have no idea how much we have been worrying about you. You must be famished."

He helped her into a chair at the head of the small dining table, reserved for small parties, pushing the chair in too tightly towards the table. Bronwen readjusted when he moved away and turned in her chair to look at her father. He had his back to her by the window so all she could see was the tense line of his shoulders.

"Are you sure you should be out of bed so soon?" Kole said, interrupting her thoughts. "Judging by the state you were in yesterday; I dread to think what you have been through."

"I am quite well, thank you, Lord Guild."

The servants began filing into the room with trays of food and tea, instructed by Mr Durward. Donovan came to sit next to Kole at the opposite end of the table from Bronwen. He was still avoiding looking at her.

Bronwen placed a napkin over her knees, wondering what she could say to coax her father out of his mood. As the last servant left, James closed the door behind them, shutting out the draft and revealing Thanatos leaning against the far wall. Bronwen jumped, hitting her knees on the underside of the table and knocking the tea that Lord Guild was pouring.

"Bronwen!" her father scolded.

"That's quite alright, Lord Wintre," Kole said as James came forwards to mop up tea from the table.

Both men looked at Bronwen when she did not speak. She was still staring open mouthed at Thanatos who was grinning at her smugly, his arms crossed over his chest so the muscles there bulged, even in the loose shirt he was wearing. Donovan turned to see what she was staring and back again, unperturbed by the demon leaning against the wall.

"What on earth are you staring at?" Donovan questioned.

"I think 'on earth' is where you are mistaken, my dear Baron," Thanatos said with a grin.

Kole turned to look as well and Bronwen almost called out to stop him, not wanting him to see the Devil who seemed intent on haunting her.

"No wonder my Lady is disturbed with you standing there, be gone with you, I doubt the toast needs guarding any more than I do."

Bronwen gasped at Kole's words, then she saw Adam Whyms move from where he had been standing in the shadows of the room next to Thanatos.

"No!" Bronwen said a little too loudly, realising that she was the only one who could see or hear Thanatos. She lowered her voice to a normal level again. "Please, Mr Whyms should stay, he just startled me, that is all. I apologise, my head is not in the right place at the present moment."

Adam's expression was unreadable and he waiting for a nod from Kole before standing in the corner again. As much as Adam made Bronwen uncomfortable, she knew he could use whatever weapons he had hidden in his jacket, whether they would work against a demon or not was irrelevant.

"It is understandable," Lord Guild replied, smiling at her. He had both hands looped under his chin and was studying her with interest.

Bronwen tried to ignore Thanatos as he did a full circle around the table and came to lean his arm against the high back of her father's chair, watching her in the same manner as Kole.

Thanking the servant who poured her and Lord Guild more tea, Bronwen brought the delicate china to her lips. Before she drank, she breathed in a heavy, hot breath of steam, filling her lungs with warmth. She took a sip and let the liquid fill her mouth with flavour. But it was not a pleasant taste. In fact, it made her want to gag.

She put the cup back down in disgust, perhaps her tastes had changed since returning. Instead, she carefully buttered a slice of toast but before she could bite into it, she saw Thanatos shake his head slowly, his expression serious. Bronwen put the toast back on her plate. She wasn't hungry anyway and the tea had put her off.

"You are not eating, my Lady?" Lord Guild questioned.

"My appetite seems to have left me, my Lord," Bronwen explained. "I shall have something later."

"Perhaps we should have called the doctor out," Kole said to Bronwen's father, who had said very little. He usually dominated conversation and she wondered if it had something to do with the altercation she had overheard between he and Lord Guild. Or perhaps it was something the demon at his side was doing, who had been watching the proceedings with a bored expression.

"No, that is not necessary," Bronwen assured them. The last thing she wanted was someone poking at her and maybe finding something that would reveal or condemn her. "They did not harm me."

"They?" Donovan said, stirring in his seat, looking at Bronwen finally as if searching her eyes for the answer.

"Are you ready to discuss it?" Kole asked gently, breaking the stare between them.

Bronwen nodded and Thanatos's interest was suddenly peeked. Kole stood and picked up his tea, his plate of food abandoned.

"Let us move to the fire where it is warmer," he said, gripping Donovan's shoulder hard as he passed.

Bronwen stood and saw that her father had not eaten anything either.

"This should be interesting."

Bronwen jumped at Thanatos's voice in her ear as she made her way to the fire. Luckily no one had seen her reaction, except perhaps Adam who was presumably still in the shadows.

Lord Guild sat on one end of the long sofa, closest to the window and gestured for Bronwen to take the space next to him. She made her way over but just as she was about to sit, Thanatos was there, grinning widely. Instead, Bronwen chose a lone armchair that faced the fire, trying to be nonchalant about refusing Lord Guild's invitation.

"When you are ready, my Lady," Kole said gently.

Bronwen nodded and looked to her father for support but he was staring away from her again. His body was tense and he held onto the sides of his own armchair, as if he were ready to jump up from it at a moment's notice.

Bronwen tried to put it out of her mind and concentrated on her story.

"After I was fitted into my dress at Mr Clare's shop, he left me alone for a moment and then," Bronwen took a deep sobbing breath. It was easy to do as she recalled the memory of her attack.

"Take your time," Kole said, his voice sounded as strained as her father's seating position. It was the first time he had sounded almost nervous.

"Someone grabbed me from behind. He had a cloth and bottle of chloroform and tried to force it over my mouth. I managed to fight him off and get away and escaped the shop using the back door."

"The back door?" Donovan said doubtfully. Kole shot him a look and Donovan gave him a steely one in return.

"Yes," Bronwen continued, wanting to finish her tale as quickly as possible with as little detail as she could get away with. "Then, I began to run through the back streets behind Mr Clare's shop. In my panic, I became turned about and disorientated in the dark. I eventually came across the river so decided to follow it through the fields. I was so frightened and did not want to turn back for fear my attacker might still be in the city.

"I was tired, so decided to rest under one of the bridges crossing the river, hoping that someone might come by who would help me. While I waited, I fell asleep under the bridge and was awoken later by a group of women. They wanted my wedding dress that I was still wearing and then pushed me into the river. I was carried away by the current and when I finally made it out, I hid in a bush, trying to get warm. I was too ashamed to be found in my undergarments in the day so stayed there until it was dark again, then I started back home and was lucky enough to find some clothing on a line by one of the farms. I feel ashamed at stealing them and even more ashamed in telling you my sorry story. I hope you are not too disappointed in me." Bronwen finished her tale, patting at the tears on her cheeks with the handkerchief Lord Guild had passed her. Her arm was sore where she had been pinching it throughout the story.

Thanatos clapped his hands slowly and laughed, "a natural."

"Lady Bronwen," Kole said after a long silence. "I am so sorry you had to go through that ordeal. We must find this man who attacked you at once." Donovan gave Kole another secret look.

"No, please," Bronwen said quickly, she had been expecting this response. "I do not want to reveal my shame to anyone else. The man is probably long gone by now. I am home and safe again."

"Well, I am afraid of what I will do if I find this cretin first," Kole said, tightening his hand into a fist.

"There are worse things," Donovan murmured, almost to himself as he stared directly ahead. Thanatos studied him curiously and Bronwen almost thought her father could see the demon.

"Well, I will have no further harm come to my betrothed."

Kole turned to Bronwen, his eyes commanding. "Mr Whyms will be *your* bodyguard now, he will guard you as he has with me, so this will never happen again." Adam appeared next to the fireplace as if he was summoned from the flames.

"Lord Guild, that is not necessary," Bronwen said. She had not predicted this. Adam was like Kole's shadow, she hadn't thought he would give up his personal bodyguard so easily. And she was very certain she did not want him. He unnerved her enough with his lingering stares, it would be worse when he was actually charged to do so.

"Lord Wintre, does this suit you? I will of course pay all expenses but Adam will need a room in your house," Kole said, ignoring Bronwen's protests.

"He has it," Donovan said dismissively.

"And you, Mr Whyms? Will you watch over my love as you have watched me and guard her with your life?" Adam turned from his employer to look sharply into Bronwen's eyes. She was caught in his gaze for a moment, before looking away with a barely hidden shudder.

Adam's eyes glinted like a hawk. "I will."

Bronwen knew it was futile to argue, especially when both Kole and her father agreed on something.

"He will guard you as well as his shadows allow," Thanatos said. His tone sent a shiver down Bronwen's spine. It was in equal measures malice and salacity. He promptly disappeared without a trace.

"I will sleep soundly tonight, knowing you are safe, especially as your father and I have some business to attend to."

Bronwen nodded as Kole stood up, rousing her father. She was used to this act of 'attending to business' and welcomed the time to settle her thoughts.

Bronwen stood with them and Kole kissed her hand before they left the room. She sighed heavily, forgetting she was not yet alone. Adam Whyms was there with her, creating his own shadows by firelight. They stared at one another again in silence. Bronwen thought she ought to say something but his look made her panic and she quickly left the living room, trying to ignore that he would follow her.

What was one more wraith to haunt her?

VI

Bronwen gratefully closed the door to her bedroom. She had told Mr Durward that she wished to rest for a while and luckily Mr Whyms had not followed her into the room. He had disappeared entirely as Bronwen had entered. She would have to speak with him eventually about what boundaries she expected but was glad he instinctively knew this was one of them.

On her small desk beside Bronwen's large wardrobe was a tray of food already brought up for her. Her half-finished letter to Josette was still sitting there – a small unfinished business.

Bronwen eyed the cakes in the tray. Though she still wasn't hungry, the light dough made her want to taste them. She lifted one to her lips, swallowed the bite and savoured the sweetness of it. It was short lived before she was gagging again and trying not to be sick. It was like each of the ingredients which made them grew and developed then wilted and rotted. She imagined that was what death tasted like.

"Perhaps you should heed my warning next time."

Bronwen's heart skipped a beat at the sound of Thanatos behind her.

"Did no one teach you to knock before entering a Lady's

room?" Bronwen snapped, feeling agitated as she wiped her mouth with a cloth before turning to glare at him.

"I have never had to before." The demon replied redolently. Thanatos was lounging on Bronwen's bed, a hand underneath his chin as he studied her.

Bronwen picked up another cake and looked at it sceptically. There didn't appear to be anything wrong with it.

"Am I unwell?"

"You will find little pleasure in food here," Thanatos explained. "It is an after effect of returning. What you taste is all that has happened to the thing you eat. Its death, in other words. Only the very freshest of food will be palatable to you, and even then, it will not taste quite right. Not for a long while anyway."

"How am I to survive without eating?"

"You do not need to eat as you are already dead."

"How am I to hide this from people?" Bronwen asked, walking away from the food and towards her dressing table on the far wall.

Thanatos shrugged, turning his body so he faced Bronwen. "It is no concern of mine."

Lady Bronwen sat down at her dresser and scrutinized herself in the mirror. Her features were the same, though her skin was a little paler. Her eyes had taken on an indifferent quality, like nothing mattered anymore and flecks of green had escaped into the brown, like vines reaching for the dark source in the centre. She always thought eyes told so much of a person. She wondered what hers would tell now.

A movement behind her shoulder caught her attention and she noticed Thanatos staring at her intently. Bronwen did not want to know what horrors his eyes would speak so tilted the mirror so she could no longer see him.

"I was not expecting to see you here," Bronwen said

tightly.

"How am I to woo you then? Send you flowers from afar and hope you fall in love with my words before my face," Thanatos scoffed. "That may be the way you have known, that love is for the poor and a man is judged worthy by his social standing. But our courtship will be somewhat different, with you being dead and me master of all things."

It was Bronwen's turn to scoff as she turned on the stool to face him and his infuriating grin.

"You would call this a courtship? Haunting me at my every turn and invading my private spaces?"

Thanatos raised an eyebrow suggestively. "I would consider it a very successful indeed, if I were already invading your private spaces."

Bronwen felt her cheeks warming and tried to hide it with a scowl. Thanatos grinned at her.

"You need me if you are to return to the living," he said. "You have just been murdered by twelve of your neighbours. Death changes everyone and life will never look the same."

"You are wrong. I do not need you."

"Not yet."

Bronwen wanted to ask more but his gaze made her squirm and she turned to face the dresser again.

There were already too many things to think about, so many things had changed and yet all had stayed the same. Bronwen weighed them against each other - she was still to wed Lord Guild and Adam Whyms was now *her* bodyguard. Her father was still emotionally deficient and she was unable to eat without gagging. Her everyday activities would return to relative normality and there was a group of Satanists in the county that she must find.

"You are not permitted to marry whilst here," Thanatos's stern voice broke Bronwen from her musings.

"I cannot see how that would disrupt things here considering I am to die soon," Bronwen retorted keeping her eyes on the desk. She wished he would leave her in peace. His presence grated on her mood – even Adam respected the boundary of her bedroom.

"It would disrupt me."

"It is no concern of mine," she said, imitating his earlier tone.

Her attention flicked back up to the mirror and her breath caught in her throat when she saw the demon stood right behind her shoulder. Wide, bloodshot eyes a menacing red, teeth pointed in a crazed snarl. Bronwen stood, making the stool she was sat on thump to the floor as she turned to face him, but somehow, he was still laying on the bed casually.

Thanatos smiled at her complacently, revealing a row of normal teeth.

"Playing two lovers against one another is not very respectable of you, Lady Bronwen."

"I have no lovers. And when were my attachments mentioned in the bargaining?" Bronwen challenged, the adrenalin from her fright fuelling her daring. The experience had been so similar to when she had seen a demon's face behind her in the carriage a few days ago, that she wondered if it had been Thanatos she had seen as an omen of what was to come.

"When I decided upon it," Thanatos growled at her insolence. It was alarming how quickly his mood had changed. "And your attachments are mine alone."

Bronwen shook her head in irritation. She did not need his provocation at that present moment and had not been considering a union anyway. She was sure starting a family would definitely defy the rules of nature, though her heart panged at the thought of never having that choice.

A choice stolen from her by *him*.

"What more could you possibly do if I disobeyed?" She raised her chin defiantly.

With inhuman stealth, Thanatos rose from the bed and

stood before her.

"Another warning, my Lady," he whispered to her. "Do not attempt to find out."

"As you reminded me earlier - I am already dead."

"Precisely," Thanatos leaned in and Bronwen stepped back, knocking a few items over on her dressing table as he placed his hands either side of her. "So, keep in mind who is in possession of your soul."

Bronwen felt herself shudder but could recoil no further. Though Thanatos's expression remained placid, his body felt as if it might topple her and she finally remembered that she feared him. A primal fear, passed through generations of teaching good versus evil, in any form they may hide.

Bronwen had the sudden urge to pinch her arm and moved one hand to do so but Thanatos caught her wrist, holding it to the side.

"Bronwen," Hearing her name on his lips made her shudder. She tried to keep eye contact, tensing her jaw.

"Devil," She said tightly.

Thanatos smiled and leant in further, as if he might kiss her. Bronwen closed her eyes tightly but felt only a cold breeze on her lips and a chill through her body. When she opened them, Thanatos was gone.

"Meeting commences," The Dux Ducis of the Secuutus Letum announced in a dull monotone.

The group of twelve seated themselves at the stone table. It was round with twelve sides, one for each of them with strange whimsical symbols chiselled into it. They all slowly removed their porcelain masks, placing them carefully on the stone in front of them.

The Dux Ducis turned to his right, where the Earl of Surrey now sat in place of the faceless wraith that had been there a moment ago. Kole nodded in acknowledgement as

Baron Wintre removed his own mask and glanced around the table at the only people he could consider friends, if he were inclined to keep any.

Eleven servants of Satan stared back at Donovan. Each had their own story to tell, their own horrors to rival Donovan's own, and he had been chosen to lead them, the twelfth member and most reluctant. He had not chosen this life; he had chosen only to love a woman who had become his wife and then mother and murderer of his only child.

He had traded his freedom for his wife's soul to be spared in hell and had since lost hope for his own salvation. He could only speculate at what his fellow condemnable's had traded.

Lord Wintre kept one hand on his mask as he addressed his group. "Lady Bronwen has returned from death."

There was a moment of silence before protests erupted around the table. Donovan allowed them to vent for a while, the news was just as much of a shock to him.

When Bronwen had walked through the door of Metrom Hall, joy at his daughter's return had not been Donovan's first reaction. It was fear that he felt. His wife's child had been no daughter to him since he had made his bargaining of souls. He had managed to keep his distance from Bronwen, knowing that one day the Devil would come for her and he must be strong enough to not only give her away, as a father might do in marriage, but take her very life and soul.

All of the twelve around the table had made deals of their own and had found themselves in this group of kindred spirits where they could all serve their Lord in whatever way he desired.

The Devil's hunters of wayward souls.

The people whom the Secuutus were ordered to kill contained within them souls that, when released from their mortal bodies, would become difficult for their Dominus to control. They did not pass on in the natural way but retained enough of their energies to have some power of their own that could not be allowed to escape.

Sometimes these would be good people who sacrificed themselves for others and were generous with their kindness, Donovan preferred not to think about what happened after the Secuutus murdered this kind of spirit and tended to send the hardiest members of the group for these deeds.

The easier to kill and most common were the evil doers, who needed to be cast to hell before they escaped their mortal bodies and wreaked havoc on the land. There were many examples in history of such a thing happening - droughts, murders, famines and possessions. Who could have guessed that the scare mongering of the church was true?

Donovan did not truly believe in heaven and hell, God and the Devil, but what he did know for certain was that souls entered a world after death and this world was governed by the creature he served. This, if nothing else, made him fearful of what was beyond life.

"No one mentioned this would happen. She was not supposed to return. Did anyone know of this?" Cornell Payton broke through Donovan's thoughts of lost things. He was a scrawny man, tight lipped and straight nosed, like most aristocrats of the era and his haughty voice chafed. He was a member of the gentry, not the peerage of England, despite the way he acted. Cornell had almost as much money as Donovan but lacked the brains to use it to progress as the Baron had.

Cornell's wife, Lindy Payton, nodded in agreement with her husband's words. She was just as grating, though she hardly spoke during the meetings.

Kenneth Quays was the next to speak. In contrast with Cornell, Kenneth had *too* much intelligence and had the look of someone who was always calculating some deprived fantasy. Even when Bronwen had stabbed his hand through to the bone with a pair of scissors, Kenneth had simply pulled the blade out and returned it to the tailor, Lowell Clare, with barely a grunt of discomfort.

Donovan had felt a small swell of pride when he had found out how difficult his daughter had been to catch but it had made killing her all the more demanding.

"Denny?" Kenneth said, addressing the man sat next to Donovan who flinched at the mention of his name. "You were the last to speak with our Dominus before the deed was done. Did he foretell of this?"

Denny Myerscough shook his head assuredly, making his thick neck wobble. He barely fit in the chair around the stone table and always wore clothes too small for him. Donovan had always wondered why the fat man was a member of the group, so frightened of everything. He could not imagine the man preforming any sin that would lead him to make a deal for his soul. Especially as Denny was still an acting Reverend in the parish of St Faith.

"No," Denny said, then continued as if to himself. "But he was not pleased with..." He shuddered at a thought.

"*With...?*" Kenneth pressed.

Denny shook his head again and looked at the table. He was the unlikely messenger of the group. For some reason, unbeknown to the rest of the Secuutus, their master had chosen Denny to receive and pass on all commands – who to kill, where they could be found and sometimes the best way to do it. *This* man, who was scared of his own shadow.

"Speak you foolish bastard, or I'll be giving that useless tongue of yours to someone what deserves it!" Haydon Stone growled, aptly named not only because he was the only stonemason in the county but also because of his stature, his body as large as Denny's but tight with muscle like a bull. His voice rasped threateningly in a way that reminded Donovan of a spitting snake, though the man himself was far from a slithering serpent, in appearance at least.

Denny shied away from him but did not utter a word; instead he looked up at his Dux Ducis which the rest of the Secuutus took as answer enough.

"Should have known who," Cornell stepped in again, voice full of meaning and his wife still nodding before she heard the rest. "He is never pleased with *you*, our Dux Ducis."

A few of the others agreed quietly but most had the sense to keep their mouth shut. Donovan had not risen to the highest position of the group through being chosen like Denny, nor was it because their master wanted *his* daughter. Donovan became Dux Ducis because he had earned it. He was shrewder, more determined and far more resourceful than any of the others - even Kole.

Donovan had needed to take control of the Secuutus all those years ago, through necessity, and he had done so zealously in much the same way he had put his mark on the business world, made his fortune and earned his title as Baron. And he would be damned if someone else sought to undermine him.

Donovan stayed in his chair and instead chose to lean forwards over the table towards Cornell, fixing him with a stare that caused the man to shy back ever so perceptibly to those watching.

"Is that a call for Lacessere?" Donovan challenged the man, allowing himself a small smile as he watched Cornell and all those around the table look away in submission. "I failed to hear you offer, Cornell."

"Or offer your own daughter," Kole added softly in a way that made even Donovan's spine tingle. He was not entirely sure which demon would have been worst to give Bronwen away to.

"Donovan was not the only one who displeased our Dominus," Maverick Townsend said, trying to distract from the subject of children being taken. His son, Kyran, was sat beside him, quietly watching the proceedings. Both had dark hair and eyes and were top heavy with muscles from farming, but did not appear as threateningly powerful as Haydon.

A few people nodded in agreement with Maverick's words and turned to the Earl, none brave enough to name him. Kole was almost as feared as Donovan but had never shown any sign of wanting the job of leader.

"Care to explain those marks you made, Kole?" Donovan asked - titles were not used in the Secuutus Letum and Donovan had no such fear of his would-be son-in-law. "You claimed you were under direction from our Dominus but it seemed that it was not arranged to happen."

"Neither was your hesitation, Donovan," Kole snapped back. "Those marks are mine alone to claim."

"But that pathetic whore was not." Everyone turned to look at the new speaker.

Velna Brinley, a young woman about the same age as Bronwen, turned her scowl on the Earl. "For whatever reasons my Dominus had to take her, you had no right to attempt to claim her for your own."

"The time set by *your* Dominus had almost passed. My Lady was fair game," Kole retorted.

"*Almost* passed. Your fair game lost us favour with him. Perhaps your Lady's return had been planned?"

"What exactly are you implying?" Donovan interrupted, sensing the conversation quickly turning and he knew Kole's patience was a fragile thing.

Clashes between Velna and Kole were a regular occurrence and he did not think he had the energy for one more, but he did want to know what Kole had been up to when carving the mark into Bronwen's stomach. Donovan knew the mark well, but even his wife had not told him what it meant and it certainly was not part of the sacrifice. Their master had been clear on his instructions of how to send Bronwen's soul to him and judging from the way he had spoken to them all after the deed, he was not pleased with Kole's interference.

Kole had told Donovan that he was to perform the pre-ritual and the Baron had taken him at his word instead of checking with Denny. If Kole had lied about it, it was something Donovan needed to investigate, but not here.

"No implications at this table, only accusations," Velna said, her voice almost yelling now. Her thick, black wavy hair made her sharp features appear sharper, like a sword or a dagger.

"Speak your mind, Velna," Kenneth said calmly.

The woman didn't turn her gaze away from Kole. Though her dark eyes burned, her hateful expression did not mar her looks. She was attractive, but plain with no distinguishable features, it bore Kole to look at her but he returned her gaze anyway, his expression equally hateful.

"You wanted to keep her here, for yourself," Velna spat.

"You think the marks Kole made kept Bronwen here?" Kenneth asked, studying the expression on the Earl's face which was as dark as the cloak he wore.

Velna rose from her chair suddenly and pointed a finger at Kole.

"You could not have done it right!"

Kole stood as well, slamming his hands down on the table, making not just the stone shudder in response.

"You think I do not know my way to a woman's heart?! I gained hers in the first place, did I not?!"

The two stared at each other, neither wanting to back down. The air fizzled with uncontained rage. Their Dominus would have been pleased with the display had he been there to see it. But he wasn't. And they still had not won his approval.

Donovan sighed inwardly. Before he could speak, another, softer voice drifted over the meeting.

"It was not Kole who struck the final blow." Everyone apart from Velna and Kole turned to Mara Brinley. A slight woman, with golden hair and blue eyes, who bore little resemblance to her elder sister, Velna.

"No," Donovan continued when it seemed that was all Mara wanted to say. He stood and though he had never surpassed the undeniably powerful aggression Kole possessed, his presence was dominant and eventually Kole and Velna sat back down. "It was *I* who wielded the knife. *I* who killed Bronwen. *I* killed my daughter and I *did not hesitate*."

The table's full attention was on him now as he emphasized each word. Donovan was careful to look each one of them in the eye, pausing lastly on Kole who nodded agreement.

"We will watch Bronwen, find out what we can. If our Dominus is unhappy with our performance, then we will do better." Donovan sat back down again, slowly and deliberately. "And if that calls for us to repeat the ritual, then I will once again claim my responsibility and wield the knife myself."

"Dux Ducis," The group said in unison, a simple gesture of submission.

He hoped the meeting could now turn to discussing ordinary business. Denny had told Donovan before the gathering that there was a man in Berwick whose dietary requirements were making expectant mothers dig out their old chastity belts. It would only need two from the group to see to him but Donovan considered sending away several of them so as to soothe the growing tension for a few days.

It was quiet for a time before Lowell Clare spoke. "What harm could a woman do?" He had been unusually quiet throughout the meeting, considering he had been particularly peevish since the sacrifice after he received a nasty bump on his head from his encounter with Bronwen.

Velna shot him a look but before she sparked another argument Haydon laughed.

"She had the best of *you* easy enough. You even put up a fight or take one look at her, hand over your balls and swoon like a girl?" Haydon laughed again and even Donovan had to hide a smile.

"How about I cut *your* balls off!" Lowell snapped back but his voice held no conviction and it just made Haydon laugh louder.

"If you can get close enough to try it, *Clare*, I might even let ya!" Haydon countered humorously, emphasising Lowell's feminine surname.

Kenneth placed his uninjured hand on the table between them to silence Haydon's chortling. "I think is safe to say that *most* of us could handle Lady Bronwen and we can assume she does not know who we all are."

"Not yet," Cornell said challengingly, looking at Donovan with expectation. He chose not to entertain the man. The Dux Ducis had decided who he would send to Berwick for the demon. He was looking forward to having Cornell, Velna and Haydon at the other end of the country for a few days and with any luck, they would kill each other and save him the job.

VII

Bronwen spent another sleepless night in her room, thankfully without watchers. She stared at the canopy above her bed for hours, listening to the distant bells of the city chiming each hour that passed, closely followed by the tall, standing grandfather clock in the entrance hall of Metrom.

Bronwen was not completely idle throughout the night. She sat on her enclosed window seat and watched the night pass, restoked the fire when she became too cold, began a new letter to Josette - though it was too dark to see well and she didn't want to light a lamp, in case someone saw the glow under her door. She even sat on the floor in front of the fire and watched the flames dance until her eyes saw nothing but red flickers and her body complained of the heat.

Mostly, Bronwen thought deep thoughts about her new life, her friends and family and the events that had led to the strange occurrences that had brought her to this dark place of foreboding.

As the clocks struck eight and the morning light filled the shadowy spaces of the room, Alda's knock on the door was a welcome interruption.

"Milady," Alda said, while she assessed Bronwen with a

worrying eye, surprised to find her Lady out of bed. "Are you well?"

"Yes, thank you, Alda," Bronwen reassured her as she let the curtain fall back into place over the window. She had been watching the comings and goings of the house staff with interest for about an hour. They all looked unexpectedly happy, joking with one another as they went about their arduous chores. Bronwen envied them for having something to do - and for having each other to joke with.

"Perhaps you should rest for a while longer?" Alda said. "I can have your breakfast brought up to you and I am sure your father will understand if you do not go to church this morning."

"No, thank you, I would very much like to go," Bronwen said, sitting down so Alda could brush her hair.

She had forgotten it was Sunday and Bronwen had no desire to stay in her room for a moment longer after her night of boredom and she thought church would be good for her. Thanatos had wanted her to return to humanity after her murder and what better place to find kindness than in the house of God. But she would have been lying to say she was not nervous.

What if God rejected her? Bronwen did not believe that a lightning bolt would come down and smite her, but she had heard tales before of people possessed who could not abide the touch of holy water or the words of the bible. She was not exactly possessed by the Devil but he was in possession of her soul and she was unsure of how that might affect her.

These thoughts swirled in Bronwen's mind even as she entered Winchester Cathedral. It had been a tense carriage ride with her father and Lord Guild, who had decided to stay in Winchester a few days longer than planned following her disappearance. No one spoke much on the journey, all lost in their own thoughts and Bronwen almost drew blood from the pressure of her nails against her skin as she pinched herself unconsciously.

The church was crowded with people, which struck Bronwen as odd, considering she knew some of them worshiped the Devil and had killed her.

She politely nodded in greeting when people acknowledged her, though they all gave her suspicious looks. At first, she felt a rising panic at the attention. Did they see something in her that was not right or holy? Then one brash woman, well known for her gossiping, came to speak to Bronwen, cornering her as she stared distractedly into the marble Tournai font near the entrance to the cathedral.

"We are so pleased that you have been found, Lady Bronwen," the woman said with false concern. Bronwen had never once spoken to her before but had seen her at many of her father's parties, along with her two daughters; the plainest girls Bronwen had ever met in both looks and persona.

"Lord Wintre had his household searching the entire city for you. No rock was left unturned, nor home undisturbed. I do hope it was not due to an argument with Lord Guild," she said suggestively, as if Bronwen would tell her some scandal that would no doubt keep the fires of rumour stoked for months.

Her impetuous manner irritated Bronwen and she was glad she had not had to converse with the woman before, but was also thankful for the insight as to why everyone in the cathedral was so interested in her.

"Mrs Franks, might I steal my fiancée away from you?" Lord Guild came to stand next to Bronwen, who was grateful for the interruption.

"Yes of course, Lord Guild." Mrs Franks blushed and fluttered her eyelids at him in a most undignified manner. Bronwen had not noticed before that others might find Lord Guild attractive and now that she was looking, she spotted a few young girls sitting on the pews, who looked at the Earl longingly and shot envious scowls at Bronwen.

Kole took Bronwen's elbow and steered her away from Mrs Franks, lest she swoon.

"Mrs Frank should perhaps turn her attention to what suppositions are whispered about *her*," Kole whispered to Bronwen when they were out of earshot. "One of her daughters is planning to elope with master Collins." He indicated to a young man to one side of the congregation, who kept scratching at his head as if he had lice. The man beside him was trying to keep his distance.

"Thank you for coming to my rescue, Lord Guild," Bronwen said as they made their way to the front pews reserved for members of the higher classes.

"My pleasure," Lord Guild replied with a queer smile.

Bronwen bowed her genuflection to the hanging crucifix on the back wall of the church - a depiction of Christ bleeding from the crown of thorns he wore. The blood was painted in such a way as to make it seem like he was crying them. It had always disturbed Bronwen. She did not see why the saviour needed to be displayed in such a way when the cross was reminder enough of his sacrifice. Bronwen preferred to know him as a smiling and kind teacher.

She wondered what he would think of her now, after making pacts with the Devil. Did it even matter anymore? Was she a lost lamb in his flock already?

No, she mustn't think that. Whatever the demon took from her, he would not have her faith.

"Lady Bronwen?" She started when Kole placed a hand on her shoulder. She was still stood in the centre aisle, staring up at the crucifix.

Bronwen shook herself and smiled at Kole.

"I was just picturing where we might stand when we are married," Bronwen explained quickly. She was becoming too good at lying.

"It would not be in this Cathedral," Kole replied casually while he ushered her into a seat. "I planned for us to marry in the church at Guildford."

"The Holy Trinity? But I thought it was having construction work done?"

"They will be finished by the time we are to marry; I will see to it."

"Is that so?" Bronwen replied, ever so slightly indignant. She did not appreciate decisions being made on her behalf, especially now that she had been murdered. Her life being taken was one decision she could not change and resented most of all, which made her all the more determined to reclaim some small freedom in her new life.

The organist began playing, now that most of the congregation were seated, cutting off any further discussion on the matter.

Lord Guild escorted Bronwen to her seat before joining Donovan, sat with the other gentlemen. It was an old tradition to seat the sexes away from one another, but the priest of the church had old fashioned ideals and he was strict in the way he conducted his sermons.

Bronwen did not mind it. She still felt uncomfortable near Kole and was glad for the time to contemplate her faith. She turned her head towards the front and picked up the hymnal from the pocket in front of her. It had a simple cross in the leather cover. She fingered it delicately as she shuffled away from the aisle, so someone else might sit in the space she left.

"Afraid I might burn you?" Thanatos was the last person Bronwen expected to take the empty seat and the least welcome.

"What are you doing here?" Bronwen exclaimed. A woman sat behind her gave Lady Bronwen a concerned look at her apparent conversing with the air. Bronwen lowered her voice and pretended to glance through the hymnal.

"This is a church."

"My goodness, it is!" Thanatos said, equally startled. Bronwen tried not to react when she saw tiny flames igniting all over Thanatos. He began patting at them comically and Bronwen had to stop herself from joining in, so she had an excuse to strike him.

"Please cease this," she hissed, earning herself another look. "Do not do this here," She murmured through gritted teeth.

Thanatos stopped the fires and turned his body towards her, draping an arm on the back of pew. Bronwen sat further forward, almost on the edge of the seat, trying not to touch him.

"Lady Bronwen, you need to learn how to enjoy this new life I have granted you," Thanatos said as the priest entered from a side door and indicated for everyone to rise. "Do not waste it on the values you held in your old life."

Bronwen rose with the rest of the congregation while Thanatos remained seated.

"It is my values that help me get through this life," Bronwen whispered while the sound of people standing muffled it.

Thanatos remained seated as the rest of the congregation turned the pages of their books to the hymn written on a chalkboard next to the altar. It was one of Bronwen's favourites, but the lyrics held different meanings to her now.

"Oh, it has been a long time since I have sat in a church," Thanatos spoke over the out of key singing. Bronwen watched him out of the corner of her eye as he glanced around himself and rested his gaze on the priest.

"For a culture so hateful of women, they do so enjoy dressing as one," he said in a way that did not seem as if he were trying to provoke Bronwen, simply stating an observation.

Bronwen struggled to concentrate on the lyrics of the

hymn and soon wished she hadn't.

{Alone thou goest forth, O Lord, in sacrifice to die}

Thanatos stood up, his very presence made the words speak to Bronwen and bring back thoughts of her death.

Then Thanatos began to sing.

{Our sins, not thine, thou bearest, Lord}

Bronwen fell silent and stared at him in shock. Of all things, she had not expected him to be able to sing so sweetly, powerfully even.

Bronwen's eyes refocused and she noticed the gentleman across the aisle from her, staring with concern.

{Till through our pity and our shame, love answers love's appeal.}

Bronwen lowered her wide-eyed gaze realising that, as she was the only one who could see Thanatos, it must have appeared as though she had been glaring through him at the man across from her.

{This is earth's darkest hour}

Bronwen tried to sing again.

{Then let all praise be given thee who livest evermore}

She was glad when the final verse came and yet felt a deeper meaning within the words.

{Grant us with thee to suffer pain...}

On the final line of the hymn, Thanatos turned his body and leant towards Bronwen, his voice made far more seductive by his singing as the sound hummed through her chest.

{Thy cross may bring us to thy joy and resurrection power}

Bronwen shuddered as the hymn came to an end. She turned to look at Thanatos just as he left the pew and strolled up the centre of the aisle. She tried to reach for him but he was already moving towards the priest standing on the pulpit, ready to begin the service.

A pat on her shoulder alerted Bronwen that she was the only one still standing. The rest of the congregation had since taken their seats.

Bronwen turned to the woman who had tapped her and sat, apologising quietly. The woman gave her a sympathetic look.

As she turned back to the front, Bronwen caught a glimpse of Lord Guild and her father. Donovan had a fearful expression again, unnatural to him, but Lord Guild's gaze was one of contemplation. Bronwen turned away and back to watch the progress of Thanatos.

The demon was looking over the priest's shoulder at his notes with amusement. The priest, as usual, plunged straight into his sermon with no introduction and Bronwen grimaced at the subject as he read lines from the Bible.

"...He it is, to whom I shall give a sop, when I have dipped it. And when he had dipped the sop, he gave it to Judas Iscariot, the son of Simon." The priest paused and looked over the congregation for effect. Thanatos nodded behind him in agreement. Bronwen couldn't take her eyes off him. "And after the sop Satan entered into him. Then said Jesus unto him, that thou doest, do quickly..."

"I have never been one to rush these things," Thanatos corrected. Bronwen breathed in sharply as if someone might have heard him, but no one flinched.

"He then having received the sop went immediately out: and it was night," the priest continued, unaware of the creature behind him, mocking his hand gestures and speech.

"Oh, my Lord, no. A gentleman should never leave one unsatisfied," Thanatos said, winking at Bronwen.

She wanted to run but was instead transfixed in shock, time slowing as she watched Thanatos move to the altar and dip his finger in the holy wine, then taste it and mock the quality. Bronwen was helpless, unable to wrestle with an invisible foe in their midst, only she could see how he mocked the sanctity of the church, like a child behind his parent's back.

She wished for God to strike him down and imagined him burning with fire. The irony of it was almost comical, imagining him burning in a fire that he owned, whilst she desperately tried to listen to the preacher telling of the Lord's love.

"...That ye love one another; as I have loved you, that ye also love one another."

"Tut tut, sir. Thou shalt not lie with mankind, as with womankind. Ah, these contradictions of the faith."

Bronwen wanted to scream for Thanatos to stop, or end the service, she couldn't take anymore. Not the depictions on the windows, nor the blessed wine and bread, the holy book in which time had made parts redundant and no longer made sense to her, not the clothing, the incense, the worshipers, the idols or the mechanical routine of the entire Mass.

If a vile creature such as Thanatos could ridicule it so entirely then did none of it mean anything? Was it all just a rigmarole? Was none of it necessary to the faith? Did God even care about what was happening in his house, or to one of his daughters? Had he forgotten Bronwen and forsaken her to her fate?

Bronwen's eyes crinkled and she thought perhaps she might cry but misinterpreted her own emotions, it was not tears that made her squint. A small gulping, breathy noise thumped in her chest and throat.

"My dear, are you well?" The woman behind her asked. Bronwen tried to nod but it was more of a twitch as she tried to rein in her emotions.

"Fine," she managed to bark out and smiled as naturally as she could, but as she turned back to the front, she couldn't get the thoughts out of her head and they eventually bubbled over. The tension was too much, it was all too much.

Instead of curling into a ball and sobbing, Bronwen began

to laugh. Fits of hysterical laughter wracked her body, the sound echoing around the cathedral so even those at the back could hear the inappropriate sound.

The entire congregation turned to her. Even Thanatos looked shocked, and then pleased, unaware that it was not *his* doing that caused her cackling.

Bronwen held her sides as she tried to regain control of herself, the sound of her cachinnation parroting off the walls. She was almost grateful when she felt a strong hand take her arm and usher her out of the church. She could feel eyes on her with mixed emotions as she stumbled down the aisle, still giggling in her crazed hysteria.

Only once she was outside and had to shield her eyes from the sudden change in light, did she look up to see who had extracted her from the service.

"Perhaps not the finest moment to gain a sense of humour, my Lady."

"Lord Guild," Bronwen said, once again sober enough to speak, her cheeks and sides aching from the abruptness of her outburst. "I am..."

"Will you walk with me?"

"You are not angry with me?" Bronwen asked warily.

"Why should I be?" Kole replied with a smile.

"My actions were hardly appropriate," Bronwen said, confused as to why Kole seemed so jovial. He gave her a meaningful look.

"Most actions are not, but one that allows an escape from a dulling situation is wholly forgivable."

He offered Bronwen his arm. She hesitated, then returned his smile and took it, grateful he did not seem to wish to chastise her for her outburst.

Mr Whyms stepped out of the shadows as they moved away from the cathedral. Bronwen had not known he was there and he faded into the shadows again at a hand signal from Kole.

116

"Might you show me how to make him disappear like that?" Bronwen said before she could catch her words. Kole only laughed lightly.

"He never goes far, as is his job and I do not want him far from you. The man who attacked you might still be waiting."

Bronwen could not argue with his reasoning and silently chided herself for not coming up with a better excuse for her disappearance.

Lord Guild led her around the side of the cathedral to the graveyard. It was peaceful with no one to watch them or study how they were together and no Alda breathing down her neck. Since Bronwen had no living mother, it was Alda's duty to chaperone and she did so with a vehemence that rivalled gladiators. Bronwen half expected her to appear at any moment, much like Adam.

The couple strolled amongst the emphatic epitaphs of the deceased in a place that often forced one to wonder what words would most describe themselves when they were gone, Bronwen especially. It was a rare thing to have the power to shape the time you had before death, the chance to influence what might be put on one's own grave.

Perhaps she should be spending her time helping people rather than enacting revenge on those who wronged her in life. But what would that matter when Hell was her destination regardless?

They stopped and sat on a bench under a large tree at the edge of the yard, sheltered from the cold breeze and looking up at the dominating spire of the cathedral. Neither had spoken and Bronwen felt Kole's eyes on her, waiting for her to speak.

"My father does not seem himself," Bronwen said, for lack of conversation.

"He was so very fearful when you disappeared. I think he worries for you," Kole said assuredly. Bronwen would almost have believed him if she did not know her father so well.

"I feel much changed since that one night," Bronwen spoke quietly, as if her voice might disturb the sleeping corpses in the ground. "I do not feel I am the same person I once was. Does that change things between us?"

Lord Guild paused for the briefest of moments before he answered.

"It does."

Bronwen turned to Kole and found a look in his eyes that she had only ever seen in Thanatos's before.

Lord Guild moved to hold the back of her neck with his hand and pulled her towards him. Then he kissed her hard on the lips. Bronwen was so taken aback by the gesture that she did not return his kiss and kept her eyes open even as he had closed his. Kole eventually released her, letting his hand slide to her shoulder, keeping his body close.

"A gentleman would apologise for that," Kole said, his dark brown eyes searching her face. "But I think you will find I am much changed as well."

Bronwen did not move from his grasp and did not motion to invite it either. It occurred to her that this was the first time they had ever been truly alone together. Even when Kole had asked for her hand, Donovan had been present to oversee it.

It had been a formal affair, without even a ring or bent knee. Not that those things mattered to Bronwen, she knew what it was to be a Lady with a social standing and reputation to uphold. She had to marry for status, not love, though she was suddenly conscious in that moment of how little she knew the Earl.

Had Kole been wishing to have Bronwen alone all this time when he knew so little of her also? Or was it only now, when she felt reborn as a new person, that he wanted to kiss her? So many questions and far too many distractions to think about anything other than how she was only borrowing time in a half living shell. Soon she would never have to question Kole's feelings for her again or worry about her own.

Lord Guild walked Bronwen home soon after. Neither of them mentioned the kiss, preferring to talk about mundane things such as the turning autumn weather and the condition of the roads, but it played through Bronwen's mind repeatedly.

"Good day, Lady Bronwen," Lord Guild said once they reached the door to the house. He had a meeting with someone in the city and had sent a servant to see his horse was ready.

Kole lifted Bronwen's hand to his lips and she blushed as he kept his gaze focused on her.

"Good day, Lord Guild," Bronwen replied, and then in a flush of impulse, she held his hand more firmly so he could not turn away. "Perhaps we could walk with one another more often? I would very much like for us to do this again."

Lord Guild smiled secretly and kissed her hand once more, slowly and deliberately this time, he maintained eye contact, making Bronwen's stomach flutter.

"We shall, my Lady," he said. "I will make certain of it."

VIII

    Bronwen's next sleepless night was thankfully less tedious than the first. This time she did light a lamp, using the curtain of her enclosed window seat to hide the light. In the burrow she had made, Bronwen read most of a book, did a small amount of embroidery, without much thought as to what she was designing and drafted yet another letter to Josette, never to be sent.

She had no idea what she should tell her friend. Josette was a liberal woman with strong beliefs about what she considered freedom in society but she was also a strong believer in God, so Bronwen was not sure how she would take the news that her friend was an undead, reluctant concubine of the Devil.

The last few hours of the night, Bronwen again spent watching the servants of the house and was found thus by Alda.

"It is not Ladylike to be staring out of the window like some love lost widow," she scolded, fully opening the curtain that Bronwen had been peering around.

"I thought that was the purpose of a woman," Bronwen replied sarcastically. "To stare wistfully upon the horizon for her husband to return to her."

"I will have less of your cheek, domina domus, the day is

still young and I am not."

Bronwen smiled at Alda, knowing she was also jesting.

"What would you like to do today, milady?" Alda asked once Bronwen was dressed.

"I thought I might take a ride along the river."

"Outside? But it looks like it might rain and it is so muddy by the river this time of year."

"I do not expect the horses will mind and I shall be back before the rain begins."

Bronwen smiled. She had been expecting Alda's answer and had prepared herself for a battle. She knew exactly how she wished to spend her time. The quicker she could find those that cursed her to her fate, the quicker she could put herself to rest and be rid of more demons than just Thanatos.

"Why not take a turn about the fields instead?" Alda suggested. She refused to ride a horse but would not let Bronwen out of her sight. Alda would rather stand sinking in the mud of her father's fields than ride a horse or let Bronwen out alone.

"Alda, I cannot have you stand in the cold and I wish to explore the river. You should remain here."

"You cannot go out on your own, not after what happened last time."

There was a shamed look in Alda's eyes and Bronwen suddenly realised that Alda felt guilty about what had happened to her in Lowell's shop. Donovan had not let her accompany Bronwen, saying that she would be perfectly safe with the carriage drivers. Perhaps her father was feeling just as guilty, which was why he had been acting so strangely since her return.

Bronwen laid a kind hand on Alda's arm. "I will not be alone. I have my own bodyguard now. Mr Whyms will go with me."

Alda gave Bronwen a sceptical look. Apparently, *she* did

not entirely trust Adam either, but Bronwen was adamant. She had had an entire night to contemplate how she might set about finding her killers and had decided to start where it had all ended; the clearing where she had been taken.

Still, it took quite a bit of persuasion to convince Alda and in the end, Bronwen had been sent with Alda's grandson Mervyn in tow to satisfy her overprotectiveness. He was strong from heaving loads and was used to riding horses from working on the farmlands attached to Metrom Hall, which provided all the household food.

Bronwen did not see the logic in sending two men out with her rather than one but was glad she would not be alone with Adam. As she settled herself onto her horse, she contemplated the ridiculous notion of being afraid of one's own bodyguard and decided that she would take this time to get to know Adam Whyms, in the hope that the unnerving feeling she had around him would ease.

Alda had been correct in saying it would rain later. Bronwen could taste it in the air and feel the moisture on her skin. The sky was a heavy grey which grew darker into the distance. She let her horse trot at his own pace so his body could warm up slowly. He was one of her father's animals and did not have a name. Bronwen had not even been allowed her own horse growing up. Her father had sold any she grew attached to so that she eventually stopped naming them and simply referred to them by their colour or temperament.

This one was sure footed in mud and was not aggravated by the cold, nor did it mind walking in shallow waters. Bronwen hoped she would not have to wade into the river but she might have to cross it if there was no bridge.

Once the quiet group of riders were some distance from the house, Bronwen turned in her saddle to look at her two followers.

Mervyn had his head down so his floppy brown hair fell

around his face and he wore the scowl of a young man who did not feel he deserved a scolding from his grandmother. Alda had drilled him before they left and the man could not mount his horse fast enough. Bronwen hoped he would cheer up as the day went on.

Adam was sat slouched on his horse, completely at ease in the saddle. He held the reins in only one hand, his other resting on his thigh as he scanned the trees and farmhouses they passed. His eyes drifted and locked with Bronwen's. Feeling like she had been caught doing something she shouldn't, Bronwen blushed and smiled at him. His eyes widened ever so perceptibly and Bronwen turned away before she knew if he had smiled back.

She inconspicuously tapped at her horse to speed him on and the animal obliged.

They soon came across the Almshouse, where Bronwen had stolen her clothes, in half the time it had taken her to walk in the dark. She slowed her horse again while she tried to find access to the river. She couldn't enter through the Almshouse garden as she had before.

Following the line of the fields Bronwen and Thanatos had walked through, a gravel path to the left revealed itself. It continued through more grassland and on towards some distant trees below St Catherine's hill. Bronwen pulled her horse in that direction and was pleased to see the path had bridges along it where it crossed escaping tendrils of the river in five places.

Bronwen urged her horse on and stopped when she reached the first stone bridge, looking greener and greyer than it had in the dark. She sat staring down at the high water, remembering its pull, how it burnt her lungs, the chill of it on her skin.

A horse nickering beside her drew Bronwen out of her reverie. It was Adam. He had ceased keeping a wary look on the trees and was now watching her with curiosity. Mervyn pulled up behind him, looking a little brighter than before.

"I am sorry for forcing you both to accompany me," Bronwen said brightly. Now seemed like a good time for conversation. She had always been awkward when it came to talking with people. Not having many friends made it difficult for her to interact with others beyond small talk at parties.

Mervyn smiled and opened his mouth to say something but was cut off by Adam.

"It's our job," he said with a slight accent Bronwen placed somewhere in the midlands. It made his words sound forced and husky.

"How long have you been in the service of Lord Kole?" Bronwen asked, wondering where he came from and why he left his home.

"Six years," he replied, offering no more information than that.

"And do you enjoy your work?"

"Mostly."

Bronwen nodded and tried to reign in her frustration. He clearly wanted to keep his secrets his, which she could understand but it was like trying to get blood from a stone. She almost asked Adam where he would take a woman to murder her - on a sudden intuition that he might know. The thought did not comfort her. Instead she tried a more open question.

"What was it about the role of a bodyguard that drew you to it?"

Adam did not reply but looked back at Bronwen while some hidden thought echoed in his eyes and his mouth quirked into a small smile. Bronwen decided she did not want to know after all.

"We should continue before it begins to rain," she said and turned her horse in the direction of the river, wishing she had tried to strike a conversation with Mervyn instead.

They moved off the path and followed the rough line of the river, Bronwen keeping a look out for any crop of trees that had the potential for a clearing but it was mainly fields in the area and none of the wooded spaces were dense enough. She could not remember hearing running water that night so turned right across the fields so as to get away from the sound, the horses kicking up loose sods of field.

They crossed a thin bit of river using a crude wooden bridge and had to stop when they reached a second wider section. The water was not deep but the bed of it was stony and had the potential to cause the horses problems.

Bronwen looked up at St Catharine's hill, looming on the other side of the water. If she made it to the top of it, she would be able to see the whole of Winchester and perhaps spot a likely place for her murder.

"I would like to ride to the top of the hill before heading back," Bronwen said, used to asking permission.

"There's a Labyrinth at the top of that, milady Bronwen," Mervyn said, brightening at the idea. Bronwen found herself smiling.

"Then let us waste no time," she said, pushing her horse forwards into the water. It lapped at the cold liquid quickly before exiting the river. Bronwen turned him around to face Adam and Mervyn. Their horses were less pleased to enter the frigid water, Mervyn's especially.

"There is a bridge upriver," Bronwen called across to them. "I shall walk alongside until we get to it."

Adam looked displeased by this and tried to force his horse across again. A breeze rolled down the water before rider and mount could enter it and the horse spooked and jumped up on its front legs in protest. Mervyn's shied away from the creature, flaring its nostrils and shaking its head, equally uneasy.

Bronwen began walking upriver without them and eventually Adam and Mervyn followed towards the bridge.

It was peaceful on the opposite side; being as on her own as was allowed. Bronwen breathed in the air and relaxed her gloved hands on the reigns, content to let her horse do the work while she tried to ignore the intense stare she was receiving from Adam through the waterside foliage.

He clearly was not pleased about leaving his charge, despite there only being a few meters between them. He tried to urge his horse on faster but Bronwen was not keen to relinquish her tenuous freedom and kept them at a leisurely pace.

A breeze creaked the bows of the shedding trees, raining dead leaves to the floor. It reached Bronwen and with it came a mild warmth and strange smell, metallic and sharp, like smelling salts – and blood.

She stopped her horse and turned to her companions but the trees at this section had become denser and she could not see through them.

The direction of the wind changed sharply and flowed unnaturally around her and up the side of the hill. She looked up at the crop of trees at the top and the blackening sky behind them. It was steep but something in her knew the horse would make it.

It was almost too convenient, Adam and Mervyn's horses unable to cross the river and the dense woodland she had been looking for suddenly appearing - as dark and terrible as a place where Satan's followers would gather.

Bronwen swayed forwards in the saddle, the movement making her horse take a single step towards the hillside. She looked down the path but could not yet see her guards and made her decision.

The horse took to the hill with the same contentment as it had the river. Bronwen knew it was dangerous to take such a steep and long climb, especially sat side-saddle, but the closer she got to the trees, the more vitalised she became, sitting up to help her horse.

Bronwen knew there would be trouble for her when the men found she was not near the bridge, but she found it difficult to regret her actions when she was feeling so warm and free.

There was something familiar about the area, besides it being part of Winchester. It was almost as if the atmosphere was personal to her. Like this should be a private place that only she should ever be in. It was strangely thrilling and she did not stop when she reached the top of the hill and pressed on into the trees, the sensation intensifying. She did not want Adam and Mervyn to find her. Why should they be here? They had no right to the place and no right to keep her constantly surrounded by watchers not of her choosing.

Bronwen had pushed her horse into a gallop and gently slowed it down as the trees became denser. Most of them still had their leaves, desperately clinging to their branches in a futile attempt to delay the winter. She had to duck her head under some of them and eventually stepped down from her horse and led it deeper into the crop, following an energy that fortified itself within her as soon as Bronwen's feet touched the floor.

Bronwen stopped suddenly. The horse huffed as it halted beside her and she let its reigns fall, not bothering to tie it to a tree, somehow knowing it would not stray. Then she stepped carefully forwards and was in the clearing.

It was empty apart from a large flat boulder in the middle. The density of the woods around it suggested the space had been purposefully cleared of trees and it was eerily free from leaves and other forest debris.

Bronwen stepped towards the centre. She knew this place. She knew this stone. It was where she had been murdered.

Strangely, it did not bother her being there. The memory of it was as faded as a dream, but she hoped that the signs of what had occurred were not.

Bronwen approached the stone stab and examined it

carefully. She had a little time before her escort panicked at her whereabouts. She felt mildly guilty at how worried they might be, then pushed the thoughts from her mind and tried to concentrate on her task.

She had no idea what to look for or what information might help her. She started with the bolder itself. There were no marks or blood stains on the rock, it was likely that a rain had washed it away. The stone was smoother than Bronwen remembered which could not have been natural. She doubted someone would go to all that effort just for her, which hinted that there was either some other purpose for the stone, or she had not been the first to suffer such a fate.

Bronwen shuddered again and heard a sound behind her. Expecting it to be Adam and Mervyn, she smiled as she turned, ready to apologise for disappearing. Instead she found Thanatos leaning against a tree.

He smirked back, so charming that it almost disarmed Bronwen, the slight breeze pulled at his deep blue shirt, revealing the hard muscle of his chest and scattering of dark hair. Lady Bronwen blushed and her smile quickly faded. She did not need this distraction and it was not ladylike to look at a man that way – especially one such as him.

"Well, I thoroughly enjoyed myself yesterday," Thanatos said with a grin.

"Am I right in assuming you are going to keep appearing at inconvenient times?" Bronwen said tightly, still angry at him for his scene in the church that had caused her such a hysterical outburst in front of the whole parish. She wasn't sure how she was to face her neighbours again and Alda had scolded her for walking home alone with Kole.

"There is nothing inconvenient about it," Thanatos replied casually.

"You defiled a holy place. A building of worship."

"So, the teachings about all creatures having *his* love were bullshit?"

"Only creatures who are not evil."

Thanatos furrowed his brow sternly, his mouth thinly set. "An evil creature, am I?" He said quietly, contemplating the sentiment before pushing himself away from the tree in an agile fluidity. "And here I was about to offer my assistance."

"You want to *help* me?" Bronwen said, watching his face cautiously as he moved to the other side of the rock from her. "After you mocked and shamed me yesterday."

"My Lady, it was not you whom I was mocking. And perhaps if you had agreed not to marry as I ordered, I would not have had the urge to shame you."

"Why should it matter if I marry? I am not to remain living."

"It matters because you are mine, Bronwen. And I do not share."

"I am not yours. I am not any man's."

Thanatos gave her a knowing look. "In this era, all women belong to someone. Very few are allowed the choice as to whom that might be."

"Or who it will not be," Bronwen said coldly. Despite her having the last word, she did not feel victorious and turned away from him back to her task.

They must have left clues; footprints, a broken branch, candle wax. But there was nothing and Bronwen had no idea what she was doing.

"You are thinking too much."

"I have no need of your assistance, thank you," Bronwen replied tersely. Honestly, she did need help, but it was unwelcome from him. She continued to examine the bolder, bending closer to it in the hope of finding something small.

"It is no good pawing around like a puppy that has lost a scent. You must feel what they felt, hear what they heard."

Bronwen sighed and closed her eyes, both from exasperation and compliance. He was right, she was thinking too hard about what was there. It would be more prudent for her to think back to what had been.

She took another deep breath and tried to recall the moments before her death. The feelings returned to her first. The fear and panic she had felt. The hopelessness and loneliness of her final hours, surrounded not as her mother had been, by family and loved ones, but by masked villains who despised her and gave her no explanation.

A cold tear fell down one of her cheeks.

"No." She heard Thanatos whisper. He had moved behind her and though she felt his breath on her ear, he seemed distant. "You are not *her*. You are them."

It was a struggle to prise herself from her own feelings and memories but she made herself pull away from the scene and watch it as if from above.

Bronwen imagined what she looked like, the woman lying in her battered wedding dress never to be used. White, the symbol for hope and purity, now tarnished with mud and blood.

"Do not feel for her. Theirs is not pity, only power."

Bronwen saw herself change again at his words. Now she saw how weak she had been, a blubbering child, desperate to hold onto life. *She* controlled the memory. *She* controlled this pathetic girl's fate and could decide so easily if this woman was to remain in this life or not.

"How many are there?"

Bronwen was only just aware of the question and she turned her scowl from the girl to the people in the clearing, drawing on deep memories she had not realised she had made.

"Twelve," she whispered.

"What do they look like?"

"They wear black robes to the floor and masks of china." She studied them each in turn, each body shape and stance they held. How their cloaks fell around their forms. "Three are women." She noted with surprise.

They all stood ready and waiting, an anticipation permeating their stares. What did they each have to gain from this?

"Good," Thanatos cooed. "Now, what did they do?"

Bronwen felt her hands rising; she could barely feel Thanatos's own guiding them. Then they met in the middle and she found a knife in her palms. It was heavy, as if the weight of it had been the cause of it falling into the woman's chest.

Bronwen looked down at her victim's frightened eyes and felt herself smirk, then she brought the knife down, feeling it sink into layers of tissue and only stop when it hit the rock beneath the flesh. She imagined she could feel the last heartbeat pulse around the blade and through her palms. This moment belonged to her now; this life she had taken was hers alone.

An excruciating pain in her chest made Bronwen fall forwards, clutching her heart. She just managed to catch herself on the rock with her other hand.

Panting, she opened her eyes again. There was a sharp prickling in her hand and a tingling up her arm. Bronwen looked at it to see a small bead of blood pooling in her palm. She studied where her hand had fallen and spotted a jagged piece of metal there, only a few inches long. The blade of a dagger plunged deep into the stone, it's handle broken off. There was also a deep hole near it and a second on the parallel side of the rock, made for something to be inserted.

This was where the metal loops that had bound Bronwen's wrists had been placed, how had she not noticed before? She was stood at the head of the rock and moved around to where her feet would have been, trailing her hand along the stone, leaving the bead of blood in a tiny smear across it.

She gathered the information she knew into her mind.

She was looking for twelve people, three of which were women. They all had black cloaks and masks and the hilt of a dagger hidden somewhere. One would have a head wound and another a wounded hand from when she tried to escape them. They must also have connections to someone who knew stone masonry and perhaps the masks they wore were traceable.

Her next move must be to question Mr Clare, who had made her wedding dress. Something was not quite right there. Why had the tailor not been there or not heard her struggling with an intruder? And if he himself had been attacked then why did he not report it and inform her father that she was missing?

Bronwen spun around, intending on heading straight there but came face to face with Thanatos again. She had forgotten about him in her musings and took a step back, her legs bumping into the rock.

"Did you find what you are looking for?" He said. His arms were crossed over his chest and his smile was unnerving.

"Not yet," Bronwen said and turned away from Thanatos. She found it difficult to look at him with his unnatural eyes. It invited her towards thoughts of things Bronwen knew she should not want.

A few droplets of water fell onto the stone in front of her. She would not be home before the rain after all.

"Do you fear me?" Thanatos said faintly.

"No," Bronwen replied just as softly and felt him move closer to her.

"Why?"

Bronwen closed her eyes tightly. His question was confusing for such a simple one. She felt like she should fear him, however, it was not him she was afraid of but what he represented - the end of her life, a future of torment and loneliness. These things were acceptable to her when she knew they would only last a single lifetime, but an eternity of it was agony.

No, she did not fear him, but she was afraid.

"Because you are not truly here," Bronwen said, confused by her own answer. Even with her eyes closed, she could sense him behind her and knew the stark realness of him. It was not like her daily life, filled with moments of dazed fantasy, where pinching herself was the only way to remind Bronwen she was awake. Thanatos was a constant reality and she hated him for it.

"Then let me in," Thanatos whispered into her ear. He was so close to her and placed light hands on her arms. She felt a shiver go up her spine.

"Let me into your mind," he continued, snaking his arms around her, one palm on her stomach, the other just above it.

"Let me into your heart."

Bronwen tried not to listen, she kept deathly still, afraid that if she moved, he would tighten his grip.

"Your soul."

He pulled her into him so his front was pressed into her back. She could smell his oaky, fruit aroma and felt his heat begin to engulf her, the light rain burning away before it reached her skin.

"Your body," he growled into her ear and reached one hand down to grab her between the legs.

Bronwen let out a small startled noise and stumbled forwards, her hands landing on the murder stone, despite the layers of her dress shielding her from being able to feel his hand at her most intimate of places.

"No!" Bronwen span around and opened her eyes to confront him, or fight him off if she had to.

Thanatos had vanished, leaving his mark on her by the stuttering of her heart and the heat of her skin.

IX

My dear friend,

I have been so worried about you! It has been over a month since our last correspondence and I have had no word other than gossip that you went missing for an entire day! Some of my more forward neighbours have even suggested that you tried to escape your marriage to Kole.

Of course, I have denied such accusations - despite how much I might wish them to be true - but we shall not go into that subject at present. For now, I only wish for some indication that you are in fact still living and if it is not to my satisfaction then I shall ride to Winchester myself and hunt you down for an explanation, and apology after letting me fret about you for so long.

I do hope to see you before the All-Hallowmas ball, as you need female conversation as much as I do.

Your ever-fretful friend,
~ Josette Emry ~

Bronwen immediately scribbled a hasty reply to Josette's letter, apologising to her friend and promising she would explain the entire thing when they next saw one another.

Then she panicked. She had completely forgotten about the All-Hallowmas ball that Metrom Hall held every year, for the workers of the estate and a few dignitaries. It was a rare night when all were treated equally and shared in scary stories, games, music, dancing and ample amounts of food. It was a much-anticipated event and Bronwen was responsible for organising it.

Bronwen's mother had been the one to start the tradition. She adored the festival more than any other and once she had died, Donovan had thought it only right to pass the responsibility to Bronwen. It was the only thing he *did* entrust to her, as even the finances and running of the household had not been passed on to Bronwen, despite Alda's multiple attempts to persuade him, arguing that Bronwen would need to know how to manage a house when she married. Alda had been allowed to teach Bronwen everything she would need to know, but when it came to Metrom, Donovan had refused, preferring to run everything himself.

As a result, Bronwen went to extra lengths to make the All-Hallowmas ball the event of the year, determined to prove to her father that she was competent. However, with recent events, Bronwen had forgotten all about it.

She rummaged in the drawer of her small writing desk, trying to remember how far she had gotten in preparations and sighed in relief when she found her notebook and her list of tasks that had to be organised. All but three things had been ticked off; make and send invitations, arrange delivery of wood for bonfire and buy an outfit and mask for herself.

Bronwen grimaced at the last item. It was traditional that everyone wears masks to the event. It assisted in the illusion that all attendants were equal, as well as the old belief that the spirits which roamed the earth on this night would not be able to recognise the living and terrorise them.

Finding a mask was one of Bronwen's favourite parts of the ball, but this year she found she had no stomach for them.

Bronwen calculated the date. All-Hallowmas was still over two weeks away, which was plenty of time to inform the guests of the change in theme. Still, she would need to send the invitations out within the next few days and had not even made them yet. At least she would have something to do during her sleepless nights.

Bronwen closed her notebook and left her bedroom to tell her father about the changes, and visit the city for supplies.

She jumped when Adam Whyms stepped out of the shadows of the landing. He had been even more watchful of her the past two days, since she had disappeared up St Catherine's Hill. Mervyn had had trouble with his horse when they tried to cross the bridge and had been forced to dismount to try coax the animal across.

Adam had waited patiently for him until Bronwen had not shown up, then, when his horse had also refused to cross, Adam had dismounted as well and left Mervyn with the horses to go and find Bronwen on foot.

The man had been almost frantic when he finally found Bronwen, walking her horse out of the crop of trees.

"Mr Whyms," Bronwen had said, alarmed to find him alone. She too had looked just as flustered as he, her cheeks had been flushed from her encounter with Thanatos and her hair had a few stray leaves in it. She had also been very wet from the rain beginning to fall, in thick droplets that simply ran off Adam's long coat.

"You were not at the bridge," Adam had said gruffly, his eyes wide as they roamed her body, checking she was alright.

"I am sorry for making you worry." Was all Bronwen had given in explanation. His gaze made her uncomfortable. "We should join Mervyn and get out of this rain."

None of them had mentioned Bronwen's escapade when they returned home. Bronwen thought Mervyn might have told Alda, but after being scolded for allowing her Lady to get caught in the rain, the man had no desire to be berated for something else.

Since then, Mr Whyms had barely left Bronwen's side. Even when she had thought to visit her father's library one night, she had found him sleeping in a chair on the landing outside her room. She had just managed to stifle a scream at his unexpected presence and silently returned to her room just as she heard him stir.

It was getting ridiculous and she hoped his obsessive behaviour abated with time or she would have to address it. Or inform Lord Guild and ask him to have a word with the man. She doubted he would do anything however, as he seemed more than happy with Adam's vigilance.

Bronwen ignored Adam as she made her way down the stairs to the drawing room where her father and Lord Guild were sat playing chess by the fire. She smiled at the normality of the sight. The two men often played chess between business meetings and the sight of her father enjoying a game lightened her heart. His mood seemed to be improving with each passing day.

Bronwen politely refused a drink from James and went to join the men by the fire.

Kole moved his queen piece delicately, with a smile of confident satisfaction, before lounging back in his chair and greeting Bronwen.

"My Lady, you are looking well."

"Thank you, Lord Guild," Bronwen said with a blush, straightening her skirts as she sat in the armchair between them. "I wish to discuss something with you both, is now a convenient time? I would not want to disturb your game."

Donovan tensed and almost tipped one of his pieces over as he moved it to mark Kole's queen.

"Now will be fine," Kole said as he contemplated Donovan's move.

"I want to begin sending the invitations for the All-

Hallowmas ball soon," Bronwen said. "And I thought that this year we could change it a little and forgo the wearing of masks."

"Why?" Donovan barked too harshly, receiving a look from Kole.

"I thought it might be different and the masks have always made me slightly uncomfortable. To wear, I mean as they make games difficult," Bronwen amended, before she revealed too much.

"Do they indeed?" Kole said with amusement then sat forwards to study the game board again. "I do not see a problem with the change, do you, Lord Wintre?"

"I suppose not," Donovan said and left his chair to pour himself a drink.

"Thank you," Bronwen said, looking at the chess board as well, thinking about what supplies she would need from the shop.

"When do you plan to hand out the invitations?" Kole questioned, leaning back in his chair again without moving a piece.

"In a few days. I should have them finished by then," Bronwen replied.

"I will go with you when you deliver them."

"That is not necessary, my Lord."

"No, but it will be good to quell these rumours I have been hearing about you trying to escape our marriage."

Bronwen looked back to the chess board, embarrassed that Kole had heard the whispers too. "I am sorry my... the incident, caused such gossiping to start."

"It is no matter. One must expect such things to circulate when in the public eye. However, I would prefer for us to appear united when others might be watching, it will be good to remind everyone that you will be marrying me."

Bronwen refocused her eyes and frowned. She was sure she had seen one of the chess pieces moving of its own accord, but it must have been a trick of the light from the fire behind it. She looked at Lord Guild and smiled as her father joined them again with a full glass of brandy.

"Yes, it will be good to remind everyone of our intentions," she said and jumped as a log in the fire cracked and fell deeper into the flames, sending sparks skittering across the carpet. The men didn't seem to notice and Bronwen had to stop herself from checking the room for Thanatos.

Donovan glanced down at the board and smiled, moving a piece and lounging back in his seat.

"Checkmate," he said, gulping down his drink.

Kole looked at the board in confusion then bared his teeth almost in a grimace, a low growl escaping his lips that only Bronwen could hear. He hated to lose but did not dispute it, despite Bronwen being sure it was still his turn. She excused herself from the room quickly, no longer warm by the fire.

Bronwen visited the city later that day, accompanied only by Adam Whyms. She had not told Alda she was leaving the house and had asked James to cover for her, explaining that Alda had very little time to herself and needed rest, so it was best not to disturb her for the sake of a trip to the shops and Mr Whyms would of course be with her.

Bronwen also planned to visit Mr Clare's shop while she was there on the pretence of needing an outfit for the ball and it would be best not to have Alda with her. Bronwen wanted to continue the search for her killers that had since been unfruitful. She begrudgingly had to admit that, without Thanatos's help, she might not even know the information she did.

Bronwen took the carriage into the city. It was the smallest of her father's coaches with only enough room for two passengers and two drivers. Adam rode in the front with the coachman, leaving Bronwen gratefully alone for the short trip to the city centre.

After posting her reply to Josette, Bronwen spent a few hours in the shops of Winchester. She bought candles, paper, paint, ribbon, small boxes and ink.

It was a dry day and not as chilly as it had been recently, but the sky was still grey enough to block the sun and very few people were walking the streets. The few that were greeted Bronwen politely, but did not stop to converse when they saw Mr Whyms looming behind her. Bronwen was glad he came in useful for something and he also insisted upon carrying her bags for her, despite them being put straight into the carriage after each shop.

Finally, she was finished and decided that she could put off the visit to Mr Clare's shop no longer.

Bronwen stepped from the carriage and took a deep breath before turning to Adam.

"There is no need to follow me in, Mr Whyms," she said, trying to sound as authoritative as she could. "I am only going to enquire about a dress for the ball and possibly have my measurements taken."

"I should be with you," Adam said, curling his hands into loose fists, ready for some unforeseen attacker.

"Please, Mr Whyms, I will not be long and I highly doubt I will be in danger in a dress shop." Bronwen tried to appear jovial but she knew better than most what dangers the place held. "If it makes you feel more comfortable, if I am not out in twenty minutes then you may come to my rescue."

Adam did not look convinced.

"Fifteen," he said, nodding towards a clock coming out from a nearby shop, instead of pulling out the watch Bronwen had assumed was at the end of the chain hanging from one of his waistcoat pockets.

"Very well," Bronwen conceded, trying to not shake her head at him as she walked away.

The well-oiled door did not make a sound as she entered

the dressmaker's shop, it didn't even have a bell on the door like most places.

Mr Clare was not at his desk against the far wall, which gave him a clear view of the window. Bronwen walked quietly over to it but didn't yet ring the bell on the desk, she doubted there would be anything of significance in the front of the shop, but studied the room anyway.

The large dresses and suits in the windows gave the room an eerie dimness, made worse by the candles that sat snugly in their holders around the walls. The soot that came off them created spectral shadows above each one and the drip trays below captured the white wax underneath, almost as if the shadows were bleeding their light away.

The room was quite large with a small seating area and a standing mirror in one corner. Most of one wall was taken up by fabric samples and hats. The opposite wall had a wirework mannequin with a measuring tape over one shoulder and a round standing block pushed against the wall. Mr Clare's work desk was scattered with various tailor's implements Bronwen did not recognise, except for one.

She reached for a pair of silver coloured scissors and inspected them. They were very sharp and looked very much like the ones she had used to stab one of her attacker's hand. Bronwen grimaced at the memory of them sinking into flesh and dropped them back onto the table.

"Can I help you, madam?"

Bronwen jumped at Mr Clare's voice and turned to greet the dress maker.

"You!" Lowell exclaimed when he saw his customer. He stumbled back a step and the fear in his voice was unmasked.

Bronwen raised an eyebrow at his response. "Mr Clare, are you well?"

"What are you doing here?" he demanded in a shaken voice, reaching behind himself for the wall.

"I am sorry, are you not open?" Bronwen asked, taken aback by his reaction. Mr Clare was usually a well-mannered gentleman. Leanly built and always well dressed, though very serious. She could not remember ever seeing him smile but he was always polite. "Shall I come back later?"

"No!" Lowell barked and tried to compose himself, blinking rapidly and shaking his head. "My apologies, Lady Bronwen. Only, I was not expecting to see you about so soon."

"So soon after what, might I ask?" Bronwen said, genuinely confused.

Lowell gave her an indignant look and began to move his tools off his desk and into a box, but did not answer her. Bronwen decided to start again.

"Mr Clare, I was hoping to employ your services in making me a dress for the All-Hallowmas ball this year. If you are not too busy." Bronwen began.

"I am too busy," he replied, not looking at her. He was being quite rude and Bronwen would have left the shop if she did not need him and any potential information he may have about that night.

"Please could I not then bring you a dress I already own and have it adapted for the night?"

"Why do you not do the work yourself? I am sure your skills with a pair of scissors will come in handy."

"Because I do not have the time or the equipment needed."

His rudeness was becoming tiring and Bronwen was becoming frustrated with his manner. Then he pulled the scissors she had been looking at earlier from the box and slid them across the table to her.

"Keep them, with my regards," Lowell said staring at her in challenge. This gesture Bronwen could not ignore.

It was then that Bronwen realized Lowell was wearing a hat and she became suspicious that he knew more than he was telling.

"Surely you should remove your hat in a woman's presence, as is polite?"

Suddenly his expression changed from menacing to fearful and then to anger.

"It is my shop." He took his hands off the table.

"Yes, it is, and I am the daughter of a Baron," Bronwen snapped back, though she hated using her father's position against people.

Lowell grimaced and put his hand to his hat, hesitating before he removed it, revealing a large cut on the side of his head. Precisely where her attacker had fallen onto the table.

"What... what happened?" Bronwen asked, her heart thumping.

"I would have thought that you of all people would know." Lowell said, his lip curled into a snarl.

"Why?"

Lowell leaned towards her ever so slightly. "Why don't you ask your master, *witch*."

Bronwen's breath hitched. "It *was* you."

Lowell responded with a satisfied smile and there was a moments pause before time sped up.

Bronwen's gaze flicked down at the scissors that were still on the table between them, Lowell saw them too and then, they both lunged. Bronwen's hand closed over them and Lowell's came down on top, his other hand grabbed Bronwen's hair in his fist and he forced her head into the table, trapping her hand.

Bronwen tried to scream for help but Lowell lifted her head and slammed it into the table again, making her ear ring. She relinquished her possession of the scissors, sliding them out so they fell onto the floor and clawed at his arm. He shoved her away from the table and she stumbled over a footstool.

There was another pause before Bronwen ran for the

door. Lowell followed close behind, grabbing the tape measure on his way, making the metal mannequin fall to the floor with a crash that Bronwen hoped was audible from outside. She reached for the door handle.

"Ada-" She just managed to yell before the tape measure came over her head and was around her throat, restricting her air. Lowell used it to pull Bronwen away from the door and back into the shop while she struggled against him, trying to pull the tape away from her neck.

"Devil whore!" he hissed in her ear as she choked. "You were supposed to stay dead. We all made our bargains; he isn't going to take away what is mine for failing to deliver."

Bronwen's vision was beginning to blur and her eyes watered.

"Go back to hell and tell him there are no returns."

Bronwen's head swam and everything started to go black. If she could just get enough air to scream...

"We are closed I'm afraid," Lowell said over Bronwen's shoulder. The distraction made him release enough slack in the tape for Bronwen to get her fingers between it and her neck and take a shallow breath.

She tried to call for Adam again but only coughed instead, not realising that she didn't have to alert him; Mr Whyms was already in the shop.

He was stood by the door with an unreadable expression on his face. Bronwen felt a wave of relief until she watched Adam close the door behind him slowly and lock it with a calm finality, trapping Bronwen inside with him and Lowell.

"I said get the fuck out!" Lowell yelled, again loosening his grip on Bronwen slightly, but she was too distracted by what Adam was doing. He looked so composed that, if not for Lowell's reaction, she would have assumed that she had been caught with two of her murderers.

Adam undid a button on his coat and reached inside, producing a slender knife from its folds. Bronwen's heart thumped painfully and Lowell actually laughed.

"That won't work on her and the bitch is mine. It was my deal! He's not taking it away! It was my god damn deal!"

"It's not for her," Adam said, ignoring the man's crazed ranting, removing his jacket then folding it neatly before placing it on the back of the sofa beside him.

Lowell laughed hysterically. "Did *he* send you? For her?"

Adam didn't reply and instead moved towards Lowell, watching him with his hawk-like eyes, the knife held lightly in his long fingers. Lowell backed up towards the wall, pulling Bronwen with him. If she could only get out of the way then maybe Adam could save her, but Lowell's grip was tight and he constricted it the more she struggled.

"Stop moving!" he screamed at both she and Adam. "She's already dead! You can't save her!"

Bronwen needed him to let go of the tape, even one hand would give her the room to get away. Lowell's back was almost against the wall now.

Adam tilted his head to one side and he stared into Bronwen's eyes. He was so unnervingly calm it was almost more frightening than Lowell. She looked away and noticed a candle burning just above Lowell's head. If only it would fall onto him, or at least drip some wax onto his hand, but she knew she wouldn't be able to reach it.

Then, everything happened at once again. Lowell cried out in surprise, loosening one hand on the tape, enough for Bronwen to duck under it. Once she had, Adam dashed forwards, baring his teeth. Bronwen fell to the floor, coughing as she crawled away. She turned to see Adam struggling with Lowell but the fight didn't last long.

Adam had already cut Lowell on the cheek and blocked a swipe from the tailor with ease before he had the man by the throat with one hand and sunk his knife deep into Lowell's stomach with the other.

Lowell coughed once and his eyes widened as he dribbled

blood down his chin. Adam let go but before Mr Clare could slide to the floor, the bodyguard swiped his knife across the man's neck for good measure. Blood spurted from the wound and poured out of his body as he landed face down at Bronwen's feet.

In complete shock, Bronwen shuffled backwards on the floor when the pooling blood began to creep towards her toes. She noticed the candle on the ground beside Lowell's body that had fallen from the holder and thought she might be sick as tears began to fall down her cheeks.

Adam bent down and wiped his knife on Lowell's jacket before he looked at Bronwen. Incredibly, he was free from blood, despite the amount of it.

Adam straightened up, making Bronwen flinch, then he held out a hand to help her off the floor. After everything that had occurred, this one action was what made her pass out.

Bronwen came to a few hours later in her carriage, dazed and confused. Apparently being unconscious did not count as sleeping but she felt less than rested.

The first face she saw was Lord Guild's and Bronwen threw herself into his arms, ignoring the stares of those around her. Kole seemed not to care either and without a moment's hesitation, wrapped his arms around her body and crushed her against his chest.

Donovan was also at the scene but was far more concerned with how and why Lowell had been killed. Luckily, the police seemed satisfied with Adam's statement of events, though Bronwen did not know exactly what story he gave, she was just grateful she did not have to explain the attack.

Yet, something still did not sit right with Bronwen. She realised what it was as she tried to loosen her corset, not wanting to ever have her airway restricted again. Lowell had not been the only person in the shop that night. There was one person missing from the story. The woman who had helped her into her wedding gown so roughly. If Lowell had been one of her murderers, then this woman must also have something to do with it.

She enquired with officers while Kole went to speak to her father, but Lowell had been the only person in the shop and as far as they knew, he had no assistant working for him.

It was almost fully dark when they finally removed Lowell's body from the shop on a stretcher, a thin white cloth covering him. Kole tried to turn Bronwen away but she couldn't avert her gaze as they placed Mr Clare's body onto the back of a waggon.

She glanced across the street behind the vehicle to a lonely streetlamp and saw a figure in the glow.

The dark creature grinned and tilted his hat to her. Then lifted a single finger before fading away.

The first of her twelve vengeances.

X

Velna stroked her rounded stomach. It wasn't too large. The baby would still only be small - a light bite really. She hummed to herself as she walked the outer walls of Berwick just one hour before midnight.

They had been there only one day and Velna's condition had already grabbed the attention of the one they were hunting. She could sense him behind her, stalking his prey.

Velna almost laughed at the thought of *him* stalking *her*.

There were no lights on the wall that surrounded the city, and this far North, the sky was always covered in clouds, blocking out the stars. Velna didn't need them, she was used to the dark and the lights from the city were enough for her to navigate her way along the deserted stone work.

Velna was singing softly under her breath now. She had not been able to get the rhyme out of her mind since Cornell had taught it to her on the way to Berwick.

{A bridge without a middle arch, a church without a steeple}

He was getting closer to her now and she slowed down to let him catch up. They were almost at the corner of the wall, right where Velna wanted to be.

{A midden heap in every street, and damned conceited people}

Velna cradled her pregnant belly in her arms as she turned, trying to look surprised to find a man there.

"Don't scream and come with me," he drooled in an accent that did not belong to the Northern city.

If they had taken any longer to arrive there, the man would have moved on again as he had in other towns, once his acquired source of sustenance had run dry. Even Velna's strong stomach for the fetishes of men found this one distasteful. She would enjoy killing him.

Velna gasped and stepped away. "What do you want from me?"

The man's eyes flicked down to the stomach she was trying to cover and licked his lips. Then he produced a knife from his jacket.

"I said come with me." He stalked towards her, brandishing his weapon.

"Oh, no, a knife, whatever will I do."

Velna placed a hand to her brow. She was a good actress, but in this instance, did not see the need to try. They were alone on the wall with no escape, so she thought she might as well enjoy herself. The man did not seem to notice her false worry, so preoccupied by the pregnancy she was trying to hide.

Velna grinned at him and then began to run. She swore a few times, not from fear but because it was difficult to run in her condition. Her front was so much heavier and it made her stumble on loose stones.

It was not long before he caught her arm in his clammy hand and pulled her to a stop. He was more breathless than she was and she supposed he relied on the women being slow and easy to catch.

"Well done, sir, you caught me," Velna mocked, not in the slightest bit tired. She was extremely fit. She had to be for her work.

"Come – with me," he panted. "And I won't – have to –."

"Cut it out?" Velna asked and he finally seemed to notice her calm manner. She smiled at his confusion and leaned in towards him to whisper. "You should let go of me now."

To his credit, he did as she asked and turned to find Cornell stood blocking his escape.

"What is this? An arrest?" The man said, holding his knife out.

Velna laughed. "No, I am afraid we are far above the police."

The man turned back to Velna and noticed another man behind her. Haydon, looking much more intimidating than Cornell.

"You bitch!" the man said and rushed at Velna before the two men could stop him, then stabbed his knife deep into her pregnant belly.

Velna gasped and grabbed the man's shoulder for support. Her eyes went wide and the man smiled at her with satisfaction before yanking his knife out and stepping back so he could see the blood and life pour from her.

A trickle of something began to fall from the wound. In the dim light it was hard to see at first. The man looked at his knife, expecting to see blood, but it was clean. He squinted at the pile of white powder at Velna's feet, still confused.

"Oh, now what shall I use to bake with?" Velna said in mock concern. Haydon chuckled and the man turned to run, straight into Cornell, who kicked the man between the legs and easily confiscated the knife.

"Where are you taking me?" the man demanded in a breathless voice as Cornell pinned his arms behind him.

Velna strolled up to him confidently, removing the bag of flour from beneath her dress and emptying the rest of it onto the floor.

"My very bad man," she said with a grin. "We are sending you straight to hell."

Velna placed the cloth bag over his head and Haydon punched him, knocking him unconscious before he could yell out.

A chill breeze came in from the window; it was rank in smell and bitter in taste. The colour of the sky was dark, Velna's favourite. Being a Lady of the night, her very essence was of the shadows. It could hide deeds that were not welcome in 'civilised society'.

The party of killers had arrived back in Winchester that afternoon, parting ways just before they entered the city again. None of the men had offered to escort Velna home, knowing her well enough to realise she would not appreciate it. She was no weak woman who needed taking care of.

Velna was ruthless and clever. The pregnancy lure had been her idea and *she* had been the one to perform the ritual that sent the Berwick killer to hell. She would have been the perfect companion for her master.

The cold air dried Velna's hair while she sat on the window sill with a vacant mind. Her room was the top floor of the brothel with an open celling, exposing beams that she hung silky fabrics and lanterns from. It also had its own bathtub set up high on a platform of floor, next to a small stone fireplace and partitioned off from the main room by thick curtains. Up two more small steps was a large round window from where she could watch the breeze stroking the treetops and forget where she was and how she had come to be there.

The alcove was still steamy from the heat of the bath water. Velna washed more regularly than most people and her body was shaved clean to avoid infections, which was why she had spent a large sum of money on the house so her room had its own drainage and pump system for water. At least no one could accuse her of being a dirty whore.

Velna's time was expensive. She chose her clients when the fancy took her. Being the owner of a brothel meant she did not have to work like the other girls, but the habit was hard to break. And truthfully, she enjoyed the company sometimes. She had fought hard to regain what choices had been stolen from her since she was a child.

Velna's father had sold her virginity to the highest paying brothel. Velna was a good little money earner for him. She soon learnt what men wanted and how to accommodate them. At the time, she had even *wanted* to be good at her job, because it kept her sister safe. As long as Velna was earning their father money, Mara would not be sold as she had been.

After a few years, Velna had started to present symptoms of a sinful occupation and suddenly the only clients that would have her were the ones that had the same sickness - among others. She became weaker and earned less money, becoming vulnerable to all sorts of depraved fantasies just so she could keep the money coming. Eventually, her father was ready to sell Mara to the same whorehouse and Velna was damned if she was going to let that happen.

It had not been this point that her Dominus had appeared to her, exchanging her soul for her sister's safety. It had been after Velna had run away with Mara to another city and spent an entire year living off scraps and what little money Velna could make from her hands and mouth alone. Soon after, her father had tracked them down.

Velna still remembered the warmth of the blood on her fingers. It had been so easy. So easy to seduce him into the alley that she was sure he did not recognise her until he asked if Mara might join them. That comment had made it easier still to plunge the glass into his neck and she almost laughed as he beat her bloody before succumbing to his own blood loss and death.

It was then, in that alley with the body of her father

staring lifelessly back at her, that her Dominus had taken her hand in his and whispered about the life she might have if she chose to serve him. He had looked so much like an angel, Velna had thought she was hallucinating. He was the first man she had ever *wanted* to touch her. He had saved Velna's life and her sister's and their servitude in exchange was a small price to pay.

One of Velna's nipples puckered, letting her know that her night gown had fallen from her shoulder. She shrugged it back on in irritation. It had distracted her from her absence of mind and brought her unwelcomingly back to the reality of her how the only lover she would actually welcome to her well-used bed, had chosen another.

That whimpering fool; Lady Bronwen.

Velna did not understand how such a prudish, naive woman could be so desired by men. What on this earth could *she* know of how to properly pleasure a man? Obviously, she was attractive, even Velna could not deny that, and she would no doubt spawn healthy children, unlike Velna, whose years of bodily abuse had made her infertile. But, what could a stupidly pure virgin do to have a man call her name out in ecstasy and vow to have no other woman for his bed?

Velna supposed she should be grateful for it. It was women like Bronwen who kept her fed when their lustful, unsatisfied husbands emptied their purses and potential heirs into her.

A change in the air made her spin around, knife in hand, up and ready to strike, should it be an intruder looking for a free ride.

Her Dominus caught her hand mid-swing. Velna's eyes widened and she dropped the knife to the floor, mortified that she had almost struck her master.

He greeted her with an intense, heated look and put her forefinger into his mouth, sucking on it gently, then more insistent, then sharp from his teeth.

Velna's breath caught in her throat.

"You were looking to be rough this evening?" her Dominus asked as he yanked her arm to pull her flush against his already naked body. The hardness of him was almost as biting as his teeth where it pressed into her stomach and she was grateful for the thin material of her gown.

"As you like, Dominus," Velna's voice hitched on the last word as he bit her shoulder and tightened his grip on her wrist. His fingers dug into her flesh where they held her to him and she welcomed it. It was never unpleasant. Velna was always amenable to his needs – she *wanted* to be the one to pleasure him in whatever way he desired. His visits were anticipated and were never the same as the last or the next.

Velna wanted him, desired him, and wanted him to desire her.

The demon of her dreams stopped his devouring of her skin. He let go of her waist and gripped her chin in his hand so she looked directly at him.

His hair was black and very short, his body tall and well-muscled and his eyes a furious heated red. He bared his pointed teeth and Velna almost lost her senses from his gaze alone.

"Is it done?" he hissed.

"Yes, Dominus," Velna said in a breathy voice, knowing he meant the man from Berwick - the would-be demon that might cause her master problems were he to die naturally.

"Good, my Servus."

Velna shivered at the name and the pleasure she gained from pleasing him.

Her master used his grip on her chin to steer her away from the window. Her feet barely grazed the floor and he moved the curtain dividing the space without so much as a glance or raised hand. When they were near the bed, he pushed her away from him and fixed her in place with blazing eyes that lit the hanging lanterns around the room.

"You have pleased me, Servus."

"I am only here to please you, Dominus," Velna said, kneeling down and bowing her head. He was the only man who could make her feel weak and want to completely submit to him.

"Is that so?" he hissed. "Show me."

Velna glanced up at him, he was holding himself tightly and Velna wanted it to be her hand around him, her mouth over him. Every detail of his body sent a shiver down Velna's spine and she felt a familiar pulse in her groin, as if it were attempting to pull her body back to him.

Velna smiled seductively at her Dominus and stood slowly. She took a step towards him but he put a hand up to stop her and she knew what he wanted.

Slowly, with practiced invitation, Velna laid herself back on the bed and pulled up her long night gown, then reached for the part of her body that men visited her for, paid money to see; to feel; to taste.

Velna kept eye contact with him while she moved her fingers slowly over herself. Just looking at him made her wet and close to climax. She wanted him inside her, wanted *his* hands on her. Knowing how the action effected human men and hoping it would have the same effect on him, she brought her fingers to her mouth and tasted herself.

Her Dominus grinned and with powerful strides, was stood in front of her at the foot of the bed. She yearned to touch him, his hard skin, as hot as a fire pit. She considered herself blessed that he had made her his bed-mate this evening. She had worried that his loss of favour for the Secuutus Letum had led her to be cast aside. More than for anything else, she hated Lady Bronwen for that.

Her master ran a finger down the front of Velna's gown and the laces came apart at his will. When he reached the space just above her pelvic bone, he brought his hands up again and the gown parted completely, revealing her naked torso. His hand reached her throat and he gripped it and pushed her deeper into the bed.

"Open your mouth," he commanded. She did so immediately and his tongue found hers, his saliva an aphrodisiac that filled her body.

"I am going to fill you and pleasure you until you wish you were dead," he whispered and Velna's hand automatically reached for herself as she groaned, needing some release from his seduction. Her master grabbed her wrist harshly and flipped both her arms above her head.

"Don't you dare!" he growled and she whimpered from frustration and the thrill his words brought. Her fast heart rate made the pulsing ache more intense.

"I want you to beg," he said, letting go of her throat so she could speak.

"Please, Dominus."

"Not like that."

His chest had been carefully avoiding the touch of hers, so he bent over her and hard muscle pushed into her with demanding pressure. Already positioned, the master thrust into Velna once, whilst piercing her palms with his nails.

She cried out in ecstasy as she came with just one thrust and he pulled out of her, hovering for a few seconds before thrusting again, sending her to a second orgasm before the first had finished coursing through her.

"What am I?" he growled at her. She only just heard him as she came down from her high, blood pounding in her ears.

"My... master..." She breathed with the hint of a smile.

He shook his head, almost irritated and dug his nails deeper and thrust again.

"What am I really?" he asked again, more loudly over her screaming orgasm.

"...Lord... of the... Under-realm."

He gave her no rest bite, still unsatisfied with her answer and sent her appealing again in agonising pleasure as only one not of earthly nature can. No human man could cause such cascading rapture and not many human women could take it for a prolonged amount of time.

"What does that make me?" He thrust three times making her whole body spasmodic.

"...A... d-de-...mon..." she could finally husk out of her spent body in a rasping breath. He *was* playing rough and her vision was beginning to blacken, blood rushing in her ears.

"This is what fucking a demon is like." He rocked his hips slowly and Velna dreaded another thrust, not sure if she could take much more. Her body was covered in sweat and her eyes watered.

"P-...lease."

"You want more?"

"Pleassse... no... no more.... please... no more."

He leant in close to her ear and whispered softly, "that is more like it."

He pumped into her a few more times, finishing himself along with her. Velna had not even the energy to make a sound and was grateful when he left her body.

The woman's eyes rolled back into her head as Thanatos watched with satisfaction. He knew he had used her as a vent for his madness at Bronwen, but she would recover. It was, so far, not possible to die from pleasure – not this time at least, he was sure.

Bronwen, he thought the name angrily. Fucking the name out of his thoughts had not worked. She still refused to obey him. Seeing her after Lowell's death, clinging to that insolent bastard Kole Guild, who had tried to take what was rightfully his, had sent Thanatos into a fury. Bronwen would not marry Kole, he would see to it. He could woo any woman and this one would be no different. He just needed to adjust his methods.

Bronwen still saw him as a demon, so perhaps he just needed time to prove her wrong. Looking down at the woman on the bed, her chest heaving, he imagined it to be Bronwen, then was briefly ashamed at how he had treated her tonight.

Thanatos was too used to being the Devil and getting his way. And while Bronwen infuriated him, he would greatly enjoy the challenge of seducing her.

Velna lifted her body up, but her Dominus was gone, leaving her empty. He was not one for pillow talk, but he did not usually disappear so suddenly.

Her body was still hot and the ache had begun, not just on her body but in her heart. She tried to stand only for her legs to tremble and give way beneath her. Velna half crawled to the still full bathtub and sank into it. Not caring it was now cold where the window had been left open.

She washed away the sweat and passion from her master and closed her eyes, reliving the love making. It had not been totally unpleasant. She would accept any abuse from her Dominus, but he had been different this night, almost cruel. She scowled, betting it was that bitch Bronwen. Her master clearly was not getting his satisfaction from her and needed what only Velna could give him.

She did not flinch as her bedroom door opened and the dividing curtain was pulled to the side, so engrossed in her thoughts of hatred.

"Good, you're alone," Mara said, using the rope on the wall to secure the curtain and walking to Velna's small clothing chest in the corner of the room. "They're waiting for you downstairs."

"Who are?"

"Who else?"

Velna shook herself and stood, cold water dripping off her

body. Mara held out a towel for her sister, unperturbed by her nakedness. They had been through too much together for such trivial propriety.

Velna wrapped the towel around herself and rolled her eyes at the dress Mara had laid neatly on the bed for her. It was respectable dulled yellow cotton, a rare heirloom they had from their mother that their father had not sold when she died. It was greatly out of fashion and far too plain for Velna.

She folded it up carefully and returned it to the bottom of the chest, instead taking out the green silk bodice and skirt that was the best at pushing her breasts to the front in a sumptuous curving.

Mara said nothing. She had known her sister was likely to change the outfit but it was a common act of hers to choose it, as if it was a way of reminding Velna who she really was. A loving, resourceful sister and not the creature of dark colours she had become.

Velna remembered something and brought an item out of her travel bags, holding it out to Mara.

"I found it in Berwick," Velna said as Mara took the book she was offering. "Sounded like something you would read."

Mara ran a finger over the embossed lettering of the cover. 'Transformation' by Nathaniel Hawthorne.

"He's American though," Velna said as she threw her towel to the floor so she stood bare in front of the bed. Mara smiled and placed the book down so she could help her sister tie up her dress. Velna often brought Mara books from her travels or when a customer gave them to her as gifts.

Velna would tell the men she enjoyed books only because she knew Mara liked them. She would sometimes ask Mara to tell her what happened in a story that interested her, or ones that her customers were keen to talk about but she had no time or wish to read them herself.

Mara loved to read. It was the education she had not been allowed to have and an escape into the life she could not lead. She did not blame Velna for their situation, but hoped that one day, an opportunity to better their lives would present itself and she wanted to be prepared for it.

Mara hesitated in tying the strings of Velna's dress when she noticed the beginning of yellow bruises on her sister's wrists and bite marks on her shoulder. She continued without comment for a while, though Velna was waiting for one.

"He visited you again," Mara stated. Velna said nothing. "You are always brooding when he has been here. Was it the same as always or did he desire your conversation for once?" The accusation was clear in Mara's voice. She saw how withdrawn her sister was every time their Dominus visited her.

She knew that what Velna did with the other men of the city was a way of survival for the both of them and Velna always had a choice, but giving herself to the demon they worshiped was not part of the bargain they had made.

"You shouldn't speak of our Dominus that way. And what I do is my own business," Velna snapped.

Mara looked away; finishing the bow she was tying on the bodice and walking to the door, the book Velna had given her clutched to her chest.

She paused with her hand on the door knob, not turning back to look at Velna as she continued speaking.

"He may be our master, but you are my sister first."

Mara left the room, leaving the door open for Velna to follow. She took a deep breath, pulled her hair up into a messy bun, loose tendrils hanging about her cheeks, and followed Mara into the dim corridor.

Velna stood on the landing. From behind the closed doors that lined the stairs, she could hear the sighs and exclamations of the punters and working ladies of the pleasure house. Her rooms were the only ones on the top floor, even Mara had taken a room on the opposite side of the house, away from the noises of the darker end.

The house had once belonged to another madam who had called it 'The Tankard'. A dull name, unimaginative and forgettable. It had been the first thing Velna had changed when she had 'persuaded' the woman to retire gracefully - as well as the substantial amount of money Velna had given her. Now the large sign above the door said 'The Siren', with the seductive and provocative image of the mythical sea nymph draped over the letters. Simple, memorable and enticing.

The money Velna had used to pay for the renovation and the brothel itself had been part of her deal with her Dominus. She had wanted Mara to be kept safe and not have to worry, so Velna had been given a large sum of money that was stolen from the poor souls they were sent to kill.

Denny was in charge of the money as well as being a messenger for their master. Velna hated that she had not been chosen to do this, considering the money she had been given, though a pleasant sum, was nothing compared to what she had done with it and now earned. She was good with money and had turned the sorry house into a thriving brothel, easily returning the funds she had borrowed in her deal.

Velna had trained the hired girls herself and they were the best. She often had men from other towns and cities visit because they could get what they wanted nowhere else. The Siren catered for many fetishes and was also the only brothel with whores that could not produce children, thanks to Mara's skills with a chemistry set. They could make good money selling the potion alone, but it would draw too much attention to themselves and Mara was still unhappy with some of the side effects.

When she was not reading, and playing at her cauldron, Mara worked behind the bar, serving drinks to customers. Velna had refused to allow her to serve them elsewhere but her sister had been insistent on wanting to help, despite Velna making enough money for the both of them.

Velna watched her sister from the top of the stairs as Mara opened the door to the bar entrance. The light from the room shone across the floor, illuminating the steps. The beam reached Velna's feet, but that was all. Then the door closed and the corridor was dark again, with only the disembodied groans and grunts as company.

Velna began walking down the stairs. One room had a woman wailing like a banshee in her faux climax. Velna shook her head at the inexperience of the girl and wished her some self-respect. She would speak to her later on the matter and have her practice her orgasms, much like a school master would have a student writing lines.

Velna took another breath of stale air and opened the tavern door. Noise and laughter hit her senses and the strong odour of beer, smoke and sweat.

Millard, the man Velna employed behind the bar to serve drinks - and to beat men senseless should they get a little over enthusiastic or refuse to pay - inclined his head towards the room behind him, reserved for gambling and special deals.

"Mr Fitz wants your company tonight, Velna," he said as she walked past him. She paused, taking the shot of spirit he had been pouring and gulping it down in one. Millard filled the same glass again.

Velna looked out across the mass of so called 'gentlemen' and spotted Fitz staring at her as he drank deeply from a pint glass. He was always anything but a gentle man. She did not mind him so much but after her earlier encounter, her usually athletic libido had gone to sleep.

Still, Velna gave him a coy smile and ducked her gaze in

the innocent way he liked. He straightened in his chair and his eyes widened in arousal - a look Velna knew well; an ancient look, of a serpent with tongue lashing out, tasting its prey before a kill.

Velna mouthed the word 'later', just in case she had a change of heart. Then she drank another shot and entered the back room, closing the door and barring it behind her before turning to see what fetid company the night had brought her.

There were three men sat around the table and her sister, who was standing behind her chair uneasily.

"Good evening, scum," Velna greeted them and made her way to the unoccupied seat next to Mara.

"Whore," Haydon replied with a nod of his head. They smiled at each other in good humour.

The other two men were Cornell - thankfully absent of his wife - and Maverick. They both had strong drinks in their hands.

"Is your son not visiting this evening, Maverick?" Velna asked slyly. "We do so like it when he visits."

Maverick didn't bristle at the implication but gave a short smile back in acknowledgment. Velna gave Mara a secret look that the men missed. Kyran and Mara had always been particularly close, a fact that Velna liked to provoke her sister about, but Mara looked too anxious to take the bait this time.

"I was not expecting to see you two so soon," Velna addressed Cornell and Haydon. They had only returned from Berwick that morning.

"Maverick has news, but like the gentleman he is, was waiting for the Lady to arrive," Cornell said, indicating to Velna. She knew he was mocking her but she didn't care and turned to Maverick.

"You will be waiting a long while if you are expecting a Lady," she said with a smile.

"Lowell's dead," Maverick stated, clearly not in the mood for word games.

The table was silent for a moment then Haydon burst out laughing, banging his large fists on the table.

"Was it his head injury?" Mara asked over Haydon's laughing, finally taking a seat at the table.

"More like a neck wound," Maverick replied with a grimace, making his meaning clear by slicing his hand across his neck. This finally made Haydon stop snickering. Lowell was no friend to them but they were allies of a sort and if anyone was going to kill Lowell, it would be one of them, anything else was unacceptable.

Velna gave Maverick a long and level look before answering, her voice no longer mocking but hard and hateful. "Was it *her*?"

"It was that bastard bodyguard Kole gave her. Bronwen weren't involved in actually killing him," Maverick said, but his own voice betrayed his belief in it.

"As far as you know?" Velna repeated. "As far as we all know, a knife in the heart should kill you."

"She was in the room but the guard stabbed him then slit Lowell's throat," Maverick explained. "The bloody idiot decided to attack the woman when she came to his shop."

"So, she *does* remember what happened," Cornell said. "She must have confronted Lowell trying to find us."

Haydon slammed his fist down on the table, making everyone but Velna jump. "The bastard better not 'ave given us away or he'll dread the day I join him in hell!"

"Yes, Haydon, you are so very frightening," Cornell ridiculed the giant man, shaking his head, but Velna noticed how his arm was now under the table by his belt, which no doubt held a knife.

"Whether she is coming for us or not, the bitch should be dead right now," Velna said sourly. "Our Dux Ducis seems content with his precious daughter and Kole won't let anyone play with his little toy."

"Kill the demon whore," Haydon agreed. "Even if she ain't the cause, she shouldn't be alive either."

Velna smiled at her ally. She could always count on Haydon to be after blood. Murder had always been his way of solving a problem. She didn't know the details, but Velna knew Haydon had been on trial for the murder of his wife when their Dominus had offered him the deal.

Amongst the members of the group, these three were the men she had the closest connection to. This was not the first time they had met together, away from the others and she knew that, should she ever challenge Donovan for his role as their leader, they would be likely to follow her. But she was far from being ready for that.

"While I am inclined to agree with you," Cornell said. "If anything should go wrong, she will know who we are and likely be a threat to us."

Velna refrained from snorting in contempt. Mara was the only one who noticed her reaction to the idea of that pathetic, spoilt, scrawny rich girl being a threat to anyone and she intervened before Velna could get overly agitated about it.

"Lady Bronwen has allies and people who guard her. It could be a hindrance when trying to protect our anonymity."

"Fuck me, don't you speak English woman?" Maverick snapped. Velna bristled and almost pulled her own knife from her belt, but her sister didn't give her the chance to retaliate, a retort of her own ready.

"Bronwen's guard, make you dead. Is that clearer or would you prefer a puppet show because I doubt writing it down would be much use."

Haydon began laughing again and even Cornell chuckled. Maverick was wise enough to stay quiet.

"We only need one of us to go, to make sure she fucking

dies this time," Maverick said. "We can hire the rest."

"I know a couple men who'll do it," Haydon added. "And I'll gladly volunteer meself to go wif 'em."

"Perfect," Velna said, already feeling victorious.

"If Donovan finds out," Cornell warned. "You acted alone, Haydon."

"When she's dead, he'll be thanking me for gettin' rid of the problem." Haydon grinned in satisfaction.

"Wait for her to leave the house," Maverick advised. "Then you won't have to worry about Donovan."

"A few men can take her bodyguard, it's Kole you have to be wary of," Cornell added.

Haydon gave him a confident smile. "Kole's on our side. He won't stop me when it comes to it."

The rest of them exchanged looks of doubt. None of them trusted Kole, least of all Velna. He had his own motives that even Donovan did not seem aware of. She knew bits of what everyone's deal with their Dominus was, she had been part of the Secuutus for long enough, but Kole had evaded her prying. Even her master refused to talk about the man, becoming agitated at the mention of the Earl who had tried to claim what was never his - asking Bronwen to marry him despite knowing she was destined to die.

"Kole cannot be trusted," Cornell said so Velna didn't have to. She didn't believe that Kole would actively protect Bronwen, but if things started to go wrong, Kole would shield his identity before defending Haydon.

"He won't stop me. She's good as dead," Haydon insisted. He was not known for his intelligence and if Haydon planned to put his faith in Kole's allegiance to the group, then Velna would have to make an alternative plan. Perhaps she would visit this bodyguard herself. Every man had his weakness and she was an expert in exploiting these for her own gain.

"Sever her empty little head from her shoulders if you

have to," Velna said with venom. "See her come back from that."

XI

A few days after witnessing Lowell's death at Adam's hands, Bronwen stood at the mirror of her dressing room one morning and ran her fingers delicately over the five lines on her stomach, wondering again at what they meant and why they were not gone like her other injuries from the day she was murdered.

It was too early for anyone in the house to be awake yet. Bronwen's only indication that it was a good hour to get up had become when Alda came for her, otherwise she stayed in her room, waiting. Her maid was getting used to finding her Lady awake, despite trying to come earlier and earlier. She had tried to convince Bronwen to take a sleeping potion but Bronwen had refused. It would likely have had no effect on her anyway.

Since finding that human sleep eluded her, Bronwen had been intrigued to note the nightly movements and habits of the servants of the house. Mervyn would sometimes sneak out at night, and return a few hours later, smiling or humming quietly.

There was a young woman who enjoyed watching the stars in the sky while she smoked. Mr Durward would also disappear out the back entrance of Metrom and sometimes had visitors, but Bronwen had yet to discover who. She had thought to follow him but decided that his business was his own.

Adam Whyms had begun patrolling the grounds before returning to his place on the landing. Bronwen had hoped to learn the times he would do this so she could leave her room and return later without his knowledge, but it was different each night. So instead, she made sure she had all she wanted for the evening before it began, like books, sewing and plenty of lighting.

Thankfully, making the invitations for the All-Hallowmas ball had taken Bronwen most of two nights and her fingers had ink stains and little indents in them from holding a quill and paintbrush for so long. It had taken her mind off the sorry business of Lowell, but she had just finished the last of the painted candles that evening and the flashbacks had started again.

It was so much worse in her memory than it had been in real life. Her imagination gave Lowell a demon's face and blood had come from his eyes when Adam stabbed him, instead of his mouth. One thing that had not been sensationalised by her mind, was how calm Adam had been, even though he had found Bronwen in the clutches of what must have seemed like a mad man. Mr Whyms had been composed, unfazed and dispassionate. He had only once looked angry and that was after the event, when he had noticed the bruising around Bronwen's neck from the tape Lowell had choked her with.

Bronwen had not been able to bring herself to talk to Adam about what had happened. Her discomfort around him had evolved into an awed fear. Not of what he might do to her, but of what he could easily do to other people. True, it made her feel safe, but troubled.

The fact that Lowell clearly had not known Adam was the only reason Bronwen did not suspect *he* had been one of her killers as well. Devil worshipers, who had carved into her flesh the five-pointed star she was currently staring at, and had watched with delight as her blood seeped from it.

"Symbols only have power for those who believe in them." Thanatos's voice drifted over to Bronwen so faintly, his unexpected presence did not startle her for once. She did, however, quickly lower her blouse back over her stomach and tie her thick night gown around herself.

"How much power do my murderers have?" She asked her pale reflection. She had looked more ghostly since Lowell's death and the dark shadows under her eyes were not from lack of sleep.

"It was one man who put that mark to you," Thanatos barked, but his agitation was not directed at her. "And he has minimal power compared to what *I* can retaliate."

"But they may yet hold more power than I." Bronwen finally turned to look at Thanatos.

He was wearing a loose grey shirt with the sleeves rolled to his elbows and black trousers with no shoes. He looked tense, with eyes more red than blue and though he leant against one of her bedposts casually, the muscles in his folded forearms were taught.

"That can be easily remedied," Thanatos was calm again, his moods changing as often as the shapes a flame might make. "Nothing comes without exchange, and giving yourself to me comes with more than just the rewards of ultimate pleasure."

Bronwen turned away from him, blushing at how his words had made her eyes roam down to where his shirt was partially undone.

Was it because he was the only man she had seen dressed so inappropriately that she reacted in such a way? Was it only a curiosity for knowledge that she could not find elsewhere which made her look at him?

"You are very sure of your abilities," Bronwen said as she tightened the sash around her waist even more.

"Very sure."

His tone had her heart thumping and she turned yet again to face him, so he could not get behind her as he had in the woods.

"Why am I unable to sleep?" Bronwen asked, if only to change the subject, feeling dizzy at her indecision of how to stand.

Thanatos shrugged noncommittedly. "You do not need to. Same as you do not need to eat or drink. A different kind of energy keeps you alive and holds your soul to its vessel."

"An energy *you* control?"

"Shape, is a better term."

"But unlike eating, I cannot force myself to sleep."

Thanatos shook his head. There was a hint of secret behind his eyes, something he was keeping hidden from her. She only detected the deception because the demon had stopped talking for once and stood staring at her instead.

Bronwen played with the tie of her night gown self-consciously. Thanatos was usually forthcoming with what he told her, so she decided that, anything he did not immediately reveal, was something she did not want to hear.

"So, my Lady, I must congratulate you on finding your first victim," Thanatos said, just as keen to move the subject. He pushed himself away from the bedpost and sat down in Bronwen's armchair in the window alcove.

"They are not my victims," she protested, moving to stand and look out of the window opposite him. There was a soft glow on the horizon, beginning to bleed into the dark sky.

"No, they are mine, and now that you have killed one of them, perhaps they will come in search of *you* instead."

Bronwen snapped her head around, concerned. Thanatos looked amused by her expression.

"It had not occurred to you that they might know you have returned? I would not worry, so long as you have your precious bodyguard around. He does watch you so vigilantly."

The way he said this did not make Bronwen feel any happier about Adam watching her. She supposed she owed him her life, but could not bring herself to be grateful enough to *want* him around her all the time.

"Are they coming for me?" Bronwen asked. She would not forsake Adam's protection if they were planning on attacking her. Hopefully, they would not group together as before. She doubted even Adam could fight off all eleven of them at once. Perhaps she needed more protection, but that would of course mean constricting her already suffocating freedom and the idea of two Adam's watching her made her shudder.

"I cannot get involved, this is your bargain to find them, not mine," Thanatos said unhelpfully.

"Cannot get involved?" Bronwen said sceptically. "And what of the candle?"

"Candle?"

"That fell out of its holder in Lowell's shop and allowed me to escape."

Thanatos raised a curious eyebrow. "Did it now?"

He stood up from his chair, moving closer to Bronwen. She turned fully to face him and backed herself against the window sill.

"Whatever happened to Mr Clare was certainly none of my doing," he said as he placed his arms on the window sill either side of her. "But perhaps you should ask your dear fiancé why he felt the need to hire someone like Adam Whyms six years ago? Was that not about the time he lost his brother?"

Bronwen frowned. How did he know about that? *What* did he know about it?

Before she could ask him, Bronwen blinked and Thanatos had gone.

Thanatos had been trying to provoke her, she knew, but

Clarence Guild's death had been a mystery and Bronwen could not get the thoughts out of her head about the stories she had heard.

Bronwen had heard bits of the story. Clarence had gone missing six years ago and had been found dead in the woods a week later. The cause and details of it were never published, hidden by the family, wanting to protect the Guild name. Kole had at one point been a suspect, but Bronwen didn't believe it.

Kole's mother and father had soon followed but less suspiciously, both had contracted some obscure illness that left doctors baffled. Despite the tragic history, Kole still had no end of suitors and Bronwen had no illusions that Kole had chosen her because of the wealth of her father.

When Bronwen arrived for breakfast later than usual, she was greeted by an empty room and cold tea. She had not seen her father but had heard him returning late in the night so assumed he was still in bed.

A couple of giggling maids entered the room through the side door and stopped suddenly when they saw Bronwen stood in the middle.

"Sorry, milady," one of them said, curtsying. "We thought you had left with Lord Wintre. Shall we bring you fresh tea?"

"My father has left already?"

The door behind Bronwen opened before the maid could answer. She turned to see Lord Guild enter the room.

"Good morning, my Lady," he said with a smile.

"Lord Guild," Bronwen greeted him with a curtsy of her own. "My father is not with you?"

"No. Lord Wintre left early this morning."

Bronwen tried not to shake her head at how hard her father had been working recently. She had barely seen him and was worried he would wear himself out.

"Please bring some fresh tea for Lord Guild," Bronwen

said, turning to the maids still hovering in the doorway.

"Yes mi..."

"That will not be necessary," the Earl interrupted. "My Lady and I shall be going straight out. If she is decent?"

Bronwen was still watching the maids, who were big eyed and blushing at being addressed by Lord Guild. Bronwen hoped she had never been so doe-eyed around him. She wondered if he liked that in a woman and felt an unexpected possessive jealously when she thought of him being with one of these girls.

Bronwen spun on her toes to find Kole stood quite close to her. In a strange impulse of appeal, she gave him her most inviting smile and blinked delicately at him. It was not something Bronwen was accustomed to and she was not sure why she acted so girlish, the maids were no contest to her, she knew. But it did have the desired effect. Kole's full attention was on her now, not the maids. His expression turned serious and his lips parted slightly.

Bronwen held her dress out either side of her in a lilac array of fabric and said, "am I agreeable enough for his Lordship?"

She immediately felt foolish for doing so and likened herself to a peacock displaying its feathers and careening.

Kole did not seem to think it so imprudent and closed the gap between them in two short steps.

"More than just agreeable, my Lady," he said in a low voice, looking down at her with intense eyes.

"My, aren't we the seductress this morning."

Bronwen flinched at Thanatos's unwelcome voice. She turned her head towards him, expecting to find him leaning against some door frame or other piece of furniture. Instead, he was stood square and tall, his arms crossed and his torso ever so perceptibly forwards, like a lion crouched in grass.

"I am positively jealous," he added sarcastically.

Bronwen turned back to Kole who was also looking in

Thanatos's direction, but of course was unable to see the demon.

Irritated by Thanatos's untimely appearance, Bronwen sought to teach him not to appear when he saw fit. If he was jealous, then it would be his own fault for intruding and she would make him sorry for it.

"Am I pleasing then?"

She teased Lord Guild with a tempting smirk.

He did not smile back but placed a hand on her cheek and a thumb on her lower lip and leaned in so close, her eyes almost went out of focus. She thought he might kiss her again and tried not to flinch away. Instead, he moved his lips next to her ear.

"If you were any more pleasing, Bronwen," he said dangerously soft, using her Christian name. "I would be forced to make my vows before these candlesticks and have you now."

Bronwen's breath caught in her throat and her heart stammered. There was a sound akin to a growl behind Bronwen. It was even audible to Kole, who checked the door with a flick of his eyes before staring back at Bronwen with a satisfied smile.

Thanatos was mistaken if he thought Bronwen's reaction was one of excitement. It was closer to a feeling of fear.

Suddenly Kole's presence felt dangerous to her, and his words a threat rather than a promise. She did not want him to be holding her face anymore, or her arm with his other hand that Bronwen had not noticed him put there. And she certainly did not want him to kiss her.

Bronwen stepped back from Kole with an easy smile.

"The candlesticks will have to wait," she mocked, to ease the blow of her refusal.

"So, they shall," Kole replied, but his eyes were no less dangerous.

A knock on the door was a welcome distraction from

whatever game they were playing.

"Lord Guild," James addressed him. "Your grooms have informed me your carriage is ready for you."

"Thank you. We will leave imminently," Kole replied and held an arm out to Bronwen. "I thought we might hand out invitations today, personally. Are they ready?"

Bronwen nodded and took his arm, once more at ease.

"I shall have to fetch them from my room, but surely you do not mean for us to hand out all of them?" Bronwen questioned as they entered the hallway. A great many people were invited to the ball and it would take far more than one day to see all of them. Especially if they all offered tea, as they surely would.

"Only the ones that matter. Mr Durward, would you please have someone fetch the invitations from Lady Bronwen's room." James bowed his head and sent someone up the stairs, then helped Bronwen shrug into her cloak.

"Wait a moment, please!" Bronwen looked up the stairs to see Alda hurrying down them, a shoe in one hand and coat in the other.

"You are joining us?" Bronwen asked. She should have expected it from her ever-watchful nanny.

"Mrs Keeper, that will not be necessary," Kole said and nodded for James to open the door as he saw the servant descending the stairs with the box of invitations. The Butler smiled in amusement as he held the door open, knowing the argument that was due from Alda.

"You are still yet unmarried to one another and until such time as you are nuptialated, milady's virtue is still under my care."

Alda was a formidable force in her duties and still seemed intimidating to Bronwen when she demanded compliance.

"Lady Bronwen's virtue is of a care to me also, I assure you, mistress," Kole countered.

Bronwen blushed at the blatant talk about her virginity.

Kole looked at his pocket watch pointedly, despite the large grandfather clock ticking contentedly in the corner.

"My concern is that patience may not be one of *your* virtues, Lord Guild." Alda indicated to his watch checking and pursed her lips as she slid out the door towards the waiting carriage. Bronwen stifled a giggle at the look of frustration on Kole's face.

Then she tried not to cringe at how close to the mark Alda's words were. Perhaps it would be best for her to accompany them, especially after what Kole had whispered to Bronwen that morning.

XII

"Thank you, Lord Banks, Lady Chloe," Bronwen said as she and Kole left the Bank's house after half an hour of tea and talk.

"Thank you for the invitation, Lady Bronwen," Lady Chloe said, while her brother, Daniel, shook Kole's hand. Their parents had been out but the siblings had been more than happy to receive the All-Hallowmas ball invitations.

Bronwen and Kole descended the steps of the town house together and entered the carriage that was waiting for them. Kole tapped on the roof for the driver to continue and they moved away.

Bronwen sighed. "Please say that was the last one."

"There is one final stop," Kole said.

Bronwen looked out of the window at the low sun, made even dimmer by the clouds. They had spent a whole day riding around the city and Bronwen's back ached from the bumpy streets they travelled. Kole's carriage was spacious and finely furnished, but human bodies were not designed to withstand constant jarring and twisting. Even the horses had been changed once in the day to allow them rest.

"We are losing the light," Bronwen commented, letting the curtain fall back over the window.

"Afraid of the dark, Lady Bronwen?"

"What can be hidden in it, Lord Guild."

"I shall keep you safe," he said with a smirk.

Kole had given Mr Whyms the day off from his duties. The man had tried to protest, but one look from the Earl and Adam had bowed his head in submission. It had reminded Bronwen of what Thanatos had said to her and she desperately wanted to ask Kole about how Adam had come into his service, but feared he would get angry at her for bringing up the subject of his brother.

"Enough of that you two," Alda snapped. She had been so quiet, Bronwen had almost forgotten she was in the carriage with them.

The woman yawned and Kole gave Bronwen a secret look. They both hoped their chaperone might fall asleep so that they could talk privately. Then perhaps Bronwen would brave asking him her burning questions.

His risqué comments that morning had been quite forgotten by Bronwen, and she had realised the foolishness of being afraid of her own fiancé.

In just one day together, the longest solid period she had spent with Lord Guild, Bronwen had learnt more about him than before.

Through observations, she had learnt that he liked dogs, but saw cats as an unnecessary indulgence and did not care for either species as companions. He was tolerant of children but had no fondness for them - something Bronwen hoped would change as he aged. He was an easy charmer of women when he wanted to be and did not suffer fools well. Kole enjoyed the winter months most and saw plants, especially those kept in the home, as pointless fancies.

They were all insignificant facts that made up a man and Bronwen wished to talk to him in depth about his interests, but other than the brief walk from door to coach, they had not had a moment alone together. And if Alda disapproved of their brief exchange about the dark, she would certainly not approve of any more intimate conversation. Bronwen had come to believe it was impossible for anyone to create a meaningful relationship with someone before marriage.

She wondered how her father and mother had managed it. From what little she knew of their marriage; it had been a deeply loving one. They had been almost obsessed with one another, despite their union being chosen for them by their families and had fallen in love long before they were wed.

Finally, the carriage came to a juddering halt and Bronwen looked outside at the solitary house they had stopped at.

It was as austere as the people who lived there. Lord and Lady Payton - an abrupt and snide couple who Bronwen always avoided at parties. She stifled an unladylike groan as the brown coloured bricks of the manor house came closer. They were her father's friends, not hers and she didn't see why they had to come to the ball.

Kole held a hand out for Bronwen and she stepped reluctantly from the carriage.

"We shall try to keep it as swift as possible, Alda," Bronwen promised herself as much as her maid. The woman nodded her head sleepily and tried to concentrate on her needles. She had dropped more than a few stitches the last part of the journey and had not gone back to fix them.

The groom closed the door and the horses pulled away to the side, until needed.

"I do not plan for this to be a long meeting, my Lady," Kole said, taking Bronwen's hand. "I do not think I could take another drop off tea, lest I drown in it."

Bronwen nodded in agreement. She had not yet managed to master eating without gagging or being sick and had managed to find ways to make it seem like she was consuming food, like hiding it in napkins and putting a cup to her lips without drinking.

A stern-faced butler answered the door to the manor and announced them through to the morning room.

Lord and Lady Payton looked startled when they saw the couple. Lindy let out a small yelp and Cornell Payton stood up abruptly, blocking his wife from view, as if shielding her.

"My Lord, I hope you do not mind us calling on you so late," Kole said as he too moved to stand in front of Lord Payton, blocking Bronwen, though his movement was more fluid. Kole held his hand out to the man and something passed between them that Bronwen could not see.

"Why should I mind, Lord Guild?" Lord Payton said tensely, before offering them a seat on the long sofa opposite them. He gave his wife a secret look and cleared his throat. "If you excuse me for a moment, I shall arrange for some tea to be brought."

Kole smiled knowingly at Bronwen at tea being mentioned and she stifled a giggle by taking time to look around the room. In the centre, above a marble fireplace, a large pair of antlers hung, which could only have been ornamental because they were far too large to be real.

There were other stuffed animals scattered around the room that were real however, from birds with impossible wing spans, to rabbits with shiny eyes that replaced their living ones. It was a little bit uncomfortable to have all of them staring into the room and every time Bronwen tried to relax, she noticed a new one. She pinched her leg to keep herself from shuddering.

She felt as though there was something out of place about the room that she couldn't quite figure, besides the macabre decorations. Perhaps it was just the initial hostile greeting they had received from their hosts, which was swiftly recovered by Lord Payton when he returned to the room.

"It is a pleasure to see you two," Lord Payton said stiffly. His wife nodded her head in agreement. She had not said a word while he was gone from the room, but had stared at

Kole intently. Bronwen had almost asked if she was alright. "The couple everyone cannot wait to see married."

"Indeed, neither can we," Lord Guild replied, unperturbed by the whole situation.

"I assume you will be moving elsewhere, once the deed is done?"

"Perhaps."

"There really is no reason for you to stay in Winchester," Cornell insisted.

"We have not yet discussed it."

A knock at the open door interrupted the awkward discussion and Lord Payton's severe butler entered the room.

"Milord, would you like me to have refreshments brought for your guests?"

"Yes, bring something," Lord Payton said with a wave of his hand. Had he not just been out to arrange tea? Perhaps he had forgotten.

"Surly you must have thought about what is to happen, after the deed is done?" the man continued to badger Lord Guild.

It was then that Bronwen realised neither of them had looked at her once since coming in. Nor had they addressed her in any manner. And the way Cornell referred to their wedding as 'the deed' perturbed Bronwen.

"I have thought about it, yes," Kole replied evasively.

"We will most likely live in Guildford," Bronwen said, trying to force herself into the conversation. "It would not be too far away to visit my father."

"It would not make sense for you to move here, Lord Guild." Lord Payton completely blanked Bronwen's comment and continued staring at Kole. The Earl seemed not to notice, or was not put out by it.

Bronwen, however, was most displeased. She looked at Lady Lindy who glanced at her and looked away again, an almost disgusted look on her face at having made eye contact with the other woman.

The tea was brought in then and placed on the table between them. Lindy poured a cup for herself and her husband but did not move to pour one for Kole and Bronwen.

"Lord Payton," Bronwen spoke pointedly, forcing the man to acknowledge her, now that she had addressed him by name. He looked at her over his china cup with a calculating look. Bronwen almost stood to leave right then, but persevered. "Lord Guild and I came here to give you and Lady Lindy your invitation, to this year's All-Hallowmas ball."

Lord Payton took a sip of tea and slowly placed the cup back on the table before speaking. Bronwen almost thought he might shun her again and realised in her haste to be done with the meeting, she had left the invitation in the carriage with Alda.

"I see," he replied. "You are still hosting the ball this year then."

"There is no reason why not," Lord Guild replied coolly. He cut a slice of cake with a knife and placed both on the plate in front of him but did not move to eat it. "Metrom Hall hosts it every year."

"Yes, but having so many people in the house, all looking to Lady Bronwen." Lord Payton leant in towards them as if suddenly interested and finally looked directly at Bronwen. Lady Lindy sat up straighter in her chair. "Will you not feel uncomfortable? All those eyes on you, watching your behaviour."

Bronwen was taken aback by the personal question and regretted wanting to be part of the conversation, now not wanting any kind of attention, but it was too late to shrink into a corner and let Kole talk for her.

"I do not know what you mean, Lord Payton," Bronwen

said in a small voice.

"I mean after your encounter with Mr Clare. Will you not be concerned about another attack?" Cornell said, his eyes alight.

"Mr Clare was not well and what happened was unfortunate and deeply regrettable." Bronwen felt her voice rising and her body getting hotter. Doubtless people had questions about what had happened in Lowell's shop, but none had been rude enough to ask. This Lord had no such qualms and his wife seemed just as morbid.

"Yes, but still, it must have been quite a thrilling experience in a usually drab life."

Bronwen said nothing and was disgusted as she looked into his eyes and saw a spark of delight there. The look was strangely recognisable. Not to look at, but the feel of it. Where had she felt it before?

"Or perhaps it was more thrilling to watch your bodyguard kill your attacker?" Lord Payton continued, delighted to see Bronwen squirming in her seat.

"Careful, Cornell," Lord Guild warned, but the man ignored his stern tone and remained staring at Bronwen.

She suddenly recognised the feeling his look gave her. She had pulled a similar expression, when Thanatos had coaxed her into picturing herself killing a young woman, strapped to a sacrificial rock, helpless and desperate to live. Completely within her power.

But why would she find such a look in Lord Payton? Was it truly the same expression? Perhaps he knew its kind from some other venture? Maybe from hunting wild animals, which he clearly enjoyed from the look of the room she was in. Or was there more to this Lord than an overbearing, rude and intrusive gentry?

"Tell me about that, Lady Bronwen." The man was unyielding under Kole's warning. "Did it make you feel powerful to murder Lowell? To watch your guard slit his throat and spill his blood!"

"Sir, you go too far," Kole stood up between them. "You offend my Lady."

Lord Payton stood up too, followed by his silent wife a moment later.

"Oh, but I would not be so brave as to upset her," Cornell said in a sarcastic tone. "Lest I be the last of us to do so!"

"If you have some accusation to make then take your grievance to the authorities, but if you should speak anymore against Lady Bronwen, then you shall upset *me*."

Bronwen thought Kole sounded surprisingly calm in front of the two and she wondered if she should stand also, but was struggling to process what was happening. As far as she was aware, she had never spoken out against the Payton's. She had barely conversed with them beyond the most minimal of polite greetings. Why did they seem so against her?

"And who would ever dare to insult the honourable *Lord Guild*," Cornell emphasised Kole's name in mockery and Bronwen wondered if Kole might strike the man. Then she was being hauled to her feet by Kole and was almost dragged to the front door.

Kole opened it himself and unintentionally pushed Bronwen through the door before he turned back to Cornell a finally time and said, barely audibly. "Watch your step in this game, Cornell. The Queen is but one pawn away."

XIII

Kole slammed the door closed behind him and joined Bronwen in the yard.

The autumn air caught in Bronwen's throat. The sun had barely moved in its decent but the ground seemed darker somehow, the shadows of the trees longer.

Bronwen breathed heavily as the carriage grooms scrambled to bring the coach over, stamping out their cigarettes. They had not been expecting the couple so soon.

Kole joined Bronwen on the stones of the entrance way and placed an arm over her shoulders.

"I do not understand what I have done to deserve such treatment?" Bronwen said, but in her heart, didn't really believe herself guiltless. She had killed a man, perhaps indirectly, but if she had not gone to seek out Lowell, then he would still be alive. Maybe this was why she had been plagued by the memory of it. But it was ridiculous to feel guilty over the death of a man who had twice tried to kill her and once succeeded.

"Lord Payton was good friends with Lowell," Kole explained.

"But he killed me!" Bronwen cried, then realised what she had said and lowered her voice. "I mean, he attacked me, and Mr Whyms was only defending me... I owe him my life."

Lord Guild said nothing as the carriage pulled up in front of them and a groom opened the door.

"It is difficult for people to see evil in the ones they care for," Kole said as he helped Bronwen in and sat opposite her.

Alda was fast asleep, she had not even woken when the carriage moved and her needles were on the floor. Bronwen picked them up and placed them on the chair next to Kole, beside the invitation they had not given to the Paytons. With any luck, they would not come.

Finally, they had some semi privacy and Bronwen did not feel like talking. Instead, she stared out the window and thought about Kole's words. She wondered if anyone could see an evil in *her* stirring. Would every kill she affected blacken her heart until she willingly joined the Devil? The Lord of death. Ruler of the Under-realm. Or whatever Thanatos was.

They passed a path into some trees and Bronwen caught sight of a doe crossing the walkway with a cautious trod. It was a little late in the year for her to be about. Hunger perhaps brought her out. Survival was always first priority for the creatures of the earth.

Kole had also been looking out of the window, a grim line to his mouth.

"Will you walk with me?" Kole asked, pulling Bronwen out of her reprieve and closing the curtain over his window.

"Now?" Bronwen questioned, looking at the setting sun. They were still a long way from the city.

"We can cut through the woods and meet the carriage on the other side."

Kole tapped a hand on the side of the carriage and it came to a halt. He watched Alda warily but she showed no sign of waking, then he gave Bronwen a wolfish grin and stepped out of the carriage.

Bronwen heard him talking to the drivers. She took one look at Alda and, despite her head telling her not to, stepped from the carriage after Kole.

He was strapping a sword to his waist, which did not fill Bronwen with confidence. Kole just smiled secretly at her and sent the carriage on its way before gesturing to the path that Bronwen had seen the deer on.

She felt foolish as they walked together in the silent solitude and twilight of the woods. Bronwen was not sure what she was doing. Her heart thumped whenever she thought about how reckless they were being, walking alone in the dark. Alda would not be pleased if she woke up. And if something happened to them. Or if Kole had a mind to...

"Do not be so concerned, my Lady," Kole said. "I said I will protect you. No harm will come to you while I am here."

Bronwen smiled at him and did feel slightly better. Shadows crowded them as they entered the trees, but the deeper they went, the more Bronwen felt at ease by Kole's side. She believed Kole knew how to use the sword at his hip and truly was glad they were finally alone. Perhaps now would be a good time to ask him her questions about his past. She had almost mustered her bravery to ask, when Kole spoke again.

"There was another reason I wanted to bring you to the woods, Bronwen."

Kole stopped on the path and turned to face her. A stream had been running to the side of them and there was a dazzling sunset behind Kole that made Bronwen squint. It gave him an unusual red halo and his eyes seemed almost the same colour.

"I wanted to ask you properly, not in a small room with someone watching, but on one knee as it should be." Bronwen put a hand to her mouth as she realised what Kole was about to do and all thoughts of questions and doubts left her mind.

Kole began to bend to the floor, still gripping her hand.

He didn't get a chance to ask her his question before Bronwen's eyes adjusted to the sudden light behind him and a new figure was blocking it. One only a few paces away and brandishing a knife.

"Kole!" Bronwen yelled and pushed him to the ground, she on top of him.

The knife came down and missed them easily. Kole reacted quickly and rolled onto Bronwen.

"Stay to the trees!" he ordered, pulling himself from the ground and his sword from its sheath.

Bronwen did as ordered and Kole engaged their attacker. He was a young man behind his short, dark beard and wielded his knife with practiced ease against Kole's sword.

A hand grabbed Bronwen from behind before she could scream.

"Now you die, Devil slut," a man hissed in her ear, his hand smelt of metal coins and smoke.

A third and fourth man appeared in front of them, one with a knife, the other a loaded pistol.

None of them turned when there was an outcry on the path behind them and Bronwen hoped it wasn't Kole's pained groan.

"D'you choose the knife or pistol, milady?" the man holding the knife asked causally, waving the dagger from hand to hand.

The man holding her loosened his grip on her mouth so she could reply.

Bronwen screamed before the hand clamped down again and his arm tightened around her as she struggled.

"Option three it is then," the knife man grinned and started to undo his belt. Bronwen struggled even more and for once wished Thanatos would appear.

"Just kill 'er already. Do what you want when she's dead!"

the man holding her said. "Properly this time." He finished just for Bronwen's hearing, confirming that this was not a random attack, these were some of the men that had killed her.

The man with the knife advanced, leaving his belt undone.

Suddenly Bronwen didn't want to die. She was not entirely sure that she would be able to return. Would it mean that Thanatos had won? Would she be his then forever? If she was allowed to return, Thanatos had warned her that she would feel all that had befallen her after death. Pain was one thing, but she was not sure she could cope with feeling herself being violated by these sick men.

There was also Kole to think about. Bronwen doubted she would return before Kole found her dead. What would he say when she rose again, a living corpse?

Bronwen saw the man lift the knife and she dropped her body slack and heavy, arms above her head to worm herself out of her captor's grasp, like a child who did not want to be carried.

The knife man stopped just in time, stilling his blade before it sliced into his comrade.

Bronwen crawled away only to be grabbed again by the man with the pistol. He flipped her around onto her back, choosing - honourably or sadistically - to look at her face when he shot her dead.

His bullet never left the barrel before Bronwen sat up and reached for it, pushing it away from her body and struggling to win the gun. He unbalanced and had to release one hand to catch himself and Bronwen took her chance, twisting her body sideways so she gained leverage and yanked the weapon loose.

She fumbled with her won pistol with the intention of firing it and had a brief smile of triumph before a sharp kick to the side winded her and she fell on her back again, the pistol scattering.

The heavy hands of her assailant pulled her arms above her head and crushed her wrists into the solid floor. He didn't reach for the gun but held her hands out of the way, leaving her body open.

Bronwen looked up into his eyes. He looked almost amused at the sport; his mouth peeled back into a grimace too close to a smile. With his large dominating statue, there was no way of escaping once he had her in his iron grasp.

"Clever little bitch, isn't she?" the man with the knife said, standing over her body, feet either side of her knees, his dagger delicately poised. "I'll enjoy fucking you. Shame though, I like a girl who struggles."

Bronwen let out a defiant squeal as she brought her foot up and kicked him hard between the legs.

The man dropped his knife to hold himself and grumbled as he fell to his knees. The giant man who had hold of Bronwen's hands laughed at his unfortunate companion as the third man retrieved the knife from the floor and sat on Bronwen's knees, not wanting to make the same mistake.

Bronwen closed her eyes ready for her finishing blow when something wet and warm dripped onto her face. She opened them again to see the knife still hovering above her, then it dropped to the floor and the heavy weight of the man fell onto her body.

Bronwen pushed the mass off her in disgust. It was only once she was free that she realised she was no longer being held down.

Dead, pleading eyes stared up at her from the body of the man who had, moments ago, been her executioner. Bronwen wiped the sticky wetness from her face and saw that it was blood - luckily not her own.

"You didn't pay us for two, Haydon."

One of the remaining men stood slightly stooping next to the giant. Both were facing the silhouette of a figure.

Bronwen couldn't see its face under the shadow of a tree but its presence sent a chill up her spine and she could almost make out demonic looking eyes and sharp dripping teeth.

Bronwen wondered if it was Thanatos, before her eyes adjusted to the light and she saw it was Kole who had saved her and it was his sword that was dripping blood - she had forgotten about him and was relieved he looked unscathed.

"I paid you for one," Haydon hissed back. "At this point, I don't care which!"

Haydon turned back to Bronwen with a furious heat in his eyes. She shied back, but the other man had engaged Kole in combat and she was on her own again.

Haydon lurched towards her. It was clear now that he had been one of her murderers, the other men were only hired to help him finish Bronwen off.

"Deal with you properly this time," he rasped and grabbed Bronwen's ankle. She kicked feebly with the other foot to no avail and he soon had his large hands wrapped around her throat. They were so large, he easily could have fit one around her neck, but both gave him extra grip and her wind pipe retreated into her throat, feeling as if it hugged against her spine. At this tightness, it would not take long for her to die.

She tried not to look into his eyes as he choked her. It was so much more painful than when Lowell had strangled her. What had she done to deserve such hatred from a man she had never met? The lack of air was making her dizzy and her eyes rolled back. It would not be long.

Bronwen focused her eyes again and saw Kole over Haydon's shoulder, his sword pressed against her strangler's neck. She could not hear what he said through the blood rushing in her ears but it made Haydon let go.

There was a brief moment when nothing seemed to go in or out of her lungs and she thought it was too late and death would come for her anyway, then she coughed and released the plug that had been holding the air back. It made a rasping noise as it filtered through her damaged throat.

Eventually, Bronwen's hearing and sight returned to focus and she saw Haydon on his feet, staring at Kole who had put his sword away.

"...protecting her? Let me end her!"

"I cannot allow that, Haydon."

The giant man growled but before he could lunge at Kole, Bronwen had reached behind her for the forgotten knife and stabbed it deep into Haydon's foot.

He yelled out in agony and turned to swipe at Bronwen, catching her on the side of the head, making her ear ring. It caused Haydon to unbalance, where he was stuck into the soil, and he fell down heavily.

He began pulling the knife from his foot with a small grunt as Kole picked up a silver object that had been partially obscured by fallen leaves and the dusk light of the evening.

Haydon dropped the bloody knife and his eyes widened as Kole levelled the barrel of the retrieved gun at the man's head.

"Kole, don't, you're on our si..." His words were shattered by the bang of the pistol. Though it wasn't as loud as expected, it made Bronwen's already muffled hearing ring in her head like a thousand tiny death bells.

Yet more blood spattered her face and some other substances she did not care to identify and tried not to look at as the back of the man's head fell open.

Kole lowered the pistol and threw it next to the dead man with a grimace, more from disgust at the sight rather than any upset at having to put a hole in a man's head.

The woods were eerily silent, all creatures disrupted in their songs and doings to listen to the danger in the night.

Then, out of the trees, made all the more prominent from

the stillness, came the sound of two distinct wolf howls before a hush descended upon the woods again.

EXODUS

Proicite quicquid feminei reservate...
{Whatsoever of the female, ye shall save alive}

I

The journey from Winchester to Guildford was long and arduous. It took most of the day to ride there with the luggage, horses and servants Lord Guild had brought with him to Winchester. Bronwen wondered how long he had been planning to stay. Surely one man did not need so much luggage?

It was difficult for Lady Bronwen to argue with Kole's plan to take her back to Guildford with him while he conducted some business. After the attack in the woods, Kole had thought it best to remove Bronwen from the gossip of the city, especially while the authorities tried to discover why they had been attacked.

Lord Guild had answered all of the police questions so Bronwen did not have to and he had tried to shield her from any detailed information, not wishing to upset her. The little Bronwen had discovered was that Haydon Stone had been the name of their lead attacker. He was a stonemason from the outskirts of Winchester, had no known family and had paid the other three men to help him with money that was clearly not his own.

So, Thanatos had been correct, her murderers knew she was alive again and they wanted her gone.

Now, more than ever, Bronwen realised the need for

protection and thought that perhaps the trip to Guildford was a wise plan after all. She needed to get away to collect her thoughts and at least she would soon see Josette.

The journey to Guildford, however, would have taken less than half the time if they had travelled by train and would have been far more comfortable than the jolting and bumpy carriage. Bronwen's hips and lower back ached from the hard-wooden chairs that gave no tolerance. She would even have preferred riding, then at least she would be able to see when a dip in the road was waiting for her spine.

Kole's argument for travelling this way was so that they might enjoy the countryside, but Bronwen would have been able to see it from a train just as easily and the countryside held little appeal to her when it was so unforgiving to a traveller's trespassing.

She pulled the curtain slightly back on the carriage window. Lord Guild had decided to ride for a while so that Bronwen could rest. Even if it were possible for her to do so, the shunting of the carriage would not have allowed her to sleep.

A dark shape blocked her view of the trees they were travelling past. It was Adam Whyms.

Bronwen had seen the barely contained rage in Adam's eyes when he had heard about the attack. So much so that she feared he would have hunted Haydon down himself if the man was not already dead.

Bronwen had yet to thank Adam for helping her with Lowell and doubted she ever would, despite realising that she had been treating him very poorly after he saved her life.

Mr Whyms turned in his saddle and Bronwen quickly dropped the curtain before he could catch her watching him. He had a certain way of looking into her eyes or giving her a small, rare smile that made her feel exposed. She remembered how his fists had curled tightly when he saw the marks and swelling to her throat from Haydon's hands.

When she had tried to tell him she was fine, her voice had come out as a rasped whisper and his eyes had flashed darkly. He had disappeared from the room for a few hours, returning later with bloodied knuckles, like he had been punching stone.

Bronwen rearranged her bodice and skirts to a semi comfortable position. She was alone in the carriage, Alda had chosen not to make the journey with her.

The maid was still a little icy with Bronwen after she found out that she and Kole had left the carriage alone the night they were attacked. Alda had been especially tetchy when Bronwen had refused to see a doctor about her throat and Kole had refused to delay the trip to Guildford until Bronwen was healed.

Kole had, of course, received the brunt of Alda's wrath and Bronwen feared she might have struck the Earl if the man had not been the one to save them both.

"You must take better care of yourself, domina domus," Alda had said in one of her rants. "It is not only you that you must consider."

Bronwen hated being on bad terms with Alda. The woman was like a mother to Bronwen, and she was correct in saying what Bronwen and Kole had done had been foolish. It could have been so much worse. Bronwen would make amends when she returned to Winchester.

The carriage flew over a bump and Bronwen almost left her seat from the violence of it. The sharp movement it caused made her neck twinge painfully and she tried not to cry out as it brought tears to her eyes.

She desperately wished she could shut her mind off for a few hours. If she missed one thing from life it was the ability to sleep. Such a strange thing to miss. Bronwen had not realised the importance of being able to have some small escapism when reality was weighing on her. The only time she had felt truly awake was in the Under-realm; with

Thanatos.

Before she could think more on the idea, the demon appeared, making her wonder if he had known it. She quickly dismissed the concept. Even if it were true, Bronwen did not want to admit that Thanatos might be aware of when she was thinking of him. It was enough he wanted her body; he could not claim her thoughts as well.

"So, you have found yet another victim," Thanatos said, hooking one ankle over his knee as if the unbalance of the vehicle did not affect him.

Bronwen bristled at him calling them her victims again, but she did not have the voice or the patience to retort. She raised a hand to her bruised and swollen neck as she thought about Haydon Stone and what the men he had hired might have done besides choke her. At least the marks would fade and her voice would return, but the damage to her mental state had they taken her body might have been irreparable. Bronwen felt fragile enough as it was.

"Is it painful?" Thanatos asked in a soft voice that had a hint of compassion in it.

Bronwen looked into his eyes and opened her mouth to speak then closed it and shook her head instead, careful not to move too much.

"I do not believe that," Thanatos said with a head shake of his own. "If you would allow me, I can heal it for you."

"*It will be noticeable*," Bronwen rasped out as best she could. She could not be suddenly healed within a matter of hours; people would question it. Thanatos had seen her wince at the pain talking caused her. The only good to come of the injury was having an excuse not to eat and drink very much.

"I can leave the marks but remove the pain and at least let me return your voice. As much as I like the sound of my own words, it does get very dull talking to oneself."

Bronwen actually had a smile at his comment and nodded

her head slowly for him to heal her. She was soon regretting her decision as he moved to sit next to her and slowly reached his hands towards her neck.

Bronwen flinched at his movements and he paused, a pained look in his handsome features.

"Trust me, Bronwen, I will not harm you," he said carefully. She did not believe she could ever trust him, but saw a small truth in that he would not harm her, not presently. Then he smiled his wicked grin and continued. "And you have but to protest and I shall stop."

Bronwen huffed at him mocking her lack of speech and stared at his hands, still hovering between them. Thanatos's comment had at least distracted her from her fear of being touched on the neck again and she wondered if this had been his intention. She nodded slowly for him to proceed.

Bronwen's body tensed as he placed his hands on her shoulders and she had to close her eyes tightly to keep from moving away.

Thanatos moved his head closer to her and she could feel his warm breath on her skin. His hands tightened on her shoulders and she could smell his fruity oak scent, so strong she could almost taste the earth. Then, he placed his heated lips on her neck and she held her breath at the sensation of her skin cooling then returning to warmth again. Her throat tickled and she resisted the urge to cough.

Thanatos lifted his lips from her and moved to the other side. This time, Bronwen leant her head over slightly to allow him access and could almost feel the smile on his lips as he kissed the other side of her throat.

Bronwen let out a quick breath from the fluttering in her stomach at how nice it felt, having his lips on her skin. She was shocked at herself for thinking it and even more startled that, when Thanatos moved his mouth away from her neck, she was confused to find she wanted him to place his lips on hers, to see what *that* might feel like.

Lady Bronwen blushed and opened her eyes to shake away the feeling and to remind herself who she was sitting next to.

Thanatos was of course smiling smugly and had not taken his hands from her shoulders.

"You should be able to speak again, but you should not underestimate the importance of body language," Thanatos smirked, making Bronwen shiver as if she was cold, when actually her skin felt incredibly warm.

Thanatos moved away to sit opposite her, hooking his ankle again. He was barefoot, with a grey shirt unbuttoned a few down, it had loose sleeves and his black trousers were tied by a rope at his waist. Bronwen envied how comfortable he looked.

"So, where are we headed?" Thanatos asked.

"Lord Guild's home, in Guildford," Bronwen replied, her voice quiet as she tested it. The pain had completely vanished but her neck still felt as if it was swollen when she touched it. She hoped the bruising was also still visible, though she dreaded to think what Josette would say when she saw it.

Bronwen shifted in her seat again and pulled at the edges of her dress where the bones of her corset were beginning to dig into her from being sat so long.

"Uncomfortable?" Thanatos asked.

"Quite."

"Lay down perhaps?"

"It will be no less uncomfortable with this motion."

Without a hint of action from Thanatos, the rocking of the carriage stopped. It was so abrupt that Bronwen thought they must have stopped moving.

She peered out of the window to see that this was not the case. The wheels of the carriage still rotated on their axels, crushing stones beneath them and bouncing over dips in the uneven road. The drivers could only just be seen bobbing in their seats and the horse's hooves kicked up wet soil onto the underside of the vehicle.

It appeared as if Bronwen was the only one to have stopped, suspended in an unmoving state. She couldn't even hear the sounds from outside the carriage.

"How absurd," she commented, putting the curtain back in place. Seeing everything but her moving was making her dizzy. Thanatos smiled nonchalantly.

"Now, you can lie down."

"I still would rather not." Bronwen looked at Thanatos suspiciously.

"This is not my way of getting you on your back, my Lady. I like to think I have more charm than that."

Bronwen cast him a speculative glance.

"It is no use when I cannot sleep."

"Lying down is not always about sleep, the same as fucking is not always about laying down." Thanatos grinned, but for once Bronwen did not feel he was mocking her, in fact his tone was strangely conversational. It would make the journey swifter having the company he offered, even if the subject was distasteful.

"Is everything about... *that*, with you?" Bronwen asked, unable to say the word.

"It is one of the many constants in my life," Thanatos replied thoughtfully. He animated his hands as he conversed, waving them in the air, keeping Bronwen's full attention. "All creatures are driven by it. They do it for pleasure or procreation. Life is fuelled by sex and the need of it."

Bronwen frowned. She could see the obscure sense in his argument, but she did not want to believe that this was the source of all motivations. She voiced her concern, for once wanting his warped view on the subject.

"It is not always the case," Thanatos admitted. "But most of the time our motivations are led by our desire. This is especially true in relationships between a man and a woman. A woman marries to procreate and a man marries for sex. There is no other reason for marriage."

"What about love?" Bronwen questioned, feeling like a young girl who had read too many romance novels as she suggested it.

"Love is another term for sexual desire. Tell me, what other difference is there between a friend and a husband, other than you have sex with one and not the other?"

Bronwen thought for a moment. She hadn't had any male friends since she was a young girl. Perhaps Lord Guild was? But, no. Despite what she had been through with him of late, Bronwen still could not say she loved him, not even after the kiss they had shared. She had always felt drawn to him for unexplainable reasons but it occurred to her then that, she did not consider Kole a friend either. Yet he was to be her husband.

"Friendship is not always present in a husband and wife," she said, not particularly answering his question but Thanatos pressed on anyway.

"Then there is only sex as a reason to marry that person. By the laws of the church you follow. Or used to." He paused with a little half smile. Bronwen narrowed her eyes at him in endearment. "Matrimony is only valid once consummated."

"Explain murder then," Bronwen said, not wanting to discuss marriage any further, thinking a more macabre subject would stop her pondering her relationship with Kole.

"You would not want me to go into detail on that," Thanatos replied, looking serious. "But you should understand that sexual desire and what some men feel when they take a life are very close indeed."

Bronwen decided he was right in assuming she did not wish to know in details and especially did not want to think about how he knew this fact. Still, she was unconvinced by his argument. There were things that were not motivated by sex and not all creatures have a need for it. Sex was primarily designed for procreation. As a way for the species to continue.

"I think that survival is what motivates us. And perhaps power. The power to survive and some people seek to use sex as a way to gain power over others." Bronwen remembered something from her childhood that gave her words clarity and she hid a shudder.

"I concede the point," Thanatos said after a little thought. "You have bested me, in our clash of tongues. Perhaps I could use that talented tongue of yours one day."

Bronwen pursed her lips and he grinned.

"Knowing what motivates a person gives us power," Thanatos continued. "You can use it to gain your own advantage or for their benefit if you are feeling particularly beneficent."

This made Bronwen wonder, not for the first time, what motivations her twelve killers had. Lowell had mentioned a deal being broken and Haydon had been uninterested in her body, he only wanted her dead for good.

"The people who hunt me," Bronwen began, not sure how to phrase the question, or if she would get an answer at all. "Do they all have their own bargains with you?"

"They do," Thanatos said. His expression betrayed nothing and he did not elaborate. Bronwen decided to press on, hoping he might give something away.

"And part of that bargain was to send me to you," she said carefully, still curious and confused at why that was so.

"No, only one man made the bargain to gift you to me. The others were only following instructions as part of serving me."

Bronwen nodded and frowned. "And this one man... do I know him?"

Thanatos smiled at her in a way that said this was all he would tell her. She nodded in submission. At least she knew that not all of them had a personal vendetta against her, but who had she wronged for them to take such measures in seeing that she suffered for eternity?

They sat in silence for a while and the quiet was welcome company. In their unmoving bubble of solitude, it was difficult to remember Thanatos was not good. Even if he was not the Devil that Bronwen's indoctrinated religion taught, Thanatos was not comparable to their angels either; otherwise he would not have locked her in a bargain she could do little to escape from.

As Bronwen surreptitiously watched him, while Thanatos stared out of a gap in the curtained window at the woods they were passing through, she found it difficult to remember he was not human either.

Thanatos's elegant fingers tapped lightly on his ankle that he held over his other leg. His dark hair looked clean and matched his close shaved facial hair. His mouth created dimples in his cheeks when he smiled, smirked or grinned, deepening the shadows of his cheekbones. In the small light given from the crack in the curtain, all his features looked soft; his lips, his eyes, his chin, his temperament.

Thanatos turned his head to look directly at Bronwen. Her lips were slightly parted where her breath was escaping in short exhalations. She closed it and looked away from him, cheeks rosy red.

Bronwen quickly found a mundane subject to talk about. He took the invitation to converse with her in everyday matters such as; how she liked Guildford, what her favourite colour was and her first childhood memory – all were questions asked by Thanatos. But, when there was a pause in their conversation, Bronwen thought she saw a satisfied look in Thanatos's expression, as if he knew she had been looking at him and knew that she had *enjoyed* looking at him.

She felt angry at herself, almost as if she had been defeated and she inwardly damned her body's reaction to him. Did all women have these sensations when around him? Was it some power he was using against her? Or was it simply that he appeared to Bronwen to be the most handsome man she had seen? Of course, it could not be natural, so could she really help how she felt? It still would not cause her to give into him. She had more self-control than that.

Suddenly, the carriage bucked like an angry horse and Bronwen bounced and fell to the side. Thinking she would soon hit the floor; she closed her eyes and a small squeal escaped her.

But the floor did not meet her. Strong hands had clasped her about the waist and a warm and solidly soft body was pressing securely against hers.

Bronwen's fluttering heartbeat from her fright soon found the rhythm of Thanatos's in a harmonic choir. His eyes caught hers in an embrace as he held her off the floor of the carriage, as easily as one might pick a flower - holding it tight enough to keep it, but gentle enough to not break its petals.

"Lady Bronwen?" a voice called from outside, in response to her audible outcry. "Are you alright?"

"Yes," she replied, not turning her gaze from the blue eyes of Thanatos. "I am fine."

Thanatos raised one dark eyebrow, giving his intense frown a softer cast. Bronwen imagined his eyes were the colour the deep ocean would be, then a storm broke and lightning cracked the sky's perfection and left red scorch marks behind.

Her sudden need to kiss his lips disappeared. His eyes were no longer human and his salacious grin no longer companionable.

II

Aterces Manor unfurled on the horizon like a scroll. The house appeared modestly sized from the front but Bronwen knew from her previous visits that it extended behind and the gardens were known for their beauty and size. The vine covered stones, used to build much of the extension, were taken from an old demolished abbey not too far from Aterces. A large tree, on the flat next to the manor, shadowed it in the evenings, making the bricks a darker, ruddy red and the white that framed the windows and entrance a dull yellow.

The carriage pulled up outside to be greeted by a line of waiting servants, their heads bowed and hands clasped in front or behind them. A man came forward to take Lord Guild's horse while he jumped down. Kole paid little attention to the procession that bowed or curtsied to him.

A footman opened the door of the carriage for Bronwen and she gratefully took Kole's hand and stepped out of the confines of the vehicle, trying to keep her aching back straight.

Lady Bronwen was also welcomed by the servants' curtsies and bows and she nodded at them in return but was distractedly looking for someone who was not part of the greeting.

"Earl Guild, Lady Bronwen," Kole's head of house, Mr Fane said. His suit was impeccable and his stern features showed no mercy for mistakes. He was thin and stood tall, despite his obvious age. Bronwen remembered him well and how the staff avoided him as much as possible, but he had always been polite enough to her.

"Fane, I assume my letter got to you in good time?"

"It did, my Lord. The rooms have been prepared for Lady Bronwen and her staff have been assigned residents downstairs. Mr Whyms' room has not been disturbed as instructed."

"Good."

A woman opened the main door in one swift motion and stood in the gap. Grinning, Bronwen rushed past the footman waiting to take her jacket and almost ran up the steps towards her friend.

Josette was not prone to gushing or hugging, and neither was Bronwen in usual circumstances, preferring to keep her personal space personal, but in light of recent events, she almost threw herself at Josette and embraced her, which her friend returned after a few seconds of surprise at the unusual gesture.

"It is a pleasure to see you too, Bronwen," Josette said in her ear, muffled by her hair. "But we are being stared at by his Lordship," Josette added in a hissing whisper when it was clear Bronwen was not planning on letting go.

Bronwen pulled back and looked at her friend. Josette had her dark blonde hair up in her usual messy manner. Her bright blue eyes shone and her cheeks heated in an attractive rosy glow.

"I have not seen you in so long," Bronwen said apologetically, her hands were still on Josette's arms.

"And now we have a whole week together," Josette replied delightedly as Lord Guild joined them on the threshold, once he had finished consulting with his people.

"Anything to report, Miss Emry?"

"All clear on the front, sir," Josette replied sardonically. Bronwen thought she might salute and recognised the iconic twitch of a smile on her features.

Kole ignored her mockery and entered his home.

Josette had been married to Kole's brother for three years before Clarence had died, yet Kole still treated her as an unfamiliar asocial, who kept his home for him while he was away. He even insisted on calling her 'Miss' like it was an insult and constant reminder that she was not part of the family. How he treated Josette was the one-time Bronwen thought him cruel and was something she would have changed if it were still possible to marry him.

Josette smirked at Bronwen, used to Kole's manner and ushered her into the house and to the back where the solarium was. She did not seem to mind that Kole had only allowed her to remain living there after he had inherited the property because of a promise he had made his dying brother. And Josette would have considered herself a burden if she had not taken it upon herself to keep the affairs of the estate in order.

It was warm and humid in the glass solarium, despite the mildness of the weather and descending sun. This part of the house looked out onto the gardens where a large lake took up most of the grass area. Swans had taken up residence on its central island and a small recreational row boat was moored by the jetty protruding from the reeds. The flower and vegetable gardens were in a walled off area to the side of the house and were mostly maintained by Josette herself. Kole had no patience for plants and spent very little time in the glass room, it was Josette's domain and she spent most of her time basking in the sun like a contented house cat.

A platter of food had been put out for them on a wooden table next to deep chairs. These were surrounded by tropical plants that were happy in the stifling climate of the room and gave off the fresh, earthy aroma of the jungle.

"Shall we have something to eat?" Josette offered, waving her hand at the food. "And you can tell me all that has happened since we last saw one another. You received my letter?"

"I did," Bronwen replied distractedly, trying to think of a reason for not eating. She failed to consider this issue before arriving at Guildford - Josette already thought Bronwen too skinny and would be the most likely to notice her lack of appetite. She would have to force herself to eat when around her friend and try not to think about the taste.

"I wonder if you would be open to a walk in the gardens instead, Josette," Bronwen said before they sat down. "I have been in the carriage for so long, the walk would be very agreeable to me."

Josette nodded. "You may rest first if you would prefer? I did not think about how tiring the journey must have been."

"I have some things to check on here. If you ladies are planning on a walk, then see that you take Adam with you," Kole cut in.

As if summoned by the mention of him, Mr Whyms entered the solarium.

"Mr Whyms has been reassigned as my bodyguard," Bronwen explained. Josette obviously knew Adam as he lived at Aterces when he was Kole's guard. Adam inclined his head in greeting and Josette returned his steady gaze. Adam had decided years ago that Josette was not a threat to him and Bronwen lost a small amount of confidence in his observational abilities, if he did not realise Josette could be a fearsome adversary when pressed.

"Reassigned?" Josette questioned. "What do you need a bodyguard for?"

Lord Guild answered the question before Bronwen could

explain. "Because Lady Bronwen has a tendency to put herself in harmful situations and her father and I felt it was necessary."

Josette looked at Bronwen in sympathy, understanding that it had not been Bronwen's choice.

"Provided you are willing to stay a safe distance from us while we talk about womanly things," Josette said to Adam. "You are more than welcome to guard our bodies in whatever way you see fit."

Bronwen knew Josette was only talking in her usual obscure phrases, but she wished she hadn't put the sentence quite like that when she saw Adam glance at her in an almost indecent way, imperceptible to anyone but Bronwen. It made her skin prickle and she was suddenly keen to be moving in the opposite direction.

"We should head out before we lose the light," Bronwen said, hooking her arm in Josette's and leaving Adam to follow behind as they casually strolled out of the solarium and down the garden steps.

"Now that we are away," Josette began, eager to talk to her friend in confidence. "What the hell has been going on in Winchester? What is this rumour I heard about you fending off a tailor? And I also heard there has been a second attack in the woods involving Kole. Are the two events related? What has your father said about it? Is he treating you well?"

"Which question would you like me to answer first?" Bronwen interrupted with a laugh.

Josette giggled in her usual girlish way; despite her being about ten years Bronwen's senior, her delicate complexion and round honest face meant she was often mistaken to be the same age or younger, but Josette was by no means youthfully naive. Her upbringing as an orphan, cared for by a begrudging and cruel uncle, had made her strong-willed and worldly wise.

"The police have not confirmed anything yet, they are still

investigating." Bronwen told Josette the story she had told Kole and Donovan about the night she disappeared, feeling guilty about lying to her friend, but she couldn't tell her the truth of it.

They were halfway around the lake by the time Bronwen had finished talking about all that had been happening in Winchester. Only the top of the house was in view, early evening shadows peering out of crevices in the old building.

"If not for Lord Guild and Mr Whyms, things could have been much worse," Bronwen finished, looking around at Adam. She caught his eye and he did not drop his gaze. Bronwen almost shuddered, remembering his murderous grin as he had run at Lowell with a knife.

"I am done talking about myself now," Bronwen said, picking up the pace of their walk, as much to be away from Adam as to be back before dark. It had been slow going due to their easy pace and the size of the grounds. Even going just around the lake had taken them an hour. Josette plunged into her own tales.

She spoke mostly about her writing; she was an author of sorts but was yet unpublished. She was struggling to find an agent or publisher who would print her book under her own name, rather than someone who had already sold copies of their own books, and Josette was stubborn on the matter. Bronwen had since stopped trying to convince her to take the advice, just so she could get some money to live off her own means, instead of Kole's and what little was left to her as Clarence's wife. Without any children to support, the compensation had been very little, most of it passing to the next male heir - Kole.

"I have heard from Lawrence recently and he tells me that a friend of his has a father who knows a publisher personally somewhere in the midlands who have only recently started out but may be willing to take on a 'small project' as he phrased it," Josette explained, becoming increasingly animated as she spoke.

Bronwen had been listening to every word, grateful for the comparatively less complicated life, but Lawrence's name had stuck in her head and she was lost thinking of Josette's younger brother.

He was still almost seven years older than Bronwen but they had been very close once and he was as youthful as his sister.

Bronwen would never forget the day they met and not only because of the tragedy that had occurred. Her father had been busy with business which had moved them to London for the better part of a year.

Josette was visiting her brother in the new year who had been living in London at the time and the three decided to go ice skating on the frozen lake in Regent's park.

Lawrence and Bronwen had bonded immediately but their otherwise joyful day had been cut short.

Bronwen still remembered the terrible sound the ice had made before it opened up and plunged the skaters into the water, entombing people beneath it who had desperately clawed at the ice to be free.

Forty-one sorry souls had perished and after witnessing such a tragedy, it was difficult not to be close to the person you shared it with. Especially as Bronwen had taken it upon herself to nurse a sick Lawrence back to health after he developed a fever from his own terrifying time in the frigid water.

"Is Lawrence well?"

"Very well," Josette replied, a sly smile on her face. "He has been made second corporal, but of course he played for modesty and said that there wasn't much competition for the role. From the sounds of it not much happens at fort Nelson, mainly drills, but he has a great view of Portsmouth if the weather is fine." She paused and looked at Bronwen. "He asks after you, on the rare occasions I see him."

Josette knew that the two had a fondness for one another and had hoped they would be married, but Bronwen doubted Josette knew that this had very nearly been the case. If Lawrence had not had a stab of conscience and more than a little fear at what Baron Donovan might do to him if they had eloped as planned, then Bronwen's life would be very different indeed.

Bronwen doubted she would have truly gone along with it in the end, too much the submissive, and she had only known Lawrence a few months. She blamed the episode on wishful youth and a want to get away from her father's house after he had shunned all other affections people had shown his daughter.

Lord Guild had still only been courting her then and a year later he had finally proposed. The time she had spent with Lawrence became a pleasant memory that Bronwen liked to recall every so often. She had not seen him in almost three years and thought he had most likely changed much since their bittersweet farewells another life ago.

They made it back to the house in time to watch the sun pass below the horizon and Josette showed Bronwen up to her room.

As anticipated, Josette had been appalled at the state of Bronwen's neck when she had removed her coat and scarf in the house. Even the immovable Mr Fane looked shocked and Adam appeared to want to punch something again.

Bronwen had brushed off the concern. She had forgotten about her neck after Thanatos had taken the pain away, it was only when she went into her room to bathe that she found a mirror and couldn't help her own gasp at the sight.

Her whole neck was swollen and had turned a greenish colour with blends of darker shades spreading out from ten distinct finger marks that were close to black. Bronwen marvelled at how defined they were and could not understand how she was not dead. No wonder Kole had wanted to take her from Winchester. There was no possible way she could have avoided gossip when her neck looked like the dark moss of a rotting tree.

Bronwen was helped to bed by one of her maids - missing Alda as she struggled with the ties of her corset herself - then waited in the dark room until the house was asleep.

Bronwen left her bed and pulled her nightgown around her, making her way over to the large bay window. It was next to the fire which was burning brightly and misted the glass quickly when Bronwen pulled open the curtain. She waited for her eyes to adjust to the gloom and looked out across the fields.

The land was mostly flat with scatterings of trees like tufts of weeds. It was not the most interesting view but Bronwen could see the driveway leading up to the house and the clouds thickening, preparing for rain. It was far from the main city, secluded and picturesque. Bronwen thought Aterces beautiful in its architecture. She would have been very happy to live there with Josette.

Bronwen curled up in the window seat and leant her forehead against the glass, enjoying the cool feel of it. It was easy here, to forget she was being hunted. She felt safer being away from Winchester. Like she had escaped her troubles for a while. She had the mad urge to go walking through the fields in the dark and let the night hide her but pushed the feeling away.

Aterces had a rich library on the floor above Bronwen's rooms and she regretted not fetching a book before bed to occupy her. She decided there would be no harm in visiting now and pulled her thick dressing gown tighter around herself then quietly opened the door.

Adam was not in the hallway as Bronwen had expected and she let out a breath of relief. The house was well guarded by Kole's other security, so perhaps Mr Whyms had not seen the need to guard Bronwen's door which she was grateful for. She might have more freedom at Aterces than her own home.

Bronwen hurried back inside and retrieved a candle and holder from her bedside table, lighting it on the fire before leaving her room. She smiled at the prospect of having free run of the house. She had been there a few times before but as she had found at Metrom, a sleeping structure was vastly different to an awake one.

If it were possible, Aterces seemed larger inside than Metrom. Her home boasted large structures in its architecture like the stone pillars outside the main door, but the rooms were confined and less numerous compared to Aterces. The painted ceilings were mostly Greek in style, depicting Gods and Goddesses draped in silk, lounging on swirling clouds and surrounded by creatures of legend. She wished she had more light to see by than her single candle.

Eventually, she found her way to the library.

The windows were floor to ceiling, as were the shelves of books. The space in the centre of the forest of knowledge, was dominated by a large wooden table, absent of chairs, and two of the walls of books had cut out alcoves housing comfortable red sofas, each with a small tea table beside or in front of it. There was a thin staircase leading to a gallery halfway up the wall, so the higher books could be reached. Bronwen scanned a shelf. Not all the titles were in English or even Latin and some of the ones that were, she did not recognise the meaning of.

This was the library Kole's brother had built Josette soon after their engagement, Bronwen remembered. It was finished before they were married so that Josette could use it immediately. It was clear Clarence had been besotted by Josette and she him.

A desk by the window drew Bronwen closer. The view beyond was of the trees and part of the garden, the brilliant orange of the leaves made a carpet on the grass and she wanted to explore outside again.

The desk itself was a stunning piece of furniture, made in dark wood with gold symbols and shapes all over it, some too faint to make out. A hidden drawer to the side had been pulled out and an inkwell in the shape of a bird rested on it.

Bronwen ran her fingers over the symbols looking for another compartment. She lit the lamp on the wall close to it with her candle, so she could see better and found a drawer with a large amount of paper inside. She carefully took out the top page, aware that she was snooping in Josette's private things, and read the first few neat lines of handwriting.

{...there is a choice for all creatures, when our master friend or foe, pulls the chain on his pocket watch and studies the hour. Do we wet the sands of our hourglass and slow the inevitable passing of life, or do we tap the top and hope to hurry the rest? For we cannot add more sand and we cannot turn the glass. It weighs too much to hold and costs too much to break. Serenely or snarled we go...}

"It is very good."

III

Bronwen only just managed to stifle a scream from the close voice, almost at her ear. She knew immediately who the voice would belong to and turned to face Thanatos with a hand at her heart.

"Must you frighten me like that every time you see fit to appear?" Bronwen accused in a loud whisper.

Thanatos smiled mischievously at her in the dim, his eyes glinting in a fiery, catlike gleam. He wore a long cloak that trailed along the floor and his feet were for once covered in high leather boots but the rest of him was dressed in his usual loose plain shirt and trousers.

"You are dead, my Lady, nothing should frighten you anymore."

"I can still be hurt," Bronwen countered indignantly. She couldn't help placing a hand at her throat. The bruising was going down surprisingly quickly but she had still covered her neck with a scarf when she went out with Josette.

"I would never hurt you. Not even to hear you screaming my name," Thanatos said in a husky voice that sent an unwanted thrill down Bronwen's spine.

"What are you reading tonight?" he asked, picking up the next page in the pile. Bronwen wanted to snatch it back from him, protective of her friend's work.

"Josette's book, I think. I only read a few lines but it certainly caught my attention."

Thanatos scanned down the page quickly. He was so expressive when he read, like he was no longer hiding behind a mask.

Bronwen realised she was staring at him and gazed out of the window again. The moon was full and the sky was surprisingly clear. She frowned and once more couldn't shake the feeling of wanting the chill of the outside on her skin.

Thanatos returned the page carefully to the pile. "I agree, it is definitely a story I would want to read. The prose is very well styled."

"You read?"

"Often. That surprises you?"

"I only assumed you would already have any knowledge you desired."

Thanatos raised his brow, amused. "You think me omniscient? Why would you assume that, I wonder?"

"I do not believe you are God, if that is what you are implying."

"I should hope not. However, my question stemmed from the very clear apprehension in your voice at thinking I know all," he smirked at her. "Is there some thought you feeling you are hoping I do not discover?"

Bronwen looked at him levelly and said sarcastically, "can you sense what I am feeling now?"

Thanatos considered her then grinned. "You want to leave the house and be outside in the night."

Bronwen's eyes widened in panic and Thanatos laughed.

"You have been staring out of windows every time I visit you at night. It is not difficult to ascertain why. I know people, my Lady, most of their thoughts can be read on their faces," he stepped to the other side of her and headed to the door, whispering in her ear as he passed, "do not worry, your thoughts are your own."

Thanatos opened the door and held out a hand to her. "Shall we?"

Bronwen looked at him sceptically. "Am I going to receive a polite conversation from you tonight? I do not want your company otherwise."

"I think we have conflicting ideas on what is considered rudeness," Thanatos said cheerfully as they both made their way silently down the stairs. She did not use the front but instead headed outside through the solarium, trying not to overthink what she was doing and glad she had thought to put boots on at least.

It was still early in the night so Bronwen had plenty of time before she needed to be back and someone noticed she was missing.

With the demon beside her Bronwen wasn't thinking about where she planned to head. She had intended on taking a short stroll around the gardens, but felt safer being out with someone, so was comfortable walking beyond the perimeter of the house and into the open fields.

Bronwen didn't know why she was confident Thanatos would assist her if she was attacked. He had shown little reason why he would.

"You would not speak to me in the manner you do if others could overhear," Bronwen continued the conversation once they were clear of the house.

"You think I would not?" Thanatos replied playfully.

"It is a very sure way of being removed from my company by either my father or fiancé."

Bronwen looked at Thanatos to see his reaction at her calling Kole her fiancé. His face appeared tenser, but it may have been the angle she was looking at him.

"I think it would depend on who I said I was, as to whether they would dismiss me," Thanatos said thoughtfully. Bronwen only partially agreed. Short of royalty, she could not see who Kole would allow to speak to her so brazenly. It was a curiosity she did not wish to nurture.

"Would you even leave if they did?"

"Of course," Thanatos said innocently. "I can always appear in your room later when they are not about." He winked down at her boyishly.

She could not get any sense of his character. He changed so often, it hurt Bronwen's head to think about how mercurial he was and she had the sudden realisation at how long he must have been on the earth for. What he must have seen in that time should surely shape his person?

"If, as you claim, you are not the Devil," Bronwen said bluntly, after a short silence. "What exactly are you?"

There was the longest pause following this question and if Bronwen had not looked at Thanatos, she would have thought he had gone. She had a moment to wonder if the question was impertinent, but if *he* could speak to her in such a brash way, then why should she not speak in kind?

Finally, Thanatos breathed in and answered her question, though it seemed to pain him to do so.

"I started human. Then I became something more... and then something less." He paused again but Bronwen didn't interrupt his thoughts while he formed an answer. It was the first time he had struggled for words.

"It is difficult to explain to you in a way your current knowledge of the world can understand. Perhaps in the insurmountable time you now have, I will be able to explain it all to you, if you wish it. Not all knowledge is desirable and once learnt, it cannot be unlearnt."

Bronwen thought about his words as they trudged aimlessly through the woods. She had found yet another thing she had not thought to consider; her own immortality. What would she do with an unlimited amount of time? Wait for the world to die? Was that even possible? And would she continue to exist, should the Earth be gone?

Would it be lonely? Would she then begin to understand why Thanatos would go to great and terrible lengths to have a companion?

The trees were thinning out and the slight uphill walk had become a downhill one, so she kept her eyes on the leafy floor.

The full moon reached the ground and provided plenty of light to see by. The sound of running water and smell of wet stones reminded Bronwen of the last time they had walked through fields together in the dark. Bronwen did not feel the breeze that brought an approaching frost. Thanatos was keeping her warm again.

She did not feel she knew Thanatos now, any more than she knew him then, though they had had many conversations. He was still an enigma, neither showing himself to be inherently evil or good – demon or angel... friend or foe.

They broke through the line of trees and Bronwen saw the river that had been producing the sound and smell. Though it was secluded, with no sign of human habitation, the bank was made of stone and was well kept. The water was wide enough for two boats to pass each other comfortably and there was a clear path alongside it. Bronwen could see for miles downriver. Upriver disappeared around a bend blocked by trees.

Bronwen sighed deeply, studying the stars and the grandness of the moon. How could one look at the vastness of the sky and not believe there was a heaven?

"Why are you marrying Kole Guild?"

Bronwen sighed again and decided to stop teasing him about it.

"I am not marrying Lord Guild. How can I? I am dead, as you say. But I must keep up the appearance of normality so as not to draw attention to myself; any more than I already have."

"Do you love him?"

Bronwen was surprised by the question and turned to Thanatos before she responded.

"Yes."

It sounded false even to her ears and she had hesitated ever so slightly.

"Could you love..." Thanatos shook his head and changed his question. "*Why* do you claim to love him? What is it about this stuffy Lord that makes you want to give him everything?"

Bronwen resented the implication that she would give Kole everything, despite knowing this to be the undesirable truth when becoming a man's wife and couldn't help giving a tart reply.

"Because he is a true gentleman. And he is real. He can be around others and does not have to hide and appear to me in the dark."

"A gentleman? Is he really? A *gentle* man?" Thanatos retorted, equally as sharp. Kole was clearly a subject that made him quick to anger and she had not yet figured out why it affected him so much. "And how are you to know that? How do you know he will not raise a hand to you once you are married or stop you from seeing your friends?"

Thanatos stepped close to Bronwen, grabbing her hair in his fist and held her chin; forcing her to look at him and answer his questions.

"How do you know he will not pull your hair while he fucks you?" Thanatos snarled.

Bronwen didn't back down and hid her fright behind a scowl, ready to bite him if he tried to kiss her.

"How do I know that *you* will not?" she asked quietly.

They stared into each other's eyes for a long moment, neither backing down. The contact was broken by a noise behind them. Thanatos let go of her and stepped back; a grim line to his mouth.

The noise became louder and they turned to see what it was.

Coming around the bend upriver was a steam boat, a small one made of wood, green with algae on most of its hull, but the ropes and various implements on it were pristine.

Bronwen moved into the shadows provided by the trees.

From what Bronwen could see in the dark and at the distance she was from it, the steamer was manned by four men. Two were stood at the wheel that steered the boat, one was watching the surrounding area and another was shovelling coal into the furnace that gave the boat its power.

There were an additional two men at the back of the ship who were only shadows, but she could tell they were fussing over something and all the crew kept looking back at them intermittently during their various duties.

Bronwen could hear them all laughing and joking but could not hear what they said. Then the vessel came closer and the moonlight showed her what they were jeering at.

Running alongside the boat, was a man. He looked tall and well-built but underfed and he only wore a tattered pair of breaches about his skinny waist. The moonlight shone off his slender body and as they passed where Bronwen stood, she saw he wore no shoes and his feet were tied with a short tether between them so it was difficult for him to run alongside the vessel.

His hands were also tied in front of him and had a line of rope that stretched out across the gap between the bank and the boat and wrapped around a peg on the hull.

Bronwen was confused. She only heard enough words from the men aboard to know that they were mocking the running man and clearly meant him ill will.

As they travelled away from Bronwen's hiding place she stepped out into the open again to watch it continue on.

Thanatos stood beside her.

"What are they doing?" Bronwen asked. It was obvious this was no game young men had invented, it was serious, especially as the man began trying to gnaw his way out of the ropes on his wrists.

"It appears they are trying to drown him." Just as Thanatos finished saying this, the men on the boat yanked on the rope hard when they noticed their victim biting at the ropes and the man unbalanced and his legs gave way. He was dragged along the bank a few metres, before slipping into the river. The speed they were travelling helped him keep his head bobbing above the water and he could be heard gasping for stolen breaths, but with his feet and hands tied, it was difficult for him to swim.

Bronwen gasped and heard men on the vessel laughing.

"Stop!" she yelled, revealing herself and running towards the boat as fast as she could. Bronwen was not sure what she could do, but the sight of a group of men torturing and trying to murder a helpless person had brought back memories of her own torment and she could not contain her rage at the sight.

The man at the stern squinted in the dim to see who had called out and turned to his friend for advice.

"Cut him loose! He's dead anyway!" one of them called.

The young man pulled a knife out from his belt and hacked at the rope until it shredded and followed the drowning man into the water before the boat sped away.

Bronwen sprinted to the place she had seen the man's head sink under the water and, without a moment's thought, dived into the river feet first.

The cold consumed her and her eyes hurt from being exposed to the grime of the water. Bronwen closed them again; it was so dark that she was unable to see anyway. She felt around her franticly, a feeling of hopelessness creeping up on her at the sensation of being trapped under the water again.

Her lungs burned and she felt a panic, still blindly feeling with her hands until finally, by unquantifiable chance, she felt a piece of rope brush past her arm. Turning in the water she grabbed hold of it like it was a lifeline and kicked her feet towards the surface.

Once she broke the water, breathing heavily, her throat making a strange spluttered gasping sound, Bronwen pulled herself and the rope to the side of the river. The mud made it difficult to get a hand hold and she was very conscious of how long the man had been under for.

A hand came out before her face and she took it, knowing it was one of Thanatos's rare acts of helpfulness. Once he had hauled her onto the bank, he helped her pull the rope until it went taut and then together they dragged the unconscious body of the man onto the grass; Thanatos doing most of the work with ease.

Bronwen turned the man over and tried to wipe away the mud and grime from his face.

"What do I do?" she implored Thanatos, who bent beside the man.

"He needs air in his lungs."

Bronwen looked at him questioningly but that seemed to be the only help he was going to give.

Uncertainly, she pulled his head up so his mouth came open and blew air into him from her lungs, not quite sure if she was doing it correctly.

"Now pump the water out." Thanatos pointed a finger at a place on the man's chest. "Here."

Bronwen put a hand on his chest and pushed, and then, finding a bit of resistance, place both hands on him and pushed with her entire body weight. She did this repeatedly as if drawing water from a pump.

"More air," Thanatos coxed.

Bronwen did as she was told, putting her whole mouth

around his and pressed harder than before on his chest again. She remembered seeing this done before, on some of the people pulled from the ice lake when she had first met Lawrence. She continued the repetition with more vigour, determined that the man would not suffer the same fate as she.

"Keep going. He is not for me yet," Thanatos said in a soothing voice when Bronwen felt tears well in her eyes from frustration.

After what seemed like an hour to Bronwen, her arms aching, a gurgled cough finally escaped the man and he turned his body to the side and threw up water from his lungs and stomach.

When he had finished, the man collapsed back onto the grass and stared up at Bronwen in confusion.

Bronwen finally had a chance to look at him properly and was astonished to realise that, it was not the mud or the night that made his skin appear dark, it was his complexion. His surprise seemed as great as hers, when he seemed to remember what had happened to him.

"It is alright," Bronwen comforted. "They have left."

"You save me?" The man asked in a thick accent that was difficult to understand.

Bronwen nodded, suddenly shy and at the same time pleased with herself. She remembered Thanatos's help but when she looked up, he was gone.

Bronwen noticed the man was still in ropes and reached out for his wrists. The man flinched and Bronwen stilled. He looked at her sceptically and she smiled in understanding.

"Please, I mean you no harm," she said and then more slowly, reached for his bonds again.

He allowed her to untie him and sat up once she had finished, moving away from her slightly. Bronwen cleared her throat and imagined what he must have been thinking.

A strange, pale woman out alone in the dead of night, had jumped into a freezing river to rescue him. It sounded absurd even to her and almost unbelievable that she had been there at the exact moment he needed her help.

"My name is Bronwen," she said, uncomfortable in the silence.

"Azubuike."

"Is that a name?" Bronwen asked. He gave her a look and she nodded apologetically. "You will have to teach me how to say it while we find you some dry clothes."

Bronwen stood, realising the need for her own change of clothing. Without Thanatos's supernatural warmth, the wet clothing and cold made her teeth chatter and she wished she had had the foresight to remove her coat and boots before plunging into a river in autumn.

Azubuike looked around him, seeming to consider his options. Bronwen thought he might bolt, but the man looked at her again and stood on unsteady legs. He kicked the rope into the water with venom and followed Bronwen into the trees. She assumed a lack of alternative and the biting cold made him follow her blindly, that and the fact he was twice her size so she posed him no threat.

They walked in an awkward silence; keeping pace easily with one another, the only sound their chattering teeth. Azubuike appeared to have difficulty walking, barefoot as he was, and Bronwen's shoes were heavy with water. She wondered if he was more or less cold than she was with his lack of proper clothing.

Finally, Aterces came into view and Azubuike stared up at it speculatively. Bronwen wondered what he was thinking and then suddenly panicked at how she was going to explain everything to Lord Guild.

"We will have to go in through the back," Bronwen said to the silently brooding man. "They do not know I left, but you can stay the night and I can explain in the morning."

The man did not reply but trudged on to the house, Bronwen considered whether offering a stranger a bed for the night was such a good idea; especially when it was not her bed to offer. But she could hardly let the man freeze, otherwise her effort in saving him would have been for nothing if he died from fever instead.

Ignoring her apprehension, she guided Azubuike to the back of the house and, checking for servants, led him through the solarium. Bronwen whispered for him to wait in the hallway as she crept downstairs into the laundry room and picked out some clothes that she thought would fit him. Then she led him upstairs to her own room. He seemed surprised that they were not going downstairs to the servant's dorms.

Bronwen did not need to ask Azubuike to tread quietly; he did so of his own accord with a stealth that unnerved her.

Once they reached her room, Bronwen closed the door softly behind them and lit a few lamps to give them some light, then rekindled the fire. Her teeth were still chattering. She needed to get out of her wet clothes quickly.

Azubuike stood awkwardly in the centre of the room, eyeing the untouched bed. In the light, it was easier to see just how dark his skin was, but instead of being disturbed by it, Bronwen was fascinated. She tried not to stare and placed the borrowed clothes on the bed, before setting some water over the fire so that he might wash.

In the morning, she would have the servants run him a proper bath and then try to explain to Kole what he was doing there. She shuddered at the thought.

A movement next to her made her start and she looked to see Azubuike holding a blanket out to her, taking her shiver as a sign of cold. Bronwen was cold, but had more pressing matters to attend to, like where she was going to put him to sleep.

"Thank you," Bronwen said, taking the blanket. Azubuike

nodded then walked to the window and peered out onto the grounds nervously.

Bronwen pulled the water from the fire and added half of it to the basin on the dresser then carried the rest to a small door at the far end of the room.

"I will change in here. Please make yourself comfortable and I will return shortly."

The strange man Bronwen had invited to her bedroom in Lord Guild's house nodded once and turned to the basin.

Bronwen left quietly and closed the door to the bathroom behind her. She placed the water in the second basin and locked the door as quietly as she could, hoping that Azubuike had either not heard, or was not offended by it.

Inside the bathroom, she quickly washed and changed into clean dry clothes, only then considering what she had done.

Bronwen had no idea why the men on the boat had been trying to kill him. What if he had done something terrible, like murder someone? And she had invited him into Kole's home with a houseful of sleeping people. And now he was in her bedroom alone with her.

Bronwen shook her head. Despite her stupidity, the memory of how the men had laughed and jeered at Azubuike, as he had fought for his life and had clearly been running for miles, still made her angry and she did not regret saving him. She would just have to be cautious in what she did next.

Bronwen knocked once on the door to the room and entered slowly, half expecting him to be gone. Azubuike was in the same place she had left him but was now dressed in the clothes she had found that were far too baggy and short, but at least they were clean.

Bronwen wrapped her dressing gown closer to her, feeling uncomfortable and exposed.

"You can sleep here," she said, pointing to the bed. "In

the morning, I shall send someone in to help you bathe and find you some better clothing."

Azubuike nodded and walked towards the bed, then looked at Bronwen sceptically. She wondered if he was maybe in shock.

"You have nothing to fear. I will be in the room next to this one. If you should need anything, please ask."

Azubuike nodded again and Bronwen left the room, smiling kindly as she closed the door. She considered locking it, but it would send the wrong message. He might still leave the house in the night, perhaps stealing expensive items to take with him, but Bronwen did not care if he did. Though, she found herself hoping he would stay, she would like to know what had happened and who this stranger was.

The night seemed to pass by slowly as Bronwen cleaned any evidence of the mud and dripping water they had brought in with them, and then planned what to say to Kole about the mysterious man she had brought home with her and what she was doing walking outside in the middle of the night by herself. Somehow, she doubted he would understand and prayed he would not tell her father of it.

In the early morning, just as the sun was stretching light across the horizon - like a painter who had lost concentration for a moment and slipped his brush across the canvass - Bronwen roused from her restful meditative state that had become her only form of sleep and made her way across the hall to the room Azubuike was staying in.

She leant over the banister of the staircase on her way and could just make out the faint sounds of servants stirring in the rooms below. She wanted to speak with the man before anyone saw him.

Knocking a few times lightly on the door, Bronwen entered a moment later on hearing no answer.

The curtains had not been drawn the night before, which gave Bronwen enough light to see by. Though the room was dim, she could see that the covers had been removed from the bed and Azubuike was not in it. She tilted her head in confusion but was not alarmed, until a movement in the corner of her eye made her start.

In a bundle on the floor were the covers from the bed, cocooning the form of Azubuike. The embers of the fire were low but there was a poker next to Azubuike's hand which suggested he had fed it at some point in the night and perhaps his exhaustion was the reason he had not made it back to the bed.

Bronwen cautiously closed the door and bent beside him. She pressed a gentle hand upon his shoulder and he immediately woke.

Bronwen flinched back and fell fully onto the floor when Azubuike turned on her, the poker now gripped in his hand and held ready above his head.

He stared at her incomprehensively in the haze of near wakefulness and she stared back calmly, finding herself unafraid of his sudden turn. Bronwen herself had had quite a few frights akin to this in her days of being alive again and recognised the kindred expression that manifested in his features.

Azubuike sobered and placed the pointy metal back by the fireplace, running a hand over his head and eyes.

"Pole," he said quietly. "Sorry," He corrected in English.

"That is alright. How are you this morning?" Bronwen asked, standing back so that he could get to his feet.

"Well," Azubuike replied, sitting on the chest at the foot of the bed.

"I am pleased to hear it." Bronwen stood by the fireplace a distance away from him, as much to give him space as herself.

"Will you tell me what happened to you?"

Azubuike looked at Bronwen carefully, as if still unsure whether to trust in this woman who walks alone at night, throws herself into cold water for someone she has never met and offers a bed to a stranger.

"I was... employed by a noble woman, now I am not."

Bronwen waited for him to elaborate but that seemed to be all he had to say on the matter. He couldn't have been a slave, it was abolished before Bronwen was born but she had heard rumours of eccentric aristocrats who still employed exotic looking men and women from Africa to entertain them, or paraded them as ornaments. It was a little outdated but was the only explanation for Azubuike she currently had.

"I have debt to pay to you," Azubuike said assuredly. "I owe you a life."

"What do you mean?"

"You save me, so I save you. A life for a life."

Bronwen smiled, she could hardly tell him that it was too late for that, but his sincerity was clear and she was growing to like him already.

She noticed now in the daylight the bruising and cuts over his body and face. His wrists had red raw marks around them and his throat was almost as damaged as her. She marvelled at how though his skin was dark, it still changed to shades of green and yellow where the damaged had been done. It was naive to think it would be otherwise, but men of his complexion were not common to her. At least not this close.

Bronwen could see the appeal of having someone so different from her mundane surroundings and she could understand the vanity in it, though she thought unpaid employment was wrong.

Azubuike would easily be intimidating at his full strength and height. He was taller than anyone she knew and broad - an attacker would think twice with him by her side.

Lord Guild and her father both said Bronwen must have a bodyguard. She would feel more comfortable if it was of her own choosing and who better than a man who claimed to be indebted to her? Could she trust him with her life?

Bronwen imagined Azubuike stood next to Adam and smiled. She would feel safer with this strange dark man than she would with Mr Whyms. She made her decision.

"My family think I am in need of a protector. I cannot say I blame them for thinking it, but if you are adamant that you owe me, then I would prefer to offer you a job." Azubuike looked relieved all of a sudden, then apprehensive again.

"You will own me?"

Bronwen realised what he was asking.

"No. You will be in my service, free to come and go as you choose. I will pay you a wage and when you feel you have fulfilled whatever debt you owe me; you can choose to go your own way."

"Paid?" Azubuike asked, as if the word was foreign to him. As Bronwen expected, his employment could not have been legitimate.

"Yes, I will pay you to be my personal guard. To keep me from harm." Bronwen realised the gravity of such a job, considering harm had already come to her and will continue to do so until the sorry business was done with.

"This I will do," Azubuike said after a brief moment of consideration.

Bronwen had not the chance to reply as the door suddenly opened and young maid walked in. She looked up. Her face dropped. She squealed lightly and left the room in a hurry.

"Oh no," Bronwen said. "Wait here, please. I will send for someone to draw you a bath and bring you some clothes while I speak to Lord Guild, the man who owns this house." Bronwen paused before feeling she should add, "my fiancé."

Azubuike did not react to the news, but as he watched her

leave the room, he had a curiously amused expression on his face.

Bronwen closed the door behind her and followed the sound of crying from down the stairs, feeling her heart pounding.

On the next floor, she could see the maid through a door that stood ajar, crying into the apron of an elderly woman who had an expression of horror across her face.

Just as Bronwen reached the base of the stairs and the women were blocked from view. The door suddenly swung open and Lord Guild strode out, his sword gripped in his hands as he stalked towards the stairs.

He only barely saw Bronwen because she held her hand up and stood directly in his path.

"Lord Guild, you misunderstand."

"Is there a man in your room?" he growled, strangely composed but clearly furious.

"Yes..."

"Then what is there to misunderstand?"

"I rescued him last night from attackers." Bronwen chose what she thought was the most important information, sensing that she had a limited amount of time to explain herself.

"And did he show his *gratitude?*" Kole stared directly at her for the first time and it took a moment for Bronwen to realise what he was referring to.

"No! No, I stayed in a separate room."

"Then why did Gretchen find you together this morning!" He pushed her to one side and stalked up the stairs like a wolf readying to contest its territory. He wasn't even fully dressed yet. His shirt was hanging out of his loose night trousers and his chest was showing. It was the barest Bronwen had seen him; even his feet were bare.

"I wanted to speak to him," Bronwen pleaded desperately while following at his heels. She had only seen him this angry when they had been attacked by Haydon and she panicked at what he planned to do to Azubuike.

"Alone?" Kole continued to accuse.

"Do you have no trust in me?" Bronwen asked and almost collided with him when he stopped unexpectedly.

His shoulders had tensed and he gripped the sword as if it were a snake trying to bite him.

When he did not speak, Bronwen walked up the steps to stand beside him.

"I wanted to ask him if he would be willing to be employed by me as a bodyguard. That is how he has agreed to show his gratitude and I plan to employ him myself, as well as Mr Whyms." Bronwen was babbling in an attempt to calm Kole. She could not see his expression from where she was stood.

"What were you doing outside?" Kole said finally.

"I wanted a walk, as I could not sleep," Bronwen explained. She had been dreading these questions the most.

"The gardens would not suffice? And why did you not take Adam with you? That is what he is there for!"

Bronwen saw her opportunity. "He was sleeping and I cannot expect him to be awake every moment I am. He will get no rest as I sleep very little. With a second guard, I can have at least one of them with me at all times."

"How can I trust that two guards will make the difference to you when you cannot respect the value of one?"

"Because this one is of my choosing and he is not simply doing it for money, he says he owes me a life debt and I believe him to be sincere."

"That does not mean he is qualified to protect you."

"He survived whatever horror his captors put him through and he looks strong enough; perhaps a little underfed, but not a stranger to labour."

Kole said nothing but looked contemplating, mulling over a decision in his head. Bronwen inwardly coaxed herself to remain strong in this decision and with what she wanted.

"I will meet him. Have him ready for breakfast and bring him down," Kole spoke to Bronwen in the same tone he used for his servants, but she didn't mind because he had stopped wanting to kill either Azubuike or her.

Kole stalked down the stairs, his sword still unsheathed.

"But if I deem him unfit or suspicious in anyway, I will not hesitate to kill him and hold you responsible."

His tone was unforgiving and Bronwen knew he meant it, even without seeing his expression. It both frightened and thrilled her that he would go to such lengths to protect her.

Once Kole was gone, Bronwen hurriedly scrabbled upstairs to do whatever she could to make Azubuike presentable.

IV

Bronwen stood in the hallway with Azubuike, trying to make his ill-fitting jacket lie straight as she braced herself for the reaction that was sure to come once she opened the double doors to the dining room.

She had explained to Azubuike that her fiancé wanted to meet him before he could start his duties as her new bodyguard. Bronwen had also asked him again if he was certain he wanted the job. She did not go into detail about how difficult it would be, but she had made it clear to him that he was a free man and did not belong to her, or anyone. If after only a few days, he changed his mind, she would not stop him from leaving.

Azubuike had considered this and Bronwen had found herself hoping he would stay. Saving his life with her own breath had somehow joined them together on a level that was beyond mere acquaintance and she sensed he felt the same. Being around him felt companionable and safe.

He had nodded his certainty in his decision to become her bodyguard and Bronwen had led him downstairs to the doors she knew Kole was waiting behind.

Azubuike put his hands around Bronwen's to stop her fretting fingers. She looked up at him, marvelling at his height and almost black eyes. He inclined his head towards the door and let go of her hands. Bronwen took a breath and nodded, then entered the room.

Kole had his back to them, so Josette was the first to spot them. A small gasp escaped her as Azubuike followed Bronwen into the room making Kole stand and turn more abruptly then he perhaps would have otherwise.

His eyes widened when he saw the blackened shadow behind Lady Bronwen. She spoke quickly.

"This is Azubuike," she said, glad she had asked him to explain the pronunciation. He had done so patiently, despite her ignorance. "While I was out walking last night, I found him in the fields after some attack. He had been badly beaten and his clothing had been stolen from him. I could not on good conscience leave him there, so I brought him to Aterces so he could get some rest and food. Azubuike was so grateful that he has agreed to be my guard, as well as Mr Whyms."

Azubuike did not disagree with the slight changes in Bronwen's story. She did not want Kole and Josette to know that she had dived into a freezing river. It was bad enough that she had been out late at night on her own.

Not one of them met the eyes of another. Josette had been nodding the entire time Bronwen was speaking and had not taken her eyes off Azubuike, who was in turn starring at Kole. Kole had his gaze fixed upon Bronwen, who was looking at Josette, not wanting yet to face Kole's disapproval. Unfortunately, she did not get much say in the matter as he took her arm without ceremony and steered her out of the room, leaving Josette alone with Azubuike.

Once the door was closed and they were far enough away to not be heard, Kole turned on Bronwen, not yet releasing his grip on her arm.

"You told me he was attacked!"

"He was," Bronwen replied, confused as to why this was relevant.

"He is black, Bronwen."

"Yes," Bronwen said, not trusting herself to not say something sarcastic in response.

"Then he is probably a slave and his owners were trying to be rid of him."

"If he is unwanted, then there is no reason why I cannot have him. Slavery is no longer legal. He is a free man and I mean to employ him."

"They are still not our equals!" Kole was very close to her face as he scolded her, but Bronwen refused to back down.

"Azubuike is perhaps no more our equal than a servant may be, but he is a man the same as you are. And if you can have such a fear of him because of his appearance, then he makes the perfect guard for me. Who would dare turn their hand against me with Azubuike by my side?"

"Your social standing will be in jeopardy. I cannot have you walking around with this man," Kole argued still, but he let go of her arm. He had blanched at the suggestion that he was afraid of a man with dark skin, but it was not what he was focused on - if he was focused on anything at all.

"What care will I have for social standing if those who wish me harm succeed?"

"You think your father will allow this and give him resident at Metrom?"

"If he will not, then Azubuike shall stay with me. My room is quite large enough to partition it in two and I shall be all the safer."

Bronwen knew she was provoking him and was suddenly worried Kole might strike her. His face was the most horrible contortion of anger she had ever seen, even on her father. Just as she thought to close her eyes from a certain blow, he said slowly, "should that happen, you will both have residence with me - in *separate* rooms."

Kole's expression had not softened but his voice was less harsh. Bronwen was surprised by his words and before he could take them back, she took them as an admission and placed a hand on his arm stepping on her toes to kiss his cheek tenderly.

"Thank you," she said and turned to go back to the room when Kole grabbed her arm and pulled her hard into him, pinning her and forcing a strong kiss on her lips. It was such a shocking and passionate embrace that Bronwen had no time to close her eyes and enjoy it before it was done and he was letting her go and stalking back to the dining room, without a backward glance at how he had left her.

Bronwen took a moment to catch her breath, certain that she had felt his tongue stoke her bottom lip before he released her. She shook herself and headed back into the room. She was surprised to find Josette and Azubuike deep in conversation and sharing a light breakfast together, not stood in the same place she had left them as she had been expecting.

The couple stood as Kole and Bronwen entered.

"My apologies," Kole said to Azubuike. "It was just a bit of a shock to me this morning, as I'm sure you can understand, Mr Buike. Finding out that my Lady has been roaming around in the middle of the night put me ill at ease. You will not be short of work, if I do see fit to employ you as her bodyguard."

Kole's tone was pleasant and polite, however Bronwen noticed he had not sought to shake hands with the man. From Azubuike's part, she assumed he had no culture for it, but from Kole, she knew he was being impolite.

"Azubuike is one name, Lord Guild," Josette corrected, trying to brighten the atmosphere. "He has no surname other than that of his previous employer."

"And whom might that be?" Kole asked roughly. Josette did not give Azubuike a chance to answer.

"I hardly think that matters now."

"It matters, if they did not leave on good terms. Tell me,

why did they sever your contract with them. Did you steal something? Refuse to work? Rape their daughter?"

"Kole!" Bronwen said, aghast at how rude he was being. Josette frowned and opened her mouth to protest when Azubuike spoke up.

"Our interests became conflicted," he said in perfect English, despite his heavy accent.

There was a loaded silence and Bronwen caught herself pinching the skin on her arm nervously. Then, Kole half smiled and nodded.

Bronwen sighed and looked at Josette, who was grinning fondly at her new friend. Azubuike was looking serious and Bronwen realised she had not seen him smile yet. But what did she expect? He had found himself near death last night only to be, what must seem to him, as recaptured into the servitude of yet more masters. It was something Bronwen would rectify as soon as possible. She did not want him to feel as though she owned him.

"Please, be seated again and finish your meal," Bronwen said and sat beside Josette who was already pouring more tea.

Kole sat at the head of the table, looking at Azubuike as little as possible.

Azubuike surreptitiously replaced the cheese knife he had been gripping back onto his plate. Thankfully, Kole did not appear to notice.

"Azubuike was just telling me about how the women of his homeland pierce their noses," Josette explained excitedly, pronouncing his name perfectly - much better than Bronwen could have. "Doesn't that sound brilliantly interesting?"

"You were not born a slave then, Azu?" Kole questioned bluntly. Bronwen bit her tongue to prevent another rebuke. She did not want to provoke Kole, now that he had agreed to her new bodyguard and hoped Azubuike did not take offence.

"No," came Azubuike's simple reply. He seemed not to care about Kole's indiscretion of words, he was just a quiet man, perhaps unused to talking.

"Azu. That will be easier for most to say," Josette added in, trying to lighten the mood. "Would you mind terribly? I personally hate it when people shorten my name. But won't it be funny to see people try to pronounce it!"

"Azu is fine," Azubuike said. He had not eaten since Bronwen and Kole sat down and would not meet anyone's eye either. He was sitting forward in his chair, looking as if he might spring from it at any moment.

There was an awkward silence whilst Josette, the main speaker, took a long drink of her tea. It was gratefully broken by servants entering the room to clear away the food.

Bronwen noticed the nervous and speculative glances the servants gave Azubuike and how they skirted around him carefully, as if he might pounce on them at a moment's wrong move. He was the perfect guard for Bronwen, in her eyes. Whilst everyone was watching Azu, she would be left to continue her hunting and she doubted any opportunistic assassins would try to attack her with Azubuike by her side.

Mr Fane entered the room to announce that Lord Guild's gentlemen friends had arrived. He was the only one who seemed unsurprised a black man was sat having tea with his Lordship.

"Oh yes, your hunt, I had forgotten," Josette said, she finished her tea almost in one go. "Bronwen and I will go for a ride and picnic today, whilst you men go and do whatever you men do."

"That sounds lovely, Josette," Bronwen replied.

"Azu can use one of my horses," Josette continued. Bronwen gave her a sharp look, knowing Josette well enough to sense what was coming next, but her friend ignored her. "It will more than keep up with yours, Kole."

"So long as it can keep up with the dogs, Miss Emry, it will be more than sufficient."

Bronwen stared at Kole in surprise. "You mean to take him with you?"

Kole took a nonchalant sip of tea before answering.

"How else can I assess his suitability as a guard? So far, the only reference I have is his being rescued by a woman."

Though Bronwen knew his words had been an insult to Azubuike, she hoped that the man saw the prestige in a Lord inviting a lowly man to hunt alongside him, let alone one of his colour.

Kole stood and turned to Mr Fane, who had returned after showing Kole's guests into the smoking room.

"Show Mr Azu into one of the bank view rooms and have some clothes for riding sent up to him," Kole ordered his butler, who inclined his head and left the room.

"Bronwen, shall we?" Josette said, standing up and almost knocking over the tea cup she had precariously placed on the edge of the table.

Bronwen nodded and looked at Azubuike who stood when Josette did. He seemed even taller and impressive in stature next to Kole. His borrowed clothes slightly too tight for him. If after today Azubuike was to stay, she would make sure to get him some proper clothing.

Azubuike looked calm and pensive and he mildly inclined his head to Lady Bronwen, telling her silently that he was not worried about being left. She hoped he had no reason to be concerned. They had known each other for only a few hours and she already felt responsible for him. The opposite to how she should feel towards a bodyguard.

Though she wouldn't stop him from going, Azubuike must surely wish to redeem himself after Kole's comments and Bronwen mothering him would negate that.

Kole let the ramblings of the men wash over him. In some part, he was pleased that the fool woman Bronwen had brought a filthy slave into his home. It was not the fact Azu was black that bothered Kole - slaves came in all breeds and Lord Guild did not want one in his presence, other than to clean his plate and his boots.

What was Bronwen doing out in the night anyway and why had that idiot, Adam Whyms, not followed her as he had been instructed to do?

However, it would be satisfying to see the look on these stiff-necked gentlemen's faces when they saw Azu. It would give them something to talk about other than how well-bred their horses were or how large their women were getting. Already there was talk amongst them of the mysterious stranger they were waiting for.

"Not another Earl who lets his dogs do all the work?" one of them jested. A man called Jonathan. Such a dull name for a man who, out of all of them, was most likable to Lord Guild. His japes and dark wit were easily more interesting than his name - as was his scared face that gave him a harsh appearance. He had a slash down one of his eyes and another smaller one on his cheek. It made him look like he had been in a great battle, which is what he liked to tell people, when really Kole knew Johnathan had fallen from a tree as a young man and nearly lost an eye and a cheek. He had landed on the fence of the house he was trying to break into, in the hope of sneaking into a young Lady's bedroom.

Johnathan never did get to see her, but had instead fucked the nurse who had been seeing to his injuries.

Kole chose not to rise to his insult and smiled slyly instead. They would soon be wishing for a snub-nosed Earl.

There were two options available to Kole to deal with Azubuike. The first was to bully him away - no slave once freed would want to enter a life of service again willingly. Kole would show him what kind of reception he would receive, should he be Bronwen's guard. The second option, if that failed, was to kill him. Hunting could be dangerous, especially to someone unfamiliar to it and it would be easy to blame one of his friends for the mishap. They might even volunteer to be accused if they were particularly hateful.

Kole quickly singled these ones out as Azubuike was shown into the room by a begrudging servant.

"Gentlemen," Kole said, ushering the man into the centre of the room, careful not to touch him and planning on burning his borrowed clothes if they ever made it back to him. "This is Azu, Lady Bronwen's new bodyguard, whom I have invited to join us today."

Azu stared at each man as they scowled at him. The room had gone deathly silent, a sweet peace to Kole. He savoured it and the scornful energy around the room, he could almost taste its sweetness and stifled a groan of pleasure.

It was a young lad called Andrew who was the first to stride forwards, hand outstretched in greeting.

"Always good to have more men," he said. Azu looked at his hand suspiciously before shaking it in a strong grip that made Andrew grimace.

Kole was almost embarrassed for the young man and knew his father, Chester, certainly was. Perhaps now he wished that his mistress had not had an unfortunate fall down the stairs, in the same year his wife had given birth to this weak-willed son - but accidents will happen.

No other made a move to shake the black man's hand, but the tension regretfully eased somewhat. Kole decided to start the hunt promptly, before the mundane discussions started again.

The men left the room, mumbling to themselves about what Kole was thinking, inviting a nigger out hunting and allowing his fiancée to be watched by the monstrosity. It was all said in earshot of Azu, but if the man cared what they thought, he did not show it; a permanently serious expression on his face, no matter his mood.

Kole waited so he was one of the last to leave the room. Andrew stayed behind too, with the intention of walking with Azubuike before his father grabbed him roughly and forced him from the room.

Kole said nothing to Azu. He just held the door and inclined his head for the man to follow before joining his guests.

Out in the stables, while the men checked their horses and had their grooms' fuss over them, Kole watched Azu with interest as he saddled his own horse, apparently well practiced at it.

The stable boy stayed to one side and watched him in fascination, occasionally passing Azu buckles and straps.

It had not been denied him the use of a stable hand, but Azubuike had shooed away help, choosing to saddle his own animal. Whether from habit of serving or from mistrust that someone would have it sabotaged, Kole did not yet know; nor could he deny that the idea had crossed his mind.

"I was hoping you had planned for us to hunt the nigger." Kole turned to find Jonathan stood next to him.

"There is no sport if your prey expects an attack," Kole replied with a cruel smile. "Best to wait until it feels safe first."

"That sounds less like hunting and more like assassination," Jonathan said, a similar smile to Kole on his grim face, which stretched the scars.

"Precisely." Kole turned back to his horse and put his gloves on before mounting, taking the reins from his groom and spurring his horse into a clear space to wait for the others.

The dogs were ready and vying to be released from their collars, muzzles dripping.

Kole took one look across the misty grass until his gaze rested on a group of walkers, making their way over the small hillock a short distance from the manor.

The winter weather obscured their feet, making them appear to be drifting over the landscape - dark wrath like creatures of the dead.

Kole knew one of them was at least.

"I was not expecting him to be so..."

"Dark?" Bronwen interrupted Josette as they continued through the wet grass to their picnic destination. They had paused briefly to look at the gathering of horses, men and dogs by the house. Azu was easy to spot in the grey light of the morning.

Bronwen hoped he would be alright amongst men who would not appreciate a dark-skinned, ex-slave joining them - a slave by definition anyway. She was sure Lord Guild would look out for him if anything happened and the hunt was the last of the season, it was doubtful they would come across anything but a late fox.

"No," Josette disagreed. "So handsome!"

Bronwen looked up at her friend a few paces further up the hill.

"You think so?"

"He is magnificent, Bron!" Josette continued, giving her friend a sly smile. "I wouldn't mind him looking after me. I have a few monsters in my own bedroom he is welcome to protect me from."

"Josette!" Bronwen mockingly put a hand to her mouth. Josette giggled girlishly, despite her age.

"Women have needs just as much as men. They are the fools that believe otherwise."

Josette stopped again and looked back at Aterces, waving the servants onwards with the supplies they carried. Bronwen knew that Josette was the perfect example of eccentric aristocrat; who would quite happily have a selection of exotic humans working for her. She would, however, pay them for their service, and well.

"Do you think it will ever be that women are treated the same as a man?" Josette mused.

Bronwen stopped beside her and turned as well to look at the charming manor house and grounds beyond it.

"In what respect?"

"Too many to number," Josette replied, more thoughtful than solemn. "A man is clapped on the back for bedding a woman, while she is called a whore."

Bronwen nodded in agreement, yet she herself was guilty of it. A woman's discretion was of the utmost importance and a man's promiscuity was one of pride. It had been bred into her that men do as they please and women follow behind. It was just how the world worked and she doubted anything would change.

"If you ever find a man who will treat you as an equal, Bron, do not ever let them go."

"Is that why you find Azubuike so agreeable? Because you can see him as your equal?" Bronwen was not sure why she had asked such a misplaced question and watched as the gentlemen rode away from the house, Azu and his brown filly to the rear.

"I consider him my equal because he is human, same as I," Josette answered, but she was not angry with Bronwen, her tone was more piteous, which Bronwen deserved. "It does not matter to me what his breeding, gender or colour might be. He is beautiful because he has a kind spirit and has a strong and agile physique. His colour just makes him all the more mysterious."

Josette turned and began walking to catch up with the servants, who had almost reached the peak of the hill and had stopped to await instructions. "Perhaps you should read more about how the world *should* be rather than listen to how fools and discriminates tell you the world is?" Josette called back to Bronwen.

Her friend had a way of criticising that never sounded unjust or mean and her comments always stuck in Bronwen's mind. Perhaps it was the writer in her, but Josette had always seemed so much more intellectually evolved than Bronwen and most other people she knew. She admired Josette and welcomed her chastisement like no other. She wished she had more friends like Josette, or just more friends that she could converse with.

She wondered what Josette would make of Thanatos and smiled as she thought about how much her friend would adore *his* physique, as well as his ideologies. Then she grimaced, knowing also how much Josette would detest his evil spirit and orchestration in the taking of Bronwen's life.

With a grim line to her mouth, Bronwen followed Josette the rest of the way up the hill.

Josette had already started helping lay out the picnic blanket. Her lips parted by the heavy breaths passing them where Bronwen's heartrate had barely increased by the time they reached the peak. Bronwen noticed now how much stronger she had felt since coming back from the Under-realm. Even pulling Azubuike out of the water the night before was little effort.

The morning haze was the same shade as the clouds and made it appear as though the fields stretched on forever. The tops of the city buildings were just visible through the grey mist and Bronwen could almost taste the calmness of the morning. She sighed in pleasure.

Once the blanket was set, Bronwen sat down on a large pillow next to Josette, who was rooting through the basket next to her and pulling out glasses and wine for them both.

Bronwen prepared her stomach for food and drink it did not want. It was an effort to force it into herself and it always settled heavily in her afterwards.

Bronwen sat with her face to the clouds. She could just

about hear the hunting horns from Kole's escapades when the wind blew a certain way. She didn't know how they planned on catching anything when they were creating such a racket through the forest. It occurred to her that you should be quiet and sneak up on the thing you hunted, much like she was trying to do with her killers.

Bronwen opened her eyes and shifted on the pillow, pinching her arm in an attempt to bring herself back to the present. Josette poured two glasses of wine and had sent the servants away while they spoke. She spilt a little on her faded dress but did not seem to notice, as accustomed to her own clumsiness as Bronwen was to *her* own frailty.

Adam was sat against a log, with a pillow to his back and his long legs stretched out in front of him. He was too far away to hear their conversation and his face was turned away from them. He always seemed on the lookout for an unknown enemy. Bronwen still felt as if he were watching her from the corner of his eye. She was becoming paranoid.

Bronwen suspected Kole had reprimanded Adam for letting her out at night. She hoped he would forgive her in time and expected that it was the end to her short freedom at Aterces and she would find him once more sleeping outside her room.

"Thank you for the notes you made on my book," Josette said, taking a large sip of wine.

"I hope I did not seem too presumptuous by making them," Bronwen said. "It was mostly my observations. It really is very good."

"Thank you," Josette said, twirling her hair in her fingers and biting on the ends of it every few minutes. It was a habit she had when she was thoughtful or nervous.

"I hope it does work out well for you, there is no reason why it should not," Bronwen said. "You have been through so much and it cannot be healthy to stay living with Kole. You are in that house on your own most of the time."

"I am hoping you will remedy that, if you still plan to marry the bastard."

"Josette, you really are biting when you want to be."

Josette bit her teeth together so they made a clinking sound, making Bronwen giggle in the way only Josette could.

"You are still certain you wish to have him as a husband?" Josette asked, once the mood had sobered again.

"If I am honest, no," Bronwen replied, at least in this she did not have to lie to her friend and could tell her everything that had been bothering her about it - almost everything. "I am just unsure that I really know him. My father will obviously not care or think that matters..."

"Fuck Donovan," Josette said, making Bronwen cringe and not at the curse word. "If you do not think it is right, then do not do it."

Bronwen wished it was that simple. "How did you know that Clarence was right?"

"I knew him well, before we were married - *very* well. And it always seemed right. I was happy and comfortable around him and he wanted me back, despite not having any money or prospects, we had a mutual *need* for one another. We just fit."

Bronwen took the time to replay in her mind her interactions with Kole. She wouldn't have used the word comfortable exactly and sometimes he had made her happy, but was it possible to be happy all the time? She didn't think so, not truly. And she wasn't sure what Josette meant by mutual need.

"I miss being with him most," Josette said, a small sad smile on her face, a mixture of pleasant memory and hurtful loss.

"Of course, you do," Bronwen replied, placing a kind hand on her friend's leg.

Josette looked at her sideways, assessing Bronwen's

meaning and deciding it differed from hers.

"I meant *being* with him," she said. "During our days, we would go about our own business, always surrounded by people; businessmen, servants, guests. But, when we were in our bed, fully alone in the dark and the quiet, no interruptions, no duties or worries... and no clothes, *that* was when we were truly together." She paused and thought for a moment. Bronwen was not sure she really wanted to know Josette's personal bed life, but it was nice to see her looking so contented.

"Sex is so much more wholesome when it is with someone you love," Josette finished, then added, "Not that the other times have been unsatisfying."

"Other times?" Bronwen blanched. "Do not tell me you pay for that sort of thing."

Josette sat up on her hands and looked squarely at Bronwen, clearly amused.

"Of course I do not pay for sex," Josette said slyly. "I am a woman, men come to me for it."

Bronwen looked at her flatly as if assessing whether she was lying. She wasn't.

"Surely you are not implying you are a... an adventuress? It is sinful."

"Bronwen," Josette said, almost in exasperation as she sat up properly and turned her whole body to her friend. "Have you read the Bible or conversed with God?"

She shook her head.

"Well then, you are only taking a human male's interpretation of what is a sin or not," Josette continued. "I have not broken any of the commandments and if sex is so wrong, why does it cause such pleasure?"

Bronwen was going to say something about temptation, but it brought up unwanted thoughts of Thanatos again. She still refused to admit to herself that it could ever be more than a mild curiosity to study him whenever his shirt hung open or when he wore tight trousers or rolled his sleeves up and revealed his muscular arms. Arms that had held her tightly in the carriage the other day.

"But, do you not worry about the consequences?" Was all Bronwen thought to say, hoping Josette would not notice her blush.

"Clarence and I tried for many years without success and I many years after. I cannot conceive."

"Oh, Josette, I am sorry," Bronwen said, but she couldn't prevent the small reproachful voice in her head that judged her friend for being so shameless. She hated herself for her thoughts and knew she did not truly think that of Josette, but it is human in nature, to think the worst at the worst times and the best when it matters least.

"It makes things easier, not having to concern myself with it. I can take as many men to my bed as I have time for."

Bronwen tried to keep the critical look from her face and almost asked what sex was like, but stopped herself. She wasn't sure she wanted to know. To her, this image of it being for pleasure didn't relate to her concept of it. Sex was purely for reproductive purposes. It was something men took pleasure in, but not a woman.

However, if Josette seemed to think highly of it, then perhaps there was something Bronwen was missing.

Delicate hooves trod the ground like poetic words softly spoken. A pair of dark eyes watched the doe – hunter's eyes - his colour making him the dark shadow of a wild animal; feline in the way his muscles flexed and tensed.

Azubuike went unnoticed by the deer, downwind from the animal, and only hoped the sound of the hounds did not alert the creature to his presence in the bush.

The men had not given Azubuike a weapon of any kind but he held in his hand the cheese knife that had been left carelessly unattended at breakfast. It was a small thing, but so was the deer. He could have used his hands if the master of this estate had been more watchful of his weapons.

A movement to the left made the doe turn and flee and the panther crouched lower and tensed.

A horse stepped into the clearing, though not nearly as full of the cautious grace that attended the doe. A man sat upon its back, the reins of Azu's borrowed horse in his hands.

He peered through the brush, but Azubuike knew he could not spot him. He considered staying hidden, his prey lost and his temporary loyalty was only to the Lady who had saved him, not this loathsome snob.

Azubuike figured it didn't matter anyway. Though he was loath to admit it - he had nowhere else to go. He had no way of getting money that would buy him passage to his homeland, and it wasn't even his home anymore. He had spent too long away, taken when he was just a young man of fifteen. Azu spoke English well enough but deliberately strived not to use it. He preferred the people around him to think he could not understand them well, so that he may learn their secrets.

Besides, he owed this Bronwen his life. He had not asked her what she was doing out there in the night and she had not pressed him for answers as to why his previous employers had tried to kill him. There was also something Azu had seen in her eyes that made him stay. A desperation, a loneliness, a quality to her that was so innocent and childlike, it made him want to shield her from harm. Especially that which might come from the man he watched now.

Saying a silent curse to all around him for his weak heart, Azu stepped from the shadows, startling the Earl atop his horse. Azubuike imagined this was one of the rare times it had occurred to the man, who was so obviously used to being in control, that the slightest offset of colour in the sky would anger him, if he had not asked God to change it.

"You will not gain the men's respect by killing their prey for them," Kole said, once he had regained his composure. "It will ruin the hunt."

Azu blinked at him and caught the reins of his horse when Kole threw them to him. He did not understand this chasing of beasts using other beasts. Hunting was all part of the catching. Yes, there was a thrill in it, but it was for the purpose of finding food as quickly as possible, so that other chores could be done. And, Azubuike very much doubted that these men would ever respect him.

Slavery was no longer a trade, but discrimination could not be eradicated completely. It was human nature to stay in groups that were similar to them in looks and temperament, just as with animals. Azu struggled to find any of them attractive, as much as a cat would find a dog displeasing to the eye.

His horse trotted beside Lord Guild while they caught up with the rest of the hunt. When they got there, Jonathan turned to them with a sneer. Andrew was beside him with a stupid grin on his face, he was covered in mud, but seemed in good spirits about it. His father, Chester, came up behind the two of them.

"Where did you two go?" Jonathan questioned.

"Azu spotted a doe amongst the crop of trees over there," Kole answered. "But it got spooked."

"I'm not surprised," Jonathan said, looking Azu up and down. The dark man returned his steely gaze.

"Good job," Andrew said cheerfully. "But without a gun or the dogs, how did you plan on taking it down?"

"With your bare hands?" Chester scoffed.

Azu turned to stare steadily at him in a way that asked for a challenge. Chester considered him for a moment and the man eventually dropped his gaze and pulled his horse away to join the rest of the party.

Azu turned back to Andrew, who was struggling to keep his mount from following. Azu looked at the man's mud-covered front.

"Fell of my horse jumping over a fence." Andrew shrugged with a small smile.

Azu blinked and pushed his horse forwards, making Andrew's horse follow along behind, which the lad was grateful for.

They caught up with the others and followed at a steady pace as the dogs eagerly sniffed out their prey.

Azu knew they were going in the wrong direction for the doe, and all the horn blowing had pushed them further away; no doubt. He kept his eyes on the trees though, and soon found himself in the centre of the group of men, together again.

One man pushed passed him, kicking his leg as his horse came close.

"Watch yourself, nigger," he said, raising his lip in a snarl. Azu ignored him. Did they really think he would rise to one insult after years of abuse? He'd learnt quickly which battles to fight and which to fight later.

It took a further half hour before someone called that a deer had been spotted and the pursuit began again.

"It could be the one that eluded you, Azu," Andrew said, trying to make conversation again. Azu only nodded. He knew the boy was being friendly and he admired his smile, but he was still not so keen on brushing shoulders with these stuck-up white men, no matter how nice they were.

"You best stay to the back then," Jonathan said to Azu. "Don't want you spooking it again."

They chased the deer across the fields with the dogs. The horses were fast, but the dogs were faster through the forest and when they found them, they had already brought the doe to heel. Attacking its legs and flank, slowing it enough for the men to take aim.

Azu watched as they called the dogs off and one man tried and failed to shoot the injured deer through the trees. It was making a horrific bleating noise as a second man's gun clipped it on the shoulder. It fell forwards on one mangled leg in an attempt to get away.

The men were laughing and jesting with one another about the missed shot, not concerned at the animal's distress. From Azu's point of view, needlessly torturing an animal when hunting was the height of cruelty. All things had to eat one way or another, but only monsters played with and tormented their food for the pleasure of it.

The horses followed the trail of blood the wounded animal made through the trees while the men tried for a cleaner shot.

Eventually, Kole tired of the game and set up his own weapon. He knew he could hit it clean through the head. The beast was worn out and had almost given up moving at all. The men watched their Lord take aim at the deer.

Kole look directly into the eyes of the doe, as he sighted down the barrel of the gun. He began to put pressure on the trigger when a black shape darted out from behind a tree and launched itself at the startled deer.

Kole opened his other eye and saw it was the slave who pinned the deer to the floor with his body. Kole's finger had not relaxed on the trigger as he watched Azu delicately stroke the deer's neck before taking a small silver knife out of his belt and, with easy precision, ended the doe's life in one deep stab to the skull. The animal's head and neck instantly relaxed and Azu placed it gently on the leafy floor, wiping the knife clean in the soil before standing up straight and looking towards the hunting party.

He spotted Kole, with his gun still raised and the two stared at each other for the longest time. It would have been easy to pull the trigger and call it an accident.

Kole lowered his gun and rode over to Azu with the other men.

"I told you, he'd use his bare hands like an animal," Jonathan interrupted, forcing Kole to lower his weapon. Surprisingly, there was an element of awe in his voice.

"Like a mountain lion," Andrew said, and to Kole's shock, everyone agreed.

They all helped strap the deer up between two horses and began the journey back to the house.

It was an understatement to say that the general opinion towards Azu had changed. Apparently, killing the doe had gained him some small form of respect. He was a long way off from being an equal or even a friend, but an unlikely ally was close.

Kole would let the Lady have her toy. He could soon be wound by a different key or be disposed of later.

Josette and Bronwen were almost back at the house when they saw the hunting party returning. They stopped on the gravel by the back door and watched with interest as the men carried the carcass of a deer into the house, clapping Azu on the back as if they were great friends.

Lord Guild spotted them and rode over on his horse.

"You best take Azu to get some proper attire tomorrow," he said gruffly. "He has my approval."

The ladies stayed silent as he rode off again to give his horse to a waiting stable hand.

Josette turned to Bronwen. "Isn't it strange, how men can bond over the killing of something?"

Bronwen looked back at the doe, swinging limply as it dangled from two wooden poles. The occasional droplet of blood dripped on the white patio stones and its eyes stared out hollowly at her. She wondered if *her* eyes had looked the same, after her killers had 'bonded' over her death and she shuddered at the thought of there being nothing more than this as motivation to kill her.

The thrill of the hunt, and the pleasure of the kill.

V

"I will not serve him. I must consider my good reputation."

Josette scoffed at the tailor's words. She, Bronwen and Azubuike had visited the city shops to have Azu fitted for clothes.

Lord Guild had recommended the place but the tall, thin, elderly gentleman had been less then helpful - once he found out his customers were two women and a man as dark as the suit the tailor wore.

He glanced at Josette and her disapproving foot tap, crossed arms, rolling eyes and impatient tutting. The man continued to watch the window nervously for anyone who might see his unwelcome customers.

Unlike Mr Clare's shop, this one had large open windows, so people passing could see into it. Modern gas lanterns lit the room where natural light could not reach. Net bouquets of lavender hung around the place to hide the gas smell and keep moths off the fabrics.

"Your reputation will not be tarnished by us, sir," Bronwen tried again. "I will be sure to tell all my friends of your professionalism and the quality of your garments."

He didn't look convinced.

"I would require triple the money for such a contract."

Bronwen's eyes widened. Azu needed a full wardrobe. That amount of money was extortion. She had little choice, besides, Kole could perhaps get it back for her later. He would not stand for this man's attitude.

"Of course," Bronwen resigned. She just wanted to be away from the shop. Being there reminded her too much of Lowell.

She was struggling to keep the memory of his terrified features at bay. The sound he made when he gurgled on his own blood. The colour and thickness of the liquid that pooled beneath him.

Then her other memories added themselves to the fray. The wetness on her cheek when her assassin's blood fell on her. Haydon's head as the bullet utterly destroyed the back of his skull. Bronwen put a popping noise to her memory, akin to a cork on a wine bottle, when really, she had not heard what horrific sound an exploding skull makes through the sound of the gun shot. Liquid Bronwen didn't know existed in the human body had left through the cavernous hole the bullet exited, the entrance strangely clean in the front of his face. At least they would not have to identify him by his body alone.

She struggled to keep the bile from her stomach down at the grotesque memory.

"Bullshit," Bronwen gasped at Josette's language. Was she the only one who did not express herself with profanities? "You are not the only tailor in Guildford, and maybe not even the best."

Josette turned to the door and held it open while Bronwen and Azu stepped out. She noticed Azu had a smile on his face - something she had not seen before. He had been silent during the visit, making Bronwen wondered if he was used to such abuse - expecting it even. Something told her he had not been expecting Josette to stand up for him and Josette hadn't finished.

"And be assured, sir," she continued before closing the door, "I shall be telling all my associates about you."

A couple were stood looking through the window and were about to walk in when Josette grabbed Bronwen quickly by the shoulders and said, loudly enough to hear but not enough to be obvious, "I cannot apologise enough, Lady Bronwen. If I had known his hands were so wandering, I never would have recommended him!"

The couple who still had a hand on the shop door very swiftly changed direction and a few people who had heard muttered and spread the man's new reputation faster than the plague.

"Was that a little too harsh?" Josette asked, once they were away down the road, the rumour snapping at their heels, begging for attention.

"Perhaps just a little, but I daresay he deserved it," Bronwen replied. "Only, what are we to do now for a tailor?"

Luckily, Josette knew one that would serve them, so led the way into the lines of quaint looking houses, away from main shops.

Azu was quiet, but Bronwen was learning there was a difference between his unhappy stern expression and his amused stern expression.

"It is just down this street here," Josette said, turning down a deserted single lane. "She likes to keep to herself."

"Herself?" Bronwen questioned. "It is a woman we go see? Is she qualified?"

Josette turned to Bronwen as they walked and gave her a pitying look, which made her rebuke somehow worse.

"Honestly, I wonder if spending so much of your life brought up by men has done irrevocable harm, Bron. You do such disservice to your own breed."

"We can be all guilty of this," Azu said in Bronwen's ear. His voice was deep and soft. It was the first thing he had said all day and Bronwen bit her tongue to prevent herself from correcting his grammar. Josette was right; she took on too many of the traits of the people around her. Too many of their opinions that left her with none of her own.

Josette stopped outside a small terrace house with a tidy, flower scattered front garden. The only indication that it was anything more than a family home was the decorated sign hanging in the front window.

The three of them opened the white painted gate and knocked politely on the door. It was opened almost immediately by an elderly woman, holding an embroidery hoop in one hand and a white cat in the other. How she had opened the door, Bronwen didn't know.

She scanned the three of them with a scrutinising eye, assessing their wares. She paused when she reached Azubuike, her squinted eyes creating more wrinkles than Bronwen thought it possible for one face to hold.

"Sir," the crone said, in a voice cracking from years of use. Bronwen held her breath, wondering what the woman would say to the dark stranger and his accompaniment of women. "That suit was not made for you."

Bronwen looked back at Azu to see his cheerful-stern expression.

"Mother," a voice from behind the woman sounded and a second lady, younger than the first, took her mother's shoulders and assessed the visitors also.

"But goodness she is right. A white shirt with such a dark complexion is an awful contrast. Please, come in, I can imagine what you are here for."

The three of them followed the outspoken woman into the house. It was clear she was the seamstress as she had a measuring tape around her neck and pins stuck into the collar of her own garment for easy use.

The house was sweet smelling and delicately decorated, with floral patterns and vases of bouquets everywhere, making the place smell earthly and sweet. After they left their coats on the hanger the woman indicated to, they were led into a sitting room, decorated much the same as the hallway.

The room was brightly lit by the large bay window, making the comfy window seat look more inviting, basked in the golden light with cream pillows. The centre of the room was clear, save for a round standing block that currently occupied a mannequin fashioning a deep burgundy skirt.

A full length, gold framed mirror dominated the opposite wall so that Bronwen caught sight of how pale she was next to Azu and even Josette.

"I shall have Millie fetch us some refreshments." A young woman who had been busy cutting fabric at the table on the far side of the room, got up and smiled to the guests as she left at her mother's words, for they were obviously mother and daughter from their golden hair and blue eyes.

"My name is Eleanor, head seamstress here," she said and held her hand out.

"I am Lady Bronwen Wintre and this is Mrs Josette Emry and, uh, Azu."

"Lady Bronwen of Winchester, and the late Earl of Surrey's wife, I am pleased to meet you," The woman said. She neither gushed nor acted awed by her customers, which was a pleasant change.

"Please have a seat ladies. No, not you, sir. I need you right here." She stopped Azu from following Bronwen and Josette with a gentle touch on his arm and pulled him towards the block.

"Will it be a full wardrobe?" The woman asked.

"Yes," Bronwen replied. "Depending on the price of it."

Eleanor nodded thoughtfully as she circled Azu, considering his size.

"I think we may have some shirts already made that we can fit to you, sir, but the jackets will have to be custom made, assuming it is a clerk suit you want rather than a workingman's?"

"Yes, that's right, one for each day including something for riding and an outfit for evenings, please."

"For a full wardrobe, including night clothes, undergarments and accessories," The woman said. Bronwen nodded - she had forgotten about undergarments and night clothes - but Eleanor appeared to be talking to herself.

"Forty-two pounds and seventeen shillings."

"Forty-two pounds?" Bronwen repeated. "So little?"

"I can assure you milady, the quality is excellent. But we must stay competitive in this gentleman's industry."

Millie came back with the tea then and a whole tray of cakes. Bronwen looked at the three women. Three generations all working together and they seemed to have done well for themselves.

"No. I will not pay so little," Bronwen said firmly. "I will give you exactly fifty pounds for your work as would be expected elsewhere."

"As you like milady, you are very generous," The woman smiled gratefully. "We can have the order done within a week for you, but if you like, we can fit a few day outfits from what we have already to take away with you now. It will only take a few hours if you don't mind waiting, milady."

"That would be excellent," Bronwen said, surprised that it would take so little time.

They spent the next few hours watching Azu be pulled about so that he could be measured. Eleanor had to use the block herself just to reach him properly. She let Azu pick his own styles where appropriate and found him to be a good judge of fashions. He preferred the darker colours of blues and greys which judging by Eleanor's expression, she approved of. He even requested that more pockets be added to the inside of the jackets.

All three ladies were very attentive and after a quick

browse at what other garments they had in the shop, Bronwen decided to ask if they would make her dress for the All-Hallowmas ball. She didn't have one yet and if they could make an entire wardrobe in a week, then perhaps they could make a dress in that time.

Eleanor was delighted that a daughter of a Baron would think to use her work and immediately grabbed a sketchpad and pencil to begin drawing some designs, while Millie worked on Azu's first ever suit.

"I was thinking about maybe having something off the shoulders?" Bronwen started as she sat on the sofa with Josette. Eleanor was sat in the centre of them, with her pencil sketching out the head and shoulders of a woman with hair like Bronwen's. Azu was sat stiffly in an armchair to the side of them. The seamstresses cat came to brush itself up against his leg and he grimaced.

Eleanor artfully drew the silhouette as Bronwen continued to describe how she wanted a bell design with puffy net sleeves and an open panel of a different colour down the front. She didn't hold back thinking about fashion, explaining that it was for an All-Hallowmas ball.

Eleanor nodded along, intent on her drawing and added a little shading of colour.

They all looked down at the picture, considering. It was cream in colour and a deep maroon on the panel down the front.

"It needs something else," Bronwen said, not quite satisfied.

"Yes," Josette agreed. "It is not quite an All-Hallowmas gown."

Eleanor nodded in agreement. The dress was beautiful but suitable for an ordinary dinner party, not a grand elaborate event.

Azu held out his hands for the pad. "Can I?"

"I... suppose so," Eleanor said, reluctantly handing the pad and pencil over.

Azu delicately put pencil to paper, trying to draw around the cat that had planted itself firmly on his lap and was purring happily. Azu handed the pad back once he was satisfied.

The women looked down at the altered design and gasped. Azu had changed the straight neckline to make it shapelier around the bosom and had added delicately drawn fabric leaves in autumn colours where the skirt of the dress separated and smaller ones across half the neckline and one shoulder. But the biggest change were the wings that came out from behind the figure. One wing was covered in cream feathers to match the main dress and the other was maroon and more bat like in design. Bronwen was surprised to find herself grinning about the connection. Azu could not know how close to life they felt to her. Half-dark and half-light. Half dead and alive.

"I think this may just be my favourite gown yet," Bronwen announced and grinned at Azu's relieved expression.

"You have an eye for this, sir. But I am afraid our skills lie in dresses, not wings," Eleanor said in good humour.

"I can make them," Azu said as Eleanor showed Millie the drawing, who had wandered over with Azu's finished jacket. She gasped in delight and praised Azu some more. He ducked his head in embarrassment at the attention but seemed pleased.

Once the deposit was paid and everything settled, they left the shop with the suit Azu had changed into and a few more items he would need carried under their arms.

A pair of shoes was the next item on the list. Josette pulled Azu into the small shop. Bronwen began to follow them, her hand on the door, when something made her look down the street. The town was quiet, with only a few hours left of the shops being open. She wasn't sure how she spotted the dark shape slip down a narrow passage between the houses. It was only there for a brief moment and at a distance but she still knew it was Adam.

Bronwen looked back at Josette and Azu in the shop, he was already being measured and Josette seemed to have everything in hand. Bronwen placed her bags inside the door and closed it quietly, then headed quickly to where she had seen Adam.

She wasn't sure why she felt like she was sneaking around. Perhaps it was the twilight making the shadows longer. It gave the town a feeling of mystery and suspense. Bronwen only wanted to ask Adam if he wished to join them on their journey home. What he was doing in the city was his business. Now that Azu could be with her sometimes, Adam had been given free days to do what he wished.

Bronwen reached the passageway and hesitated. Alleys had become a place of wrongdoing in her mind. Only people seeking to hide lurked in the back streets of cities. They were dark, damp, smelly and a maze to get lost in.

Trying to look as inconspicuous as she could, and not like she was hiding something, Bronwen peered around the corner and squinted in the dark. It was empty, of course, no demons, hellhounds or Adam.

Her feet took her down the passage before she could stop them. There really was no reason for her to travel this way. She should have gone back to Azu and Josette who would wonder where she had gone and Azu would feel bad for not looking out for her.

A murmur of voices stopped her before she stepped out onto the other side of the alley. She used the wall to press her body into the shadows, cringing at the slim on them and the drip that fell on her head from a drain above.

She could see some small stalls down this dim, narrow street. People were selling out of the back of their houses and they looked to be just setting up, rather than packing their wares away.

Bronwen spotted Adam a little way down the lane. He was talking to someone; a woman in an elaborate dress. It looked dark in colour, as did the woman's unconfined hair.

They didn't seem to be hiding what they were doing and didn't look worried as people passed them. Adam even laughed at one point, something Bronwen had not seen him do before.

Bronwen chided herself for being so suspicious. She almost decided to join them, when Adam passed a small package to the woman which she tucked into her bosom and produced her own. She had it clutched in her hand and placed it in Adam's pocket herself, whispering something in his ear and smiling like a satisfied fox that had just killed a coup of chickens.

Her smile was what made Bronwen stop and she blushed and looked away when the woman bit Adam's earlobe gently. When Bronwen looked back, the woman was gone and Adam was walking straight towards her. Suddenly, she didn't want to be caught. She began back down the alley a step and calculated that she wouldn't make it before he got to her.

On the verge of an unreasonable amount of panic, she pressed herself against the wall and hoped Adam would pass the alley by. She prayed he wouldn't notice her and had just enough time to realise how ridiculous she was being, thinking that flattening herself against a wall was a brilliant solution, when Adam was in the alley with her.

Bronwen held her breath and scrambled for an excuse, when Adam walked straight past her and out the other side of the passage.

Bronwen's mouth fell open slightly as she moved away from the wall and realised that she was still holding her breath. She let it out in a relieved sigh and shook her head in disbelief.

Adam had been less than a hands width away from her

and didn't blink an eye at the strange woman on tiptoes against a wall and stiff as a board. It wasn't possible.

A noise behind her connected her to reality again and she headed back towards the light to join Azu and Josette.

Bronwen squealed when someone touched her arm as she left the passage. She looked up to find Adam stood there. He had quickly removed his hand at the noise she had made and looked taken aback.

"I am sorry, Mr Whyms," Bronwen said quickly.

"I frightened you, milady," He stated blandly.

"No, no," Bronwen explained, her heart still hammering and her cheeks growing hotter at the girlish sound she had just made. "I just thought you had not seen me."

"I always see you," he said, in a way that didn't lessen her anxiety. She just stared at him mutely. "It's my job, milady."

"Right, of course," she said, shaking herself. "I just thought I saw you and wanted to ask if you wished to ride with Azu, Josette and I. We will be heading back to Aterces soon and we have a carriage waiting in town."

"You were down there?" Adam asked, looking concerned. His hand moved slightly towards his pocket. Bronwen tried not to look at it.

"No, I could not find where you had gone."

"Azu let you go on your own?"

"He does not know I have left the shop."

"Then he was not watching."

Bronwen grimaced. She didn't want to get Azu in trouble. It wasn't *his* fault a group of satanic worshipers kidnapped and murdered her and was the cause of her paranoid curiosity and tendency to misjudge levels of danger.

"Shall we?" Bronwen asked, in an attempt to change subject.

Adam indicated with a swing of his arm for her to lead the way. She swallowed and headed back towards the shoe shop, with him following closely behind. She managed to mostly forget he was there, always a few steps behind her, but she didn't like him being at her back. Bronwen had an uncomfortable sensation that he was staring at her the whole way. It made her conscious of the way she walked and the pace she breathed, so much so that she almost tripped and fell, she was concentrating so hard on which foot went where.

Unfortunately, her small stumble had only reddened her cheeks and caused Adam to walk even closer behind her, as he hadn't managed to grab her the first time. The way back to the shop seemed to take twice as long.

When they got back, Josette asked her where she had been. Both she and Azu looked uncomfortable when Adam followed in behind her. Bronwen quickly explained and the four of them collected their bags again and left for the carriage.

Azu took Josette's bags from her and Adam took Bronwen's before she could protest. His hands lingered on hers as he took them and he leaned in closer to her than he needed to. His jacket hung open enough for Bronwen to see the pocket the mysterious item was in, but not what it contained.

VI

The cold of an approaching winter sent the leaves into angry protest; their cheeks flushed with the fury of knowing they fought a losing battle and fisted ends curled as they swore their return to the branches in the summer.

The church bells chiming seemed less dramatic, as they told all who were listening, that the midnight hour had begun.

"Perfectly on time," Earl Guild said, once the bells had finished. He turned from watching the clock tower in the distance, just visible beyond the stone pillar he was stood by.

"Coming late can be just as rude as coming prematurely," Velna said, making a show of stepping from the shadows.

The Earl gave her a smile that lasted only the briefest of moments, then scowled and got on with business.

"Attacking Bronwen was a fool thing to do," He scolded, knowing his voice would not be overheard. "Why did you not consult the Secuutus?"

"*I* called a meeting with *you* tonight," Velna said. "So, I will ask the questions. I didn't come for a lecture, especially from you. Besides, it wasn't me who tried to kill her. *I* would have succeeded in ending the little wretch."

"Then what brings you all the way to Guildford, if it was

not for my council?" Kole said in a mocking tone. It was no secret that he and Velna despised one another, but this was not the first time the enemies had allied or sought advice. They both saw the value in the other's skills and mutually agreed to come to the other's aid, for as long as it did not affect their own goals.

Velna gave Kole a coy smile and leant up against the pillar, pushing her chest out so her breasts were hard to miss. A move Kole was certain she had used many a time. He was not sure if Velna was even aware when she did it anymore.

"I wanted to know what you plan to do about the problem we face, because the more our people die, the more they will bay for blood."

"And blood they shall have, once Donovan sees fit to give it to us," Kole replied. "You heard him at the last meeting, if Bronwen needs to die, then he will do it."

"And do you really trust his word?" Velna hissed, pushing off the pillar and leaning towards him. "He has said nothing to indicate he knows what happened and why she is back, nor that he plans to do anything about it." She leaned in and lowered her voice, though there was little need in this abandoned part of town.

"Some of the group are wondering if he is fit to lead us in this matter. They are looking for someone who will call him out - someone who will call for Lacessere."

Kole looked at her seriously, but could find no hint of mockery. "You surely cannot be considering it."

"If someone doesn't come forward soon, I might."

Kole scoffed. "You could barely make it past the first trial last time."

"That was then," Velna growled. "I'm stronger and smarter now. And just because I call it, doesn't mean I seek to win. I just think that, in this matter, Donovan is not in his right mind."

"The same could be said of you," Kole snapped back. It

was obvious Velna's main flaw was her jealousy. He had, at first, marked it as her weakness but as the years went on, he knew it could be a very dangerous strength. She was cunning and ruthless and brutal sometimes, but he had found that even Velna's reckless behaviour was not her biggest weakness, it was their Dominus.

"Your own involvement could also be called into question, Kole. I have noticed the Lady has two nice new bodyguards to help defend her, we shall have to see how long that lasts." She looked smug, but Kole wasn't interested in what she was up to. He hired Adam because he knew he could take care of himself and because he knew he would loyally tell Kole whatever he found out about Bronwen. As for Azu, if Velna planned to kill him, then it would be one less thing for Kole to do.

"What of our master?" Kole asked. "Has he no words for what he wishes us to do next?"

"We don't exactly do much talking together." Velna smiled satisfactorily, though there was a hint of hurting behind her eyes - her biggest weakness.

"How convenient."

"*You* could just as easily summon him of you wanted to," Velna snapped. "Or..." she paused and looked about, as if the trees and cobble stones around them listened. She leant in closer to Kole, her voice barely a whisper. "We could summon something else."

Unexpectedly, Kole hit her across the face with the back of his hand. Her hair whipped the air from the force of her head turning. Velna recovered quickly and looked back at him, not even putting a hand to her reddening cheek.

"That is not and never will be an option," Kole hissed, in a voice that was surprisingly shaky. "Do not *ever* dare to speak of it to me again."

"Is your stomach too weak to do what needs to be done, milord?" Velna spat back, the blow had only angered, not silenced her. "Or is *your* heart not fit to lead us either?"

"I do not need a demon to take care of one weak woman."

"And yet, you also have done nothing about her, just like Donovan. Instead you bring her here and play the doting fiancé and defend her when Haydon had the chance to kill her." Kole's palm twitched but he did not hit her again. Not yet. "We know you were there with her. Haydon hired three other men. I don't believe that she would have been able to fend off all of them without help."

"Haydon foolishly tried to kill me first and you cannot kill Bronwen," Kole snapped. "She returned here because our Dominus sent her back, and he will continue to do so until he has satisfied himself with whatever game he is trying to play."

"You cannot know that. We have only tried the once to kill her..."

"I *do* know that. I know it as certain as I know summer follows winter. You will not kill her and the more people that try, the more people will be killed and Bronwen will find the identity of each and every one of us. Do not think for one moment our deaths will be as precariously final as hers was."

He stopped talking, hoping he hadn't revealed too much of what he knew, but it was all true and he was not yet prepared to let Bronwen find out who he was. The time would come, but he still had far to go.

Velna crossed her arms and looked up at him steadily before she spoke in the most dispassionate voice she had ever used.

"Then we must summon something that *can* kill her." Kole did not hit her this time, but his eyes darkened monstrously. "If you do not call Lacessere, then I will. And if I must lead us to rid us of this blight to our group, then I will face the trials with fervour."

She turned away and began walking back into the

shadows, apparently done with the meeting. This angered Kole more than anything else that had been said, but a small pulling feeling at the back of his soul forced a confusing mix of emotions in with his anger. He didn't know if he felt fear, hatred or sadness in his claustrophobic body. It made his voice tremble as he called after her.

"You cannot control what you might summon!"

Velna paused in her retreat to the darkness and looked back at him.

"I do not seek to control it," she said calmly. "I only need *her* to be the first thing it comes after."

Over the next few days, Bronwen spent her daylight hours with Josette, going for walks or rides in the woodlands, shopping in the city and doing a vast amount of talking - about everything they could think of. Kole mostly left them to it, joining them for the occasional meal and treating Bronwen equally as indifferent as Josette. Apparently, his warmness towards Bronwen was reserved for Winchester. In Guildford, he was the Earl of the county again.

Bronwen's spent her evenings exploring the house with nothing but candlelight to guide her. Occasionally Thanatos would appear and she found him to be quite companionable during her lonely nights. Their relationship had shifted slightly since the night they saved Azubuike. Bronwen's remaining fear of him had almost completely dissipated and she began to treat him as an acquaintance.

Thanatos had a vast knowledge on many subjects and even listened with genuine interest as Bronwen discussed the differing qualities of fabric around the house. A subject which would have bore anyone else but Thanatos never gave her that impression. He asked questions and offered his own insight to the otherwise mundane topic.

His company was unexpectedly welcome during the nights

she could not leave her room because Adam was patrolling the corridors.

Mr Whyms appeared increasingly ill at ease since the day in the alley. His lingering stares were more intense and he seemed to have lost all sense of personal space whenever an opportunity to be close to Bronwen presented itself.

When Adam helped her into a carriage, he held her waist as well as her hand. When she walked past him through doorways, he showed no inclination of moving aside, so she had to shuffle past, their bodies almost touching. On the stairs he was so close behind her she worried she would trip and fall into him.

Bronwen was not the only one to notice Adam's strange behaviour. She often caught Josette looking unimpressed and sometimes she would clear her throat by way of warning Adam that he was becoming too friendly, especially as he did not act this way when Lord Guild was around. It almost made Bronwen want to spend more time with Kole, just so she could breathe a little.

Even Azu, who Bronwen was still getting to know, had started to put himself between them at every opportunity, much to Adam's distaste.

It was ridiculous needing a bodyguard to protect against her other bodyguard. But there was little she could do about it until Azu was fully settled into the role, then perhaps she could request that Adam return to his usual duties as Kole's guard.

When not wandering the dark corridors of Aterces and avoiding her intrusive bodyguard, Bronwen read Josette's manuscript at her request.

The story was about a man who, after a tragic accident on a ship, had woken to find his wife and son missing. He dropped everything in his life in order to find them again and on his travels, he unwittingly falls in love with a woman claiming to be able to help discover where his family have gone.

The twist to the story was that the man is actually hallucinating, from a fevered illness caused by the shipwreck. His wife had died in the accident and turned out to be the woman in his dream. The story ends with him having to make a decision, whether to die and go with his wife to the next place or to fight his fever and live so he can look after their son.

Bronwen thought Josette's book was fantastic and had cried from a deeply felt compassion towards the characters.

Bronwen decided she would invite a selection of publishers to the All-Hallowmas ball and introduce them to Josette. If her status was to be useful to anyone, she wanted it to be this.

Finally, it was time to leave Aterces and return to Winchester to begin preparations for the All-Hallowmas ball.

Bronwen had been pleased that Josette had agreed to travel back with them early and spend some time at Metrom.

Unfortunately, Adam Whyms was also returning with them instead of staying with Kole who was remaining in Guildford for a few more days. Bronwen was glad about this, as it meant she would have more time to spend with Josette and Azubuike alone.

The door closed on the train compartment just as it pulled away from the station.

Josette and Azu sat across from Bronwen in the large train compartment they occupied for the journey. Bronwen was beside the window with Adam the other side, looking out at the auburn leaves under a dark sky that threw rain across the glass and threatened night. Gas lights lit the room, the smell of it and colour of the velvet chairs reminded Bronwen of the theatre. Perhaps she would take Azu and Josette to a play one day.

The journey was far shorter and more pleasant than being in a carriage and Josette produced a pack of cards and proceeded to teach Azu her favourite game. He picked it up quickly and was soon in competition with Josette and Adam, who was taking it very seriously, thinking about each turn while they stared daggers at one another. It was clear that Azu and Adam were not going to be friends.

"Do you have any family, Mr Whyms?" Josette asked during a game.

"No, ma'am," he replied. "Not anymore."

"I am sorry to hear that," Josette said genuinely. "Have you been a bodyguard before?"

"Yes, ma'am. Twice before."

"And I hope they ended well?"

"Well enough."

Bronwen gave Josette a knowing look. It was clear that Josette was trying to get the measure of the man and she wasn't ready to give up yet, despite his resistance to engage in conversation.

Josette scanned the man, not noticeable to anyone but Bronwen who had seen Josette's interrogation tactics before and knew what was coming.

Adam's jacket sleeves were rolled up in the warmth of the carriage. There were marks on his forearms and the back of one of his hands was a different shade to the other. The skin looked tight and smooth.

"How did you come to have so many scars?" Josette asked; propriety now lost.

Adam actually smiled. "A fire, ma'am - mostly. And fighting. I can shoot straight and I'm good with a knife, but my hands are my best weapons."

He flexed his fingers with a grin then glanced at Bronwen with wide eyes, as if he had only just realised who he was in the carriage with. Josette continued quickly, not wanting to spoil the first sign of interest she had been able to get from him.

"Where did you learn to fight?"

"From my brother," Adam continued, reverting back to his short replies.

"He used to fight too?"

"Only me and my father - a fight shouldn't really be one sided. They both died in a fire."

"The same fire that burnt you?" Josette didn't give her condolences, reading from his tone that he wouldn't have cared for it anyway.

"Not quite the same, no," Adam said cryptically, the satisfied smile on his face made Bronwen uncomfortable and she decided to excuse herself to find them some refreshments.

Adam and Azu immediately stood to go with her.

"I can manage quite well on my own, thank you," Bronwen snapped. "I am on a train in first class. What could possible befall me here?"

Bronwen slid the door open and left the compartment before they could protest. She hadn't meant to snap but, in truth, she wanted to be alone to think about what she was going to say to her father when he met Azu. He would not be pleased, she knew.

Donovan had not sent a reply to her letter explaining about her new bodyguard, and that was before he found out about Azu's heritage. She had not found the right words to describe it to him. Bronwen had not wanted to blurt out that Azu was a black man, she didn't see why it should matter. She would not have immediately described someone else as being white, so why should Azu's dark skin define his description?

Still, she dreaded her father's reaction. She may have said to Kole that she would keep Azu in her own room if Donovan refused to give him residence, but she knew she would not put up much of a fight if he commanded her otherwise. It was not that she feared her father's wrath, it was more that she had spent her whole life wanting his approval. Wanting him to show her attention. Wanting him to be proud of her. Wanting him to be her father.

The corridor of the train was empty and Bronwen walked quietly past the compartments, pinching her arm and trying not to look inside as she forced down her curiosity. One room had the curtains pulled and she blushed as she heard giggling coming from inside it. She hurried past, trying instead to listen to the rain as it trailed chaotic lines across the window.

Soon there was only empty compartments and the locked entrance to the baggage cart was ahead of her. She must have gone the wrong way.

Bronwen turned around to try the other end of the train, when an arm flew out in front of her and placed a hand on the window. She jumped at the sudden appearances of another person.

"Oh, I am sorry," Bronwen said to the floor, not sure what she was apologising for. The figure didn't move and she looked up to find a man wearing the hat and uniform of a train guard.

"Excuse me, sir," she said and stepped to the side. He moved in front of her, taking a step closer and raising an eyebrow at her.

"I need to see your ticket, miss," he demanded in a gruff voice Bronwen didn't appreciate.

"Of course," Bronwen said sweetly and got her ticket from her pocket.

He snatched it from her and examined it, then ran his eyes over her critically before crushing it in his hand and shaking his head.

"This will not do," he said over Bronwen's indignant complaint. "Come with me, miss."

"Is there a problem with my ticket?" Bronwen said,

confused at this rude man and refusing to move until he gave her an answer.

"Perhaps."

He put a hand on her arm and opened the compartment next to them, gesturing with his other hand for her to enter.

"What do you..."

"Come with me now," his voice rumbled in a low growl and his hand slid to her waist as he nudged her gently towards the sliding doors. Bronwen began to feel threatened and her heart beat faster. She tried to push back but his grip on her was strong.

"Remove your hands, sir, or I shall scream for my guards," she said with determination, wishing she *had* taken one of them with her and cursing her imprudence.

"If they can hear you over their card game," he grinned, using his other arm to wrap around her upper body and he forced her into the dark compartment.

Bronwen gasped and was ready to scream when his palm pressed just below her throat, over her collar bones and she couldn't speak, as if her voice had been stolen.

"Unless you plan to scream my name, I would not recommend causing a scene," he whispered into her ear. His voice had changed and she recognised it immediately.

Bronwen squirmed free of his grasp and stood with her back to the window so she faced him.

"Disappointing, my Lady," Thanatos mocked, shaking his head. "No biting, scratching. Not even a knee to the groin. If I had been so inclined, it would have been minimal effort on my part to take you."

Bronwen tried to speak but nothing came out. Thanatos smiled and Bronwen felt her breath pass through her lips and her throat tickle.

"Why did you do that to me?" she accused, her voice returned but croaky.

"I could not have you screaming the carriage down for no

reason."

"You know that is not what I am referring to."

He looked at her levelly, his expression so smug, she could have slapped him.

"Anything to get your heart racing."

Bronwen scowled, then turned to the window and looked out. The lack of lighting in the compartment made it easier to see outside. The sky was pink on the horizon but the rest had heavy black clouds that did not seem to show signs of abating soon. She hoped her father would have a carriage waiting in Winchester.

Thanatos joined her and stood close, their breath misting the cold glass.

"Do you forgive me?" he asked, not sounding the least bit sorry.

"I suppose I shall, considering I owe you a gratitude for saving Azubuike's life. He has quickly become a good friend, one that I desperately need."

"I could not on good conscious let him die."

"Good conscious? Is that so?"

Thanatos looked at Bronwen seriously.

"Yes, my Lady. You see, I must be both the good and the bad for my occupation. I assist souls in finding a place in the Under-realm. There is a place for rewards and for punishment and then there is the rest. I could show you if you like?"

Thanatos held his hand out to her, palm up and she pulled hers away against her chest, as if he had bitten her.

"No!" she said, louder than she meant to, and there was a small amount of hurt in his eyes. "I... I am not ready to see," She admitted honestly.

Truthfully, she was still holding onto the idea that hell was below her; ruled by Satan who was evil, and heaven was above; ruled by a benevolent God. Things appeared much more complicated than that and she wasn't yet sure if she wanted to start seeing Thanatos as being capable of feelings... capable of love.

Already she was finding it difficult. For the moment, she was content with pretending that the evenings they had spent together were a way to pass the time and perhaps get to know one another as friends.

His fingers folded back into his palm and he lowered his arm and looked back out of the window.

The dark blue of the approaching night hovered over the red of the sunset, reminding Bronwen of his eyes.

"I did not know you were able to change the way you look," Bronwen commented.

"I can appear as anything I choose as long as it is a living thing."

"Even an animal?"

"Yes, but it is not a painless process to change one's energy so dramatically."

"Is it possible for me to?"

"Not while you still live. At least, not without my help."

It would be nice to have that ability. She wouldn't have to concern herself with the people hunting her. She could even make herself into something large and dangerous, like a lion. She indulged in imagining it, having strong muscles to pounce, and claws that could rip out a man's throat. Then she scolded herself for thinking such a cruel thought. The price for such a thing would be too high in any case. His gifts always came at a price and the darker the gift, the darker the price.

"Are you... dead as well?" Bronwen asked. She had assumed that he had been born the way he was, but he had mentioned the night they saved Azu that he had once been human and this intrigued her.

"I am very much alive. Far more alive than anyone, in fact. But I am not human. I do not occupy a human body and no longer need one."

"And," Bronwen turned to look at him in the fading light and he turned his body towards hers. "Is this what you truly looked like? When you were human?"

A pained expression crossed his face and he turned away to the window again. "No. It is not."

Bronwen did not press him further. It was clear by his frown that it was not a subject that he favoured. Interesting, that he of all people could let vanity concern him. He was far more human than he made out.

Bronwen did something then that surprised even herself. She placed a gentle hand on his arm and stepped onto her toes to kiss him lightly on the cheek, then moved away shyly. Thanatos looked just as shocked as she did, and stopped his hand halfway to his cheek as he turned to stare at her.

"Please, take that to mean my gratitude only. For saving Azu. I have not properly thanked you for it," she said when he didn't speak, feeling the need to justify her action.

"For one man? I wonder how many I need to save to get what I really wish from you," Thanatos said softly.

Bronwen shook her head and smiled. "I doubt even you could rewrite all the wrongs of the world."

"I would turn the very world upside down."

Bronwen's lips parted as he gazed at her intensely, trying to show her that he meant every word of it. Yet, she couldn't understand why he would feel that way when they had not known each other that long. She could not understand why she was starting to feel things she was desperately trying to ignore.

"I should be getting back to my carriage," Bronwen said after a long while. "We will be arriving soon."

She walked away and slid the compartment door open when a hand fell over hers.

"Wait," Thanatos said softly. Bronwen looked up into his eyes. His profound, blue, human eyes.

Was he going to kiss her? Did she want him to?

"Do not forget your ticket," Thanatos finished, producing the intact piece of paper. She took it from him and he let go of her other hand as he stepped backwards into the shadow of the room and disappeared.

VII

The All-Hallowmas ball arrived quickly. Bronwen had had little time for anything else in the week leading up to it, organising decorations to be put up, food to be prepared, games set up, music arranged and the huge bonfire built ready in the field outside Metrom Hall.

Josette and Azu were invaluable in helping her with it all. Rushing around to Bronwen's orders. Josette had even mocked that being a General suited her.

Donovan had been expectedly furious at Bronwen's new bodyguard but unexpectedly, not because Azu was black.

"I will not have someone in my home whom I cannot trust. You don't know anything about this man," Donovan had raved at Bronwen.

"I know him very well father, and Lord Guild has approved him."

"Has he indeed."

"Please, give Azu a chance and if he does not prove himself honourable, then I will dismiss him myself." Bronwen had almost fainted when her father had agreed that Azu could stay. He was always in an unusual mood around All-Hallowmas. It reminded him of her mother and Bronwen had spotted him shed a tear on many a year previous when the bonfire was lit.

She wondered if she would see him do so again and once more wished for her courage to be with her, so she might embrace him and share in his grief. It was something she planned every year, and every year, her fear of his rejection had prevented her from doing so. More than ever before, Bronwen needed her father this night.

She thought about that deeply, sitting patiently on her stool, as Alda and the other maids flitted about her bedroom, deciding how she should wear her hair, what jewellery would best match her outfit and what embellishments should be applied to her face.

Her dress had arrived from the seamstress in Guildford one day ago, as well as the rest of Azu's clothing and Bronwen was delighted with the results. The fabric and the colours were rich and elegant. Alda, of course did not approve and she tried to convince Bronwen to wear something else, right up until the moment she was being laced into it.

After admiring herself in the full-length mirror of her bedroom, pleased that the bruising on her neck had completely disappeared in time for the ball, and ignoring a disapproving sigh from Alda at the inappropriateness of colour and style, Bronwen was ready for the final touch of the outfit - her wings.

Azubuike had presented them to Bronwen that morning and she and Josette had gasped at the beauty of them. Each feather had been lovingly stitched to the fabric frame of the cream wing and the maroon one was made of stiff fabric stretched over the black bones of the limb. It had a few black feathers stuck haphazardly to it as if the wing had wilted away with the autumn.

Even Alda did not make a negative comment as she helped Bronwen into them and they marvelled at how well balanced and comfortable Azu had made them, with what little material he had requested for the project. He truly was an artist of great skill.

Bronwen was surprised that Thanatos was still nowhere to be seen. A ball seemed the perfect setting for his usual irreverence. She had not seen him for an entire week, not since the train and the longer Thanatos was absent, the more Bronwen thought about him. It was infuriating to her that her mind was allowed to wander.

Bronwen left her room and found Azu waiting for her in the hallway outside. She knew Josette would not be ready for another hour yet.

"Azu!" Bronwen exclaimed. "You look dashing."

He was wearing a full suit for the evening, one that Bronwen had had specially made for him. His long waistcoat made him look even taller and he pulled at his blue necktie uncomfortably.

"Thank you," he replied, then admired his handiwork. The wings only came down to Bronwen's waist so they were not too heavy to wear and did not stick out very far, like they were folded in on her back.

"You will be easy to find," Azu said, a small smile on his lips.

"Thanks to you, Azubuike."

Azu nervously laid a gentle hand on Bronwen's arm, as if not certain the contact was allowed.

"You are the most dashing, Malaika," he said, kindness and fondness in his eyes.

"Mala - ee - kah?" Bronwen sounded out. Azu smiled at her without explaining its meaning. She hoped it was a good thing.

They had quickly grown closer than a professional relationship. Bronwen now considered Azu a friend as dear to her as Josette.

He still spoke very little, but Bronwen had realised that was just part of his stern countenance and actually Azu could speak perfect English, when he wanted to, apart from the occasional grammatical error or mispronunciation.

Azu could read better than he could speak and not only in English, he also read in Greek, Spanish and even Latin. Bronwen had given him run of the library and he spent more time in there than she did. He had other surprising skills as well. Azu's few drawings he had done were incredible, so lifelike and intricate and he had a clear eye for artistry.

On discovering this, Bronwen had endeavored not to generalize what she knew about her friend and protector. The only skill she didn't know about, was his fighting abilities. Azu did not seem to favor weapons like Adam. Bronwen wondered if she should give him money to acquire some, since he had not asked and Mr Fane had been most put out to find that Azu had used one of the silver cheese knives to kill the doe in Guildford.

Azu had not told Bronwen of his past yet, and she had not told him hers either, which suited the both of them. There would no doubt be a time when it was necessary to share their stories, but not knowing hadn't affected the bond between them.

Bronwen descended the stairs with Azu and entered the dining room, which had been filled with food to accommodate the many guests invited. The décor was minimal in this room, the intention being that the food was the decoration. Each dish had been fashioned beautifully by the kitchen staff, from roasted nuts dripping in syrup, to carved pumpkins filled with red fruit and all were covered in cobwebs made of pulled wool and yarn.

Lord Wintre lifted his head from staring into the fire as Bronwen entered. He pulled his usual disapproving expression at Azu's presence and started when he noticed Bronwen's wings. He recovered himself with a cough before speaking.

"There are distinguished guests attending tonight,"

Donovan said, looking her up and down with a stern line to his mouth. "Go change into something more appropriate."

"It is All-Hallowmas, father. It is my intention to turn a few heads in my direction," Bronwen asserted herself. She would not be discouraged by her father's disapproval.

Donovan was wearing a plain dinner suit with no decoration. The Baron did not normally dress too lavishly for the occasion; his mask was always the most elaborate thing and usually the most horrific looking. It had previously been a challenge of the invited guests to outdo Donovan's horror masks and every year they had failed. With Bronwen's proposed change in theme to have no masks, he just looked dressed for dinner.

"That beast that follows you will turn heads enough," Donovan growled and for a moment Bronwen thought he meant Thanatos, before she remembered how others saw Azu.

"Do not speak about Azu in such a manner," Bronwen snapped, before she could stop herself, but he had made her angry. She did not care how her father treated her, but she would not tolerate him dishonouring the man who had sworn to protect her.

Azu had carefully blended himself into the background. Something he was even better at than Adam.

"I will do as I damn well please and you should be grateful I allowed him in this house to begin with!" Her father was yelling now and slammed his empty drink down on the fire surround. Bronwen was momentarily worried he might strike her, as he once had when she was little.

"You will soon be my problem no longer," He finished, a little calmer.

"I never have been your problem, father," Bronwen added solemnly.

Donovan looked up and met her eyes in a rare moment. Bronwen could count on one hand the times she had felt any form of connection to her father, however small, and this one significant look would be added to the tally.

Lord Wintre opened his mouth to say something when the door was slowly opened and James stood in the doorway. He sent a wary glance between the two of them before speaking.

"Lord Guild has arrived, Milord."

Donovan nodded and their moment was broken, Bronwen feeling the familiar loss, like when a sentence is left half said.

They both made their way out to the hallway to greet Lord Guild, who was in his best black suit with a cream coloured waistcoat, including a dark red cape across one shoulder that hid his arm. He raised an appreciative eyebrow at what Bronwen was wearing.

"It appears we have come matching, Lady Bronwen. How appropriate," Kole said with a half-smile.

"My father thinks the design is inappropriate," Bronwen said lightly as Donovan stood beside them, feeling braver with more people around.

"Surely not. On the night we should remember the dead?" Kole said as he shook Lord Wintre's hand firmly. "It seems very appropriate indeed."

Bronwen saw her father grimace as the first guests began to arrive.

Bronwen could see them through the little window next to the door. As expected, everyone was out to show themselves off, all dressed in their finery, most of the women wearing so much jewellery it was a wonder they made it up the stairs and through the door at all. The men, meanwhile, seemed more concerned by how fine their carriages and well-groomed their horses were compared to other guests. Bronwen was pleased to see no sign of a mask but heavy makeup and elaborate attire instead.

Each one of the guests greeted the three hosts, bowing and

shaking hands with them in turn. Bronwen shuddered when one man came dressed completely in a black cloak and was pleased when he removed it to reveal a brown suit covered in orange and yellow fabric leaves. Every one of the guests complimented Bronwen's wings that moved so fluidly with her that they appeared to truly be part of body.

Finally, Bronwen greeted the people she was really waiting for, the publishers who had replied to her letter. They were a pair of men who owned a small and fairly new company in London. They had been the only ones able to attend on short notice. Being new to the south of England - both coming from Durham and moving to London only a year ago - they were keen to make some powerful friends.

Bronwen was quick to greet them, once she heard them introduce themselves to James at the door.

"Mr Patel, Mr Lawnem," Bronwen said, taking their hands in turn as she stepped towards them. "I am so pleased you could attend. I am Lady Bronwen and this is the Earl of Surrey, Lord Guild, my fiancé and Baron Wintre, my father."

They shook hands with each other, though Kole and her father were stiff and suspicious.

"Please, make yourself comfortable and I hope to be able to talk with you soon," Bronwen said, hurrying the men inside the ball room before either could ask about Josette and reveal who they were. They thanked her again with large friendly smiles and entered the room.

Bronwen resumed her position next to Kole.

"Who are they?" He asked in an accusing voice. Bronwen opened her mouth to make a quick excuse when she was thankfully saved by Josette coming down the stairs.

Josette pushed ahead of another group of guests and stood in front of Bronwen, who was pleased to see she was looking very presentable in a pastel green dress. The pointed green hat Josette wore, decorated with spiders and gold stars, was surprisingly modest.

"You made an effort," Bronwen teased Josette as they gave each other a brief hug.

"*I* am not the one ready to fly away," Josette winked at Bronwen before being shunted along by the never-ending train of guests behind her. "See you in three hours," Josette whispered as she entered the ballroom.

It certainly felt like three hours by the time the final guests arrived and Lord Guild took Bronwen's arm as they were announced into the ballroom together, as the future Earl and Countess of Surrey.

Bronwen hid a cringe at the title as everyone clapped and cheered their hosts. The music became louder and Bronwen and Kole began the dancing. She hated all the eyes on her, it made her feel self-conscious, especially the way Kole held her pressed flush against his body, possessive and inappropriate in front of so many people.

Bronwen's attempts to pull back from him were met with a tightening of his grip on her waist, so she could not do so, without making it obvious to everyone that she did not feel comfortable with the proximity of her future husband.

Instead, she kept her eyes averted and concentrated on her feet to keep the blood from rushing to her cheeks.

Thankfully, she was only made to suffer one dance before Kole released her to the masses, to socialise with too many people for Bronwen to remember in one evening. She was pulled into joining all the many parlour games that had been set up around the ballroom and was pleased she was only made to observe most of them.

Finally, Bronwen made it to Josette and was relieved to see her friend was flourishing in the environment, socialising with everyone she came across and quickly becoming very popular. Bronwen envied how easy she made it look.

"Josette," Bronwen grinned and gave her a warm hug.

"Countess," Josette mocked, equally pleased to see

Bronwen and laughing at her friend's scowl. "Come for some civilised company, have you?"

"It is greatly appreciated. And, I have a surprise for you." Bronwen led Josette over to two men laughing in a small group happily. Bronwen was thankful they seemed nice on first impression and were clearly having a good time, with full mugs of ale in their hands.

"Mr Patel, Mr Lawnem, this is Miss Josette Emry, the author I wrote to you about," Bronwen said in a break in conversation. The rest of their group dispersed, leaving the four of them to talk.

"Miss Emry," They said in unison, smiling at her and Josette's eyes widened.

"Patel and Lawnem? From PaL's publishers?" Josette said, a hint of wonder in her voice.

"You have heard of us?" Mr Patel said, with a smile of gratitude.

"Of course. You have published some of my favourite books; 'Little life giveth', 'The trees of Eden's garden', 'The iron mirror.'"

"That last one I can vainly lay claim to," Mr Lawnem said with a grin.

"Yes, of course it was," Josette stumbled. "Forgive me."

"There is nothing to forgive for inflating a man's ego, but we are interested in your book ma'am. Lady Bronwen has teased us with it. We have been given the basic plot and I must say we are intrigued. Have you put it forward for publishing before?"

Bronwen subtly slid away and left them to talk, feeling pleased with herself. She hoped it would work out for Josette, her novel was easily good enough and if Bronwen could use her undeserved higher class to help a friend, then she would.

She walked over to the table at the far end of the hall and picked up a glass of wine, for images sake.

"I am surprised your fiancé allowed you to wear such a risqué dress, my Lady," Thanatos said, appearing beside her with no warning, as was usual. He admired her wings with an expression full of pensive amusement.

"I did not give him a choice. And he would not have objected anyway."

"No, I imagine he would not have."

She looked at him and saw he was wearing formal attire and had a drink in his hand. His skin was not as pale as it usually was either. In fact, it was mildly tanned. She wondered why, but did not ask and hated herself for feeling so pleased to see him.

Thanatos looked very dashing, having changed from his usual loose trousers and half unbuttoned shirt. He looked positively regal in his dark blue suit, with a lighter blue sashed cape across his chest and one shoulder, similar to Kole's. He also wore gold bands on his forearms and a gold belt. The buckles on his black boots were gold too and he had the golden hilt of a dagger tucked into one. It did not look completely out of place in the room, but if it were possible to see him, he would have stood out.

Thanatos took a sip of his drink and casually scanned the room.

"How is it that you are able to drink here?" Bronwen asked him, jealous that he did not seem to gag at the taste of the wine like she did.

"Because I always get what I desire," He replied casually, looking down at her with amusement.

Bronwen scoffed but could not help the smile pull at her lips. There was something about his confident manner that made her feel at ease, which was part of the reason she had missed him.

Bronwen looked away, noticing a few people had turned to watch her. Then she saw Kole gazing at her with expression of confusion. Bronwen ducked her head into her chin and tried not to make her lips move as she spoke.

"I must look mad, talking to myself."

"Only because it is rude not to make eye contact while you do."

"What do you mean?"

Thanatos didn't get a chance to answer as Lord Guild strode up to them purposefully.

"Sir, I do not believe we have met?" Bronwen blanched and almost spilt her drink.

Had Kole really just addressed the man beside her as if he were a real person?

Thanatos laughed humourlessly. "You should be careful what you believe."

Lord Guild held his hand out in greeting, which was met by a solid and very real one. Bronwen almost let go of her drink, blinking furiously as if it would change what she was seeing.

Kole was shaking hands with the Devil.

VIII

Bronwen's eyes widened as she watched the men and saw Kole grimace at the strength in Thanatos's grip. He was real. He was here. Everyone could see him.

"Indeed." Kole tried to let go of Thanatos's hand, to no avail and pulled himself free with visible force. "Lady Bronwen, are you going to introduce us?" He said testily, flexing his fingers out of sight of the mysterious man.

Bronwen closed her hanging mouth and was stuck for what to say. "Uh, well this is... uh, he..."

"Very well," Kole interrupted Bronwen's stumbling. "Please, allow me to introduce myself, as something seems to have struck my Lady." Kole looked pointedly at Bronwen and she cowered below his gaze before he turned it to the very real man by her side.

"I am Lord Guild - the Earl of Surrey and Lady Bronwen's betrothed."

"Lady Bronwen's betrothed *and* Earl to the whole of Surrey? Well, you are a man of wealth and taste indeed." Thanatos grinned, his tone sarcastic, and it did not escape Lord Guild's notice. His eyes barely hid an angry scowl, that Bronwen had quickly learnt meant danger and the corner of his eye twitched.

Thanatos took no notice and sipped his wine. He had a

tinge to his voice - a mild accent that only showed itself when he spoke lengthy sentences.

"Yes, Lady Bronwen has been fortunate to secure such a bond," Kole said in irritation.

"Strange, she failed to mention it." Thanatos smiled a secret smile and Bronwen found herself obscurely grateful for him mocking Lord Guild, though she was uncertain as to why and she could not help worrying about the consequences. If she did not step in soon, there would be a brawl right there and then.

However, Bronwen still could not speak, she was reeling from knowing Lord Guild could see Thanatos. As could everyone else for that matter, judging by the curious glances they were receiving.

"And you are, sir?" Kole drew himself up to height, but was no match for the man whose dominating presence had turned more than a few heads, especially from the women of the room, who fanned their faces furiously and no doubt whispered about his handsomeness.

"I am sorely needed on the dance floor, if you would excuse us." Thanatos took Bronwen's drink and placed it down on the table, then gripped her gently by the elbow and led her to the dance floor. He twirled her around to face him with finesse and held her tightly to him as they blended with the other dancers.

Still in a daze, Bronwen had allowed him to lead her away and only now came back to herself.

"What was that? You can be seen now?" Bronwen accused, looking over her shoulder to see if people were perplexed that she was dancing with an invisible partner, but the looks they gave her were ones of intense curiosity.

"If I so choose," Thanatos grinned, with obvious delight.

As they changed position with ease, Bronwen saw Kole walk up to her father and discuss her dancing partner in hushed tones.

"What will Lord Guild think?" Bronwen worried aloud.

"What do you care?" Thanatos replied bitterly, swinging her roughly so she could no longer see Kole and her father.

"You are jealous?" she exclaimed, scolding herself for feeling pleased by the idea.

Thanatos frowned. "What is there to be jealous of? I could cart him off to the Under-realm with barely a blink if I wanted to."

He sounded like a spoilt child and Bronwen couldn't help tease him further for it.

"I have no doubt, but you are not jealous of any power he may have, you are jealous that he won my affection."

Thanatos looked momentarily irritated then regained control and smiled down at her.

"For now."

Thanatos held Bronwen at a respectful distance from his body and executed every move with ease, so much so that, all she had to do was follow his lead and not have to think about where she was putting herself.

Bronwen's face reddened at all the staring eyes around her, all intrigued as to whom her partner was, who was not her betrothed. This man was beyond a doubt the most finely dressed of anyone and easily one of the finest looking, with his tanned skin and dark hair and eyes. Thanatos had obviously changed his appearance to make himself look more human and it had somehow had the opposite effect.

Bronwen caught Azu watching her from one corner of the room, just as intrigued as the other guests. Then, Bronwen caught Adam's eye, stood on the other side of the hall. He was tense and had one thumb hooked in the pocket of his long jacket, having not made any effort to change for the occasion.

"Why have you revealed yourself?" Bronwen asked Thanatos in a hushed tone.

"You asked me to," he replied, unperturbed by the

attention they were receiving.

"I did no such thing."

"Not in so many words, but you expressed an opinion that Lord Guild is a real gentleman, and I am not one."

"And you thought I meant I wanted you to be real also? A gentleman?"

Thanatos acted offended. "I have always been real, my Lady, it was you who chose to deny it. But I thought I would show you that I too can be a gentleman, if you so desire."

"And you begin by offending the host?"

"The Earl of Surrey, you mean?" Thanatos somehow made the title sound humorous. "That was just for my amusement. And I think your affections for the Earl have been too long uncontested."

"Uncontested?"

"Yes. You see, I have not gone to all this effort for one night of frivolous fun, despite it being my nature. I have revealed myself so that I may court you openly, Lady Bronwen, as a gentleman would."

Bronwen's eyes widened and she stopped dancing. "You are going to court me? Now?"

"When better than the night of All-Hallows, when the souls of the dead gather in the shadows." He grinned at his impromptu rhyme, not letting go of Bronwen.

"This is my life. You cannot invade it like this," she said, exasperated and alarmed that he wanted to court her. *Him.*

"I believe it is *my* life. To invade as I see fit."

Bronwen shook her head, knowing he was right and wanting to be away from him. "You change the rules too often, on this deal of ours."

"It is my game to play, Lady Bronwen."

She shook her head again and pushed herself back and out of his arms. "I will not be a willing pawn in it, for you to sacrifice to the knight." She turned her back on him and hurried away, head bowed and arms tight by her sides -

straight into the path of Lord Wintre.

"Father," Bronwen breathed in surprise.

"Baron Donovan," Thanatos said behind her, coming to stand beside Bronwen, saving her from facing the look Lord Wintre was giving them. "I apologise, I have not been able to introduce myself sooner. Your delightful daughter has captured my attention since I arrived. My name is Thomas Nasta, I am visiting from London and a friend invited me along to this fine ball."

Bronwen inwardly cringed at his last name - an anagram of Satan. She knew he meant for her to figure it out and was no doubt amused with himself for it.

"And is there a title to accompany your name?" Donovan asked icily, clearly, he did not appreciate the arrival of this new guest.

Thanatos leant in towards him conspiratorially. "Prince, milord. Prince Thomas, of the Hellenes."

Donovan's eyes widened as much as Bronwen's did.

"The new royals of Greece?" Donovan asked, stunned.

"I had business with the Queen," Thanatos replied calmly, his faint accent Bronwen now knew to be Greek.

"Business with Britain's Queen?"

"Unless you have another?"

"Of course not, my apologies, your Grace." Bronwen had never seen her father so flustered. "We are honoured to have you here. I hope my daughter has been treating you well?"

Donovan did not look at Bronwen, but kept his wide eyes on Thanatos as he moved around the Baron and picked up two glasses of wine from the table. He handed one to Bronwen with a smile and she took it mutely, out of habit.

"Better than well, milord, I only wish I had met her sooner, before she was swept off her feet by the young Earl. I hope I have not offended Lord Guild by taking his fiancée away, and for not introducing myself. I was trying not to reveal who I was so soon. I now realise this was perhaps a foolish indulgence, but, as only second in line to the Grecian throne, I despise being called highness."

"Not foolish at all," Donovan said. "Lord Guild was just being protective of Lady Bronwen, as you can understand."

"Yes, I can understand that very well," Thanatos said, looking directly at Bronwen.

She swallowed hard and stared at the floor, pinching her leg absently, still holding the wine glass aloft.

"I must introduce you properly, if I may, I am sure Lord Guild would be delighted to make your acquaintance."

"I am sure he would," Thanatos said slyly. "But it would not be *gentlemanly* of me to leave a Lady alone."

Bronwen looked up again to see Thanatos staring at her and she couldn't help staring back.

"My daughter is hardly alone, your grace, in a ballroom full of people," Donovan said, but Thanatos ignored him, still captivating Bronwen with his eyes. She felt hers watering and glanced at her father before stepping away.

"Excuse me, please," Bronwen said and unceremoniously removed herself from the two men. Thanatos watched her go and only turned back to Donovan when the Baron began asking him about the politics that had brought a Grecian Prince to England.

Bronwen wasn't watching where she was going and looked up when a hand grabbed her arm. She was only half aware she had stopped moving when Kole pulled her close to him, almost roughly.

"Who is that man?" He demanded.

Bronwen looked around in a daze to see her father laughing heartily with Thanatos.

"That, would be Prince Thomas Nasta of the Hellenes," Bronwen replied and continued walking to the door of the ballroom and out into the hallway, then through another room and finally out into the gardens of Metrom Hall, ignoring the guests still enjoying the ball.

A couple were giggling and hushing one another behind a tree somewhere. Bronwen made sure to walk in the opposite direction, her shoes clicking on the cobbles of the pathways through the house gardens.

Eventually, in an area where light from the house had almost faded to nothing, Bronwen came to a bench under a canopy of dying leaves and collapsed into it.

The music and guests were a distant sound and the voices of the outdoors began to compete for her attention. The bench was cold and the unlit bonfire loomed in the distance. Her life had turned into an opera, without the uplifting aria or the peace of knowing it had some sort of catharsis.

Bronwen stared into the glass of wine she was still gripping tightly in her hand. She wanted to drink it, to let it make her numb, and she didn't care what it tasted like. She lifted the glass to her lips with the intention of gulping it all in one.

"Put that down this instance, young Lady!" Alda's voice startled Bronwen so much, she almost dropped the glass.

Alda swiftly took it out of her hands and sat down next to Bronwen, whilst pouring the liquid out onto the floor. For some reason, Bronwen's first assumption was that it must have been poisoned. Why would Alda think it was poison?

"If you wanted to be rid of it, there are easier and surer ways," Alda said quietly, putting the glass on the ground.

"Be rid of what?" Bronwen asked, thoroughly bewildered.

"There is no need to lie to me, domina domus. I have known you all your life, did you think I wouldn't notice your lack of appetite, your restless sleep and change of mood. And with no indication to prove me wrong in my reasoning."

Bronwen almost ran from Alda. The woman had somehow figured out that Bronwen was dead and the man inside claiming to be a prince, was in fact ruler of the Under-realm, not Greece. Then sensibility shook her from her panic and she considered each thing Alda had said.

She thought Bronwen was pregnant!

"Oh, Alda no, you are mistaken, I am not..."

"I told you there is no need to lie to me. I know the signs and I have been through it. All I need to know is, do you want to keep it? Then, we can begin to make plans."

Bronwen thought carefully about what she said next. It was true that her recent actions fit the condition and if she denied it, she would have to explain what the real reasons for them were. Apparently, she hadn't gotten away with hiding them like she had hoped. But, if Bronwen claimed she was pregnant, then what would happen? The lack of a baby would obviously be a problem, but maybe she could say later that she lost it.

"What sort of plans?" Bronwen asked, stalling for time while she thought about what to do.

"If you want to keep the baby, then we need to hide the pregnancy until you are married, and that needs to happen as soon as possible. But if you want to... unburden yourself, there are ways to do it."

"Like a doctor?"

"No, not if you are early enough. You can simply take a medicine, which works most of the time. It will make you sick for a week or so, but we can easily hide the reason for it."

That was it, the perfect excuse. Bronwen would simply take this medicine of Alda's and she would be none the wiser about whether a child existed in the first place.

"You would help me with this Alda? Get rid of the baby?"

Alda nodded thoughtfully. "It is not Lord Guild's then."

"Why would you assume such a thing?" Bronwen replied, a little offended by the nonchalant way Alda had presumed she had been frivolous, not just with her virginity, but with her faithfulness.

Bronwen desperately forced thoughts of Thanatos from her betraying mind.

"I apologise, but after what happened in Mr Clare's shop and after your disappearance, well, I thought that he might have... forced himself upon you."

"No, Alda, nothing like that."

"I believe you. Kole does not know about the child then. It is for the best. Your reasons are your own and of course, I will help you. After all, it is my lapse in vigilance that put you in this position."

"Please do not think that, this is my fault alone."

"You cannot be wholly to blame, innocent as you are. It should have been obvious to me that after all the torment you have suffered recently, you would want to seek the comfort of your fiancé. *He* should have known better than to have taken advantage. We will say no more on the subject. Leave it to me."

Alda stood up and Bronwen followed.

"Thank you, Alda," she said and gave her a hug, touched that Alda would do this for her, and be so kind about it, considering her opinions on immoral women.

"Nonsense," Alda said, brushing off Bronwen's gratitude. "I must begrudgingly admit, you have been engaged for the longest time. Not many would have expected you to act otherwise. I suppose there is no need for me to explain things to you now, about your wedding night. I had planned to tell you the eve of the wedding, if you wished to know."

"I appreciate it," Bronwen said, slightly regretting the lie, as she would desperately have liked to have asked a woman about these things. She had shrunk from asking Alda before, but sexual relations had been an unavoidable subject since Thanatos and a time would come when she wanted to know more.

Josette was her only female advice on such matters now.

Bronwen made a mental note to attempt the subject when they were next alone. It might embarrass her immensely, but there were things she needed to know.

"When did you first begin to suspect?" Bronwen asked, curious.

"It was when the certain tell-tale sign failed to appear and then I began to notice the other symptoms, and you and Lord Guild have been getting closer and closer. Oh, domina domus, do not look so terrified, all will be well, and it is between you and I." Alda patted her on the hand and left Bronwen alone.

Lady Bronwen fell back onto the bench. The look of horror Alda had seen on her face was not because of a baby that was not there, but because Alda had made her realise that she had not had her monthly cycle.

Bronwen had been due just under three weeks ago, but nothing. She knew she had not had sex and tried to rationalise it. It made sense that, as she did not need to eat and drink, she did not need to reproduce, but a small part of Bronwen whispered doubts about how a force other than nature could have made her pregnant.

A force that had the power to change the way it looked, travelled to places in seconds, took life like it didn't matter. Was it possible it could give life where it did?

Was it possible Thanatos had made her pregnant?

Bronwen pushed herself from the bench and almost ran back to the house to find the demon and confront him, but when she made it to the ballroom, she found him surrounded by people, all laughing and fawning over him. He looked every bit the popular aristocrat - charismatic, confident and charming. And, breathtakingly handsome.

Thanatos looked up, as if sensing her presence and met her eye. Her breath caught in her throat and he smiled like a satisfied cat. Then, she fled from the room again, deciding instead to be alone.

Bronwen opened the door to the servants' entrance, knowing no one would find her down there and sat on the stairs in the quiet dimness. The night was not going how she had hoped.

She had just been getting back to some semblance of a normal life. She had friends again and hosted parties and she could pretend that the nights she spent with Thanatos were nothing but a dream. Yet here he was, reminding her of the stark reality of her situation.

It was not long before a figure opened the door and almost fell over Bronwen.

The mass of fabric began to giggle as she apologised and Bronwen knew it was Josette and felt her heart lighten just a little.

"Bron, what are you doing here in the dark?" Josette's words slurred and she giggled again as she slid onto the stairs to sit beside her friend. Bronwen had to grab her to stop Josette tumbling all the way down and couldn't stifle her own laugh.

"Don't you know there are goats about tonight?" Josette scolded her.

"I think you mean ghosts, Josette," Bronwen corrected with a laugh.

"No, I mean goats," Josette said seriously, nudging Bronwen playfully. "A very grabby one with horns, have you not seen him? I think he arrived with the other witch. Witch - *which*, is why I don't think it good to be alone."

"Then why are *you* down here?" Bronwen countered, nudging her back.

"Because I am a witch too, of course!" Josette put a hand on her head and patted it, then looked around her. "Where have I put my hat?"

Bronwen laughed and it felt good. The heaviness she had been feeling since seeing Thanatos was almost all gone. Josette had distracted her and she always knew how to make

Bronwen laugh through the darkest of times. Josette very rarely took life too seriously and had a way of bouncing back that Bronwen envied and admired.

"Oh, yes, I remember now, I gave it to Mr Lawnem, who promised to keep it for me until I returned with the manuscript."

"Josette! They want your novel!" Bronwen exclaimed, finding yet another reason to shake her melancholy.

"They want to read it. Of course, why should they not want it, I am, after all, a writer of great talent." Josette's flushed face turned serious again, but her pout made it funnier, then she grinned and leant in close to loudly whisper the next part. "Or so Mr Lawnem says, and my intuition tells me that he is a man of great talent too." Josette winked and Bronwen's sides hurt from laughing so much.

"Then, what are you doing here, Josette! Get back to the talented Mr Lawnem and retrieve your hat."

"Right!" Josette said and lifted herself unsteadily from the stairs, using the banister and Bronwen's head for support. "But first, to my manuscript!" She started down the stairs and Bronwen quickly grabbed her arm and helped her before she hurt herself.

At the bottom, she let Josette lead the way into the servants' quarters of the house.

"Where are we going?" Bronwen asked.

"Azuboo has my manuscript. He was reading it."

Bronwen shook her head at the ridiculous name and pulled Josette in the other direction. She had made sure Azu was given a nice room with its own bathroom. The house was just as well designed in the lowest floor as it was above, only lacking all the furnishings. Bronwen very rarely came down here, but knew where Azu's room was from when she had gone to see if he was settling in.

"We should not be going into Azu's room without him,

Josette," Bronwen said as they reached the door, feeling like she was invading his personal space, then she rolled her eyes as Josette dangled Azu's room key in front of her. Bronwen took it, doubting Josette would be able to locate the lock in her condition.

"I hope you did not steal this key."

"Never." Josette placed a hand over her heart in mock offence. "To think I would need a key to break into somewhere. I am insulted you would think so, Brony," she said with a sly grin as she entered the room.

Once inside, Bronwen thought it wise to light a candle and the small room filled with its soft glow. Josette looked about her in momentary confusion at the sudden brightness, then shrugged and located her manuscript on Azu's small desk.

Bronwen couldn't help looking at the room. Azu had pushed his neatly made bed against the far wall under the small window, a wooden chest at the foot of his bed. There was not much of a view, but Bronwen knew it faced the sun when it rose. The walls were bare of decoration and it made Bronwen sad to realise that Azu truly had nothing, when she had everything - even a second life. Perhaps she should start being grateful for it.

Josette gasped at something on the desk and Bronwen rushed over, suddenly worried something had happened to the manuscript. Then she inhaled with her friend when she saw the images there. On the few blank pages, that had been tucked in with Josette's book, were beautiful drawings in charcoal.

Two of them Bronwen recognised clearly as scenes from Josette's book. The part when her main character gave his son a compass to guide him and when he said goodbye to his wife in a vison.

The feelings had been captured perfectly, but it was the third picture that truly made her gasp. It was of a young and beautiful woman, looking directly out at the viewer. She had a small, sad smile and her hair was stuck to her face in places. It was clear that the woman was Bronwen, especially as she realised that this was how Azu had seen her when she had saved him. It made the hint of wings behind her back more profound.

"Wow," Was all Josette could say.

Bronwen nodded and placed the paper down reverently. This must have been why he had suggested the wings for her costume. She was not sure how she felt about being seen as an angel, but she was awed by Azu's talent. If he could achieve this with charcoal and scrap paper alone, what could he do with a canvas and painters' equipment?

"Come on, Josette," Bronwen said, pulling her friend out of the room and locking it securely behind them, being sure to blow out the candle.

Bronwen went with Josette to give the publishers her book, worried she would fall at their feet or drop the folder. She had little to worry about, as the two men seemed just as drunk as Josette. Mr Lawnem even held her hat out of reach, making Josette jump for it with flailing arms.

Smiling at the happy energy of the festivities, Bronwen found Azu and returned his key. He looked slightly worried at the idea of Bronwen being in his room and seeing his drawing, so she smiled at him and placed a grateful hand on his arm.

"Malaika?" Bronwen asked and Azu nodded. She tried not to cringe at realising now that it meant angel. Azu didn't know how wrong he was but it made him smile back at her and their bond strengthened even more.

They walked outside together when James announced the bonfire was ready and watched in silence as everyone gathered around the pile of logs and one large circle of people lit the candles from their invitations in an illuminating loop, then all stepped forwards together and lit the bottom of the pyre with differing success.

One side went up before the rest, but it didn't take long before the whole thing was alight, bathing the guests in warmth and radiance. Bronwen grinned at Josette as she joined her and Azu and they all looked to the sky as ash, glowing like fireflies, drifted upwards to join the stars.

Bronwen closed her eyes and sighed, sending a silent prayer to her mother, asking her to watch over her father.

When she looked again at the guests, watching them dance around the fire like sprites, it was Thanatos she sought and Thanatos she found. He was stood a small distance from her and was gazing at her, not the fire. His eyes blazed stronger than the flames and she felt her heart thump in her chest.

Then she found herself wondering what it would be like to kiss him. What it would be like to give into his dark life. His wants of her. What their children would look like...

Bronwen pinched her arm and forced herself to look away, a common rhyme coming unbidden into her mind.

{On All-Hallowmas night, when shadows dance in firelight, demons prowl the earth till day, to hunt themselves unwilling prey}

IX

Bronwen, Josette and Azu had spent the next day in quiet solitude while Josette recovered from the ball - with no regrets. Not even after Bronwen told her about how she had removed Mr Lawmen's tie and whipped him with it.

"At least he will remember me," Josette had said with a satisfied smirk.

Bronwen was just pleased her friend had had a good time, even Azu had enjoyed himself. He and James Durward - of all people - had gotten along very well and had spent most of the night talking to one another in hushed whispers.

Donovan seemed in higher spirits too. Bronwen had tried not to grimace when her father had told her to treat Prince Nasta well, should she see him again. The two had arranged a business deal during the party - a hefty commission of fabrics for the Prince's new home he was having built in England, as a gift from the Queen.

Thanatos had played his part all too well. Nothing won Donovan over like a business connection. No doubt the information about fabrics Bronwen had given him came in very handy.

It was a rare, dry day and Josette and Bronwen decided to show Azu around Winchester. They set out on horses and made light conversation as they toured the little streets and old architecture. They briefly went into the cathedral - which made Bronwen feel uncomfortable and walked along the river - which made Azu feel uncomfortable, then ate a light lunch in a quaint café.

Bronwen was surprised at how easy it became to ignore the glances and stares Azu was getting as they rode. It was not so rare for a dark-skinned person to be seen around the city, but one accompanying Lady Bronwen Wintre, who already had so many rumours surrounding her, was something that would be whispered about over tea.

Bronwen decided that it did not matter to her what others thought. She wondered why it ever matter to her at all and relished the freedom in not caring. It gave her a confidence that she had not experienced before and she realised with crushing disappointment that she never wanted her friends to leave and never wanted to leave them; knowing one day she would have to.

What would become of Azubuike when Bronwen returned to death? Would Josette take him in? She doubted Kole would allow that. And would Josette always be stuck being a privileged servant for Lord Guild? It worried her as they walked the horses through the city centre and took Bronwen a moment to realise that Josette had stopped next to a boarded-up shop. It was beside an alley and had a decorative arch bridging the gap, with a clock in the centre.

"What are you looking at?" Bronwen asked, as she manoeuvred her horse to stand beside Josette.

"How much do you think that house is?" Josette asked without looking away from the windows of the place above the shop that were so grubby, you could hardly see the sign that announced it as being for sale.

"I could not say. Why?"

"Just curious. I think it might be larger than it appears from the outside is all."

Bronwen considered the house again. She knew the property prices in Winchester were high, due to its boasting heritage - having once been the capital of England - and its flourishing trading market from the textile industry, which had been one of the reasons her father had settled there and helped it grow.

Soon afterwards, they began to head back to Metrom Hall, mounting their horses once away from the shops and traveling down the back streets laden with houses.

"Alda thinks that I am pregnant," Bronwen said as she rode between Josette and Azu. She had wanted to say something all day, no fully shaking off the thought that she indeed might be. The opportunity to ask Thanatos about it had not presented itself and she had no way of getting into contact with him. She could hardly address a letter to the Under-realm, whereas he could appear to her whenever he desired.

Bronwen expected her friends to ask her for the truth of Alda's theory, but instead, both of them laughed in unison.

"What?" Bronwen demanded.

"You are not pregnant, Bronwen," Josette said when she had finished laughing.

"You have not been with a man, Malaika," Azu said, using the endearment as a way to soften his words.

"And how, might I ask, would you know that?" Bronwen said indignantly, letting go of the reigns so she could place her hands on her hips. They slid away but she was not worried, still between the other two horses who kept hers in line.

"You are far too innocent," Josette said with a giggle. "And Kole is far too stern to have been between your legs."

Bronwen's offended cough was drowned out by Azu's renewed laughter. It was good to hear him laugh, serious as he usually was, but it did not feel good with it being at Bronwen's expense.

"I am not as innocent as you two believe me to be," Bronwen said, now crossing her arms.

"Really," Josette said with a wink. "Care to make a wager on that?"

Bronwen looked at her friend directly and stuck her chin out in challenge. Josette grinned.

"If my book becomes published, then you, Lady Bronwen Wintre, must come with Azu and I to any establishment I choose."

"That is hardly a difficult bargain, Josette. How does it prove your point?"

"Do you accept?" Josette insisted.

Bronwen studied her friend who smiled innocently. She could not fathom what Josette hoped to gain. Surely the most she could do was take Bronwen to a place that had a reputation for being dirty, and seeing as she never became ill, the cleanliness of such a place could do little harm to her.

"Fine. I accept," Bronwen said, squirming at the thought of being trapped into another deal, but it bothered her that Josette and Azu thought her so meek. Perhaps it was because she did not want them to think her feeble like everyone else did.

"Catherine!"

The shout startled the three of them and their horses unsettled. Azu and Josette quickly gained control of their mounts and Bronwen reached for her missing reigns, but was too late as a small shape ran in front of them and Bronwen's horse whinnied and rose slightly on its front legs.

Bronwen held on tightly to the horse's mane, hearing a frightened squeal. A second, larger figure darted past and grabbed the smaller one to move it out of the horse's way, but the beast was too disturbed without a rider to properly command it and bucked again.

Bronwen tried to soothe it with her voice, then felt a

strong arm grab her around the middle and pull her off the animal. Bronwen let go reluctantly and allowed the horse to bolt away as she was pulled against a solid body onto the front of another horse.

Bronwen looked up to see it had been Azu who had pulled her from the spooked beast. She thanked him breathlessly and he helped her slide to the floor, jumping off his horse as well to stand beside her.

"I am so sorry, are you alright? Oh, Lady Bronwen, oh my, we are so sorry. Please forgive us." A woman was saying, flustered at finding it had been a future Countess that had almost been thrown from her horse.

Bronwen vaguely remembered her from some distant meeting at church and when a man joined her, pulling a young girl roughly along beside him, Bronwen recognised the family as the Huddersfield's.

All three of them had pale brown hair and dark eyes. The girl, Catherine, had tears in her eyes and looked terrified.

"Lady Bronwen," The gentleman said in a gruff voice. "I cannot apologise enough for our daughter. She just ran from us before we could stop her."

"That is quite alright, no harm done," Bronwen said kindly, now that her heart had calmed down.

"But your horse, milady," Mrs Huddersfield said, panicked. Bronwen looked down the empty street and knew her horse was long gone. She had given Josette the calmest of the three, knowing her friend's clumsy reputation.

"Not to worry, it will find its way home and I will ride with Azu." Bronwen turned to her friends who had been patiently stood with their horses. "This is my friend Josette Emry and my friend and bodyguard, Azubuike."

The two stepped forwards as Bronwen introduced them.

"Bodyguard?" Mr Huddersfield blanched and seemed about to say something more when he remembered who he was talking to.

"And might I ask what Miss Catherine was running from?" Josette said sweetly when she noticed the girl was sobbing quietly. She smiled at Catherine who rubbed her tear-filled eyes and shook her head.

"She does not want to go to her piano lesson," Mrs Huddersfield explained. She was softer spoken than her husband.

"She must learn an instrument if she is to be an accomplished young woman," Mr Huddersfield directed at the girl, who tried to turn away.

"Well, I have never been very good at playing instruments," Josette said to the child, trying to coax her out. "And I consider myself very accomplished."

The girl rewarded Josette with a small smile and her hiccups stopped. Bronwen's heart ached seeing Josette with children and knowing she would never have any. She would have made such a lovely mother. Kind and intelligent and accepting of others. Her children would have been very lucky.

"Yes, well," Mr Huddersfield said testily. "We wish for Catherine to learn the piano. And I know that Lady Bronwen is a skilled player also, which is why we chose the same tutor for her."

Bronwen felt her whole body go cold. A queasiness began in her stomach and her smile faded.

"Mr Quays is her tutor?" Bronwen said, swallowing a hard lump in her throat.

"Yes," Mr Huddersfield said, though Bronwen already knew the answer, she could see it in the girl's eyes. "He is the best in the city, Catherine has leant very quickly in his study."

"I have no doubt she has," Bronwen said quietly. She barely felt Josette's hand on her arm.

"Yes, but she is a little out of practice lately, which is why I think she does not want to go today," Mrs Huddersfield said, smiling at her daughter indulgently. "We may have to reschedule for tomorrow morning."

"Really," Bronwen said through gritted teeth, her voice didn't sound like her own. "Is that the only reason?"

"Bron," Josette whispered beside her, pinching Bronwen's arm to get her friend back to the present, knowing it was how Bronwen coped. But the Lady had looked into the young girl's eyes and felt all the sorrow of her own childhood flood back. How she feared the people around her and was terrified of the life that the world had given her.

If Bronwen's higher born station could not protect even *her* from malevolent forces, what hope would someone else have? What hope did this innocent have?

Bronwen saw this fear and hopelessness in the girl and wondered if her eyes had looked the same all those years ago. She too had once hoped that someone with the power to end her suffering had understood, as she understood the plights of this small, blameless child.

"Do not send Catherine back to him, Mrs Huddersfield," Bronwen said, appealing to the kinder of the two parents. "He is not a suitable tutor."

"He was suitable enough for you, your ladyship," Mr Huddersfield snapped, clearly irritated by Bronwen's tone.

"I assure you, he was not," Bronwen said and pressed on, finding courage somewhere within herself. "Do you not wonder why the man does not take adult students? It cannot be that his stool is too narrow for two."

"Whatever do you mean?" Mr Huddersfield bristled and Josette finally let go of Bronwen's arm, sensing her friend needed to do this.

"And a man of his standing and age should surely have married long ago. Yet his affections are directed towards his young students, rather than the women that present themselves to him."

Mr Huddersfield shook his head in incomprehension. "A

man's inclinations towards marriage are no concern of mine."

"It is his *other* inclinations that should become of a concern!" Bronwen could not help raising her voice and Mr Huddersfield looked about him conscientiously, not wanting to draw attention to their talking, though the street was still empty.

Mrs Huddersfield hung on every word Bronwen uttered, however. The evidence of her understanding was seen by how she clutched Catherine to her side, as if the swift breathlessness of a crib death might strike her from the world at any moment.

Bronwen saw her chance to protect the girl and flung her will upon it.

"Have a care with your precious child," Bronwen said. She reached out a hand and held the woman's arm. Mrs Huddersfield's eyes widened. "Take note of her and you will see a change."

The woman looked down to see Catherine was crying silently and some small realisation crossed her features. This produced tears in the mother's eyes too, though the father was still blinded, from all but that Bronwen had been the cause of the sorrow in his two girls.

"Enough of this!" he snapped and pulled his wife away from Bronwen's kind hand. "Lady or not, you have spoken out of turn and your father will be hearing of it!"

"It is of little matter to me, as long as Catherine is taught by Kenneth Quays no longer." Bronwen stepped away, her voice lower again, now that she was sure at least one of the parents understood.

"Who are you to say how I choose to have my daughter taught?" The man was unrelenting, feeling as though some slight had been made against his integrity, but he did not yet comprehend how. "Mr Quays is a fine tutor and now that his hand is healed, he will be able to continue teaching

Catherine."

Bronwen's eyes widened. "What did you say?"

"I said that he will continue..."

"No, his hand! What happened to his hand!"

"I said he has been unable to teach due to his damaged hand. He hurt it in some accident a few weeks ago. Managed to fall on a branch of some kind while out riding. It went right through his palm, or so I have heard. But I do not see what that has to do with..."

Bronwen did not hear the rest as she began backing away, until she felt the body of a horse behind her. A rushing in her ears made her deaf to Azu's worried questioning and she was only barely aware that she had mounted the horse and pulled it around.

"Let her go, Azu," Josette said as Bronwen kicked her heels into the horse and galloped away as if her past was hounds nipping at her ankles and ravens ripping at her hair.

Kenneth Quays was one of her killers.

And why should she be surprised? The man who had ruined her childhood. Stolen it away from her. It made sense that he should steal her life also.

Bronwen remembered how the scissors had sunk into the flesh on the hand of one of her attackers, between bones and tendons. That hand that had touched her so long ago which she had buried with her other demons.

It was too much of a coincidence otherwise and something in her was certain of it. That grunt he had made when he let go had played in her mind too many times and she only now made the connection.

She was not sure where the horse was taking her. Was not sure if it were her who guided it. Finally, her mount began to slow and Bronwen found herself beside the river.

She dismounted and walked for a bit; wanting to rid herself of the excess adrenaline which had caused her to run from her friends.

It was quiet out. Most people walked the city streets where they could duck into a warm shop. Few people strolled along the banks so late in the day.

Bronwen bit her lip in an attempt to hold back tears and finally stopped and stumbled down the bank to a hidden fishing alcove at the water's edge, leaving her horse on the bank.

She knelt down and caught her reflection in the ripples as they distorted her expression. She looked so frail and wretched and pathetic. She tried not to splash the reflection away in anger and began to weep instead.

Her tutorage with Kenneth Quays had started as anyone would have expected. He was a kind teacher, always encouraging and softly spoken. The change in their lessons had begun so subtly that even Bronwen had taken a while to realise what was happening to her.

First, Kenneth would sit too close, then he would place his hand over hers to guide it at the piano, then he would have her sit on his knee so he could play along with her.

It was only ever touching. She knew some girls had it much worse and she had blocked out most of the details but seeing the broken soul behind Catherine's eyes had brought it all back. How he had praised her for doing well and stroked her hair, her arms, her legs...

Bronwen felt sick thinking about it. It was because of this early experience with Kenneth that Bronwen struggled trusting people and her body would go cold when they came too close or tried to touch her. It had taken her years to stop cringing every time Kole kissed her hand or stood close enough to brush arms with her.

It was especially confusing for her to realise that what she felt around Thanatos was different. He had made it clear to her from the beginning that he would do her no harm and that she was completely in control of their encounters, despite all his power. No other person had made such promises. At least, none which she believed.

"Malaika?"

Bronwen looked up to find a white handkerchief dangling from Azu's beautifully dark hand.

Bronwen took the cloth from him mutely and wiped away her tears.

"May I join?" Azu asked. Bronwen nodded and he settled down next to her silently, watching the sparrows dive down to the water, causing little ripples.

The canopy of a maple tree over their heads dipped its bare branches into the water; as if testing the temperature before dropping its orange leaves onto the surface.

Bronwen was glad for Azu's company and that he asked no questions and expected no explanations. Not all men were cruel, some were kind and did not expect things from a woman that she did not want to give.

"Where is Josette?" Bronwen asked.

"Went back. With the horse."

Josette knew about her past with Kenneth. Bronwen had told her friend on one of the rare occasions she had been drunk. The two had enjoyed far too much wine one evening in the absence of her father and Lord Guild. The story had come flooding out of Bronwen in a rush when she had refused to play piano for Josette.

Josette had been very serious when she offered to kill Kenneth for it. Bronwen now wished she had agreed, but she would not have risked Josette being caught. It was her burden to bear and her guilt to carry after finding out that Bronwen had not been a rare impulsion of Kenneth's. The man had committed these horrific crimes before and would again.

Unless Bronwen put an end to him.

"If you could prevent a bad person from doing bad things but you would have to do something equally bad or perhaps worse to stop them, would this be just as terrible a thing?"

Bronwen found herself asking.

Azu took his time in answering, considering how to phrase his response. "My opinion had no matter. If a kindness to a kind person needs a cruelty to a cruel person then the giver of the sentence must decide if it be correct. It is this person who will feel good or bad."

What he said made sense to Bronwen and in her heart she knew it was what she had already chosen to do years ago if she had the power to.

Still, there was something that held her back. She dug deep and found what it was.

"Do you think God would judge that person for it?" she asked Azu who was threading pieces of river reeds together.

Azu snorted. "People should do good things because they want to be good people, not to go to heaven."

He looked at Bronwen carefully. "And people who do bad things to good persons have no place here."

Bronwen nodded solemnly, understanding his meaning. She shivered, now cold from sitting on the floor so long.

Azu stood, helped her to her feet and threw his pleated reeds into the water. They watched them float downriver before finding Bronwen's horse and heading back.

Bronwen felt lighter as they rode but she still had a decision to face. She knew what sentence she would pass to Kenneth, but was she strong enough to pass it herself?

They found Josette near the entrance to Metrom's grounds. Her horse was grazing on a small patch of grass and she sat on a low wall, staring up at the bare branches and daydreaming.

Azu and Bronwen dismounted to join her.

"I am so sorry I left you," Bronwen began but Josette waved her off, standing up as well.

"Do not be silly, Bron."

"Have you waited out here all this time? You must have been freezing," Bronwen said.

"I thought it best to wait for you. I did not want people asking questions as to where you were and get you into trouble for leaving," Josette explained.

Bronwen smiled and they began to walk towards the house, keen to get inside where it was warm and comforting.

Josette walked alongside her while Azu fetched the other horse and caught up with them.

"Did you go to *his*?" Josette asked as delicately as she could, glancing at Azu.

"No, I did not. And it is alright, I do not mind if Azu knows," Bronwen said, smiling at him.

"You do not have to tell me anything, Malaika," Azu said, a stern line to his mouth. "I can know most of what happened."

Bronwen nodded and felt tears in her eyes, that she fought to keep inside. She had done enough crying.

"It was a very long time ago," she said.

"I will kill him," Azu stated, so matter of fact that Bronwen believed him.

"Not before I get to him first," Josette added, equally serious.

"No," Bronwen said. "I am not sure I want that and I cannot put either of you at risk. If you were caught, you would be put to death and I will not forgive myself. If I go, I must do it alone."

"You certainly will not go alone!" Josette snapped, sounding like a scolding mother.

"Josette, I..."

"No, Bronwen, you stopped me before from ending the sick bastard, so you will not put *yourself* at risk either, not for the sake of him. And, meaning this in the kindest sense, you will not be able to do it on your own. Taking someone's life is not something you can just decide to do, no matter how evil the man. You are too kind to do this deed."

So, her friends did believe Bronwen to be weak and

incapable. Perhaps they were right to think that. She never stood up for herself, Haydon and Lowell would have easily killed her for the second time, if she had not had help. Why was it that she could not defend herself?

But this was different. This man, Kenneth Quays, did not just ruin her life, he was continuing to do the same to other girls. It was clear this creature would not stop until he died and she could not go to the police about him either. She had no evidence, and truthfully, she did not want anyone else to know what had happened to her. There was no way she could keep something like this from the public eye and it would require his other victims to come forward and testify against him as well.

And then, there was the fact that he was, most likely, one of her killers. She would not be free of Thanatos if she did not do something about Kenneth.

But, could she face Kenneth again? Could she stomach her fear of him long enough to look her abuser in the eye and then gather the courage to put a stop to him?

X

Looking up at the house of her former piano instructor, Bronwen felt a sense of foreboding discomfort in the pit of her stomach that spread like a disease, making every hair stand on end and her skin feel hot.

The smell of the nettle bushes, hugging against the wall of the front gate, made her want to gag and her breath quickened. It had not changed by one brick or leaf.

Bronwen had left her horse tied to a lamppost near the house, ready for a quick getaway and had tucked a knife from dinner into her boot. It was cold and uncomfortable there and she was still unsure if she would be able to use it, but the sun was creeping higher over the horizon and she had little time to decide.

Lady Bronwen closed her eyes slowly and took a deep breath before walking through the eerily silent gate. She tried the handle of the door and was relieved to find it unlocked. She stepped inside quietly and stood in the hallway of Kenneth's little town house. He did not have a permanent housekeeper, only a woman who cleaned the house every other day, so she knew they would not be disturbed.

It was possible to hear the faint sound of piano keys from

one of the upper floors. From the simplicity of the tune, Bronwen guessed it was a student which surprised and worried her, considering how early it was in the day.

The ascension up the stairs to the first floor was a bitterly long one. If it were possible to be dragging her feet, she would have been, but Bronwen felt safer knowing Kenneth did not know she was there, as if that would give her the upper hand with this man who filled her with so much dread.

The door where the soft, sad melody came from was open. Bronwen quietly stepped into the doorway and looked into the room, finding some inner strength to face her childhood demons.

The music room hadn't changed either. There was a small red sofa on the back wall, next to a modest fireplace. A desk was pushed under the small window, its thick net curtains always closed so the room had to be constantly lit by lanterns and candles. There were metal stands for holding music in one corner and a bookshelf in the other. The black piano was still shiny and dominated the centre of the room and sat on the stool in front of it was Bronwen's nightmares.

Mr Quays was sat with his back to the door speaking to a young girl next to him. She had pale brown hair like Bronwen's and she recognised her to be Catherine.

Kenneth placed a hand on the young girl's lower back - too low. The girl cringed but could not move away and Bronwen felt an equal measure of disgust and fear. There was another feeling as well, creeping into her stomach and it took her a while to realise what it was - an unwanted pang of jealous rage.

Bronwen felt sick at her own confused emotions. Why would she ever feel jealous that he was abusing this young girl and not her? Was it because she was no longer his favourite student? But that was absurd and nonsensical - irrational even. Perhaps it was because this had been the only reason Bronwen had not been completely broken from their lessons together. If there was a reason for what Kenneth had done, if he had just been so pleased with Bronwen that he could not help himself, then it was a little more bearable.

Seeing Kenneth giving this girl the same affectionate caress and watching him lean his body into hers as he used to do to Bronwen, shattered every reason she had rationalised in her youth and just made her even more enraged.

"Take your hand from her," Bronwen's voice was barely audible, but she knew Kenneth had heard it from the way his shoulders tensed.

"Bronwen," Kenneth replied.

The girl turned to look at Bronwen still stood in the doorway. It was Catherine and there was a brief expression of guilt in the little girl's eyes that made Bronwen's heart ache.

Kenneth's hand moved from the child's back to her knee where it gripped her leg tightly, the fabric of her cream skirt creasing. The girl turned back to the piano and quickly continued to play, clearly more afraid of the man beside her than Bronwen.

Kenneth had still not turned to face her.

"I am afraid you will have to wait your turn, Bronwen."

"I am no longer your student, Kenneth," Bronwen replied tightly. "You will address me as Lady."

Kenneth laughed. "You will always be my student."

He turned his body to look directly at her and did not flinch from the hateful look in her eyes. "There is still more that can be taught."

Bronwen's muster faltered for just a moment under his scrutiny. A wrong note played by the girl at the piano broke the tension between them. She turned to look at Bronwen again and seeing the fear and helplessness there, returned enough of the Lady's bravery to step into the room fully.

Unlike the girl, Bronwen had some power now and was perhaps the only one that could put a stop to the piano teacher's *lessons*.

"Go home," Bronwen told Catherine. "Tell your parents that Mr Quays is no longer able to tutor you."

Catherine hurriedly stood up but Kenneth's hand fell on her shoulder. She froze, utterly terrified.

"I think not," Kenneth said, so calm and controlled.

He stood up as well and pulled Catherine towards him. She stumbled out from behind the piano, her lip trembling as he held her in front of him and stared at Bronwen.

"We have yet to finish our lesson. I feel a demonstration would be beneficial, if you would be so kind, Bronwen. Won't you come play for me again?"

Bronwen scowled. When she didn't move, Kenneth's arm snaked across the girl's neck. Not enough that he would hurt her but his meaning was clear.

Bronwen couldn't fight him while he held Catherine to ransom. She slowly made her way towards the piano, stalling for time. She sat on the edge of the stool and stared at the white and black keys in front of her, able to create the most harmonious sounds or with one misplaced finger, create a horrible mixture of contradictory notes.

"Let her go, Kenneth. This is between us."

"Continue," Kenneth instructed, ignoring her and Bronwen lifted her hands to the keys.

Her thumb easily found middle C and she gently pressed it. The piano made no noise, she had pressed so lightly, but her imbedded memory of the notes engaged in her mind and she merely glanced at the sheet music in front of her and began to play like an expert.

She had not played in so long and had once enjoyed it before Kenneth had begun his torment.

Bronwen turned to look at him and forced herself to smile. "Will you join me?"

Kenneth grinned and Bronwen tried not to shudder. He didn't let Catherine leave as she had hoped and instead forced the girl to sit next to Bronwen while he came to stand behind them.

"Continue," Kenneth repeated. Catherine hesitated and Bronwen nodded to her to do as he asked.

Catherine started to play along with Bronwen supplying the upper cords.

Bronwen skipped a note when Kenneth's hands stretched around her to join her at the keys, his long arms encasing her which made it much harder to play.

Bronwen was captivated by his hands and she noticed the mark. A scab that flexed as the bones beneath it moved while he played. It was the exact same place she had stabbed her attacker.

Kenneth's body pressed into Bronwen's back as he reached from natural to sharp. Bronwen could feel the contours of his shape through the fabric of her dress. *Every* contour.

Bronwen stopped playing and began to stand up, but his arm wrapped itself around her waist.

Bronwen froze as he knelt one foot on the stool behind her and pressed himself against her.

"I have never forgotten the smoothness of your skin or how your little fingers played," Kenneth murmured against the bare skin on the nape of her neck.

Bronwen felt herself shaking. She considered calling for help but the house was well insulated to keep from disturbing the neighbours with the lessons.

She kept thinking someone would walk in. Her father will come searching for her. Josette will come storming in with Azu. Thanatos will appear to mock her.

Bronwen realised that none of these things had ever happened before. Why should they now simply because she was older?

And she still had to consider Catherine who was still playing and trying not to notice what was happening beside her.

If Bronwen could just get her out of the room, she could deal with Kenneth.

"Do you think of me?" Kenneth continued. His hand slid lower over the silk of her dress. His other hand pressed into the keys of the piano as if he was struggling to contain himself. "We no longer need to fear how far we go."

Bronwen swallowed down bile.

She had always been weak willed. Her thoughts were strong and she always imagined herself defending those who mattered; when in reality she shied from confrontation. She kept quiet, nodded politely, bit her tongue. Had she really changed at all? Was Josette right when she said Bronwen would not be able to do this? Now was the time to decide.

Bronwen looked at the hand that was still holding onto the piano, the hand with the scar from the wound she had put there. An act of bravery.

It could not be coincidence that she had stabbed *him*, out of all the other people who had murdered her she had injured one of the hands which had haunted her for years.

She met Catherine's frightened gaze. Bronwen placed her hands on the fallboard of the piano and something passed between them.

Catherine slowly slid her hand off the keys.

Bronwen pulled down the fallboard of the instrument, crushing Kenneth's fingers.

He yelled out in pain and yanked his fingers out roughly, pulling Bronwen backwards over the stool so she toppled to the floor.

Bronwen hit her head hard on the ground and gasped in pain. She rolled onto her side to scramble to her feet.

"G—oouh..." her voice broke off in a wheeze when Kenneth kicked her hard in the stomach and she rolled onto her back.

She was pleased to see that Catherine didn't need telling twice and had run out of the room.

"This is why I prefer them young," Kenneth said, uninterested in the fleeing girl as he put his full weight onto Bronwen, pinning her arms with his knees. He was still cradling his hand, his fingers not quite aligned how they should be.

Bronwen struggled beneath him but he was too heavy for her and it hurt where his full weight cut off the blood to her arms.

"You didn't struggle half this much when you first started learning. Nor did you put up much of a fight when strapped to that rock."

"Get off me!" Bronwen screamed. "I know what you did! I know who you are!"

"Do you indeed? And what was your plan in coming here? To kill me?"

"Yes," Bronwen hissed. "Like you killed me."

Kenneth laughed. "You won't kill me, Bronwen. You aren't strong enough."

"She is strong enough."

Kenneth yelped as a hand dragged him up from off Bronwen and across the floor. The figure punched him a few times and then grabbed up the piano stool and pinned Kenneth underneath it.

Bronwen sat up, confused and gaining the feeling back in her arms.

Azu was sat on the stool, keeping Kenneth captured there.

Bronwen stood up and joined him, amazed that he had managed to arrive on time. She took the knife out of her boot and Kenneth laughed again, spitting blood from his split lip onto the carpet.

"Whatever next, Bronwen?" he mocked though his chuckles. "Will you have one bodyguard for each of us?"

"I am going to kill you, Kenneth," she said with such venom that he sobered and became serious. Like a teacher scolding his pupil.

"You did well today, Bronwen. But now, it is time for you to leave," Kenneth said calmly.

"I cannot allow you to harm another child!"

"No one will believe you if you tell anyone. Only yesterday I convinced the Huddersfields that you have not been well since the attack. And no doubt someone would have seen your man here enter the house. Your father may help you escape the noose, but someone has to hang."

Bronwen frowned and looked at Azu. He was right. This was a busy area of the city. Even if no one saw them enter, they might see them leave.

Azubuike frowned back at her. "I am no mind in this, Malaika. You must choose for you."

Bronwen looked back down at Kenneth, conflicted. He grinned and spread his hands out either side of him. She knew that he was mocking the way she had looked the night he had helped kill her.

She would have perhaps interrogated him as to the identity of the others but could not do that with Azu there. He had already heard too much that was, so far, obscure enough to explain away. If Bronwen started talking about sacrifices and knives, he would be unlikely to ignore that.

She gripped the knife in her hands and Azu moved the stool out of her way so she could bend down to hold it against Kenneth's throat. He stared at her, keeping eye contact.

"Do it," he murmured.

She hesitated and he grabbed her wrist. Azu readied to grab him again if needed but he only moved Bronwen's knife down over his heart. Where they had stabbed her.

And she couldn't do it. She couldn't take his life while he lay there prone like she had.

Bronwen stood again and stumbled backwards. She wanted to be out of the room. Anywhere away from Kenneth and the piano. She had always dreaded her lessons, had always wanted someone to rid her of her teacher. Some knight who would rescue her. Now, it was in her power to do the same for the other children he had harmed and she couldn't do it.

Kenneth pulled himself upright and stared at her, a smug look on his face.

She couldn't do it.

The sick feeling in her stomach never failed to show itself whenever she was close to other men. It warned her to trust no one and it was his fault.

Yet, she could not kill him.

Bronwen dropped the knife and Kenneth started to laugh again.

Azubuike grabbed him by the collar and punched him hard in the jaw a few more times until he was knocked out cold.

Bronwen's hands were shaking and she barely registered Azu taking them and guiding her out of the building, helping her onto her horse and leading them back towards Metrom.

Lady Bronwen felt a sob escape her and she began crying, the weight of her life since her death becoming too much. If the pressure of it had been a corporeal creature, it would have been *its* pushing on her shoulders that made her crumple over the neck of her horse.

Azu reached over and pulled her onto his horse. She cried into her friend's chest all the way back, digging her nails into her skin and feeling like she had failed.

She may as well give into Thanatos if she could not face her killers. What use was she in this world?

"I could not do it," Bronwen said once her tears had run dry, feeling desolate.

"No, not this time," Azu replied. She wasn't sure there would be a next time but his confidence in her was a soothing balm.

"What are you doing here?" Bronwen asked, wiping her tears away on her sleeve.

"I let you face him alone, but you will not go alone," Azubuike said calmly. "I saw the girl come out and had to see."

"Thank you," Bronwen said, his heartfelt reply making her want to cry again. "I suppose that frees you of your obligation to me. You saved my life so now we are even."

"You were not in danger," he insisted and looked down at her. "And I will like to stay."

"Why would you, when I get myself into such trouble?"

Azu laughed lightly. A rare occurrence for him. "You think this is trouble?" He shook his head.

"I will stay."

XI

      In the large windowless study of his home Donovan stood, slightly hunched, next to one of the shelving units that lined the walls. Behind its glass doors showcased many ornaments that he had collected on his way to success and power.

Across from him, barely a few paces, one of the cabinets stood open. There was a gap in the display, between the Grecian depiction of a tempting demon and the relief of an innocent maiden that his wife had bought him, before she died.

He had never noticed the irony of the two items before, for the gap in the centre of them was reserved for the knife that had sliced open his daughter's heart and soul. Perhaps on a subconscious level, he had been aware of the connection. And, oh, how he was painfully aware of it now.

A bell chiming merrily at the door to the study, alerted Donovan that there was someone in need of his attention. The room was well soundproofed. It was where all the Secuutus's business was conducted, when not at the meeting place. The little bell was how servants contacted Donovan when he was in his study.

He opened the door slightly to find James waiting patiently outside.

"Reverend Myerscough is here to see you, milord."

"Bring him to me," Donovan ordered gruffly.

"Very good, milord." James acquiesced as Donovan closed the door again.

Very good. Was it?

Donovan breathed deeply and moved to close the cabinet with the missing dagger. The hilt was all that had been left of it after their Dominus had broken the blade off; in the rock they had killed Bronwen on. They had been unable to free the blade and Donovan had hidden the hilt in his secret cupboard in the wall of his study.

He did not want to imagine what might happen if Bronwen found him in possession of it; if she even knew it existed. He did not know what to think anymore.

Donovan was supposed to be leader of the Secuutus Letum, but since he had murdered his own daughter, he had lost his drive to keep things in order. Lord Guild had taken it upon himself to do that and while he was grateful for it, he also had to wonder at what the young Earl's motives were.

The bell chimed again and Donovan let Denny into the room. The fat man looked out of breath and sweaty from holding the folders he had brought with him. He eased himself into the chair by Donovan's desk that creaked in protest. Donovan sat in the chair on the other side.

Besides Kole, Denny, surprisingly, was the most tolerable company out of all the members. Yes, his cowardice was infuriating at times, but he was not a threat and occasionally had good advice, though Donovan would never admit this.

"I have Haydon and Lowell's accounts for you to go through," Denny said, pulling out papers and passing them to Donovan. Denny kept all of the Secuutus's money in order. It had been stolen over the years, from the victims their Dominus told them to kill and now, the funds were bulging.

On the rare occasion a member died or left the Secuutus Letum, any benefits they had been given as part of the deal with their Dominus, was returned. All Donovan as Dux Ducis had to do was approve any movement of money and sign for it to enter the bank account that was in his name. It was one of the risks of being leader. If the money were ever traced, it would find itself back to him and not the rest of the members.

Neither of the dead men had much. Some of the property passed to family members and most of the money went back to the account, so it didn't take long to go through everything.

The two daggers that bound souls to their master's realm disappeared when a member died. Donovan had seen it happen once when an assignment had gone wrong and their target had gotten the better of one of their new members. Donovan had held the man while he bled out from the wound in his neck and the dagger in his hand seemed to fade away to nothing as the man's life had. It had spooked Donovan for weeks and he was convinced that each blade represented the soul of the person who had made their deal.

His suspicions were further confirmed by how unique to the individual all the blades were. They all had indecipherable symbols engraved into them and coloured stones in the hilt. They were short and thin and had never once blunted or stained, even after all the blood they had seen.

He supposed that was why he had never found his wife's blade when she died. The dagger which had taken Bronwen's life the first time. Of course, none of the Secuutus knew about this and he planned to keep it that way.

Donovan's eyes drifted over to the painting of his wife on the wall. She had been so beautiful. Curvy in all the right places. In the painting, her hair was modestly pinned up, thick and dark brown like coffee. The cream dress she wore and her shy downward look portrayed an innocence Donovan knew she hadn't possessed. She had been feisty and lustful, a brutal warrior who took what she wanted and sent men wild with wanting. More like the hidden painting that was behind it; on the side of the secret room built beneath the stairs which held all the gathered occult objects the Secuutus acquired.

Donovan had paid a large sum of money to have it built as well as for the second painting. It was almost identical to the public one; except his wife had no clothes on.

There was another chiming at the door, making Denny jump and Donovan stifled a growl as he got up to answer it.

"Milord, Mr Quays is here to see you. Shall I tell him you are indisposed?"

"No," Donovan replied curtly. "Show him into the drawing room and have Ruth fetch some drinks."

Donovan turned back to Denny who was struggling to get out of his chair.

Denny followed Donovan out of the room to meet with Kenneth. Donovan was not keen on the man and did not want him in his study if he could help it. The drawing room would be private enough.

Donovan employed his staff for their trustworthiness and ability to not ask questions. They must have overheard some things over the years, seen some things too, like blood stains on his clothing and bandages changed from wounds he had gotten.

And why did they keep his secrets? Money, of course. Donovan's money did not belong to the Secuutus, it belonged to him alone and he paid his staff well and often employed people based solely on how unfortunate they were before moving to his house.

James Durward was the most loyal. He had been a butler before, but his employers had had him arrested for indecent activities with men. He had been due to hang when Donovan saved him and offered him a job. He didn't care who people fucked, that was there business and James had proved himself invaluable, strictly keeping his house and staff in order.

Donovan's choices were not always so perfect. He had before employed the wrong type of person, who threatened to report him for things they had overheard and Donovan had to either be rid of them himself, or had to use his contacts within the authorities to hide whatever accusations were made against him.

It was a necessity to have such contacts within the police and had been especially useful in preventing any detailed investigation into the two attacks on Bronwen.

Walking down the hall and entering the drawing room, Donovan's eyes immediately settled on his visitor. Kenneth had a steady and demanding hand on Ruth's hip, a servant of the house. She was incredibly young, far younger than Bronwen, with a sweet face that the man obviously agreed with.

Ruth looked highly uncomfortable being alone with this man, as she shakily placed a tray on the table, full of tea and some light cakes.

Donovan cleared his throat. He did not like someone touching his property. Safety, as well as money, was what he offered his staff and Kenneth's wandering hands threatened to break that contract.

The man looked up, but did not remove his hand from where it had languidly drifted to the girls behind.

"Baron Wintre, Revered Myerscough," The man said, with a friendly smile and a hint of self-satisfaction.

"Kenneth," Donovan replied for the both of them.

He inclined his head for Ruth to leave before she could pour the tea. She gratefully removed herself from beside Kenneth and left the room.

Kenneth pouted and Donovan took the seat on the sofa opposite him. Denny took it upon himself to serve before Donovan had to ask and he planned to tell James to give Ruth a day off as compensation.

"Quite a cute little thing that one, Donovan," Kenneth said as he picked up a spoon and began stirring sugar into his tea. Donovan noticed he was using his left hand to do this. Two fingers on his right hand were bound together tightly.

Denny passed Donovan a tea and then sat down in the largest armchair farthest from the fire.

"Have you come here to admire my servants, or does your appearance have a purpose, Kenneth?"

Kenneth smiled, tapped his spoon on the side of the cup and sat back in the chair without drinking the tea.

"Your darling daughter just tried to kill me."

Donovan paused in his drinking and had managed to keep enough composure to not spit it out.

"I daresay you deserved it," Donovan replied, nonchalant. It was a mannerism he had been forced to practice since Bronwen had returned from... whatever they had done to her. Kole had been an excellent role model for him. "Did you scold her for missing a note again?"

Kenneth smiled a secret smile, that only he knew the meaning of.

"Oh no," he said and held up his injured hand. "She found them all quite expertly."

Donovan had to smother a smile that threatened to surface. It was barely a week ago that Kenneth was saying what little harm Bronwen could do, and while a few broken fingers was not a grand display of prowess, it *was* harm.

"I see," Donovan said.

"I would apologise for the multitude of bruises I gave her in return, but I am not feeling particularly contrite in the circumstances." He finally picked up his tea and drank deeply, struggling to hold the cup with his left hand.

"Does she know about us?" Denny asked.

"She said nothing to indicate it," Kenneth replied. "But that does not mean she does not know."

"I think I would have heard about it if she did," Donovan mused. "She is not so good an actress as to be the same around her own father, knowing *I* was the one who struck the final blow."

"Perhaps she is though. There was something different in her eyes. Something darker. She is not a child anymore." Kenneth paused and stared off to the side. "It was almost like looking into a mirror." He added in a light voice, as if the thought amused him.

Donovan raised an eyebrow at his comparison. He could not deny that he had noticed there was some quality that was different about his daughter. He had paid enough attention to her over the years to at least notice that.

There was also the lie Bronwen had told about being attacked in Lowell's shop, as if she had forgotten all that had happened to her after the event. Kole had told him to let it be until they calmed things in the Secuutus Letum but Lowell's death had caused a disturbance amongst them. And then Haydon had taken it upon himself to try and kill her, though Donovan did not believe the man acted alone. Haydon was not the brightest of them, but he could not prove anyone else's involvement in it yet.

He had since tried to keep them all busy, sending them on errands for the Secuutus, anything he could legitimately thing of. It would have been easier if their master had demons they needed to hunt, but Denny had confirmed that their Dominus was silent on the matter, as if he wanted them all in Bronwen's path.

"I think she is hunting us, seeking us all out," Kenneth said. "She found Lowell very quickly."

"Lowell was a fool that none of us will miss," The Baron

retorted. "He was quick to scare and no doubt has himself to blame, as does Haydon. None of this proves she is after us."

"And what of the attack on me?" Kenneth asked. "It was, for the most part, unprovoked."

They were interrupted by a knock on the door.

"Enter," Donovan called.

James opened the door and bowed his head apologetically for the intrusion. "Milord, Lord Guild is here. May I show him in?"

"Yes, immediately."

Donovan remained seated as Kole strolled in. Kenneth and Denny stood and nodded to him as he reached the table.

"We may have a problem," Donovan said to Kole, before he had even settled into the chair he had moved in front of the fire, so his back was to it.

"When do we not?" Kole replied, a slight smile on his face as he undid a button on his jacket and sat, waving dismissively at Kenneth and Denny to sit.

"Bronwen is more than she seems," Kenneth said.

"Lady Bronwen has always been more than she seems, or our Dominus would not have wanted her in the first place," Kole's tone was intolerant. Perhaps Kenneth's company was unwholesome to him as well and Donovan knew he found Denny revolting.

"What do you mean by that?"

"I am just making conclusions based on what we do and do not know," Kole clarified. "Our Dominus could have made that deal with any one of us, anyone on earth in fact. I cannot imagine that Donovan's deal would come at a greater price than any of ours, and even if it did, it is still a very specific thing to ask for."

The two men thought about this for a moment. Only Donovan knew what deal he had made, he had not divulged it to any member of the Secuutus Letum, just as they had not told him of theirs, but he knew that Kole was right. Their Dominus could have asked for anything of him, but this was premeditated. It was not a typical handing over of a soul where Denny gave them a target and they simply used their knives to kill them. No, he had been very specific with Bronwen's sacrifice.

It had never sat right with Donovan that Bronwen had been returned for only twenty-five years, but agonising over it wouldn't have helped, so he had chosen to see his daughter as a business transaction and nothing more.

"What difference does this information make?" Kenneth asked.

"None whatsoever," Kole answered. "Other than we cannot kill Bronwen in the ordinary manner and anyone who tries to do so, will meet a very sorry end."

"How do you know we cannot kill her? None of us has succeeded yet. Do you think our Dominus sent her back on purpose?" Kenneth asked, now looking tense.

"Why not?" Kole replied casually. "He was displeased with us and even if that is not the reason, he could just have easily made a bargain with Lady Bronwen, like we all have."

"Make a bargain with her?" Donovan said indignantly, a sick feeling in his stomach at the thought. "To what end?"

Kole shrugged. "We may never know, not unless we ask her, which of course we cannot."

"Can't we?" They all looked at Denny, who had said very little so far. "I think Lady Bronwen is lonely. She does not have a group like we do. She is seeking friendship." Denny gave Donovan a significant look.

Bronwen had come home with Azubuike and Josette when she returned from Guildford. They all seemed very close, spending their days together, where Bronwen had before seemed content to be alone.

"Perhaps then, one of us should get close to her?"

Kenneth mused. He hooked one leg over the other and leant back into his chair. "If we did the ritual correctly, then Bronwen..."

"*Lady* Bronwen," Kole corrected icily.

Kenneth smiled sweetly at the Earl. "Lady Bronwen, is in fact dead, so we can assume that she made a deal with our Dominus to return here. In which case, she is aware that she is dead and knows that she is in the midst of those who killed her. It would not take much for someone to get close enough for her to confide in them. I know from personal experience that it is very easy to get into that sweet little head of hers."

Donovan considered his words as he drank more tea. What Kenneth said had merit, though he loathed admitting the man was right. If they could get Bronwen to confide in someone, then what would they do with that information? Perhaps they could find out what deal she had made with their Dominus and use that to their advantage. Whatever this gained them, it would be better than the not knowing.

He even entertained the idea of having Bronwen join the Secuutus, then dismissed it. He didn't want her involved in that... didn't want to reveal to her what he had done to her and what her mother had done to her.

Now, the only thing left to consider was; who was close enough to Bronwen to break down her barriers? It was obviously not her father; they were not close at all and Donovan's immediate thought was of Lord Guild. He knew that Bronwen had never been fully pleased with marrying Kole. There was no love there, but he also knew that Kole had kept a reasonable distance from Bronwen, at least until she had died. Then, there had been a subtle shift in their relationship. Kole had changed almost as much as Bronwen appeared to. The Earl had seemed physically stronger, but more conflicted with how he acted on his desires. Again, Donovan wondered what the man's motives were.

Kole met Donovan's eyes and smiled knowingly.

"It would be little effort to gain her trust," Kole said with a sly glint in his eyes. "Once she is isolated from her friends again, Bronwen will come to me easily. So long as I am given the time and the freedom to do so."

"Take whatever freedom you need," Donovan confirmed, though he had to shove his sudden uneasy feeling to one side. He did occasionally feel as though he were a father, but always quelled the sensation quickly.

"Permission from the father," Kole jested. "How honourable."

Donovan rolled his eyes at the man and left the sofa to pour himself a glass of something stronger than tea.

"The only matter left to settle is keeping the Secuutus from attempting to kill her again in the meantime," Kenneth said, indicating to Donovan that he would like a glass too.

Donovan tried to refrain from breaking it over his skull, but the brandy was too nice to mix with brains and bone, and he was tired of cleaning blood off everything.

Despite his dislike of the man, Kenneth was one of Donovan's allies. The group was clearly split into two allegiances. Velna's allies and Donovan's. So far, he had lost one in Lowell and she had lost Haydon making them even again with Maverick, Cornell and Mara with Velna and Kenneth, Kole and Denny with Donovan. He preferred not to count Cornell's useless wife or Maverick's useless son. Especially as they would both no doubt choose Velna.

"Velna came to me in Guildford," Kole said, as if he had been reading Donovan's thoughts. "She wants to call Lacessere."

Kenneth laughed and Denny tensed.

"She wouldn't," Donovan said. "She almost died last time, what makes her think she will succeed?"

The trials of Lacessere were a way to decide on the Dux

Ducis. If someone called the challenge, the trials were started on the next full moon and each of the members brought a trial to the circle, designed to knock out their opponents. There were very few rules and things always became increasingly difficult and dangerous, as was its purpose. Leaders did not want their rule easily challenged when the work they did was so risky and the Secuutus as a whole could not afford a weak leader.

Velna had been a worthy opponent in the last trials, but had almost bled out when one man, no longer with the group, had made them all cut themselves repeatedly to see which one of them fainted first. Donovan still had the scars on his arms from it and the stupid woman had refused to give in. He was certain Velna would not call Lacessere herself.

"You know what she is like with her jealousy, which is further evidence of our Dominus's interest in Lady Bronwen. We all know how Velna worships our Lord," Kole said. It was no secret that their Dominus visited Velna for his pleasure. She delighted in reminding them all that he favoured her.

"I do not believe she would go to such lengths, regardless. She protects that sister of hers fiercely and wont risk her being harmed," Donovan said firmly.

"She seemed desperate, even for Velna and she was very smug about something. I think she plans to try and kill Bronwen herself."

Donovan tried not to smile at the thought. Not of Bronwen dying, but because, if the last failed attacks were anything to go by, Velna would be killed trying and that would solve one problem for him. However, the Secuutus Letum was becoming smaller and smaller, which was not a good thing. They may soon have need of more members which was a trial on its own.

The four men sat and thought for a moment. If Bronwen

could not be killed, as Kole suggested, then what were they to do, other than wait for her to hunt them all down and kill them. Haydon and Lowell had been a fluke, but Kenneth had been sought out by Bronwen. She needed to be watched carefully, or sent away entirely.

"Perhaps, we should send her away until we know more?" Donovan suggested, having a sudden idea. "We could fan the interest this Prince Nasta has shown her..."

"No!" Kole yelled, slamming his drink down on the table. "Bronwen is *mine*."

The other men stared at him, surprised by his vehemence. His voice had changed into a low growl that seemed inhuman and Donovan could have sworn the fire behind him blazed brighter.

"Oh, please," Kenneth scoffed, recovering faster from Kole's outburst. "Lady Bronwen belonged to her father and now she belongs to our Dominus, it was your attempt to claim her that made him so displeased with us. Perhaps if you had stuck your cock in Velna instead, our Lord would not have sent the girl back to haunt us."

Donovan thought Kole might beat the man to death on the drawing room floor. It would be entertaining at least. But instead, the Earl visibly shook himself, like a dog shaking out his coat, and then took a long breath before speaking.

"I can handle Bronwen. She will soon come to heel and tell me everything we need to know about why she is back."

Kenneth finished his drink and put down his glass. "If you think that will alleviate the tension in the Secuutus. Not all of our group are as level headed as we are."

XII

"You have not been with us lately, have you?" Josette said to Bronwen in the carriage on the way to the station. Josette had received a letter from Mr Lawnem asking her to meet with them to discuss her book. The letter had not given much away and it had taken a while for Bronwen to convince her friend that it could only be a positive thing, if they were asking her to travel all the way to the capital.

"Have I not?" Bronwen replied, in a voice that even she was aware sounded distant.

"Are you sure you will not come with me?" Josette tried again, looking concerned for her friend. "It is not too late to send for your things."

"I am sure, Josette. I have too many things to do here and you will have Azu to keep you company."

"You should keep him here, if you are determined not to come," Josette dropped her voice, even though it was unlikely Azu would hear them above the horse's hooves. He was riding with the footmen at the front of the carriage. "Not that I am complaining about being left alone with him." Josette winked, making her friend blush.

Bronwen had refused to allow Josette to go all the way to London without a chaperone and she wouldn't send her with Adam, most likely for the same reasons Josette didn't want to leave him with Bronwen.

She had chosen to remain in Winchester for a few reasons. She did not want to have that discussion with Lord Guild about her leaving the city without him and there was nothing to do in London at night - at least not without roaming a dangerous city – and, she really did have things to do.

"Should not be leaving you," Azu said when they got to the station and stood on the platform while Josette went to buy the tickets. He had been sulking since the moment Bronwen had asked him to go with Josette.

"Please Azu, London can be dangerous for a woman on her own."

"Here is dangerous for you." He gave her a pointed look.

They had both been wondering if Kenneth would take action against them for their failed attempt at killing him and it was one of the reasons Bronwen wanted Azu out of the city.

She didn't care if she was implicated but if things went askew, she wanted him to be able to run. Bronwen had even explained what had happened to Josette and given her extra money to take to London with them, just in case.

Josette had of course agreed, after berating Bronwen for not taking Kenneth's life and for not planning things better before going to his house. The way she spoke about killing a man was so blasé, it had at first shocked Bronwen. She knew Josette spoke her mind but this was murder; evil person or not. It made Bronwen again wonder if she was too weak to do what she needed to do.

"You know Josette well enough now to see that she would be a risk to herself in a big city alone," Bronwen continued to reason with Azubuike.

"I heard that!" Josette said indignantly as she returned from buying their tickets. The protest in her tone was ruined when she tripped over her travel case and Azu had to catch Josette before she fell onto the tracks.

Bronwen shook her head. "Besides, I have Mr Whyms to watch out for me while you are gone."

They both gave her the same sceptical look they had given her in Guildford.

"Oh, please, you two. I have survived so far without you, I am sure I can manage a few days more," Bronwen said, knowing this was not strictly true.

"Just, be careful, and do not be so trusting of that bodyguard of yours," Josette said seriously. "He is Lord Guild's man after all."

"No, he is my man now, he is under my employment. And what precisely do you mean by that?"

"I shall tell you when you are older," Josette said smugly, placing her hands on her hips and grinning.

They hugged each other goodbye as the train was ready to depart.

"And do not come back without a book deal!" Bronwen called to Josette where she hung out the window. The train pulled away from the station, trailing clouds above it that wisped in air currents.

"Or a husband!" Josette called back, making Bronwen laugh.

Bronwen waited until the train was out of sight before returning to her waiting carriage. She missed them already as she stepped inside the coach and did not like the thought of being alone with Adam. He had been unusually absent in recent days, ever since they had returned from Guildford.

She wondered if he perhaps wanted to be released from his duties and thought about how she would approach the subject. She guessed that Adam would inform her or Lord Guild if this were the case.

At least he had stopped watching her door at night and she had been able to visit the library to read. It was nice to get away from her room which had begun to feel like a prison; her sentence lasting through the darkness until the sun finally rose.

The second night without Josette and Azu's company, Bronwen was once again in the library, passing her time without them by searching for something that could tell her of how her nightmare had begun. She had decided to try and discover what the mark on her stomach was and why it might have been put there. So far, Bronwen had found nothing in her father's collection of books. It wasn't as well organised as Josette's and it didn't help that Bronwen's thoughts were distracting her work.

She had two prominent things in her mind, her failed attempt at stopping Kenneth and a possible life growing inside her. She wished again she had a way to call for Thanatos. Bronwen had no way of speaking to him and she had seen no sign of him since the ball. Was he planning on only seeing her as his alias, Prince Nasta? She had so many questions. Including if she was pregnant with his child by some magical means.

She scolded herself for dwelling on it as she reached for books on a shelf at head height, not aware of their covers or relevance to her. She dumped them on the library desk, pulled closer to the fire for warmth in the cold night and walked to the ladder, occupying her mind with climbing instead.

Barefooted, Bronwen found it needed her full attention and she chose the largest book on the highest shelf to pull out into her arms.

She began descending the ladder. The awkward weight of the book and her inattention threw off her centre of balance and her foot slipped away from one of the rungs of the ladder. She dropped the book to grab for a handhold and was relieved when strong arms wrapped around her waist and caught her - she knew who it would be.

"You could have caught the book as well," Bronwen breathed, as she listened a moment to see if the huge thump of the book hitting the floor had woken anyone in the house. Luckily, her father was away on some business and she could handle any of the servants.

"I've only so many hands, milady," her captor replied, as he placed her back on solid ground.

Bronwen was taken aback to find it was Adam, not Thanatos as she had been expecting. She recognised his drooling midlands accent immediately.

"Oh, I thought it was..." She paused and stared at him. He was stood quite close to her, but then, he had just caught her from a fall. Bronwen swallowed. "I did not mean to mock. I thought you were asleep."

"I was. The rest of the house went to bed hours ago."

"I see," Bronwen said and slid sideways away from him, on the pretence of picking up the book she had dropped. The pages were folded over one another and she frowned as she tried to straighten them. "We should both be getting to bed too, I suppose. I just wanted to get this book while I thought of it."

"Are you not cold?" Adam said, stepping in front of her.

"I will not be, once I am in bed," Bronwen replied. She had the book clutched to her chest and became aware of what little clothing she was wearing. She had removed her thick night gown when she became too warm from lifting books and was stood only in her white silk night dress.

"Here, take my jacket." Adam shrugged off his overcoat, which he always seemed to wear, to reveal a thick brown shirt underneath. Unusually, it didn't have any sleeves. It showed the muscles in his arms and the scars on them. Burn marks were prominent on his right arm in particular. Bronwen tried not to stare.

"There is no need. It really is not a long walk." Bronwen smiled and walked past him, trying to relax her shoulders.

She felt a weight on them as Adam placed his jacket on her anyway. It was large and heavy and smelt of smoke and of Adam's musty scent.

Bronwen rolled her eyes while he couldn't see her. She shifted the book in her arms and reached for the handle of the door. Adam made it there first, and held the handle unturned.

"I am very tired, Adam. Please let me go to bed."

"I want to speak to you."

Bronwen turned to face him and resisted the urge to look in the pockets of his jacket.

"And it could not wait until morning?"

"I have waited long enough."

"Then please, let us sit first and get warm." Bronwen was stalling for time and she wanted him to move away from her. She wanted something other than a book between them, like a table - or another room. He bowed his head which gave Bronwen the opportunity to move around him and step into the centre of the library, hoping to bring him away from the door, should she need to escape.

She contemplated calling for help, but Adam seemed genuinely distressed as she didn't want to upset him further.

"I will not be warm again," Adam said, so fervently that Bronwen looked seriously at him. He was still facing the door and clearly something was troubling him and she couldn't find it in her to ignore his distress, despite how uncomfortable he was making her feel.

"Are you unwell?"

"I feel unwell when I am around you; feverish and heartsick."

He turned around and took a step towards her. Bronwen took a step back reflectively.

"I do not understand," Bronwen said, even though she knew where the talk was headed. She had known of his feelings for a while now.

"I cannot be without you, milady," Adam said, putting a hand to his heart and taking another step, which Bronwen countered with one of her own. "I am always cold without you in my arms."

"Mr Whyms, this is mad and inappropriate behaviour," Bronwen said firmly, trying to stand tall and wishing she could put the book down that was weighing in her arms. Perhaps she could throw it at him?

"You would deny a dying man his cure?"

"Do not be ridiculous. You are hardly dying and you do not know me well enough to warrant such feelings. Never mind how improper this is. I am willing to forgive you and forget the whole thing..."

"Forget?" He said, now stalking towards her so she was backed against the bookcase, the shelves shaking a looming fist above her, threatening to offload its books onto her head. "Would you rather I made you forget?" His voice was pained and pleading. He looked so weak and yet this made him more dangerous.

"I would rather you stepped away and stopped all this nonsense. If Lord Guild hears about this..."

Adam laughed a short bark that made Bronwen jump. "Lord Guild hired me to keep an eye on you, to tell him where you go and who you see."

"What?"

Bronwen was confused. Why would Kole need to know where she was? Surely Adam only meant in a way that would keep her safe, not that Kole was spying on her.

"That was before I realised my feelings for you. I will not betray you to him. I want you to run away with me. You know I can keep you safe - safe even from Kole. He will never find us, I promise. I can make it so he will never lay a finger on you again..."

He trailed off and left Bronwen to fill in the blanks. She shuddered as the peril of her situation was dawning in her.

She changed tactic.

"If you care for me, then you will let me go to my room now. I am so very tired."

"You do not understand how much I need you, Bronwen." He leaned towards her, grabbing her face in both his hands and kissed her on the mouth. She kept her lips tightly closed and dropped the book she was holding. It fell on his feet, but in his heavy boots, he didn't feel it.

Bronwen pushed his hands away from her face and released herself. Her expression was disgusted and she rushed for the door, wiping her mouth with her sleeve.

She turned the handle and tried to pull it open, but it was locked. When had he locked it without her notice? She began to search the pockets of his coat that was still around her shoulders, when a hand clamped over her mouth and she felt a sharp pain in her neck. She tried to scream past his palm and elbowed him in the ribs.

Adam moved back, an empty syringe in his trembling hand. Bronwen put a hand to her neck and found a small drop of blood on her fingers.

"What did you do to me?"

"To make you sleep," Adam said quietly.

"What was..." Bronwen reached for the wall as she stumbled forward. She tried to take another step but her leg went out too far and she unbalanced and fell.

Adam caught her in his arms, the syringe abandoned on the floor. He cradled her head and caressed her cheek. She tried to push him away, but her arm swung out dramatically and missed. He caught her wrist in his hand and placed it across her stomach.

"Don't worry. It is only so you don't feel the pain of your first time."

Bronwen heard a belt buckle and her heart began to thump, which only increased the speed of the drug coursing through her system. She opened her mouth to scream and her throat filled with fluid. It bubbled out past her lips and down her chin.

"Bronwen?" Adam said, concerned for her suddenly.

Bronwen's body shuddered, then convulsed. She spat out the froth in her mouth so she could breathe as her muscles began to spasm out of control. She was mildly aware of Adam above her, looking more panicked than she was, before her eyes rolled back into their sockets and she struggled to breath.

Bronwen tried to put a hand to her throat, but her arms were useless and her muscles burned over every inch of her body. She could hear herself wheezing and coughing and Adam speaking frantic words she couldn't comprehend, while he tried to hit her on the back and shake her. She wanted to be sick, but even those muscles eluded her brain's command. It was the most intense pain she had ever felt in her living life and seemed to go on for hours.

What on earth had he done to her?

Finally, Bronwen couldn't get any air into her lungs and her body stopped writhing on the floor without her commanding it to, her eyes stared up at the ceiling without her seeing it and her ears did not hear Adam crying and leaving the room and the dead Lady on the floor.

XIII

Bronwen opened her eyes to a darkness, which retreated from her once it knew she was awake. Her arms were above her head and without seeing it, she knew they were chained together. For the second time, she found herself hanging in a void - the place she considered the Under-realm's version of purgatory.

Bronwen let out a small frustrated squeal that was unlike her and tried to pull at her bonds, before she remembered the pain it caused to fight them. She winched as her muscles clenched and realised reluctantly that she would need Thanatos's help if she wished to get down.

Stubbornness allowed her to hang for a moment before calling for him. She took the time to think about what had just happened to her. As with the first time Bronwen had died, the stark realness of her condition hit her. She still felt far more awake in this place than in the living world.

From her memory, Bronwen was sure that Adam had not meant to kill her. He had drugged her, but Bronwen didn't think that the intention of the substance was to kill her. She wasn't sure if the alternative scenario was better or worse than the current and shuddered at the thought of what he had planned to do to her. She was glad that her final fading memory was of him leaving the room.

Bronwen squealed again in frustration and it felt good to do so, even though the movement caused her pain. She dropped her head to her chest and grimaced.

This was it. She had lost. She was lost to the world and would have to spend eternity with a demon. She tried not to sob. Tried to be brave and not think about who she had left behind, ashamed that this had been her end.

"Thanatos!" Bronwen yelled into the darkness, her voice loud but muffled as it drifted into the mists. There was little sense in delaying her eternity.

"My Lady, how nice to see you again."

Thanatos was beneath her with a smug smile on his face, the vapours swirling around his bare feet. He looked victorious.

Thanatos lowered Bronwen down slowly and she looked away from him like a petulant child. He walked towards her, leaving her dangling, her toes only just grazing the floor.

"I like you like this very much," he said, appraising her body, dressed in the thin white dress that seemed to be the compulsory attire of the Under-realm.

"Please, do not do that," Bronwen murmured. She was already feeling vulnerable. She couldn't even trust those who were paid to protect her.

"I am sorry. Would it help if I were naked?"

Bronwen didn't reply but shifted, trying to reach the floor and only succeeding in swirling the mist around and sending lancing pain from her wrists to her toes.

She winced but didn't make a sound. Thanatos saw her pain regardless and gripped her about the waist before she could object, then lowered her into his body tightly. Taking her wrists in his hand, he dissipated the chains and her pain with it.

"I am sorry," Thanatos said, sincerely this time, placing her feet on the floor, though he didn't let go of her entirely.

"Adam attacked me with something," Bronwen said.

"Yes, poison it seems," Thanatos explained. His eyes went misty and unfocused as he elaborated. "Strychnine mainly, mixed with cyanide and arsenic. Someone must really despise you, and have an incredible talent for potions. To mix all three and have them act independently from one another. Even I am unsure as to how this might be achieved."

"That is indeed comforting to know," Bronwen said sarcastically. She pushed Thanatos away from her, or more, herself away from him as he was unmoved by her shove.

"Shall we get you back to find out?" Thanatos said, holding his hand out to her. She looked at it sceptically.

"You will let me go back?" Bronwen asked, her heart lifting.

"This time, yes. But I do not want to encourage this kind of reckless behaviour."

"Reckless!" Bronwen said, indignant. "I was attacked in my own library by my own bodyguard!"

"Yes, but your encounter with Mr Quays was reckless. That could just have easily been your death."

"You know about that," Bronwen said, sounding like a child who had been caught doing something wrong.

"Yes, I know how you went there, without any plan in mind, with what I can only assume was a kitchen knife. It takes much energy to send you back to the living and the longer you stay dead, the harder it will be on you. The most disappointing part is that the event with Mr Quays was entirely unsuccessful, even with the help of Azubuike."

He stalked away from her and Bronwen rushed to keep up, not wanting to be left behind. The void changed almost instantly into a room with a roaring fire and large inviting armchairs. There were candles all around the room, but the light seemed blue in tone, contrasting with the red wallpaper and carpet. The centre was taken up by a pile of pillows and fluffy throws and blankets in various shades of blue. Bronwen wondered what they were for when Thanatos sat on one of the large pillows and looked up at the ceiling, totally at ease.

Bronwen looked up as well and gasped. The entire ceiling was made of glass and looked out upon the great expanse of the sky, clear of clouds and filled with stars. So many that it seemed there were more stars than empty space and they all appeared closer than possible. Bronwen briefly thought it was just an incredible painting when she saw a star shoot across the expanse.

"Join me?" Thanatos requested; his voice full of mellifluous seduction. He was staring up at the night sky, his hands behind his head and a small smile on his face.

He looked so serene and Bronwen blinked rapidly, trying to dispel unwanted feelings towards seeing him lying there, in all his unnatural, attractive splendour. His shirt had pulled up slightly where he had his arms up, revealing a small section of his hip.

Thanatos watched with amusement as Bronwen blushed and she scolded herself for being so pining.

"I could not kill Kenneth," she said, finally sitting down on the pillows opposite him, staring at the floor rather than Thanatos.

"And why not? I told you the best way to punish them was to send them to me."

"I will not apologise for not killing a man – even one such as Kenneth."

"Then why return? Why go back to the land of the living if you do not plan to free yourself from me? Does my gift have so little meaning to you?"

"It is not a gift if there is an exchange. And it may be akin to your character - all this evil - but I was not born or raised this way," Bronwen argued, more passionately because she did not want to answer his questions. She did not know why she had returned, knowing she would eventually have to come back to the Under-realm.

Was her fear of Thanatos so strong that she could not give herself to him? Was it because he was a man that she dreaded being touched by him, as Kenneth had touched her? If it were Josette sitting opposite him now, would she have already given in and shared his bed?

Thanatos was quiet for so long that Bronwen thought he might have left her. She looked up and met his eyes.

"You think me evil then?" he asked her finally and she looked away from his accusing and almost pained expression. It made her regret saying such a thing, even to a creature like him. A creature who had men like Kenneth serving him.

"It is not all damnable and pernicious, what I do. But it is an occupation nonetheless and a choice that should not be made lightly," Thanatos continued, when she did not answer his question. "You think me the Devil, but tell me, if you met God and he looked like a man, would you not deny your belief in him too? So, why should I be the Devil, simply because you find my way of life distasteful? What I do has its purpose and I would have explained it to you, if you had shown any inclination of wanting to know, but instead you insisted on calling me Satan, despite my numerous attempts at proving you wrong."

Bronwen looked at Thanatos guiltily, but he had gone back to staring at the ceiling, a deep frown on his handsome face. He could seem so human sometimes, especially when his feelings were hurt.

"Why did you come to the ball and reveal yourself?" she said in a soft voice.

Thanatos sat up and looked at her, his voice still bitter. "You said you wanted a gentleman. So, I gave you one."

"That was not what I meant, or wanted."

"And yet, that is what you have."

"And what of when I *choose* to have you?" Bronwen said in the hope of steering the subject elsewhere. "You may come

364

and go as you please, yet I have no way to contact you, should I need you."

"Need me?" Thanatos said, intrigued.

Bronwen looked away. "When I have questions to ask you," She muttered.

"Questions," Thanatos said, disappointed. "You finally have questions for me?"

Bronwen braced herself and asked the one question that was burning her from inside. "Am I pregnant?"

"Who has touched you?" Thanatos growled, making Bronwen lift her head.

"No one," Bronwen stumbled, shocked at his sudden change and ferocity. Did he not know about what Kenneth had done to her as a child or was he only talking about sex?

"Then you cannot be with child," Thanatos said and his eyes went back to normal, where they had momentarily flashed a lethal red.

"Then *you* have not..."

"Put a child in you?" he interrupted, sounding irritated. "No, your bleeding has stopped because you have stopped. I said before, you are no longer part of the nature that rules the world above."

Bronwen blushed at his blunt mention of her female condition, then felt an unwanted rush of disappointed despair.

"So, I can never have children?" she whispered to herself. Bronwen was not sure why she thought she might still be able to and felt stupid for thinking it. She had always wanted children to keep her company and wondered if this was how Josette felt.

Of course, she would not be able to have children. Bronwen's life was only temporary. Did she really think she could leave them behind when she died?

"Not unless you want them with me. And it is... complicated," Thanatos said, but this did not alleviate

Bronwen's despair.

She pulled her knees up to her chest, making sure the fabric of her white dress was tucked around her and looked at the stars in the roof above.

"And should you have need of me, you only have to ask," he said. "Daemonium, et opus vestrum."

"Daemonium?" Bronwen questioned.

"Demon, I need you," Thanatos explained. "Have they been neglecting your Latin studies, my Lady?"

"I know what it means," Bronwen snapped. She was just confused at Thanatos calling himself a demon, considering all the time he spent trying to convince her he was not one.

When she looked into his eyes for an answer, she realised that he had said it to mock what she thought of him, like when he had used the anagram of Satan for his alias Nasta and it *did* pain him.

It was strange that she could discern all that in one patient look. Bronwen comprehended then that she was beginning to know Thanatos - his personality in all its unpredictability.

Bronwen shifted uncomfortably. "Why Latin?"

"I like the way it sounds," Thanatos said casually. "And it is useful in cases where we would not want our meanings to be obscured." He gazed at her knowingly.

"I assure you, there will not be an occasion where that is true," Bronwen said icily.

"Of course not. But a man needs solid words, when a woman distributes her kisses so freely."

"Do you delight in torturing me?"

"It is the only time I have your attention, and that is what I delight in."

"Do not be so petty," Bronwen snapped, tiring of him.

Thanatos sat forward on his hands and crawled towards her. He pulled on her ankles so her knees were no longer by her chest and hovered above her, so his hands were either side of her shoulders and his arms encased her.

Bronwen tried to shuffle away, but was trapped. She turned her face to the side in discomfort at looking into his eyes, at how they swirled with more of the world's knowledge then anyone should possess.

"I am master here, Lady Bronwen," Thanatos murmured in her ear. She could feel his words on her neck. "It is impolite to insult a man in his own home."

"You should not presume to lecture me on propriety, *Prince* Nasta," she said the faux name bitterly, but he only laughed at her.

"Ah, Thomas is of course a gentleman, but as you have so many times made plain to me, *I* am not."

He used his knee to gently, but insistently, push Bronwen's legs slightly apart, enough for him to put his own knees there. She glowered up at him and yet, Bronwen still did not feel afraid. Despite her inability to move, she felt anger more than fear when he was like this.

"You no longer intimidate me. Whatever form you take."

"But, how am to tell you do not want me, when signs of your desire are evident?" Thanatos pressed his full body onto her so his whole form could be felt against hers. He still held his weight off her, but she gasped as she felt his chest, stomach and hips pressed against her breasts and stomach, and then felt another hardness between her legs and blushed deeply as her stomach fluttered and there was a strange singular pulse between her legs.

Bronwen turned her head away again, trying to make her body move.

"You think my teasing is a torture? You have no concept of the word. The true torture is resisting something that you know you want - that you know you can take but choose to deny yourself," His voice was soft and his lips were so close to Bronwen's skin that her scalp prickled. "You make yourself suffer for no worthy cause, my Lady. Stop resisting, let the darkness in and suffer in pleasure, forever and ever."

Bronwen shuddered and her muscles clenched in places she wasn't aware she had any. He kissed her neck and shifted his hips, barely a scrap of cloth between them.

"You cannot make me," Bronwen whispered, more to herself than to Thanatos.

"Agree to be with me," He whispered in her ear. "Give me your permission. That is all you need say - habes meum consensum - and I will release you from the life you have been shackled to and take you into mine."

Bronwen scrunched up her eyes and balled her fists. Her breath caught as he moved his hips again and her nipples seemed to itch in a way that said they needed to be touched.

Bronwen had never felt this feeling in her body before and wondered if this was what it was like when two people desired one another. Was it this feeling that led a woman to cast aside her reputation, just to satisfy a lust?

Somewhere in her mind, Bronwen found a small voice that told her it had found where her strength had retreated to and was ready to lead the charge.

"No," she said in an exhale.

"Bronwen," Thanatos breathed in a smooth voice.

"No!" She said louder and moved her legs finally to close him out.

Thanatos laughed and immediately removed himself from over Bronwen to sit opposite her again. She sat up and straightened her skirt in embarrassment and frustration.

"I would not have taken what you were unwilling to give, my Lady. But you must start fighting for yourself. What are you so afraid of, Bronwen?" Thanatos said silkily. "Is it I? Or your own desires?"

"I would like to return now, please," Bronwen said shakily. She didn't want to be near him, afraid he might touch her again.

"Bronwen..." His voice was soft and unusually delicate. "Why do you fear being touched?"

Bronwen looked at him, her knees wrapped around herself and felt tears well in her eyes again. Did he know? He couldn't know. Would he care if she told him? He wouldn't care.

"Ask Kenneth Quays," she said angrily and Thanatos's eyes flashed. Bronwen looked away again before she could see if he had figured out what she wasn't saying. "Please, I want to go home."

Thanatos held out his hand to her. "As you desire."

Once Bronwen had left his company, Thanatos struggled to contain his rage. The walls shook with it and the starry sky above him turned black.

The kiss that Bronwen had given him on the cheek in the train carriage had been all he could think about for weeks. It didn't make sense to him. He who took women whenever he wanted and loved to explore every part of their bodies. Yet, this one chaste and innocent kiss from the Lady had him filled with more wanting than he had ever experienced before.

It was because of this kiss that Thanatos had entered the living world as Prince Thomas Nasta, in the hope that he might gain another favour.

He felt so foolish, especially as his little display with Bronwen a moment ago might have destroyed yet more of their precarious relationship. But he had to know what was holding her back. He had to know why she was so scared so he could protect her... no... so her could take what was his, he had to remind himself.

And her words. Her small figure closing up protectively as she revealed her most inner feelings.

Kenneth Quays. Thanatos had never suspected and he felt a fool! He prided himself on knowing people and spied on the human world regularly. He even knew of the man's inclinations, even knew that he had taught Bronwen. But he had not known this. Had not thought that he would dare do this!

This insolent bastard had touched Bronwen as a child, knowing that she was meant for him. Kenneth had broken his deal to serve his Dominus by taking what rightfully belonged to him. Perhaps if Kenneth had not broken the woman's spirit, Bronwen would still be beside Thanatos - or beneath him.

Thanatos told himself that it was for this reason alone that he did what he did next. And not because it might result in another kiss from Bronwen and perhaps her forgiveness and elusive affection.

LEVITICUS

Nec polluamini in omnibus his quibus...
{Defile not yourselves with any of these things}

I

Ping.

Kenneth turned to his piano - to the light sound of a key playing of its own accord. He was unperturbed by the phantom sound. Often it might happen that a string is plucked by whatever force coursed through the air. Like the memory of heat a ceramic pot retains or the twitching of a muscle too often used by a repetitive action.

Or perhaps it was in his mind.

Kenneth turned away, back to his desk and his paperwork.

PING.

A cord this time.

Kenneth reached for his lamp and turned the gas up fully, so the light passed over the whole room. He stood and walked the few paces to his piano and lifted the fallboard off the keys. They were white and glossy, the black blocks leering over them, they jeered at him, as mute as a mime. He put the lantern down on the hood of the instrument and lightly pressed down on a high cord, too lightly for any sound to come of it.

Its deeper brother cord answered.

The teacher stared at it a moment, then swiftly rounded the piano and lifted the entire top off, knocking the lantern from the table. He was lucky it did not smash, the flame simply extinguished and it rolled away to the wall, making the room darker but for the light of a streetlamp outside.

There was nothing inside the piano. None of the hammers were out of place and the strings were not vibrating.

It was a trick of the mind from his weariness. Ghosts and ghouls did not worry him, there were far more terrifying things that could lurk in the darkness and in the darkness of one's mind.

duuuhhhnnndonnndinnnnn....

BANG! The hood of the piano slammed closed as Kenneth let go of it. A painful thump in Kenneth's heart turned into a lump in his throat, plugging his scream back down into his stomach. In the brief second before the lid hit into place, he had seen his sister on the shiny surface of the piano, as if she were sat there.

The music ceased the moment the lid had closed, but he had seen that not a single hammer had moved when the music sounded. The noise still rang in Kenneth's ears; his muddled brain grasping at what the tune had been, at the same time as rejecting that he knew it.

When he finally felt able to breathe and move again, Kenneth sided around the piano and picked up the fallen lantern.

There were too many shadows that could dance to and fro with the small amount of light, and cause an agitated mind to see things. Kenneth thought the best thing to do was leave the room and go to bed as planned.

He lit the lantern again with the matches on the mantel piece. Someone was playing a trick on him and he refused to be scared in his own domain.

Not glancing back at the piano, or closing the lid to keep dust off the keys, Kenneth strode to the door. Just as he reached for the handle, the music began again. He had been expecting it this time however and smiled with one edge of his mouth.

It was obvious who would want to frighten him and who potentially had the unearthly power to manipulate a piano to play on its own.

Lady Bronwen would have to do better than that if she wished to unnerve him.

"You have been practicing," Kenneth smirked, not turning back from the door.

"Are you impressed, brother?"

Kenneth dropped the lantern again, this time it did smash before the flame extinguished, oil dripped from it onto the carpet.

It had been the voice of his sister. A person he had not spoken about to anyone. Bronwen could not know of her. He had been meticulous in his suppression of why he had really moved to Winchester and even if she did know, she would not have known her voice. How softly sweet it sounded when she had sung by the piano as he played.

Kenneth turned on his heel with great courage. The room was empty. The light was low and every shadow seemed to grab his attention as he tried to focus on all of them at once.

He felt behind him for the handle of the door, but couldn't find it. The wood felt smooth and lacked calluses or grain from the varnish.

Without an escape, Kenneth stepped into the centre of the room as bravely as he could manage.

His sister was long dead. There was nothing she could do to harm him, even if she was a spirit.

"You abandon me so easily?"

Kenneth shook the voice from his mind. As he did, he saw a shape in his peripherals. The figure was gone before he could focus on it, moved to the other side of him; first white and delicate, then dark and threatening. It was more unnerving than if he could see the thing properly. The voice followed it when it moved around the room.

"You have others to replace me, now. I wonder if father would

374

have done so, when I became too old for his bed, as mother had."

The piano started playing again. Kenneth knew the tune now. It had been a common one when he was young, that he had played and sung with his sister often. But the notes were disjointed and the scale it was played in too high. Some notes were added to it as well, so it gave the tune an uncomfortable resonance - a tingling up the spine.

"Is that why you let father kill me, brother?"

Kenneth was stuck in his place. There was a sickness in his stomach while he tried to focus his mind on the solid things in the room, to pull himself back from the paranormal happenings that threatened to cascade forbidden memories into the sane part of his consciousness.

'You should have let mother kill me, as you told the police. Such lovely police officers. They were so thorough when they checked my carcass for any sign of life.'

Kenneth shook his head, but it only replaced the room with the image of his sisters back, moments before his father had come at him with a knife. The dead weight of her had brought him to his knees, then, just as quickly, he had launched himself at his father with the knife that had been in the girl's chest moments before.

"THE SON TAKES THE SIN OF THE FATHER!"

This shriek was so close to Kenneth's ear that he crouched down into a ball, hands over his head. It was his mother's voice - the woman who had beaten his sister, blaming her for their Father's misplaced attentions. It had made her seek out Kenneth's bed instead, and it was only right he should comfort her as she asked him to. They had to stick together.

The cry had stopped the music at least and shocked Kenneth enough to gather his wits and stride for the door.

The handle was there. Freedom from the reliving of a nightmare. A recurring terror and desperate loss.

duuuhhhbuhhhrrrrraaa...

The music was played sweetly now. More perfect than was

humanly possible to play. Every note in the correct place, with the precise amount of emphasis where needed. It would not have been possible for Kenneth to play better himself after a lifetime of practice.

That fact made it more terrifying than the deliberate attempt to demoralize him. He wanted it to stop... immediately. It had to stop!

With wild intentions, he turned back to the empty room and almost ran at the piano.

Kenneth pulled off the top and yanked furiously at the hammers, when that didn't stop the music, he ripped at the strings in frenzy. The taught wire resisted him and cut open his hands. The thinner ones he succeeded in plucking retaliated by whipping his face, lashing at his skin and making deep welts in his flesh. It was a wonder how they missed his eyes.

Soon Kenneth's hands were wet with blood, too slippery to continue his assault and yet the music refused to cease.

He looked down at his hands. His bloodied hands. The same shade as they had been when his sister had died and he had murdered his father in revenge.

Kenneth fell to the floor, crumpled into a tight ball of blood and tears as he wept hysterically, injured hands over his ears, desperately trying to block out the music.

His weeping gave over to a repetitive wailing when the voice of a long dead girl joined in.

{When the soft dews of kindly sleep, my wearied eyelids gently steep. Be my last thought, how sweet to rest, forever on my Saviour's breast}

"Ahgh... ahgh... ahgh..." Kenneth cried out until his throat was dry and hoarse, so he could only whimper as he listened to how horrifically the lyrics took on their own meaning.

{Abide with me from morn till eve, for without Thee I cannot live. Abide with me when night is nigh, for without Thee I dare not *die!}*

Kenneth could not form words, even if his mind had let him think for a moment.

{If some poor wand'ring child of Thine, has spurned today the voice divine, now, Lord, the gracious work begin...}

{LET HIM NO MORE LIE DOWN IN SIN!}

Kenneth let out a strangled scream and tore at his ears and face and beat his head with his fists in the hope the pounding would drown out the song. A sweet song turned sour like rotting fruit.

Eventually, he clawed his way to the piano stool, his energy ebbing with his sanity. Kenneth wished there was something there he could fight with. Something in the room human enough in shape that he could gain some satisfaction in destroying it.

At the keys, he beat his bloodied hands down upon any note, trying to break the tune, but the thing was too damaged from his attack that only one note, deep and ominous, would submit to his command. He played it over and over again, beating his fist on it until it had become part of the illusory song. Blood dribbled onto the carpet and into the cracks of the piano, so a squelching accompaniment joined the composition.

He didn't know how long he sat playing like that, tears pooling in his eyes and joining the blood. Exhaustion slowed his hammering and Kenneth opened his eyes he had not realised were closed. He had lost much blood and the smears on his face had long crusted over.

A white hand slid silently along the keys towards his. A small, delicately young hand, perfectly manicured and clean. It was not quite solid but lucid in its creamy texture.

Kenneth dared not look directly at it, lest it disappear.

"*For without Thee... I dare not die.*"

Slowly, Kenneth moved his deadened hand across the keys towards it - only noticing then that all music had ceased -

then took the coiled and abnormally lengthy piano wire from the apparition's hand.

"For without Thee, I cannot live," Kenneth whispered to himself in a trance and repeated the mantra in his head as his numb fingers uncoiled the wire then, made a loop in one end and threaded it to create an unbreakable noose.

II

The news had reached her by accident. Bronwen had been stood on the first-floor landing outside her bedroom, taking pause at the window to view the crescent moon and its glowing shimmer in the clouds, its true shape obscured by them.

The sound of a weak knocking on the front door made her lean her head over the banister. It was very late to be making a house call.

Even more unusual was that it had not been James who answered it but her father.

"Kenneth is dead," said a man, pushing his way through, before the Baron had a chance to invite him in or send him away.

A hat low over his face meant Bronwen could not see who it was from above and did not want to move from her current position, lest the wood creaked and alerted them to her watching.

"Already?" Donovan said, in a tone that did not portend to caring about the loss of life, more an inconvenience at the timing of it.

The man shrugged off his coat, without waiting for admittance from Donovan.

Bronwen bent down lower but she only caught one word,

"...suicide," before the door to her Father's study was closed.

Bronwen considered sneaking up to the door and listening, but decided it was not worth risking being caught and knew that the door was well soundproofed. Besides, she had all the information she needed. Kenneth was dead, by a supposed suicide.

The details did not matter, either way Bronwen knew it was unlikely to have been Kenneth doing it to himself. She would have suspected Josette or Azu but they were still in London, not due back until the morning. Besides, Bronwen doubted they could have arranged for it to look like suicide, even if they had arrived early to do it.

She thought about how Thanatos had reacted when she had implied Kenneth's inclinations and something deep within her made her certain it had been him.

Bronwen couldn't help being pleased that the man was finally gone. She caught herself smiling about the death of another and judged herself for it. That was a downhill slope of evil that she wished to avoid at all costs.

Her soul belonged to her no longer, but she would keep it from being tainted nonetheless.

She had returned to the living a few nights previous; mere moments before a maid had walked in the room.

There had been minimal pain this time. The poison's work had stopped the moment her heart ceased pumping it through her system, and the lingering effects of it hadn't had time to settle in. All she felt was the numbing stiffness of being dead for hours on a hard, cold floor. And of course, the searing pain of her spirit becoming one with her body again.

The maid who opened the door looked shocked to find Bronwen there and apologised with a look that said she wasn't really sure what she was apologising for.

Bronwen excused the maid in a strained voice, trying not to draw attention to the syringe that had killed her, lying like a beacon on the floor. Once the maid had left, Bronwen picked it up carefully and wrapped it in a handkerchief, then made her way to her room.

Once the door was closed, Bronwen checked her bedroom for any sign that Adam might have hidden there. She even checked under the bed and inside her wardrobe, though she was sure he would be long gone by now, thinking he had murdered her. He obviously hadn't gone for help or she would be in a morgue right now, rather than staring at the wrapped syringe in her hand.

Bronwen wasn't sure what to do with it. She certainly couldn't have anyone find it. She had the idea of pulling up one of the floorboards, but dismissed it and stuffed it in the thin decorative box kept on her mantelpiece, turning the key for the first time in years. Then, she put it snugly in one of her mother's hiding spots - a hinged panel on one of the thick bedposts that was hollowed out. It was one of the few places Bronwen was sure only she knew about.

That done, she sat on her bed and thought about a number of things like, whether to find Adam, what Josette and Azu were doing, what Kole and her father would say about her disappearing bodyguard, but most of all she thought about Thanatos and how it had felt to have his body pressed against hers - which was why she was grateful when Alda burst into the room and began to complain about her lack of sleeping and the mess she had created in the library.

Events over the next few days had been slow. Her father returned from his business and they had a discussion about Adam's runaway. Donovan didn't appear overly concerned - not even surprised - only inconvenienced and frustrated that he then had to allow Azu to be sole guardian of Bronwen.

Mostly Bronwen spent her time in the library, the only book she found remotely related to her was a beaten copy of 'The Iliad of Homer' which irritated her even more because it only reiterated some of the things Thanatos had said about his Under-realm, and she desperately wanted him to be wrong.

{Why so much grief for me? No man will hurl me down to Death, against my fate. And fate? No one alive has ever escaped it, neither brave man nor coward, I tell you - it's born with us the day that we are born.}

Bronwen had scoffed at this line in the text, but had found herself keeping the book in her room.

The day Josette and Azu returned couldn't have come sooner. Bronwen would have gone to the station to get them if they had sent word. Instead they found her in the library, surrounded by a pile of books and papers.

"It happened!" Josette exclaimed as Bronwen got up to embrace them both. "I am a published author!" Josette was beaming, and Azu was smiling as well.

"Congratulations!" Bronwen gushed and hugged her friend again, then embraced Azu as Josette began talking about everything the publishers had said and what was to happen next.

"They were clear on not putting my entire name on the cover. They assured me that it was not to do with me being a woman, but because of how it looked. We settled on 'J B Emry', doesn't is sound so professional."

"B?" Bronwen asked. "But your middle name is Mary."

"The B stands for Bronwen," Josette announced proudly. "It was all down to you that this happened and I am so grateful."

"Nonsense, I did not write it," Bronwen argued, even though she was immensely touched. "I did nothing other than add my family name to an invitation."

"And all I have done is add your name to a book," Josette countered firmly. "It is done now, so consider it my thanks. It is only an initial."

"Thank you, Josette," Bronwen said, truly touched by the

sentiment. "Now, we must go and celebrate. Where would you like to go? My treat and I will have no arguments on that."

"Well, you owe me a debt Lady Bronwen, you claimed you would go to any establishment of my choosing should I secure a book deal," Josette said mischievously.

"And I shall keep my word, Mrs Emry," Bronwen said, but the look in Josette's eyes made her apprehensive.

"You say that now, but it is not a place where people like you are seen, or rather, *can* be seen."

"Just because I am wealthy does not mean I am some obscure creature," Bronwen's sentence trailed off as she realised, she might be.

"I know that, but I worry I might be pushing your boundaries a little too far with this one."

Bronwen frowned at this. After Adam had successfully killed her and Thanatos's words about her not fighting, she had felt even more vulnerable than before and even more determined to prove she was not as delicate as everyone seemed to think she was.

"Josette, I made a promise and I intend to keep it. What is our destination?"

"A brothel," Azu answered before Josette became too flustered.

"Oh," Was all Bronwen could reply, giving herself time to process the information.

"I do not want to go there for that," Josette quickly explained. "Well, not just that, it is also because the drinks are inexpensive and well, it is not as stringent as other places. No one is afraid to be who they are or do what they want to do. Not like an upstanding establishment where you have to act the part and are always observed and judged. It is just good fun."

"What do you think, Azu?" Bronwen asked her serious friend and bodyguard.

"I go where you go," he said unhelpfully, and then added. "Fun is much needed."

"Very well. I said it was your night, Josette. And I shouldn't worry about me being recognised, I do not think you will find anyone there who will know me."

Bronwen heard Azu chuckle behind her quietly.

"Still, perhaps it would be best to go in disguise," Josette said, stifling her own laugh for her friend's sake. "We do not want to tempt thieves by wearing fine clothing."

Before Bronwen could ask if that was likely, Josette had her off to her room to change. The plainest clothes Bronwen had was ironically her church outfit, which was mostly black with white lace sleeves. Josette undid the top of it when Bronwen came out from behind her dressing curtain, so the top of her breasts could be seen making a smooth arch above her bodice.

Josette ignored Bronwen's complaints and set to loosening her hair and tying it in a messy bun at the top of her head, then added various cosmetics to Bronwen's face, lips and eyes.

She presented Bronwen in front of the mirror proudly.

"Josette! This is far too much eye paint. People will think I am a fallen woman!" Bronwen complained.

"Perfect," Josette said with a grin, then went behind the curtain to put on her own attire.

Bronwen looked at herself properly. She didn't look anything like herself and she smiled at that. The black dress made her look pale and morbid and her brown eyes had more of the otherworldly blue in them each day. She promised herself that this night, she would be a different person, not some weak-willed Lady - just for one night.

Josette came and stood beside Bronwen. Her dress was more flamboyant that Bronwen's and even showed a bit of her leg when she moved.

Bronwen made room for her at the mirror, then answered

the door when she heard a light knock. She used the door as a barrier to hide her clothes, afraid her father or Alda would see her dressed so strangely, but it was Azu.

Bronwen ushered him in quickly and closed the door.

They appraised one another at the same time. Azu wore his normal dark coloured shirt and a waistcoat but with no tie and his collar was unbuttoned. He also had a gold earring in one ear that looped around his ear lobe. He looked like a sailor or, more likely, a pirate.

Azu nodded at Bronwen in approval and she curtsied in an exaggerated manor which earned her a rare smile.

Josette pulled them both over to the mirror and the three of them looked at their reflections.

What an unusual trio. A pirate, a courtesan and a... a demon.

Bronwen wondered if they were perhaps overdoing it, but the costumes made her feel new. Like hiding behind a mask.

Bronwen and Josette giggled as they snuck out of the house together. Her father would not notice her disappearance anyway and Bronwen left a note for Alda saying she was having dinner with Josette and Azu to celebrate and wouldn't be back until late. The three of them took horses from the stables and headed out, following Josette closely through the twilight.

Bronwen breathed in the night. She had yet to tell Azu and Josette about Adam disappearing. She didn't want to ruin the night by making them worry. And she did not want to see the look in their eyes that would say that they had been right, and Bronwen had been wrong – very wrong.

Josette became increasingly animated as the got closer to their destination and she talked almost nonstop about her time in London. Mr Lawnem had taken the two of them out to see the landmarks of the city and had gone to dinner with Josette after the contracts were signed.

"Josette, I believe Mr Lawnem was quite taken with you,

perhaps you could have come back with a husband," Bronwen teased.

"He was only being friendly to a client, is all," Josette brushed off Bronwen's remark with a wave.

"I doubt a publishing house generally put their authors up in the Star and Garter, he must be very friendly indeed."

"Nonsense. Tennyson and Dickens frequent the place and they are both authors."

"And they are both quite well established in the literary word now. I heard one of Alfred Tennyson's poems sold over ten thousand copies in one month."

Josette only smiled in response, no doubt imagining doing the same thing herself one day.

The building they arrived at was obviously old, and so tall, it looked about to topple, without any houses either side to hold it up. It was very oddly shaped and had more chimneys sticking out of its multiple levelled roofs than windows. The large sign above the entrance was lavishly painted with the image of a naked woman with the wings of a bird and tail of a fish draped seductively over the name of the brothel, 'The Siren'.

A couple of men laughed as they walked through the main door, removing their hats, and Bronwen had a pang of apprehension at what she was doing. What if her father found out? What would she see and hear going into a place like that?

She didn't have long to find out as they tied their horses next to the others, under a crude shelter with a trough of water that looked surprisingly clean. Bronwen wasn't pleased about leaving her horse there but begrudgingly did so with Josette pulling on her arm in an excitement that was infectious.

They were let through the large door without question by a smiling woman who offered to take their coats and hats. They handed them over gratefully.

The bar was stuffy and full of so much smoke, that it gave the room a haze that obscured most of the people's faces, which Bronwen was glad about. The smoke also helped cover the smell of beer and sweat and other things.

Josette marched straight up to the busy bar at the back of the room and waited to be served, while Azu and Bronwen surveyed the room for different reasons.

The two corners of the room nearest the door seemed to be the busiest tables. One table was so surrounded by men and the women serving them, that it was impossible to see who the people were that had everyone flocking to them like birds to seeds, all trying to push into the middle.

At the other table, people left it as much as they arrived, and through the gaps in bodies, Bronwen could see a group playing cards on a round table, piled high with coins and papers.

The rest of the room was full of noise and laughter and shouting to be heard above the other shouting. Bronwen was surprised to note that not all of the women in the room were working. Some were there for the enjoyment of the company. A smile actually lifted Bronwen's frown. She looked at Azu before turning back to the bar and paying for the drinks Josette had ordered, careful not to show all of the money she had brought with her.

Azu appeared to relax too and they picked up their drinks and slid away to an open booth at the far edge of the room.

It was a good vantage point to watch the various happenings and had a straight view to both doors.

Once they were sat down, Bronwen finally looked at the drinks Josette had bought. One was a frothy dark beer, in a tankard that looked surprisingly well kept, and the other was in a small glass and contained a green substance that seemed more solid than liquid and was only filled halfway. Bronwen had never seen anything like it before, even in her father's collection of drinks.

"It is called absinthe," Josette yelled to them both, looking pleased with herself. "It is strong and supposed to be drunk in one go." She demonstrated by tipping her head back and downing the lot. She made a sour face as she put her glass down again and grinned at the other two.

Azu and Bronwen looked at one another, then down at the drink and simultaneously poured theirs into Josette's glass, filling it to the brim. Josette giggled at the two of them.

"More for me then," she said and drank some of her beer.

Bronwen pulled hers closer to her and planned to pour it into Azu and Josette's tankards when she got a chance. She doubted beer would taste any nicer to her than tea or water.

It only took another round before Josette was becoming merry, and Azu too, Bronwen presumed, by the way he smiled. Josette talked nonstop again and eventually she excused herself to go speak to some people at another table whom she had met at the bar and were beckoning her over to them.

Bronwen and Azu declined joining her and said they didn't mind her going when Josette said she would not leave them. It was her night and they told her to be careful and not to leave the place without them.

Bronwen slid closer to Azu so they could talk.

"You can go with her if you wish," Bronwen said close to his ear. "I will be fine here."

"I don't think I'd be welcome," Azu said, his accent thicker now he was on his third tankard and second absinthe, that Josette had forced upon him and he found he actually quite liked.

Bronwen looked over at the two women she had noticed staring at Azu earlier. It was by no means unfriendly, in fact they kept trying to beckon him over and we're flaring their skirts to show off their legs and busts.

"You should go with them." Bronwen gestured with her head at them. "I will pay, and they seem very taken by you."

Azu scoffed and drank again.

"Are you not tempted by them?" Bronwen teased, trying to ease the lines in his forehead. He shook his head and she followed his line of sight to where a man was sat on the far wall. He kept looking over at Azu with a shy smile.

"Perhaps the company of that gentleman would suit you better?" Bronwen joked but stopped when a fearful look entered Azubuike's eyes and he lowered his face to the table.

Bronwen looked back at the man and wondered why Azu had reacted like that. She had only been joking with him. But her mind did not want to admit what her eyes and heart suspected.

Before Bronwen could ask, she was soon distracted by the doors opening to let in a new gang of people. There were four of them and they strolled in like they owned all they saw. She felt Azu tense beside her as the men walked straight up to the cards table and spoke with the players there. Then, it was time for Bronwen to tense as a fifth man entered and marched directly to the bar.

It was Adam Whyms. His hair stuck to his face and he had dark rings around his eyes. He looked like he was on a mission from God and struck his fist on the counter as he demanded something from the barman, who gave him a warning scowl and left for the side door.

"We need to leave," Bronwen whispered to Azu, turning her face away. She wouldn't be recognised in a crowd but with Azu stood next to her, she would certainly be spotted.

Azu nodded stiffly. He was still staring at the other men who had entered just before Adam. Bronwen looked at them more closely. She was sure she recognised them but was not sure from where. Then they laughed loudly and Bronwen didn't need to see the look on Azu's face to realised who they were.

"Get Josette and meet me by the horses." Azu hesitated, not wanting to leave Bronwen alone. She gave him a meaningful look and he didn't need to be told twice and slid out from the booth to head to where they had last seen Josette.

Bronwen kept her eye on both sides of her now. The men in the corner, who, she remembered with dread, had been the men trying to drown Azu the night she had saved him from the river. And Adam on the other side, who *had* actually succeeded in killing her.

Bronwen kept her eyes on him as she moved towards the door and watched as a woman entered the bar from the stairs and began talking to Adam. She had her hands on her hips and Adam was clearly shouting at her, though even he could not be heard above the other sounds around Bronwen.

Bronwen wondered whether it would be a good idea to find out what they were talking about when Adam shifted slightly so she had a better view of the woman. It was the same woman he had met with in Guildford down the dark alley.

Bronwen froze and watched the two. Her escape forgotten as an image of the woman slipping something into Adam's pocket flashed across her memory. Could she have been the one to give him the syringe? Had she known it was poison? Was she the one to have concocted it and if so, why?

Bronwen truly looked at her, now that she was closer and the room lighter. She was not much older than Bronwen, plain in complexion but with a shapely figure, which would make any man admire her. Bronwen was sure she recognised her from somewhere other than the alley, but could not place it.

The woman looked up then, straight into Bronwen's eyes and gave her a look of such terrible coldness, that Bronwen first thought she must have been looking at someone else. She had never met this woman before and couldn't understand what had caused her to show such passionate hatred towards someone who was only looking in on them. It made Bronwen look away swiftly and when she had the courage to look up again, Adam was also staring straight at her.

She backed up and bumped into a table, barely registering the people complaining about their drinks being spilt as she stared at the changing expressions on Adam's face. First horror, then shock, relief, anger and finally - possession.

Bronwen turned to see that the door was too far away for her to escape and the mass of people by the popular table had spread like a virus across the space. She turned back and saw Adam had halved the distance between them already.

Bronwen's heart fluttered and she shuffled around the table she had been holding onto. Adam pushed a man out of the way and was only a few paces in front of her when a mass of darkness was stood between them - black arms and shoulders tense with muscle.

Bronwen peered around Azu's imposing form as Josette held her arm.

"What the hell is going on?" Josette asked, speech slightly slurred.

"Move nigger, this doesn't concern you!" Adam spat with malice, still looking at Bronwen.

Azu refused to back down; a solid shield of strength between Adam and the two women.

Bronwen wasn't sure what to do except try to get out. They were drawing attention to themselves and soon Azu would be spotted by his own attempted murderers. Bronwen couldn't let him get hurt on her account.

"We need to leave," Bronwen said in a quiet voice, placing a hand on Azu's arm.

Adam's eyes filled with a terrible anger at her touching Azu and he growled as he made a grab for Bronwen. She closed her eyes, but Adam didn't get far before Azu punched him hard in the face, knocking him completely to the ground.

Bronwen looked just as shocked as Adam as the man wiped away blood that was coming from his obviously broken nose. She gently tried to turn Azu towards the door, knowing that now, they really needed to leave.

Azu backed away slowly, keeping his eyes on Adam, still on the floor, then turned away and the three of them retreated to the door.

Bronwen looked over her shoulder at Adam and was glad she had when he lifted himself off the ground in an easy movement and began to pull out one of his many weapons from beneath his long coat. She just had time to squeal incoherently and push Azu aside when the knife hurtled past them and into the wall, right in front of the face of a man who was about to lean in and kiss one of the serving women. She screamed shrilly at the sight of the blade.

The bar was silent momentarily and everyone was staring at them – including the men who wanted Azu dead.

"You!" one of them said, standing and reaching for his own knife. His comrades noticed and stood as well.

Now the three of them were caught between two enemies and a tight mob of people, keen to watch the events.

III

"What the hell is going on?" Josette said again, quieter now that no one else was talking.

The silence didn't last long, but it was not Adam, Azu or the other gang of men who started it. Instead, a third party jumped in – the man who had almost had his nose sliced off by Adam's stray dagger. He had pulled it from the wall and ran yelling towards Adam.

Bronwen didn't see how it happened, or maybe didn't remember, but soon after this enraged charge, the whole room was in a raucous mess. Women were squealing, men were yelling, glass was being shattered, tables toppled.

The moving crowd separated Bronwen from Azu and Josette in the confusion and she found herself backed up against a wall with wide eyes. She couldn't understand what had happened to cause such chaos and desperately tried to spot Azu and Josette in the crowd, calling out their names only to be lost as well.

She found another name forming in her throat. "Daemonium, et opus vestrum."

Bronwen flinched when a bottle smashed near her then suddenly all appeared still and quiet, for nothing else occupied her mind in that moment. Not the men beating each other's faces and filling their tankards with blood, or the women retreating up the back stairs. For there, the furthest from where she stood, was Thanatos. He was coolly stood amidst the destruction with an amused smile on his face, his arms crossed and staring directly at her. He was wearing a dark red shirt with black waistcoat and black trousers that fit him snugly and tucked into his high boots.

Bronwen pinched her arm as she stared at him in his appealing attire - the only calm looking person in the tempest around them. The fighters didn't seem to go anywhere near where Thanatos stood and as he moved towards her, the crowd parted of its own accord to let him through, the brawl filling in the spaces he left.

His steps were controlled and Bronwen's heart beat faster at the look in his eyes - a heated, wanting look. She realised her mouth was open but couldn't close it. Why did the sight of him put her at ease?

Bronwen fell to the floor when a man barrelled into her as he tried to hit another. The glass on the floor crushed into her hand where she caught herself and she hissed at the pain while she crawled away under the table, like a child frightened of a storm. She pulled out the larger pieces of glass she could see through the blood, wincing at the pain.

Once done, Bronwen peered into the fray of legs and liquid, spilt from the tables, and tried to see where Thanatos had gone. A bloodied face appeared in front of hers, making her jump and hit her head on the table.

"Found you," the face growled and an arm reached out for her. Bronwen screamed and tried to back away but his arms were longer than the table and he grabbed a thick tuft of her hair and dragged her out from under it, kicking and screaming wildly.

Once out, he turned her to face him, still holding her hair. She hardly recognised Adam Whyms through the sadistic glaze in his eyes. He looked almost feverish, more frightening than the night he had attacked her. Bronwen squirmed and tried to get away.

"You're mine!" He yelled into her face.

"I think you will find yourself mistaken," A smooth growl sounded from behind Adam, who turned to find Thanatos staring at him with all the look of a Devil in his eyes.

"Fuck off!" Adam yelled at the demon, and even Bronwen was fearful for the weak man that held her.

Thanatos grabbed Adam by the collar and pulled him easily away from Bronwen, who fell to her knees again.

"Oh, I intend to," Thanatos hissed at Adam who was finally focused enough to feel frightened by the demon with the pointy teeth, bulging muscles and red coloured eyes. It was truly intimidating and even Bronwen looked away. From her cowering position on the floor, she saw Adam's feet leave the ground.

Bronwen thought she heard Adam actually yell out in fear and decided not to look to see what had made him react that way. He was then dropped to his knees and scrambled away as fast as he could.

A hand extended at eye height to Bronwen and she looked up timidly into Thanatos's eyes, afraid of what she would see, but he was his normal self, a small self-satisfied smirk on his lips and a glint in his eyes.

"As much as I like you on your knees before me," he said playfully and she wanted nothing more than to leave the bar, with him there to protect her.

Gratefully taking his hand, it wasn't until he had guided her all the way outside that Bronwen realised she had given him her injured hand with the glass still stuck in it.

She pulled her hand away and noticed small pieces of crystal fall from it. She brushed them off her palm and found no wound or glass there at all.

Bronwen looked at Thanatos in wonder but before she could speak, Josette ran over to her with Azu behind. Her friend embraced her.

"What the hell is going on?" she said for the third time that night. "We were about to go in for you when..." she trailed off and looked at Thanatos, who was leaning against the fence with ease. Josette looked at him sceptically.

"Josette, Azu, you remember Thomas Nasta, from the All-Hallowmas ball," Bronwen introduced him, which snapped Josette out of her stupor, but didn't alleviate the suspicion in her voice.

"Yes, I remember, a Prince are you not?" Josette said, perhaps a little rudely.

"Do not doubt it," he said smoothly, a wicked look in his eye as he glanced at Bronwen, who felt a shiver go up her spine.

"We should leave before Adam or... anyone else comes outside," Bronwen said, glancing at the door.

"Yes, but only one of our horses are there," Josette said gravely, swaying slightly on the spot. "The other two are missing. Sorry Bronwen, this is my fault entirely."

"It is alright, Josette. Azu and I were the ones attacked, how could that be your fault?"

"What about the horses?" Azu asked, also looking nervously at the door of the bar. It sounded as if there was a re-enactment of a civil war inside.

"Allow *me* to escort you home, my Lady," Thanatos cut in, his faint Grecian accent back. "I have a horse here, so we can have two on each."

The three looked at him silently. Josette was cautious, Azu confused and Bronwen suspicious that Thanatos might have had something to do with the horses' disappearance simply so he could escort them home.

"Thank you, your grace," Bronwen said, with a biting tone at his fake title. His eyes flashed red and salacious at her words and she thought he looked far too pleased with himself, so she changed the rules of the game he was playing.

"I shall ride with Azu and Than... Prince Nasta, with Josette," Bronwen smiled sweetly at the spike of anger in his expression, which he swiftly calmed.

"Very well," he said and led them to where the horses were.

His horse was much larger than Bronwen's little brown one and was all black with a shiny hide, tense with powerful muscles. It didn't look natural and Bronwen felt guilty at the look in Josette's eyes when she saw what she would be riding.

Thanatos untied the horse and held a hand out to assist Josette onto the beast. She hesitated, then grabbed his palm, only for them both to pull away again as if a static charge had passed through them.

Josette took a step back from him and Thanatos looked irritated.

"What is it?" Bronwen asked.

"Nothing," they replied simultaneously.

"I will ride with Azubuike," Josette said, pronouncing his name in the perfect way Bronwen couldn't quite manage.

"Josette, what is the matter?" Bronwen mumbled quietly. Even Azu was looking at Thanatos with trepidation.

"I cannot ride a horse that large," she said stiffly, avoiding Thanatos's eyes.

Bronwen conceded when it was clear she would say no more and allowed herself to be helped onto Thanatos's horse, feeling nothing in her own hands at his touch, other than warmth and a tenderness she tried desperately not to think of.

Once they were away, Bronwen asked quietly. "Did you do anything to Josette so that we would have to ride together?"

"No, I did not," Thanatos replied firmly, stiffening slightly. "Your friend has had too much to drink."

Bronwen looked back at Josette on the other horse, but she was her normal bubbly self again, riding side saddle and talking animatedly to Azu, while he tried to keep her from falling off the horse.

Thanatos had his hands low around Bronwen so he could relax his arms whilst holding the reins. His strong forearm steadied her back where she was sat side saddle, so she couldn't fall off and she tried to ignore whenever his hands moved to adjust the reins and stroked her leg.

Bronwen could feel his heart beating against her arm and was surprised to find it so steady, though she wasn't sure why she expected it to be otherwise. In fact, she hadn't expected him to have a heartbeat at all.

"Were you in the bar the entire time?" Bronwen asked him.

"I was," Thanatos replied. "By the door."

Bronwen looked ahead in the darkness. So, the faux prince was the one with all the admirers.

"Did you know I would be there?" She asked quietly.

"No," was all he said. He had seemed tense since they had mounted and Bronwen stayed quiet for a while, waiting to see if he would say something further, which he didn't.

"Why were you there?" She said finally, not liking the atmosphere.

"I enjoy the people," he said, smiling.

"Were you there for..." Bronwen trailed off. She wasn't sure why she was asking him these things and even less sure why it mattered to her, but it did. She could feel him looking at her but refused to meet his eyes.

"I do not need to pay for sex," He answered. Bronwen realised she had been holding her breath and tried to let it out slowly, so he wouldn't notice.

"But... you do..."

"Fuck other women? Yes, I do."

He shifted in his seat uncomfortably and Bronwen adjusted herself as well so she wasn't leaning against him so much.

"Does that bother you?" he asked.

"No. Why should it?" Bronwen said but even she was unconvinced by her tone.

"I can stop. If you ask me to." Thanatos seemed genuine, which confused Bronwen even more. He was a man. What say did she have who he chose to have relations with?

"What you do is your business. I can make no claim over you, even if we were married."

"Why do you think that?" Thanatos asked, surprised. "You think because I am a demon that I would not honour any vows of fidelity made between us?"

"I think because you are a man you do not need to uphold such vows," Bronwen sounded bitter. She had always known that when marrying Lord Guild that he could take a mistress if he wanted and see little consequence for it but she as the woman had to remain faithful.

"There is a difference between fucking and making love and not every man is so frivolous with their affections. When you choose to be mine, then I will give you the same exclusivity. You shall be all that I desire, Bronwen."

Her name on his lips was softer than the rest of his words. Like saying it was a caress to her spirit and she was shocked to find she believed him.

Azu and Josette's horse pulled up beside them when the path widened enough in the city proper. They trotted past the quiet houses, under the clear sky and glow of the streetlamps. The air was cold but Bronwen was again warm beside Thanatos and wondered if he extended the same warmth towards Josette and Azubuike as they did not appear to be shivering.

"I have not yet thanked you for pulling us out of the fight, your grace," Josette said, back to her normal self.

"Thomas, please, I hate my title. It makes people forget that I am just a man."

There was more meaning behind this, Bronwen knew, but

didn't comment. Instead she said, "you pulled them out?"

"I did, my Lady," He replied.

"You must call us by our names also, if we are to use yours," Josette said, matter of fact, despite the look Bronwen threw her. Her father would not be pleased to hear another man call her by her first name.

"Our Christian names it is then, Josette," Thanatos said, with a smirk Bronwen had come to realise was the one he used when he was thinking his own private joke.

Josette blushed shamelessly at how he said her name and looked at her with his intense eyes and seductive smile. Bronwen hated herself for feeling possessive and jealous that he was showing her attention.

"Unafikiri ya England, Azubuike?" {What do you think of England, Azubuike?} Thanatos said to Azu in his own language, perfectly pronounced, shocking all of them. Bronwen did not even know what language Azu spoke.

Azu studied Thanatos carefully with wide eyes before he replied.

"Ngumu na baridi." {Stiff and cold}

"Mgumu, dhahiri," {Stiff, definitely} Thanatos laughed. "Wakati tukio wito kwa ajili yake." {When the occasion calls for it}

Azu laughed loudly, something he rarely did and it was a good sound.

Josette gave Bronwen a surprised look and raised an eyebrow. Bronwen was just as stunned. Not that Thanatos had spoken to Azu in his own language, but that Azubuike had clearly been won over by the man in only a few sentences.

They continued talking to each other in the language as they left the city and followed the path to Metrom Hall. Josette had run out of conversation as she was almost asleep in the saddle, resting her head against Azu's solid chest. Bronwen briefly played with the idea of doing the same with

Thanatos, wondering how it would feel and what he would smell like, before she mentally slapped herself.

What was wrong with her tonight? Had dressing up caused such a change in her that Bronwen had forgotten how Thanatos had treated her in the Under-realm on only a few days ago? Or was it because he had saved them all from a potentially dangerous situation with no gain on his part for doing so?

Bronwen did not want to interrupt Azu and Thanatos talking, as it was the most she had ever heard Azu say, but they would be at the house soon and there were a few things to consider. Donovan would be back from his business meeting when they returned without two of his horses.

"What are we to tell my father?"

"I am so sorry for our manners," Thanatos said. "Azubuike and I were just discussing it and it was rude of us not to talk in English, but he has been away from his country for over seventeen years, he tells me."

Bronwen did not know this and tried to hide a scowl. In the weeks she had known him, and even after saving his life, Azu had never once spoken about his past. A ten-minute conversation with Thanatos and he disclosed everything.

"You are forgiven," Bronwen said bitingly. Thanatos must have noticed her tone, as he let one hand go of the reins and held Bronwen tightly to him around her waist, as if consoling her. He hid the motion from the other two with his arm.

Bronwen's breath caught in her throat at the closeness and she said nothing more.

"Do not worry about Lord Wintre," Thanatos said calmly, as if he thought nothing of how intimately he was holding her. "I shall speak to him and he will be none the wiser to where exactly we crossed paths."

The other two seemed content to let him do this, but Bronwen was still concerned. She could not predict what

Thanatos was likely to do in any situation. He always surprised her, and not always in a pleasant way.

They reached the door of the house and found her father waiting for them, a crushed piece of paper in his hand. His face was one of fury but it quickly softened when he saw Thomas sitting behind Bronwen. Then he looked confused at why they were riding together. Thanatos had let go of Bronwen's waist, which was still warm from his touch.

"Greetings, Baron Wintre," Thanatos said pleasantly, jumping down from his horse with ease and helping Bronwen slide gracefully to the floor, as if she weighed nothing. They were hidden momentarily by the horse and Bronwen felt his hands slide low to her upper thigh, before he let go and headed towards Donovan. Bronwen hesitated while she waited for her blush to subside.

"Prince Nasta," Donovan said, still confused.

"Lord, I am afraid I found your daughter in an unfortunate state," Thanatos said, walking up the stairs of the house confidently, his hands behind his back. "Two of your fine horses were stolen whilst Lady Bronwen was enjoying a meal with her two companions, at the same establishment I was dining at and I insisted upon taking them home. I hope this was not a presumptuous thing for me to do."

"Of course not," Donovan stumbled in a gruff voice and Bronwen saw him stuff the note she had written for Alda in his pocket. "Only, I was not expecting to see you."

Bronwen tried not to laugh at how her father was acting. If only he knew whom he was really talking to.

"His highness came very much to our rescue," Josette said, awake and clear headed again.

"Then you must come in and allow me to thank you over a glass of brandy," Donovan said, now recovered from his surprise.

"I am afraid I will have to decline the offer, as it is late for all of us."

"Then please, let me invite you to a small gathering I am having next Friday, to show my gratitude for taking such good care of my daughter."

"It was for my pleasure also, I assure you," Thanatos said, glancing once again at Bronwen. He caught her eye with a flash of fire, making her tremble - not with fear but something else. If Donovan thought what Thanatos said was odd, he showed no sign of it. "But I would be honoured to join you, Lord Wintre."

Donovan looked delighted that the Prince accepted, even after they said their goodbyes and he closed the door.

Bronwen was stood on the stairs. Donovan saw her watching.

He stared at her for a moment, his pleased expression changed to regret, softness, then irritation. He opened his mouth to say something then closed it again firmly and marched away to his study.

Bronwen kept to her room that night, trying to lose herself in a book but found her mind wondering to places she despised herself for visiting.

If she was not careful, she would forget what Thanatos truly was and allow herself to be lost to his depths.

IV

"That creepy sadistic evil slimy disturbed creepy bastard!" Josette said after Bronwen was forced to explain how Adam had attacked her.

She hadn't told them that Adam had killed her, only that he had injected her with a sedative which she had reacted to.

"You said creepy twice," Bronwen said.

"That is because he is twice creepy. I knew there was nothing good about him. If my stomach wasn't churning right now, I would go to kill him myself."

"There is no need. He is gone now and there was no harm done."

"No harm done! He drugged you Bronwen!" Josette exclaimed, further hurting her head. She was still suffering from the absinthe, having not been warned that one sip was usually enough. She had been violently ill all night and the next morning. "What if you had not had a reaction to it? What if he hadn't cared if you were dead? He could have taken full advantage of you and one day I shall kill him for it... just as soon as the room stops spinning."

Bronwen couldn't help giggling at Josette. She doubted Adam would come near her again, not soon anyway, not after what Thanatos did to him. She had never seen a man so terrified.

After Bronwen's tale, Azu finally told them about the men that were after him and why.

"Your leaders banned slavery, but some people still have them," he began, not looking at either of them as he spoke. "I was taken from my country when I was fifteen. I was walking in a field on my own and they thought I had no family. I couldn't speak English, but I fought them. They took me anyways and put me on a ship with another boy and two girls. It was a long journey. We were put in same rooms and became good friends, but the men who took us did not like that we talked in our language, they beat us till we understand and then one day..." Azu paused and looked at both of them carefully, not sure whether to continue.

"You can speak to us about anything, Azubuike," Bronwen coaxed.

Josette nodded. "We are not as delicate as we seem and we are here for you."

Azu nodded and opened and closed his fists nervously. He spoke slowly and quietly, only his tone betraying his difficultly in telling his story.

"They made us... ubakaji..." He shook his head, trying to find a polite word in English to say what happened. But, not finding one, he pressed on. "They made us rape the girls, me and the other boy."

Josette had a sharp intake of breath in horror and Bronwen had time to wonder why she was not as shocked. She was horrified, of course, but she was not shocked by what the men had done. Perhaps she was getting too used to evil - too used to sex being used as a weapon against people. It just re-established her want to stay away from it.

"Most everyday they made us do it, not always with same girl. They spit on us while they watched. 'Beasts only fuck other beasts' was the first English words we learnt. They still put us in same room and we couldn't help them when they cried, or when *we* cried. One girl killed herself soon as she got to the country. Cut her arms." This part made Azu put a hand on his head, as if holding in the horrific memories that hammered to escape his mind and infect others with its poisonous nightmares.

Bronwen and Josette said nothing, allowing him, and themselves, a moment to recover. Neither had moved, so intent on the story and their friend's pain.

"In England, we were taken to same house owned by a Lord and Lady. We were washed and dressed nice and had our own rooms. Then we was taught lessons; music, painting, singing and shown about at parties like decoration. Us boys tried not to learn English because we didn't want to know what the people said to us, or about us. The other girl learned. She learned all she could and was nice to the men, to survive, I think.

"Then, many years gone, the Lady of the house tried to get me with her in her bed. I said no and she come to *my* bed instead, but I locked the door. She just tried harder and took away the locks. So, I held the door closed. One night, she got drunk and hurt herself outside my room. I helped her back to her room, into her bed and one of the Lord's men saw us. He was on his way to her bed as well and became mad. He beat me and put me up by my wrists on rope and when the Lord come home, the Lady said she was forced by me. I think he wanted me dead, but the Lady wouldn't let him kill me, so they kept me and beat and starved me for weeks.

"She still come to visit when I was tied up and got angry when I didn't show her attention, but she tried anyway. Her husband caught her and he beat her too, but mostly me, even though he knew what his wife did. Then, he ordered his men to take me out, far away, and kill me. When I fought to not get on the boat, they made me run, all day and night. There was fishers and people, but they not stop them, just turned their heads away." Azu's lips twisted into a hateful scowl, then his face softened slightly.

"Then, Bronwen found me. She saved me." Bronwen didn't smile, not feeling that it was the right moment to do so. Azu didn't speak for a long time, a faraway look in his eyes as he stared at the carpet.

"What happened to the other two? Your friends?" Josette asked in a whisper.

"The girl got pregnant and was still there when I was. The man..." he trailed off and looked out of the window. Bronwen noticed a tear form in the corner of his eye and he brushed it away. "He was killed as well, so the Lady had no more men around. The men hung him with the rope they tied me up with. I couldn't help him. I couldn't get the rope off. I try to jump up to loosen the rope, but was not enough. Kutomba! I tried, but still watched him die." A sob escaped him and they were silent again. Bronwen wasn't sure if she should reach out to touch his arm, but she didn't move a muscle, except to blink away her own tears.

"What were their names?" Bronwen murmured, as softly as she could.

"Sanaa had the baby, Nomusa was the other girl and," Azu's voice became softer, "Faraji was the man."

They were all quiet again. It was clear that Faraji had been more to Azu than a friend. It confirmed Bronwen's suspicions after she had joked with him in the brothel at how he had looked at a man. She should have been horrified by this, but she wasn't. Bronwen's feelings towards Azubuike had not changed. She still loved him like a brother, no matter where his affections lay.

Bronwen looked at Josette and saw her eyes were red from crying, as she was sure hers were too. She wanted to do something, somehow. Make the world better. But she knew in her soul, that it would always be full of cruelty and hardship. She might have had to suffer the loss of her mother, but she had been very young and it was a different ache to losing a lover.

Bronwen almost told both of them, in that moment, what had really happened to her. Wanting the relief that showed in Azu's face, when he realised he was finished with his story and that he had friends who cared about him greatly. Josette spoke before Bronwen's mouth took over.

"Should you ever need protection, Azubuike, for who you are," Josette said carefully. "I offer you my hand in marriage. I would never ask anything of you and, as I am unable to bare children, nothing will be questioned. We can be free to live our lives how we wish to, with none the wiser."

Azu looked heartened by this proposal and even smiled slightly through the sadness in his teary eyes.

Bronwen decided it would be a bad idea to ruin the moment they were all sharing by adding more darkness to it. And truthfully, she was afraid they would both reject her.

She was a Lady like the ones who had abused Azu and she could not offer protection to either of them that didn't involve using an evil power. Bronwen supposed she really was a demon and the truth of it would come out eventually. She doubted she would age and her friends both would. Or maybe one of the people who murdered her would reveal what she was.

For now, Bronwen would cherish the time with them and be grateful to have that much. There were far worse things in the world.

Once Josette was over the worst of her drink induced sickness, the three of them spent the day in the city.

Josette bought a ridiculously large, floppy brimmed hat with peacock feathers in it and insisted on buying Azu a top hat.

Bronwen bought art supplies for him which he was overly grateful for. He carried his new easel and paints with a care to rival a new mother and Bronwen made him promise that his first painting would be for her, to display in her own room.

Despite the joviality of the day, both Azu and Bronwen were constantly on the lookout for those who wished to harm them. She didn't really believe that Adam was gone, and after hearing Azu's story that morning, she also didn't believe that the men who tried to kill him would stop, now that they knew he was alive.

They were both being hunted.

Bronwen nodded as she pretended to listen to the woman sat beside her, when actually she was listening to Thanatos, having a discussion on the other side of the table. He was sat exactly opposite her; only the tall gold stem of a candelabrum between them.

Bronwen wished Josette or Azu were there with her, or better yet, she with them. But neither of them had been invited and would not want to be there anyway. They were both spending the evening together, playing cards in Josette's room and Bronwen envied them. She wished she could sneak out and join them. Surely no one would notice her missing? She knew Thanatos would.

Throughout dinner Bronwen had watched Thanatos carefully and from the way he looked at her, or smirked in a certain way, it was obvious he knew she studied him and he enjoyed it, as much as he enjoyed the attention of the other guests, from which he had plenty.

Even Lord Wintre seemed taken by him, engaging in conversation enthusiastically with the man and delighting in telling all of how his Grace came to his daughter's rescue. Bronwen felt slightly embarrassed for her father, knowing he would react differently if he knew the man posing as a Prince was really the Devil in disguise.

Only Lord Guild was not seduced by Thanatos's company

and sought to undermine him whenever he had the chance, becoming increasingly frustrated when he could not succeed, even when the subject was controversial.

"And what is your opinion on this college for women being opened in Cambridge, your grace?" Lord Borthwick asked, while having his wine glass filled yet again by Mr Durward. He didn't notice that the shrewd butler only filled it halfway. "Are your women allowed such reckless freedom in Greece?"

Bronwen actually turned away from the woman who had been talking *at* her. It was rude, she knew, but she was far more interested in what Thanatos had to say.

"I would hardly call your women free, let alone reckless. I would go so far as to call them, diffident." Thanatos looked at Bronwen steadily, until she was forced to look away. He himself had called her reckless in the Under-realm not too long ago. Did that mean he did not consider her shy and restrained? She doubted it.

"And, so they should be," Borthwick said, to nods of agreement from the other gentlemen.

"I am not so sure I agree with you," Thanatos said and Bronwen looked up at him again. "I think I would prefer it if more women were freer with their love and reckless with their virtues."

This met with raucous laughter from the men at the table and stern disapproval from the women, but of course they said nothing, including Bronwen who scowled at him.

Thanatos grinned back and she knew he had been baiting her into saying something and stand up for her gender. To not care what these people thought. Kole spoke before she could even contemplate what she would say.

"This is hardly a subject for the dining room."

Thanatos held up his hands in apology. "You are right. That was rude of me. I have actually read an interesting essay recently, by John Stuart Mill. 'The Subjection of

Women' it was called and described many values that I myself hold."

Again, he had the whole room's attention as he continued.

"He believes that equality for the genders will lead to the intellectual advancement of the species and ignoring half of the potential of humankind is detrimental to its development. Mill presses the view that intellectual pleasures can achieve greater happiness than pleasures of the senses. I am not sure I wholly agree with him on that point, as I think both are as important as each other. How can one enjoy the sweetness of a fruit, but not need to understand why it is so delicious?"

Thanatos met Bronwen's eyes as he said this, taking a deep drink of his wine. The way he licked it off his lips afterwards made Bronwen's body go hot and the passing between them did not go unnoticed by some of the other guests.

The dinner plates were removed and the guests drifted over to the fire with their drinks. A modest band played for them in the corner while they all split into various groups of conversation, the largest being Thanatos's, who stood next to the fire, unperturbed by the heat that kept the rest at a distance.

Bronwen's group was the smallest, containing only three women, including her. The other two discussed Thanatos shamelessly and desperately tried to get Bronwen to reveal things about him.

"Is he married yet?" the elder of the two whispered to Bronwen.

"I do not know," Bronwen replied.

"Perhaps that is why he has come to England, to seek a virtuous English wife," the younger girl giggled.

"He shan't turn his eyes towards you then, Lillie," the elder teased. Lillie pouted, then grinned.

"But my very name means purity," she dropped her voice

again. "And I would not mind it spoken from his lips."

The two women giggled and Bronwen glanced over to Thanatos. He appeared deep in conversation with two men, but something in his expression told Bronwen that he had heard every word.

Bronwen remembered how he had murmured her name against her skin and she shuddered and looked away again.

"I have heard the art of Greece is quite vulgar, with naked statues everywhere. You must ask him if it is true, Lady Bronwen, he seems keenest on you."

Bronwen simply told them they should ask the Prince themselves and eventually, they tired of her answers and lack of interest. They excused themselves from her lacklustre company and Bronwen once again wished she were upstairs with Azu and Josette.

She was pleased when she was finally sat alone. Only Thanatos seemed to notice her solitude and kept looking over at her, almost longingly. He was still at ease with the company. He looked to be enjoying himself even, expressing himself with small hand gestures that were characteristic of his good-humoured mood.

Bronwen noticed the expression of boredom on his face when women approached. The look and talk of the women appeared not to entice his attention - not when Bronwen was in the same room.

The Lady pulled her gaze away at the sight of a woman giggling and leaning in close to Thanatos. It was not because of jealously, as she had seen how Thanatos cleverly deflected the woman by passing her another drink and introducing her to a gentleman on his other side. Bronwen had looked away because she was embarrassed for her.

Bronwen had never acted that way around a man, not even Lord Guild, and didn't think she would have, even if she had met Thanatos in different circumstances. Like if he really were a Prince and she just a Lady with everyday problems like finding a husband and worrying she could not have children.

She put a hand on her stomach wistfully as she stared at the floor unseeing.

"Perhaps Lady Bronwen would delight us in playing something instead?"

Bronwen looked up at the mention of her name. All had turned to look at her expectantly. Apparently, Thanatos had been asked to play for them and he had offered Bronwen's skills instead.

Bronwen shook her head but made no move to join them by the fire. "Your grace, I have not played in a long time and I am afraid I would not do the company justice."

"Bronwen, surely you would not refuse the request from our prestigious guest," her father said with a tense authority and she dropped her gaze, trying not to scowl.

Thanatos waved a hand in the air. "I would not want to force the Lady into something she does not want to do."

Bronwen gave him a sardonic smile and stood. "But, as my father said, *how* could I refuse?"

Thanatos matched her smile, feeling as though he had won, and she walked to where the musicians were sat. The pianist had moved out of the way for her already.

She pictured Kenneth's fingers playing across the keys; shook her head and turned to the other instruments. One stood out to her like a rose in bloom. The violinist held his instrument with such care, Bronwen almost didn't ask him for it.

"May I?"

"Of course," he said, handing it to her. "You play, milady?"

Bronwen felt the weight of it in her hand and the smoothness of the wood, compared with the sharpness of the strings.

"We shall see," she said quietly and stepped to a wider

space.

She had never touched a violin before. It had always fascinated her to watch one being played and how they made it sound so light and easy. Bronwen wanted to play it, but wasn't sure what had possessed her to take it up in front of all the guests sat waiting.

She glanced up at all of them - directly into the gaze of Thanatos. His half smile was confident and his manner unassailable.

Bronwen's eyes narrowed as she smiled mischievously and expertly placed the violin on her shoulder and tucked her chin in. She noticed her father's confused expression before she closed her eyes, tuned her hearing into the crackle of the fire, breathing of the guests and her own heartbeat.

It started slow, each note clearly defined, then, her hand found the tempo of her nervous heart and sung for it.

The Lady played for what Adam had done to her, for Azu's lover Faraji and for the twelve Satanist that haunted her. She also played for Josette and her book, for her husband Clarence and her brother Lawrence, for the time Bronwen had spent with Azu, for who she used to be; and she played for the woman that she was becoming.

Bronwen didn't open her eyes until she was finished with the final long sorrowful note, trailing it off at the end. It was her own version of a song, filled with all the long-suppressed feelings she had harboured over the most evolving few weeks of her short life.

Bronwen lowered the violin and scanned the congregation of guests. All were speechless and silent in shock. She hadn't played badly, in fact every note was perfect and blended into the next one flawlessly, but it had not been the conventional, parlour melody that they had been expecting. It was complicated and foreign sounding - otherworldly.

A few people jumped at the deafening sound of an applause. Everyone looked around at Thanatos who was grinning and clapping his hands slowly and enthusiastically. Eventually, the rest joined in, all except Lord Guild, whose blank expression seemed all the more menacing when Bronwen couldn't tell what he was thinking.

Bronwen hurriedly handed the violin to its owner who had a look of wonder on his face and then she turned back to the guests and curtsied politely.

"Excuse me," she said, and left the stunned room.

Bronwen walked up most of the stairs at a stumbling speed and sat at the top, just before the landing, her head in her hands.

She wasn't certain how long she sat there, but it was long enough that the chill air began to make her skin prickle.

The door opening below made her stand and move to the upper landing, so she could not be seen easily.

It was Thanatos who entered the hallway and he didn't need to see her to know where she was. He began to walk up the stairs towards Bronwen with a slow, controlled pace, as if approaching a flighty animal.

Bronwen leant on the banister and watched him.

"Thank you, for livening up what was turning into a dull evening of talking politics and business," Thanatos said.

"Were they talking about it for very long?"

"They are still talking about it now. You would think they had never heard a violin before."

"I doubt they have heard it like that."

"Then, they are missing out."

He reached the top of the stairs and stood with Bronwen. She pushed herself back and stood straight to face him.

"I have never played the violin before. Was that some trickery of yours?"

"Not mine, my Lady. That was all you."

"How?"

"It is part of our bargain. You can expect to enjoy some of my power. Of course, not all of it. Not yet."

Bronwen crossed her arms and turned to look down into the hallway. The sound of the party was just about audible. She knew no one would be able to hear her conversation with Thanatos, unless they were stood in view of the stairs.

"You are not pleased by what I offer?"

"I cannot control it," Bronwen replied. "And that concerns me."

"It should not be concerning. You may not be conscious of the decision, but your soul is. It will help you when you most require it."

Bronwen turned to face him again.

"How can you talk of us having souls?"

"Because we do have them, perhaps more so than anyone who is alive. A soul is the energy that animates your body, which is what makes you who you are. It can never be destroyed and it is for you to harness alone."

He stood up straight and faced Bronwen. She had to look up slightly due to his height and she unfolded her arms and placed one hand on the banister to steady herself.

"You still hold on to the ideology of religion," Thanatos stated, rather than asked.

"No. Not in the way you think, but I do still believe in good and evil and that what I do makes a difference, even if it does not change where I end up after all of this. I want to be a good person because that is what I think is right, not because a preacher has told me I should," Bronwen echoed the words that Azu had said to her by the river. "You may not be the Devil that I was raised to fear, but the things you have done still make a difference, whether or not you are good or evil and *that* matters to me."

"You would not take my word for it, if I told you there was a good reason for what I do?" Thanatos asked, his voice solemn.

"Not if you could not tell me that reason,"

Thanatos looked away. "And what of atonement?"

"If that is what a person truly and honestly wishes to achieve, then they can."

"And forgiveness?" his voice was quiet and he closed his eyes a long moment, before looking back into Bronwen's.

"That would depend on the wrongdoing and the apology," Bronwen replied, just as quietly.

They were silent for a long while, then Bronwen asked, "did you kill Kenneth?"

"Kenneth killed himself. I simply showed him why he should."

Bronwen nodded and looked down at her feet. "Thank you."

"You do not consider *this* action evil?"

"I did not say that," Bronwen answered, then grimaced. "But no, I do not."

Thanatos looked at Bronwen's hand on the banister and hesitantly placed his lightly on top. She allowed it, noticing how warm it was compared to her skin.

"I hope that one day I can explain to you my reasons behind the evil I do. And perhaps you will see fit to forgive me."

His eyes were intense and he moved a slow step closer to her. "Yours is all I need. I have a hole in my soul, Bronwen. Where you should be."

The few inches between their bodies seemed to boil and Bronwen's hand tingled to her fingertips where Thanatos still had hold of it. He reached his other arm up and held her warming cheek, his fingertips buried in her hair and he pulled her face closer to his, so their lips almost touched - but not quite.

"Thanatos," Bronwen breathed, so quietly it was almost a sigh.

"Please," he begged. She could feel his warm words on her lips. "Do not tell me to stop."

Then, their lips met. Bronwen's stomach surged then

melted and an invisible magnetism drew their bodies flush against one another as they kissed. She could feel every part of him against her. His chest, his arms, his stomach, his hands in her hair, making her scalp prickle and her stomach turn over. And when he sought out her tongue with his, a pleasant throbbing between her legs startled her.

"Nasta!" someone barked from below them and Bronwen turned her face away hurriedly, her fingers finding their way to her tingling lips and fluttering stomach.

"The gentlemen are moving through to play cards, if you care to join us?"

Bronwen recognised Lord Guild's voice, even though she was turned away from him. Her heart hammered as she wondered if he had seen them kiss. There were no lights on the landing, only what had drifted up from downstairs and he didn't sound angry or appalled, but his voice was strained in an unusual manner.

"That sounds to my liking, Lord Guild. I shall join you imminently," Thanatos called back, his voice showing no sign that anything was amiss. There was a long pause where no one moved, before Kole spoke once more.

"And if Lady Bronwen cares to join the party again, the women are calling for some tea in the morning room."

Bronwen closed her eyes and cringed. There was a subtle note hidden in the sentence and Bronwen knew he had seen her and Thanatos together.

"Thank you, Lord Guild. I shall join them," Bronwen called down as calmly as she could but knew her voice wavered.

It was silent again and Bronwen startled when a hand was placed on her arm. She turned and saw Thanatos smiling at her, a quick glance over the banister revealed that they were alone again. Bronwen had half expected Kole to come charging up the stairs to drag her away from Thanatos.

"You must excuse me, while I go act the gentleman once

more." He bowed low to her, one arm dramatically out to the side. When he spoke to Bronwen, his voice was almost as quivering as hers. "I hope we can speak again soon, my Lady."

He strode away down the stairs and disappeared from view.

Bronwen made it a few steps down and found herself sitting again. Her arm wrapped round one of the decorated poles of the staircase. She rested her head there as she caught her breath.

She wasn't sure what repercussions might come from her indiscretion, but was certain no good would come of it. A shadow moved somewhere on the landing and she focused on Azubuike stood there.

Bronwen straightened up and turned to him. He was carrying empty plates and glasses to take downstairs and had been smiling before he saw Bronwen sat alone in the dark.

"Is you alright?" Azu asked, in his broken English; made worse from his drinking with Josette.

"I expect I shall be," Bronwen replied and gave him a genuine smile, which didn't make him look any less concerned, but it stopped him from asking any questions as he watched her walk downstairs and away to the room the other women were in.

V

Bronwen did not have to wait for long to find out if Lord Guild planned to confront her about kissing the false prince. She had spent the rest of the dinner party distracted, thinking about what might happen. Luckily, the women didn't appear to notice and she was grateful when they all left, despite her father's offer at having them stay. She thought Thanatos would jump at the opportunity, but he declined, saying he had a room booked in the city.

Bronwen bid her father and a cold Lord Guild goodnight and retired to bed, changing out of her dress and into more comfortable night clothes. Once she thought everyone was asleep, she headed to the library, planning on reading for pleasure to take her mind off of how her body had reacted to Thanatos's kiss. It had not been this way when Lord Guild had kissed her, or anyone else in her short experience.

Was it because he was a demon? Or because she found him undeniably attractive? Though she hated finally admitting it to herself.

Bronwen closed the library door silently and jumped when she noticed a hand protruding from the large armchair opposite the fire, a glass of dark brandy gripped tightly in its fingers. The high back of the chair was facing her, so she could not immediately see who it was.

Bronwen considered leaving before she was noticed, but the figure spoke first.

"So, it appears your virginity is not exclusive," Lord Guild said from the chair. He had not turned around but he somehow knew it was Bronwen.

"Excuse me?" Bronwen said, affronted by his tone, but her voice was not as strong as she had hoped.

Kole peered around the chair at her, the fire behind his head made his face dark in shadow.

"I saw you kiss Thomas Nasta," He accused. "So, how did he compare, my Lady?"

"Compare to what?" Bronwen crossed her arms, finding the tone she wanted. She may have been the one in the wrong, but he did not have to be so harsh and brazen.

"To me, of course," Kole said, getting up from his chair in one movement, his brandy swirling in his glass. "Or am I so forgettable?"

Bronwen sighed. "Lord Guild, please, I did not mean for it to happen. I have not encouraged his affections."

"But you have not been rejecting them either."

"There is no need to be jealous."

"Jealous!" Kole growled and slammed his glass down on the table. He stalked closer to her and Bronwen tried not to cringe. "I am not jealous; I am indignant at someone touching my property without permission!"

"Your property?" Bronwen found herself getting angry. "I do not belong to any man."

"Not yet, but I have made my claim on you and you will respect that."

"I have a right to change my mind," Bronwen argued bravely, despite the darkening look in his eyes but she could feel her blood boiling.

"You will marry me because you love me, Bronwen."

"What makes you think I love you?" Bronwen couldn't stop herself and resisted the urge to hold a hand to her mouth. It was too late - the words were already said.

Instead of yelling, as she had expected, Kole turned on her with a swiping blow that did not fail to hit its target.

Bronwen's voice caught in her throat from the shock and pain of his hand across her face. Before she had time to register the sting, his hands grabbed her upper arms; his fingers digging into her flesh.

"You're lying!" Lord Guild hissed as he shook her.

"Let go!" Bronwen squealed. He was strong and she had become scared and the sting of her face made her eyes water.

"I have every right to put my hands wherever I choose to," Kole growled and pulled the edge of her nightdress off her shoulder.

Bronwen lifted her hand to slap him but he caught her feeble wrist and struck her again, once on the same cheek, then again on the other in a blow that forced her to her knees with a whimper.

Kole grabbed her hair in his fist, giving her no respite and pulled her face closer to his as he bent towards her.

"Love, honour and obey," Kole murmured through gritted teeth. "I will settle for two of the three."

He pulled her up to her feet and bent her neck back uncomfortably.

"Do not force me to beat the compliance out of you, Bronwen. I have played nice so far and once we are married, things are going to change."

He studied every inch of her face. Her bottom lip trembled and she had her hands out in front of her, as if that might stop him.

Kole grabbed her chin and kissed her hard on the lips. Bronwen struggled with him, then managed to connect her teeth with his lower lip and bit hard, cringing at the mild taste of blood.

Kole groaned, almost pleasurably, then let go suddenly. In her disorientation, Bronwen was almost glad when he struck her a fourth time, this time with his fist clenched. She felt as if her eyeball had been wrenched from its socket and her head hit the library table on the way down.

Her eyes watered and her mind span, making weird observations, like how rough the carpet felt and how this had been the second time she had been attacked in the library.

"Do not think it pleases me to see you like this," Kole murmured, bent down close to her ear. "But if you ever think to defy me again, I will not hesitate to beat you so hard, you will wish you were dead."

Bronwen cringed when he moved and just managed to register him leaving the library before she blacked out.

"Malaika?" Azubuike's voice was the first thing Bronwen heard when her fuzzy head started to clear.

She was cold and her head and face throbbed, particularly her eye.

Azu helped her sit up as she groaned back into consciousness.

"You're bleeding," Azu placed a gentle thumb on her lip and she remembered biting Kole, surprised that she had been that feral.

"It is not mine." Bronwen shook her head and immediately regretted it. She thought she might faint again and used her hands to hold herself off the floor.

"And what of this?" Azu asked, hovering a hand over her cheek but not touching it.

Bronwen stood up, with much help from Azu, and stumbled towards the table where she picked up a silver plate and could just make out the semblance of a reflection. Her cheek was swollen and had turned a purple shade. Red veins crawled in the whites of her eye, trying to feed off the colour in her pupils.

Bronwen groaned again.

"Was it *him*?" Azubuike's voice was aggressive and protective at once.

"No," Bronwen answered solemnly, knowing he meant Adam.

"The other then? Guild?"

Bronwen bowed her head in acknowledgment. "It was my doing. I should not have said what I said."

Azu came around the other side of the table to face her.

"Bullshit! You a fool to believe it, Malaika. I don't care who he is."

She knew he was right, but her thoughts were too muddled to think about it. The only thing she seemed to manage was an inappropriate laugh.

Azu helped her over to a chair by the fire so he could look at her face better. Bronwen was still in a daze and didn't notice when Azu left and returned with a cloth and two bowls of water. He put one over the fire for a few minutes to warm it.

Bronwen winced when he dabbed at her face as gently as he could. Her head was pounding and she felt sick. She was fed up of being so easily attacked by people. If only she were stronger, or knew how to fight. If only this mysterious power Thanatos spoke about had chosen to help her.

Azu placed a soaked cloth across her swollen cheek and eye. It was freezing cold and the water dripped onto her shoulder that she realised was still exposed. She pulled it up absently.

Despite the cold of the cloth, the throbbing of her face began to subside and it occurred to Bronwen that Azu was no stranger to fighting. The blow he gave Adam couldn't have been from strength alone.

"Azubuike, will you teach me how to fight?"

"I can teach you," Azubuike said with a nod. "But women do not fight here. They will not like it."

"We shall do it in secret," Bronwen said firmly, convinced this was a great idea. Azu consented then helped her back to her room.

"I suppose I shall have to tell Josette what happened," Bronwen said as Azu pulled the covers over her, to stop her shivering from cold. "We will have to stop her from killing Kole."

"Mimi mpango wa kumsaidia," {I plan to help her} Azu mumbled in his language and Bronwen could guess what he said.

"Thank you, Azubuike."

"Sleep, Malaika. I will watch tonight."

Donovan left his driver to deal with the horses and carriage as he stepped up to the door of his home, peeling off his gloves as he walked inside.

Lord Wintre loved his home. It was where he and his wife had planned to grow old together. And though not all of the memories there were happy ones, like when his wife had killed their only daughter and then died years later, he could not see himself living anywhere but Metrom Hall.

The servants would be asleep at such a late hour, but that would not have prevented Donovan from calling them for tea. Lucky for them, he only wanted a brandy and headed for his drawing room.

The fire was still burning low, he was pleased to note. This room was his second favourite, used as the main living area of the house. Donovan had spent many an hour talking, playing games, eating and drinking with his wife by the fire. His first favourite room was of course their bedroom. He knew many Lords and Ladies who did not share a room with their spouse, and he pitied them. They had no idea what they were missing.

Heading straight to the glass decanter he kept on the table

by the door, Donovan again found himself thinking about what he was to do with his daughter. His dead daughter whom he had killed.

He had been content thus far to let others make the decisions for him. To see how things panned out. To let Kole do what he felt was best. But after seeing the bruises on Bronwen's face that she had tried to hide with cosmetics and the mysterious disappearance of Adam Whyms, a man Kole had been using to keep track of Bronwen's whereabouts, Donovan knew it was time to step in. He just had no idea how.

Donovan wasn't sure what would happen if Bronwen were to find out about his involvement in her death. Could he explain it to her somehow? He doubted it. If she remembered what happened to her as all evidence suggested, there was no reason for Bronwen not to kill him in return. That's what he would have done.

But, Bronwen was not like Donovan; not like her mother even. She was quiet and reserved and skittish. Or at least she had been before all this messy business had started. Perhaps she *would* find the strength to kill him. He had been no father to her. He hadn't allowed himself to be.

"Pleasant travels, Lord Wintre?"

Donovan turned around to find Prince Thomas Nasta sat in an armchair by the fire. Donovan tried not to look phased, as he was sure the room had been empty when he entered and the hour was very late. He looked at his pocket watch to reiterate this as he walked over to the fire.

"Quite pleasant, I would say," he said conversational. "I apologise, James did not inform me you were here, your grace. He should have stayed awake to offer you a drink."

Nasta waved a hand in the air to dismiss his apology, a strangely unnerving smile on his face as he stared at Donovan who stayed standing by the fire, warming himself after his travel. The winter was closing in and he wanted to

426

retire to bed. He was in no mood to receive guests - even a Prince. A Prince who, in normal circumstances, he would have wanted to marry Bronwen.

Donovan was still unsure why he had suggested to encourage the Prince's affections and send Bronwen away to Greece. It was not in his nature to ignore his problems, but when it came to his daughter, he had always struggled knowing the right thing to do was.

"Is there something you wished to speak to me about, your grace?" Donovan asked when the silence grew too long and the man's smile was becoming uncomfortable.

"It is about your daughter, my Lord," Nasta said mildly and Donovan tried not to smile; his reservations quickly forgotten. He had been waiting for this. Kole had told him about seeing Nasta and Bronwen on the stairs a few nights ago which had no doubt been the cause of Bronwen's bruises.

The Earl was an associate, an ally in the dark. He had a good name and station and Donovan knew Kole kept his property protected. But here was a royal, a prince. Yes, perhaps it was only of a small country, but it was still far above Countess. Bronwen would be a Princess, perhaps even a Queen one day, brushing shoulders with the royalty of all the other countries, including England. It would do wonders for Donovan's business. And perhaps then he could put her out of his mind and the Secuutus would settle back to how it had been.

If Nasta offered a marriage, Donovan would not turn it down and Kole would just have to understand. And, if he were being honest with himself, Donovan had come close to killing the Earl for hurting his daughter. It was nonsensical, especially as Donovan had killed her himself and he had, after all, given Kole permission and freedom to break Bronwen, he just hadn't expected that to mean physically.

"I do not think she has been quite herself recently," Nasta

continued, a thoughtful hand tapping the glass he held. Presumptuous of him to help himself, but Donovan supposed he was used to it; being a prince.

"Love will do strange things to women," Donovan took the liberty in saying, with a secret smile. He would provide the push needed, if necessary.

Nasta raised an eyebrow. "Love is it? Not death then?"

Donovan stiffened and gripped the glass in his hand tighter.

"Death? I am afraid I do not understand your meaning, your grace," Donovan said, trying to calm his nerves. He was sure the man had only gotten the word incorrect, but it still made his insides turn at the mention of it and he couldn't help remembering the feel of the knife's slight resistance as it plunged into the flesh of his daughter's chest. He put his drink on the mantelpiece and kept a hand there for support.

"You know my meaning exactly, Dux Ducis." Nasta's lips curled up into a snarl and he hissed the 's' on the title.

Donovan swallowed and shook his head slightly, getting a grip on himself. This was not the first time someone had gotten close to discovering the Secuutus Letum and the work they did, but it was the first time anyone had called him by his Latin title and something in the man's eyes sent a shudder up Donovan's spine. It was so familiar to him.

"How do you know that name?" Donovan said in a small voice as the Prince drank deep and precise from his glass. Donovan contemplated if the glass was sturdy enough to smash the man's skull, then ran a plan through his mind on where and how to hide the body, how to make him disappear and cut all ties to the house, where to hide the weapon.

Nasta laughed loudly, throwing his head back and barring his teeth, which Donovan was sure had become much longer and sharper. He hoped the volume wouldn't wake anyone, as it would make it much more difficult to dispose of the man.

"Because I gave it to you, Dux Ducis," Nasta said and Donovan's knees almost gave way. He shook his head again, not wanting to believe that his master was currently sat in the chair before him.

"Oh, you do not believe me," the man mocked and suddenly, without so much as a blink from Nasta, Donovan staggered back as the fire roared in the hearth, spitting embers that fell onto the carpet, only to become snakes that reared up and spat fire at Donovan.

{For the return of a soul and salvation of another, the servitude of the husband and father}

A small sound escaped Donovan and he fell into the chair closest to him, a hand on his heart.

He had not heard those words spoken in twenty-five years. No one knew of them; they were *his* words. *His* personal nightmare. The deal he had made with the Devil. The demon sat across from him smiling and enjoying the pain he inflicted on his servants.

"So quiet, Donovan?"

"You were Thomas Nasta? The entire time?" Donovan said, running through every conversation he had ever had with the man.

"I am and plan to continue to be."

"Bronwen," Donovan breathed. "Does she know? Does she know any of it? All of it?"

"You could always ask her yourself. After all, she is your daughter. Perhaps if you treated her like one, she would have told you about the deal I made with her."

"You made a deal with my daughter!" Donovan growled, a fist forming in one hand.

"So sentimental over her now, are we?" Nasta growled back, far more threatening, and a flash of red in his eyes made Donovan adjust himself and remember who he was really talking to.

"Dominus," he said in respect. "Why have you sought me out this night?"

"As I said, Bronwen is not happy, though we can hardly blame her. She has many enemies and few friends or family. I believe I can help her with one of those things. Bronwen needs her family, she needs her father, as do most women her age. And I find that this is something I can give her."

Nasta put his glass down carefully on the table and in a blink, he was standing behind Donovan's chair. Donovan tried not to flinch as his Dominus leant in behind him to speak softly in his ear.

"Your wife is unconfined, as promised. And I release you from our bargain. Our deal is complete. Vacat vobis, liberum." {You are free}

Donovan let out a small cry of relieved anguish. He was free. No longer did he have to lead the Secuutus if he didn't wish to. No longer did he have to do the demon's evil bidding and fear the consequences if he refused or displeased him. He had been living under this shadow since his wife's death. He had killed his own daughter to keep his one true love safe and now it was all over in a few words. As if it has been nothing.

Nasta moved to the fire and stood facing Donovan directly.

"I have always wondered, Baron, why you never asked me for my reasons for choosing your daughter in particular? Or why I only gave her back for twenty-five years instead of just taking her from you as a baby?"

"I did not think you would tell me, Dominus," Donovan said, he was reeling from his new freedom but had just enough of his sense left to answer the demon he still called master. "And, it was not my place to question you."

"No, it isn't. And no, I would not have told you. But this would not have stopped another from asking."

Donovan looked down at his hands, a weary slump to his

shoulders. "I have spent a great many sleepless nights wondering."

He put his head in his hands as he stared at the carpet and remembered how his wife had looked when she was alive. Her almost black hair that came in waves and made her cheeks paler. She was beautiful. Even when covered in blood that had not been her own; a mad look in her blue eyes. Her teeth bared. The knife slick in her fingers. A small form lifeless on the stone.

Donovan's shoulders heaved and he whispered her name to the floor. He no longer believed in a benevolent God but suddenly felt the need for confession to the only deity he had known.

"Bronwen became very ill the weeks after my wife's death, when she was a few months shy of her sixth birthday. The doctors said she was in a critical state, despite all they did to save her. They could not figure out what was wrong.

"My wife did not have any illness that they knew of either, she had just seemed heartsick and wasted away over the years but Bronwen was young and strong and knew nothing of the world other than her mother was gone. It was one of the few times I saw her as my child, so sickly and helpless in bed, crying for me to hold her. She was in so much pain and yet, I wished she would die. I wished she would slip away in her sleep and wake no more because then I would not have to kill her myself. I would not have had to..." Donovan's voice broke and he held his face in his hands in shame.

The demon was silent but Donovan sensed he was still in the room; attentive as Donovan bared his soul.

"Bronwen recovered fully the very next day. It was like a cruel joke of fate, dangling redemption before me. The doctors could not explain it either but I had always suspected there had been more hand in it than science. Your hand."

He looked up at Nasta but his expression was unreadable.

"It was that moment that I realised, if I did not begin to distance myself from Bronwen, I would never have had the strength to kill her."

Donovan sniffed and sat back in his chair, looking at the painted ceiling of the golden rimmed clouds of heaven. The roof seemed so high and far away to him. Unreachable.

"I should not have asked it of you."

Donovan frowned, surprised that the devil he had called master for so many years; had feared and served without question would admit a fault of his own.

He sat up again and looked at the creature across from him. The light from the fire lighting one side of his dark features and leaving the rest in the cold of the night. Donovan almost laughed at the ridiculous poetry of it.

"Why did you choose her?" he found himself asking but not really expecting an answer. "Why choose Bronwen? Cornell has two daughters or there is Mara or Velna. You are powerful enough to have any woman you choose, so why her?"

The demon looked irritated by the question. He turned his face towards the fire and Donovan was sure he would not speak anymore but Nasta surprised him again.

"I find myself caring for her for reasons I cannot fathom. And I want her to choose me in return."

"You killed Kenneth for her."

"I did."

Donovan was lost for words.

The piano instructor had been found hanging by the neck by one of his piano strings. It would have severed his head if he had jumped but Donovan had been sickened to find out that Kenneth had lowered himself off his own banister carefully so that his death was slow and painful. What manner of beast could have convinced him to do that to himself?

So, he had never even considered that the Lord of the

Under-realm might want Bronwen to like him. Maybe even love him.

And would she? Surely not. Not Lady Bronwen Wintre, whom Alda had taught good from evil and abstinence above all things.

Yet, his daughter had not attended Sunday mass after her hysterical outburst and had kissed that very Devil on the stairs; after playing a violin in such an unnervingly skilful way that Donovan had even had to hide the tear from the raw emotion it evoked in him.

Bronwen was changed from the meek and quiet Lady Donovan had ordered others to make her. Her soul was being darkened and tainted and it was not wholly Donovan's doing.

This creature had no reason to make his deal and send her back to the living other than to hope that the Secuutus would attack her and force her even closer to him.

Which is exactly what they had been doing. A realisation came to him with sudden clarity and he couldn't stop the words from leaving his mouth.

"You are planning to use me. You think when Bronwen discovers what I did, what her mother did and even the betrayal of her fiancé, she will follow you willingly to the darkness."

The demon's eyes flashed a wicked red and the ever so subtle smile that touched the corner of his mouth made Donovan feel sick.

Perhaps if he had revealed himself to Bronwen, rather than relying on Kole's methods, she would have told him everything herself and he could have prevented this. Could have helped her.

Maybe if he convinced her of his reasons? But no, it was too late. He doubted Bronwen saw him as a father any more than Donovan saw her as a daughter.

First, he would have to rebuild the bridge between them.

He would have to make her trust him again and then ask forgiveness and hope she was too weak-willed to kill her own father.

If she was strong enough to resist this devil before him, perhaps there was a chance.

Nasta stood and stepped over to the fire. He turned back to Donovan who was gripping the edge of his armchair tightly; as if afraid he too might be dragged to hell.

"Should you see that fiancé you mentioned," Nasta said. "It might be wise to remind Kole that what I have claimed as mine will always be *mine* and should he think to touch it, harm it or take it in anyway, he would do well to remember his own Devil's bargain."

The fire blazed again and Donovan shielded his eyes with his hand. When he looked back, all the flames had been sucked away with Nasta and left creaking icicles in its wake that clung to the marble of the mantelpiece, along with all the charcoal and wood that had been burning only moments before.

The lamps had gone out and Donovan sat stunned in the gloom. He sat there for the whole night, staring at the same space. He may have fallen asleep at some point with his eyes still open while the ice thawed. It brought cold shivers to Donovan's exhausted body and by the time the servants walked into the room, it was but a puddle of water on the stone that Donovan could almost imagine himself to have cried there.

VI

"I will not be gone so long this time, if all goes to plan," Josette said to Bronwen as they oversaw her luggage onto the train destined for Guildford.

"What plan?" Bronwen asked.

The time for Josette to return to Aterces had come around too soon and she would desperately miss her friend and her dramatic ways. What she had been going through had only been bearable because of Azu and Josette. If not for them, she might have joined Thanatos weeks ago.

Josette tapped the side of her nose. "I do not want to jinx it by giving it away so soon or ruin the surprise."

The train whistle blew, signalling that it was ready to pull away from the platform. Josette hugged Bronwen and Azu fiercely.

"Guard yourself, friend," Josette murmured in Bronwen's ear and suddenly Bronwen didn't want to let go.

"Josette..." she began.

"Do not fret," Josette interrupted. "I will be back soon and all will be well."

Bronwen reluctantly let go and the train pulled Josette and her secrets away from the station.

She knew that Josette had been referring to the marks that Kole had left on her face. It had been a struggle to keep her from throttling the Earl and Azubuike had been no help. He too had wanted nothing more than to throw Kole through a window.

Bronwen had seen her would-be husband in a new light and truthfully, it had terrified her.

She had not planned on marrying him anyway since she was not to remain alive but the way he had spoken to her and had ripped her gown from her shoulder and forced his mouth on hers had her worried that she would not be able to delay breaking the engagement. Though, she was fearful about how he would react.

Would he strike her again? Tie her up and steal her away? Or something far more drastic, like impose a marriage between them by forcing himself on her?

Azu stood next to Bronwen as Josette's train disappeared from sight. Bronwen felt a shiver go up her spine.

"Are you alright, Malaika?"

Bronwen nodded. "Just cold. Perhaps I should not have sent her on her own."

"I am not leaving you again," Azu said firmly.

Bronwen smiled and put a hand on his arm, then walked with him out of the station back to the waiting carriage.

Bronwen insisted Azu ride inside the carriage with her and they made their way through the city slowly as the afternoon faded into evening.

Azu had already started to teach Bronwen to defend herself a little each day. He had taught her how to punch without breaking her fingers and Josette had laughed at the two of them one rainy afternoon as Bronwen had struggled to get out of Azu's strong grip around her waist.

Bronwen doubted she would stand much hope against a real attacker but was willing to take any help she could. Too many people had tried to harm her and too many had succeeded.

At a crossroads the carriage waited for a farmer moving a

flock of sheep through the city. Bronwen could hear the coach drivers yelling at him to move and it was obvious that it would be a while before they could continue their journey.

She lazily looked out of the window at all the houses. The city looked like it was leaning, built uphill as it was. The buildings had been placed so they were against one another as if holding each other up.

Under the shadow of a public house, a group of people caught Bronwen's attention and she felt her stomach sink. She sat straight back in the carriage to hide herself, after recognising the men who had been after Azu, stood in a group and looking like a mob.

Azu leant forwards after seeing the look in Bronwen's eyes and hearing the small squeak she had made.

Bronwen gently held him back from the window. He took her warning and leant far back against the chair and used a small crack in the curtains to see out.

He too stiffened when he saw the men and watched them intently. Bronwen prayed they would not notice and damned the drivers above, still yelling at the farmer and drawing more attention to their carriage. She wanted to move the herd herself. It would have been quicker as it seemed like an age before they were finally pulling away.

Bronwen let out her breath as they disappeared from sight.

"Don't fear for me, Malaika," Azu said, though his shoulders were still tense.

It was not only seeing the men after Azu that had made her so nervous. It was also the company they kept. Bronwen had seen both Lord Guild and Adam Whyms among them, laughing and shaking their hands.

What was Kole doing? Did he know they were after Azu? Was he trying to be rid of her friend so Azubuike could not be there to shield her if Kole became overly friendly with his fists again? And Adam had declared that he would protect her from Kole before he unwittingly killed her. Anything that had brought them back together as allies could not be good.

"I will settle this, Azu," Bronwen said assuredly. "They cannot get away with what they did to you."

Azubuike remained silent the rest of the way home while Bronwen thought about what she was actually going to say to Kole. She was feisty when discussing an action, but when it came to real confrontation; Bronwen had to be pushed to her limit before she would truly say anything. But this was her friend and she would be damned if she was going to let anything harm what few she had.

When they arrived back, Kole's horse was being brushed down and fed. Having taken the shortest route for a single horse, he had beaten them back to Metrom.

Bronwen kept her mind furious when she entered the house to give herself strength.

"It would be better if I go in alone," she said to Azu before she entered the drawing room.

"I should stay," he protested.

"I will call if I need you and my father will be in the room with us. He will not let any harm come to me."

This made Azu even less convinced, but he went downstairs to his room regardless.

Bronwen braced herself and marched into the living room. She found Kole stood by the fire alone, string into the flames.

He looked up before Bronwen could retreat. She did not feel safe facing him without her father or Azu being present but his satisfied look at the bruises on her face, which she had been unable to completely cover with makeup, made her angry.

She straightened and closed the door behind her so she had something solid against her back.

"I saw you with those thugs that have a vendetta against

Azu," Bronwen started, not bothering with a polite greeting, worried she might lose her nerve if she did not confront him now.

"Yes, you did," Kole said, taking a sip of his wine.

Bronwen took a brave few paces closer, even more irritated by the nonchalance in his tone.

His eyes seemed to roam Bronwen's face and her darkened cheek and bloodshot eye. She couldn't quite tell what emotion crossed his features as he studied the marks he had put there. Was it compunction or delight?

"I would like to know why you are associating with them when they mean to do my friend harm."

"A friend, is he?" Kole said tightly. "And do you know whom you are associating with, my Lady?"

"Azu has told me, yes. He told me of how they kidnapped and tortured him like a slave, which is illegal in this country."

"There are a great number of things illegal in this country."

"Then why were you speaking with the men who did such horrendous things? What could you possibly have been speaking to them about? I demand to have an answer from you."

"You *demand* it, do you?" Kole put his glass down and turned to face her fully, clearly unhappy with the tone she was using and struggling to keep his self-control.

"Yes, and I demand to know why you hired Mr Whyms to spy on me and report to you," Bronwen continued, his rising anger adding fuel to her own.

"I think we both know why I needed to." Bronwen tried not to wince at the terrible wrath in his voice.

"No, I do not. You hired him as my bodyguard *before* I kissed Prince Nasta. And I think in the circumstances it might be best for us to break our engagement amicably."

"If you think this mishap lets you escape from our

marriage; you are gravely mistaken. And I will have a lifetime to break you like I would a horse until you finally admit you are mine."

Bronwen was shaking she was so angry yet at the same time, she was struggling not to flee from the cold, fevered look in his eyes.

"That will never happen. You cannot force me to marry you."

"You think not?" Kole sneered. He stepped closer to her and Bronwen only just managed to stand her ground. "Your father has already given me his blessing, Josette will be gone and as for your little pet, well, I have it on good authority that some old friends are looking for him and I just so happened to provide them with the information they needed on his whereabouts."

"You bastard!" Bronwen swiped her hand towards Kole's face with the intention of striking him. He caught her wrist with ease and yanked her towards his face.

"Without your disgusting slave to protect you, you have *nothing*," Kole hissed in her face. "You are just a weak female who should do as she is commanded."

Bronwen tried to get out of his grasp but he held her tighter. It felt as if he wanted to prise her hand off or pull her arm out of its socket.

"If I command you to do something, you will only ask how I would like it done," Kole continued, his face so close to hers it was just a featureless blur, somehow making him more menacing so that Bronwen was forced to turn her head away. He grabbed her by the throat and made her look into his eyes.

"And, if I see fit to beat you, you will take the beating without complaint..."

Bronwen's hand began to tingle, not the one Kole was holding, but the one that was free. She felt something cold brushing her palm. The air there was gaining solidity and weight in her hand.

"...and when I decide I want to fuck you, wherever and however I choose, you will sigh and moan and beg me to take you again and again until you are sore and I am satisfied..."

The thing in her hand had almost finished materialising and Bronwen was certain she knew what it was and had no doubts about how to use it.

"Kole," her father's voice came from behind her. The dagger that had begun to feel solid in her palm fell away to smoke as Donovan moved slowly beside them.

"I would politely like to request that you remove your hands from my daughter," he said in a strained voice; trying to contain his own ferocity but also very aware that Kole had a tight grip on Bronwen which could easily tip in his favour if the situation escalated.

"No, Donovan, your daughter needs to be taught some respect and perhaps if you had been more of a father to her, she would have it."

"My father taught me that you do not need to raise a hand to someone to teach them respect," Bronwen hissed when Donovan did not defend the slight to his integrity.

"Well, we will not know until we try it," Kole growled, shaking her. Bronwen raised her chin in an incredible act of rash courage fuelled by her rage.

"Do it my Lord and remember it well because it will be the last time you ever touch me."

"You defiant bitch!" Kole raised a fist and Bronwen closed her eyes, waiting for the blow that never came. She heard the sound it made, flesh on flesh, but didn't feel a thing.

Kole grunted and when Bronwen opened her eyes, he was stumbling back and someone was stood between them - her father.

Kole moved his hand from his face and it came away bloody. Dark red liquid came from his nose and it looked crooked. His eyes watered from the pain of it and his anger was evident.

Kole straightened from where he held the mantelpiece.

"Move away, Donovan, and I will forgive you this once."

Bronwen was confused. Her father had struck the Earl, but why? He didn't care for her and never had.

Her father moved closer to the fire for a moment and Bronwen's heart fell, thinking he was moving out of the way and allowing Kole to have her but Donovan was only moving to reach for the sword he kept on a stand over the fireplace. He unsheathed it with a practiced air which told all watching that he knew how to use it. He held the sword up towards the Earl.

Kole was unflinching and wiped his bleeding nose on a handkerchief with a wince he could not hide.

"Are you sure this is the choice you wish to make?" Kole said with a cold sneer. "I will not hide this incident from the others and there will be repercussions."

"There are reasons I am leader and they are not," Donovan growled back, his voice was as steady as his hand. "I should have made this choice from the beginning, when you first tried to claim her."

"Your sentiment will get you killed."

"Death is not the final justice."

They were speaking as if Bronwen were not in the room and she had no idea of the meaning of their words to one another, but she didn't care. Her father was still defending her and it meant more to her then she thought it would. Bronwen had for so long considered herself an orphan, her father always distant, always away on long journeys. She thought he saw her as an inconvenience that he needed to marry off. She could never have imagined he would stand by her now.

The Earl had a title and lands and contacts and perhaps could have given Donovan channels into higher society. He hadn't so much as commented on the black eye Kole had given her previously as if it was to be expected.

The standoff between the men ended when it became clear Donovan would not back down. His raised arm showed no signs of lowering.

Kole scrunched up his handkerchief and moved his body forwards. Donovan tensed, but the Earl simply threw the blood marked fabric into the fire and walked, straight backed, out of the room. He left the door open and a cold breeze entered after him.

Bronwen's skin prickled from the chill and from the tension of the situation. Her father lowered his sword only once he had heard the front door open and close again. Then, he turned to Bronwen, a grim line to his mouth and concern in his thoughtful eyes.

Bronwen threw herself at him. Tightening her arms around his middle and burying her face in his chest. His arms were limp by his side, but when she didn't let go, he placed the sword back on the mantelpiece and put his arms gently around his daughter, uncomfortable at first from the uncommon gesture before they both warmed to it.

Bronwen breathed in steadily, feeling safe and comforted. He smelt like burnt wood, damp horses, lavender from his clothing and something spicy in the brandy he always drank.

Eventually, Donovan put his hands on Bronwen's shoulders and she reluctantly pulled away. Both had tears in their eyes.

"I will make it right, for as long as I am allowed to," Donovan whispered to her. Bronwen didn't ask him what he meant. She thought that if she spoke, she might burst into sobs so nodded instead.

Donovan pulled her into a quick embrace again and thought about the repercussions Kole had mentioned.

He could not leave the Secuutus Letum as he had planned. Donovan knew of all the horrific things the

Secuutus members could do to Bronwen and her unclaimed soul. He most likely knew more than they did about what atrocities could befall his daughter despite her being dead. He would not take that risk.

He would continue to lead the Secuutus, only, it would be to lead them astray and he would have to hope to God and the Devil that they would not challenge him.

Josette looked down at the wheel where it had rolled a distance from the carriage, snapping cleanly away from the axel.

"I am sorry, Mrs Emry," said one of her drivers who had come to pick her up from the station. "We only just had it fixed and Lord Guild checked it himself before he went back to Winchester."

"Did he indeed," Josette mumbled to herself. She put her hands on her hips and looked back at the carriage, now tipped over on one side in the dirt, her luggage strewn across the muddy ground. The other driver gathered up her things after he had tied the two dazed horses to a tree. They had calmed since the incident and appeared to be in good health as they grazed the sparse grass that lined the rough forest path.

"Well, there is nothing to be done now," Josette sighed and headed for the horses. "I will go and fetch another carriage and some help from Aterces."

"You can't go on your own," the carriage driver argued as Josette chose the calmest of the two horses and untied it from the tree.

"You must stay with my things," Josette ordered. "Make sure they are not stolen. I will be perfectly safe. The house is not far from here."

"Mrs Emry," the man said uncomfortably. Josette used one of her fallen chests to get onto the horse, tucking her dress in under her legs to make it easier to ride.

"No one is going to come by here so late in the afternoon except people who wish to do us harm and I do not plan to wait for that to happen. If I am not back in two hours, then abandon the carriage and go for help. Should anything happen to me, you will in no way be held responsible."

With that, Josette kicked the horse into a trot, not wanting to push the animal before she knew it was completely unharmed from the carriage tipping.

The sun was low in the sky and she knew she had to hurry if she wanted to get back to the broken vehicle before nightfall.

Josette felt uncomfortable out there in the woods. They were Kole's woods. They had never belonged to her husband Clarence, even when he had been the Earl of Surrey.

Josette remembered Bronwen's bruised face and ground her teeth together. She wished she had had the time to speak to Bronwen before she left. She should have told her friend everything years ago, about what she suspected Kole was and how she knew.

At first, Josette had kept her silence because she had hoped Bronwen and Lawrence would wed. When that had been averted by Bronwen's fear of her father, Josette had said nothing because she did not want Bronwen to reject her or her brother. Lady Bronwen's small-minded upbringing posed a barrier to her understanding.

Yet, when Bronwen had come home with a black man, whom she had rescued, and her parochial attitudes appeared to be vanishing, Josette had still kept her secrets because she was terrified about what Kole would do to Bronwen if he discovered she knew the truth. Josette couldn't yet take that chance. She had to prepare first. Had to make sure they were all safe. Had to be closer to them.

Which is why she had purchased an apartment in

Winchester with the advance from her novel and the other money she had invested. She had planned to return to Aterces only to set her affairs in order then return to Bronwen and Azu. Already she had set things in motion for if the worst should happen.

Josette sped her horse on a little, wanting to be free of the trees that loomed bare branches over her, like the bones of the dead trying to pull her to the afterlife with them. The wind changed direction and Josette's inner sense knew something was coming. Something dark and deadly and deranged. Something that was angry beyond reason and wanted someone dead for it.

Josette grabbed for the cross around her neck with its silver circle of coloured stones and prayed for protection.

The wind changed direction again and her horse whinnied in alarm. She pulled on its reins to keep it under control.

Josette's horse jumped up on its hind legs as something darted out of the trees in front of them. A fox? No, something larger, like a wolf. But there were no wolves in this part of the country. Josette's horse did not care about this fact and bolted down the lane. Josette leant forwards on it. Trying to keep a grip on its reins, her thumping heart kept time with its pounding hooves.

Josette could see something moving in the trees. Keeping time with them. Changing shape. Bringing the darkness behind it.

She began to shout her prayers above the roaring wind in her ears.

Josette knew it was too late. She was not afraid of dying, she would be with Clarence again and her soul was safe - Bronwen's was not. Josette could only hope that Lawrence would finally admit what he was and still had enough feelings for Bronwen to help her.

Josette whispered one final prayer into the horse's mane and closed her eyes.

VII

Bronwen almost burst into tears all over again when her father told her he would give Bronwen her dowry for her own use. She could marry whoever she chose - or no one at all. She was her own woman, like Josette.

Father and daughter had spoken for many hours. A longer conversation she had ever had with him her whole life. The bridge between them was by no means built, but they could see one another now, across the gap that had divided them for so many years.

They built the fire back up and Donovan had food and drink brought for them, which neither touched, but the formality was necessary to make both more comfortable - unfamiliar in the act of being a family.

Donovan apologised a number of times for being a bad father and Bronwen was sorry for being a bad daughter to make him feel that way.

"I never believed you fully recovered from mother dying," Bronwen said gently. Donovan had stiffened at that and looked away. "It is nothing to be ashamed of, she would be proud of you and your grief, I think. I have always wondered why you did not find another wife and mother for me."

Donovan didn't say anything for a long while. Bronwen was wrong if she thought his wife would have been proud and there were other more obvious reasons he had not brought another woman into his life. It was difficult enough keeping Bronwen from it all. Donovan had invited women to his bed, of course, but he had found none quite like the love of his life. She was, quite simply, irreplaceable.

"You look so much like her, Bronwen. It has been difficult for me."

This was only a small part of the reason Donovan had pushed her away for years. Every time he had looked at her as she aged and matured, Donovan saw the past repeating across her face. He could almost smell the blood again. The only thought he had pushed into his mind when he plunged the knife into Bronwen's heart, the only way he had known how to get through the ordeal of killing his daughter, was by reminding himself she was already dead.

When Bronwen was a baby and his wife still alive, Donovan had revelled in the little creature. Often taking the girl into his arms or out on rides with him or simply rocking her by the fire while his wife mostly ignored them, refusing to even hold Bronwen.

Bronwen had been a difficult infant, never wanting to eat or sleep, sending the household into despair at the child. She would not take the nursemaid's milk and would cry if she was left alone when put down to sleep. Donovan had thought the demon had sent her back broken, to deliberately punish them. Until one day, Donovan had found his wife finally holding their daughter in her arms.

Bronwen had been so quiet, Donovan feared his wife had killed her again. Instead, he found them in an armchair by the fire, the baby happily suckling at her mother's breast, gazing up at her with big blue eyes. It had made Donovan stop regretting the deal he had made, if only to see that look in his wife's eyes, so full of love and tenderness that one would never have believed that she had killed the child.

Despite this change, his wife had still wasted away from

some unfathomable heartache. It had happened so gradually, over many years. Donovan had first thought she simply could not take the pain of knowing she had killed their daughter, but he was fooling himself and suspected that something far more grotesque had been eating away at her mind.

Donovan doubted Bronwen remembered any of it and decided to let her continue to believe their distance was because of her mother's passing.

The next day, Donovan joined Bronwen for breakfast and asked if she would ride with him, as he had some business outside the city. Bronwen was genuinely delighted by the offer and told Azu he could have the day for himself. He deserved a day off and she would not need him if she were with her father.

Mr Durward helped Bronwen into her coat in the hallway while Donovan shrugged on his own. He still seemed awkward around her, but she hoped a day with him would alleviate that.

James opened the door for them and Donovan made a strange strangled gasp as he looked out into the misty morning.

Bronwen had never heard him do such a thing before and stood next to him to see Thanatos on the doorstep. She too made a noise – a sigh of exasperation.

"What are you doing here, Nasta," Bronwen said, ignoring the disapproving look from Mr Durward.

"I came to see you, my Lady," Thanatos said with a grin. He had discarded his accent and looked more like Bronwen knew him. Even his eyes seemed to have returned to their deep blue and red shades, unnatural for a human.

"I am afraid I am indisposed. I am spending the day with my father."

"Are you indeed?" Thanatos said with slow amusement and looked at Donovan, who had not taken his hand off the door frame. "Perhaps I might join you?"

"No, you may not," Bronwen retorted. She wouldn't let him ruin a rare day with her father.

Thanatos still had not stopped staring at Donovan who spoke in a low and fearful voice that took her aback.

"Do not speak to him like that, Bronwen."

She looked up at her father and saw a small terror in his eyes.

"I do not want to be any trouble. I shall go," Thanatos said graciously and began to leave.

"No, your grace," Donovan said, with a strange emphasis on the title. "You and Bronwen could go on ahead of me. I have business that would only bore both of you. Perhaps we can have dinner together this evening, Bronwen, if that suits you?"

"It suits me greatly. You are very kind, Lord Wintre," Thanatos answered the question meant for Bronwen with a secret smile. "And, my Lady?"

Bronwen was frustrated but could not say so in front of them and was even more frustrated at how torn she was over who she wanted to spend the day with.

Donovan was her father, finally wanting to take the job, but it would be a strained day for the both of them as they tried to fit back into each other's lives.

With Thanatos, it was easier being herself and she felt comfortable with him; saying whatever she thought without unwanted consequences. But it was strained for other reasons. She would have to spend the whole day resisting him and his strange and intriguing ways.

"I suppose it shall have to suit me. But I think it best Alda accompany us," Bronwen said, feeling triumphant at ruining his plans.

"If that is Lord Wintre's wish?" Thanatos said, staring at Donovan. Bronwen was sure she saw his eyes flash red.

"No," her father replied and stared at him just as

intensely. "I believe you to be an honourable man, Prince Thomas. If I have your word that you will bring Bronwen back whole, I will allow it."

"Oh, I always keep my word Donovan," Thanatos said and shifted his gaze to Bronwen. "Every one."

Bronwen pushed past both of them, out the door and towards the waiting horse, knowing she had lost. She heard Thanatos chuckle and she gritted her teeth.

Thanatos's large black stallion nudged Bronwen with his nose as she came close. No carriage was waiting and there was no second horse for her. Bronwen crossed her arms. She knew Thanatos planned for them to share the ride, no matter how she argued. She considered fetching a horse for herself or refusing to spend the day with him, but it would do no good, he would only appear to her in her room no doubt.

"Might I assist you?" Thanatos held out his hand to her as Bronwen looked up at the giant horse. "Something so large can be a little hard to mount."

Bronwen pursed her lips and looked back at her father for help. He made no move to argue about the arrangements. He had defended her against Lord Guild, but had no such desires here. Bronwen made an indignant sound and stomped away from the two men on foot.

Thanatos laughed again and Bronwen sped up to get away from the sound of it. It took her a moment to realise that there were hoofbeats close behind her. They stopped when she heard a growl from Thanatos. She refrained from turning to see. Had his horse been following her and not waiting for his master?

This thought made her feel less defeated and she smiled. There were some creatures Thanatos could not control.

"Do not look so concerned, Donovan," she heard Thanatos say far behind her now. "There are worse things."

Bronwen continued her furious pace even when she heard

the horse and rider galloping to catch up with her. She was by the gates of the estate when the black mass pulled up beside her.

"Is it your intention to walk the entire way?" Thanatos mocked. Bronwen ignored him and continued through the woodland path outside the gates that led to the main road.

"Bronwen, stop." She didn't. "I said stop."

"Why should I?" she snapped. Bronwen knew she sounded like a petulant child and she didn't care.

"Because I asked you to."

"And if I refuse your order?"

"Then I will politely request again," Thanatos said, exasperated. She glanced up at him, he was frowning deeply, unsure about what to do with her. She raised an eyebrow at him and he narrowed his eyes.

"Please, my Lady Bronwen, will you stop for just a moment so that I might speak with you?" It sounded like it physically hurt him to say the words. He was so ridiculous that Bronwen did as he asked.

Thanatos dismounted and stood in front of her. Bronwen turned her face away, wanting to stay mad at him, despite not being entirely sure what she was angry about.

"Thank you," Thanatos sighed, then he grabbed her chin in his hand and turned her face to him, his expression turning dark.

"Who did this to you?" he growled.

Bronwen had forgotten about the bruises on her face. They had faded almost completely, but nothing escaped Thanatos's notice.

Bronwen pulled her chin from his grip. "I walked into a door," she said, making it sound sarcastic somehow.

His eyes bled red and his mouth turned into a snarl. "Qui autem in infernis arderet!" {He will burn in hell}

Bronwen shook her head at him. Thanatos knew it had been Kole, she could see it in his eyes and hear it in his words.

"You have your wish. I will not marry him now."

Thanatos looked at her levelly, his eyes back to normal. "Is this why you are displeased with me?"

"Because you said I could not marry?"

"Because I did not stop him from hurting you."

Bronwen stared at Thanatos. He truly did believe it was his fault. But why? She looked away.

"No," she said. "I am not feeling myself recently, that is all."

It was the truth. Since the incident with Kole, Bronwen had been feeling as though her frustrations were always to the surface, waiting to bubble over. There was little reason for it and she had never felt this way before. Angry, sometimes. Frustrated, yes often, but never so pent up with rage that grinding her teeth and pinching her arm was the only thing stopping her from biting someone's head off.

"Bronwen, will you please get on the horse with me?" Thanatos asked gently. She nodded.

He helped her up and mounted behind her and she felt a little better as they set off again.

"To where are we headed, your grace?" Bronwen said the name sarcastically and he actually laughed, deep and resonating against her straight back. It made her relax again.

"We are going somewhere different today."

"Somewhere far?" Bronwen asked hopefully.

"No," Thanatos said with a smile and pulled Bronwen into him so her breath caught as he murmured in her ear. "Not today."

"Where then?" Bronwen asked, her voice coming out strangely breathy.

"Wolvesey Castle."

"Oh," Bronwen said, slightly disappointed that they would be staying in Winchester. The castle was a ruin and though she had not visited it before, she wasn't excited by the idea.

Thanatos chuckled at her response as if he had been expecting it.

It didn't take them long to get to Wolvesey with it being very close to the cathedral. The clouds were a uniform grey above them, making the broken stones of the outer castle wall monotoned.

Bronwen felt herself getting angry again at the disappointing trip. Thanatos tightened his grip on her waist and she felt herself calm. She wondered if he could sense her feelings and decided she didn't care.

Bronwen closed her eyes and felt herself relaxing back into him, listening to his steady breathing near her ear and strong thumping heart against her back. She shook herself and sat up again to view the rest of the area.

Thanatos took them to a low section of wall and his horse stepped over it easily. They strolled through a crumbling arch into the courtyard and stopped. Thanatos dismounted and reached up to help Bronwen down.

"Does your horse have a name?" Bronwen asked, concerned it would wander off.

Thanatos smiled mischievously. "Kharon."

Bronwen recognised the name and laughed. "The porter to the underworld?"

"You have been doing your research, my Lady. It is difficult to find an animal that can cross the ways after death, so I thought it a suitable name."

"Why not use a real horse while here?"

"Kharon can appear wherever he chooses, as I can. Having to find an alive horse every time would be tedious. Also, he is much faster. His only vice is he keeps eating in this world and being sick."

Bronwen patted the horse's neck. It snorted in contentment.

Wolvesey Castle was called a ruin for a reason. It had been mostly demolished long ago. Only the roots of the structure remained. Everything was very square and grey. It matched the newer building attached to it where the Bishop of Winchester lived except that had a brown roof and well-kept garden.

Bronwen left the horse in the courtyard and headed for the largest of the square structures. Thanatos followed her through the weathered doorway, looking far more interested in the place than Bronwen.

"Do you remember things like this being built?" she asked as she watched him place a hand on the stones thoughtfully.

"If I was around at the time, but there are so many things that have been built over the years across the entire world, so unless it is significant to me, then I do not care to witness every structure humankind deigns to erect. I would never get any work done."

Bronwen thought about the expanse of the world. It was difficult for her to imagine. She had seen the globe her father kept in his drawing room and had always been amazed by how small Britain was compared with other countries. To her, it seemed huge and the distance to Guildford was long enough. She imagined there were places in the world that no human had ever seen and she would like to see them one day, just to know she had been the only one there.

"Have you seen everything on earth?" Bronwen asked. He laughed as they moved through a wider gap in the wall towards a taller, square tower.

"Even I have not seen all the world has to offer and I like that thought."

Bronwen smiled, she liked that thought too, knowing that there would always be new things happening that not even Thanatos could predict or witness. "If I had experienced everything possible then I would struggle to find a reason to stay here."

"You can leave?" Bronwen asked. Stopping to look at him.

"In a sense."

"What do you mean?"

Thanatos smiled at her. "You gave me the impression you did not want to know, my Lady."

Bronwen looked at the walls of the castle, wondering who had lived there and what they had done with their short lives. "I do not want to know all of it."

"Why?"

"For much the same reason you are glad you have not experienced everything. If I knew all the secrets of life, then there would be nothing for me to stay living for."

"I understand more than you know," Thanatos said quietly. "And yes, I can leave, but I would not want to. I enjoy what I do. It may be cruel at times but there is also beauty in it and I believe in the value of my occupation. Things would be very bad if I stopped.

"Everything works with the energy of the Earth; its soul. It has to remain balanced at all times, constantly moving to where it needs to be. Or else things will simply cease functioning. The world would die."

Bronwen wondered if that would be better. For everything to just end. In her current mood, she would have liked to have been the one to do it and struggled to keep such thoughts from consuming her.

She turned to the tower and wanted to be at the top to see the whole castle. There was a small door in the bottom and inside the shadowy, musty block, there were narrow stone steps.

Bronwen began up them carefully. Thanatos stayed close behind her in case she fell.

Bronwen smiled when she reached the top and looked out at the ruins below her. She felt like she was being adventurous. Like how she used to be when she was a child. She used to have to entertain herself during her father's absence. When she wasn't being forced to learn things like dancing, sewing, music and numbers, she would explore for as long as Alda allowed her missing.

One fortunate thing about having a father who ignored her was the freedom that came with it, more than the other girls her age with important parents. At least until Bronwen became a Lady and was expected to stand in line and look pretty.

Alda always scolded her when she came back with cuts and bruises and dirt on her clothes from climbing trees and wading through streams in the woods.

"I should be thankful for your boyish figure, else the neighbours would think Baron Donovan's daughter feral," Alda would say as she scrubbed burrs from the girl's hair. Those had been good days.

"Why did you send me back at all?" Bronwen asked. "Why not simply keep me in the Under-realm with you?"

"I will not make the mistake of keeping someone against their will again. And, I had hoped that after seeing the hardships the world has to offer, you would come willingly."

"Affection does not work like that. Love does not come from a lack of choice. It is the opposite, in fact."

Thanatos watched her thoughtfully. "Do you miss anything of your life?"

Bronwen sighed and looked at the courtyard reclaimed by nature and the Under-realm horse grazing on the grass there. Her life was an adventure now. "I do not think I do. Not truly. This life is restricting and cruel. At least my eyes are open to it now and I have more freedom than I ever had before, despite the deal you and I have made. I am not glad that I was killed but no, I do not miss being alive either."

Thanatos looked at her steadily. He seemed pleased by what she had said, as if she had relieved a burden of his.

"Do not assume that to mean I wish to be with you," Bronwen said quickly, looking at him sternly.

"I would never dream of assuming that," Thanatos said

with a grin as he walked past her and out onto the crumbling wall, up to the very top of the tower. Bronwen followed him, less gracefully. The wind was stronger at the top and pulled at her every way as if deciding the best angle of attack.

"Actually, I lied. I miss being able to sleep and dream."

"Dreaming is not always what you wish. Why wake up to know you cannot have what you desire or suffer in a nightmare you cannot fight or escape from?"

"But you can do things in dreams that are not possible in real life. Even things that *you* are not capable of," she said quickly before he made the point she knew he would make.

"There is very little I am not capable of, my Lady."

Was he capable of love? Not just between a man and a woman, but between friends or family. Bronwen didn't voice her thoughts. She didn't want to add it to things that were already very complicated.

She thought about what Thanatos wanted from her as they stood on the tower together. His whole motive was to have her in his bed, but there was more to it than that. He had said in the beginning he wanted her companionship, in whatever life he was leading, and gave the impression that in the bad times, his role in the world weighed down on him. Perhaps he was looking for someone to relieve that pressure by sharing it?

Bronwen imagined herself in that role, to see how it would feel. She didn't feel strong enough for that. How could she be when she struggled fighting the simplest of conflicts. She had gotten away through luck or help in every situation and had shied away from confrontation if she could help it. But, the more Bronwen studied Thanatos, the more time she spent with him, she knew she was able to comfort him if she was to be dragged back to the Under-realm. The one certainty was it would be on *her* terms; *her* decision to see him.

Bronwen moved to the edge of the tower, looking over the side, down to the hard ground below. It was not so far but she felt an excitement at the danger. Thanatos watched her from the wall where he leant against it, the wind flicking his hair around his head. He smiled at her affectionately when she looked over her shoulder at him, her own hair tickling her cheeks. He looked so youthful and human.

"I understand how lonely you must feel, Thanatos," Bronwen said suddenly.

His expression darkened and he looked away from her so Bronwen couldn't see the hurt in his eyes - the weakness there.

Bronwen turned back to the scenery, feeling giddy at the height. She could see the river Itchen, Winchester Cathedral, St Catherine's Hill. This city had so much more meaning to her now. All these places that had changed her.

"I used to stand on the edge of the balcony at Metrom and lean out until my nerve failed. It wasn't as tall as this, but I knew I was likely to die if I fell in the wrong way. I wondered what it would be like, just to let myself go and tumble through the air. What thoughts would come to mind before death."

"Why did you not jump?" Thanatos's voice was soft and distant. As if he wasn't really there.

"I knew there would be no one there to catch me and that is all I really wanted; a saviour to rescue me from my loneliness. I used to pretend I was a princess trapped in a tower and one day a prince would come and climb to my rescue." Bronwen looked over her shoulder, expecting Thanatos to be laughing at her whims, but his expression was serious. "What foolish things we do when our emotions get the better of us," she said. This time he did smile and pushed away from the wall to stand next to her.

Thanatos held out his hand to her. "May I?"

Bronwen looked at it in confusion. Did he mean to jump

off the edge with her? She found herself reaching out to him and gasped as the ghostly vision of the castle appeared on top of the ruins. It deepened in colour and texture the longer she held his hand. The moat below the building disappeared as the walls became solid.

Thanatos steered Bronwen around so she was looking into the courtyard. It was so busy. Full of people carrying things in and out of the buildings, laughing and talking. Then that wall became solid and Bronwen was inside the tower. It looked so real, just like a dream. The tapestries, the carvings, the smells of meat cooking and the sound of people going about their lives.

She wondered if this had been how he had convinced Kenneth to kill himself. Had he shown him things from the past that he did not want to see. She couldn't imagine what would make Kenneth feel guilty enough to end his life.

The heavy wooden door to the room opened and a young couple entered, holding hands. They looked so happy with one another's company and they embraced and kissed. Bronwen blushed and as they moved towards her, she took her hand back from Thanatos and stepped backwards before he could stop her.

The walls faded away and Bronwen realised too late that she had stepped backwards into empty air and she was falling.

It was too late, she had let herself go, over the edge, her limbs flailing out of control as she spiralled through invisible air currents.

It took a moment for Bronwen to realise she wasn't falling anymore and she opened her eyes, expecting to wake up in the Under-realm like before and instead found Thanatos looking at her with intense eyes.

She looked above her and saw the grey stone of the castle. She was stunned at how far she had fallen and amazed that Thanatos had caught her.

"That was quite a fall, Princess."

Bronwen was breathing heavily through parted lips and hung onto Thanatos's neck tightly. Her cheeks were flushed and hot from the blood rushing in her ears and through her body. She felt tense and relaxed at the same time and she had the irrational need to be with him. To be held and kissed and loved by this demonic creature. To have him protect her and need her - only her.

"Let us return somewhere warm," Thanatos said when they had been staring into each other's eyes for a long while.

Then he leant in towards Bronwen's ear as he murmured the most erotic words she had heard anyone say to her before.

"You are trembling, Bronwen."

VIII

Donovan watched the unholy horse carrying his only child away with the Devil.

Perhaps his future son-in-law? He laughed humourlessly. It was like killing her all over again.

He waited on the porch while the thing went out if sight, just as another rider came trundling towards the house from the opposite direction.

Donovan squinted to see who approached and knew from the large size and dark clothes of the rider that it was Denny.

"Donovan," he said, puffing and out of breath even though he was on a horse.

"What are you doing here?" Donovan demanded. Denny never came to see him during the day and even at night, he only came when it was something important. Donovan's immediate assumption was that someone else in the group had died.

"A... meeting... has been... called," Denny puffed as he dismounted with a thud, the horse complaining as the man yanked on its mane to steady himself.

"What does Velna want now?" Donovan said gruffly.

"Not Velna," Denny said as he awkwardly tried to tie his horse to the marble pillar at the bottom of the porch stairs. He gave in trying to reach around it and loosely knotted the reins to one of the potted trees next to the door. "Kole."

Donovan eyes widened and he turned back into the house, cursing profusely.

"James!" he yelled in the hallway as he headed for his study.

"Yes milord?" Mr Durward entered the hallway, looking anxious from his master's tone.

"Send someone to cancel my meetings for the day and I will not be back tonight." Donovan went to his study, then added in a more regretful tone. "And tell Bronwen I am sorry, I cannot spend the evening with her."

Donovan didn't wait for the butler's reply and locked the door to his study behind him. He knew Denny would wait outside and he wouldn't be long.

He picked up the letter opener on his desk, pulling it out from underneath the ornament of a unicorn, stood protectively above it. He went to the picture frame on the opposite wall, ignoring the portrait of his departed wife staring down at him and ran the letter opener down the side of the picture frame, through the hidden seam that entered the wall.

Donovan heard the lock click as the knife moved it and he used the frame of the picture to turn the painting like a handle and pull the secret door open.

There were no windows in the study, so Donovan didn't have to worry about onlookers as he walked into the hidden room, looking lovingly at the opposing portrait of his wife behind the door, wearing no clothes at all, a subtle smile on her red lips and a crimson cloth pooling at her feet. Despite her being naked, this was the more comfortable looking picture of her. She had been unbearably beautiful and the wicked glint in her eyes always made Donovan's groin stiffen and his heart break.

He turned away, closing the door behind him. There was light in this room, it had been specifically designed for it in an elaborate and intelligent architectural design that could not be seen from the outside of the house. One of the long windows on the landing above was slightly longer than the rest and the bottom of this served as the window to the secret room. From the inside of the house, the wall cut off the bottom of this window and it was not possible from the angle to see that it extended further. Then, from the outside, it just looked like an ordinary decorated window, too high up to get close enough for anyone to see inside.

The room itself was small, no more than a cupboard and full of the darkest implements imaginable; poisons, various knifes, a small chemistry set for making the poisons, vials of different blood samples with labels Donovan had never known the meaning of. The room also had a secret tunnel that led out of the house and came out at a small stone building next to a woodland stream. It was how his wife had snuck out in the night without anyone knowing.

Donovan walked to the back of the room and opened the wardrobe there. Inside was his black cloak and ceremonial mask of the Secuutus Letum.

Donovan looked at it with mixed emotions. It was the symbol of his damnation, his prisoner's garb. He pulled it off the hanger and stuffed it into the bag waiting beneath and left the room hurriedly, making sure to lock the door behind him.

Outside, Denny was sat on the steps, drinking a glass of wine that James had given him. His butler had also had a horse prepared for Donovan.

The two mounted quickly and sped away to find out what the Secuutus had in store for them.

The meetings were held far away from town in an old abandoned water mill and warehouse, once used for grinding grain into flour and storing it in the large barn attached. It took a good few hours to get there and Denny was out of breath again, so they spoke very little. Donovan mainly thought about what Kole was planning.

Kole wouldn't use the fact that Donovan had struck him in the meeting. The Secuutus didn't operate that way, but he could certainly fan an already present lack of confidence in their leader and push Donovan into action over Bronwen. He wasn't sure what he could say if they asked him what he planned to do about her and there wasn't much use in planning something that hadn't been asked yet.

He and Denny stopped by the side of the abandoned mill and dismounted.

Only a few other horses were waiting outside in the cold - Kole's included.

"I will stand by you, Donovan," Denny said before they went in and Donovan was surprised to realise how comforting it was to have Denny as an ally.

They walked through the wooden door and into the room on the left of the mill that used to serve as a living area. Here they changed into their robes in silence.

Donovan was a different person when in his uniform. The mask changed him. All his fears went away. He was in charge of this domain. These people were under his command, *his* orders.

He strode past Denny confidently, who was still trying to squeeze himself into his robe. Donovan didn't blame him for being overweight. If he had spent years only eating porridge and water, he would have taken full advantage of the freedom too, he just couldn't understand why he chose to fool himself by wearing clothes far too small for him.

Outside the door of the meeting room, Donovan spotted two black figures talking. Despite their masks, Donovan knew one of them was Kole, he had spent long enough around the man to recognise the set of his shoulders and the high tilt of his chin. The other must have been Velna as it was distinctly female in shape and she held herself like she knew all men watched her.

Velna saw Donovan coming and swirled away like a wraith into the room. The two of them were never usually allies but when they were, it was well known that trouble would follow. Something dark and dangerous for all.

Kole turned his dark eyes on Donovan.

"I hope the call for this meeting is not personal," Donovan muttered to him.

"*You* made this personal," Kole replied; soft and biting. "You should pray a meeting is all I call."

Donovan allowed himself a grimace behind his mask before he followed Kole.

The room opened up into a cleared space with a high ceiling, criss-crossed with wooden beams covered in green ivy that slithered around the dying wood and down the walls. The floor was clear enough of debris and the only thing in the large room was a sturdy stone table. The only legacy Haydon had left behind. He had hand chiselled the table with its twelve sides from the old grinding wheel of the mill. The black chairs that surrounded it had been donated by Cornell from his own home.

Donovan took his place and studied the others as they entered. He could tell each one of them apart just by the way the stood or walked, hung their heads or held them too high.

He hated every one of them.

Once they were all seated Donovan waited for a crow in the rafters to cease its cawing at some trespasser, then spoke in a voice that was clear and unassailable.

"Meeting commences."

They all removed their masks and placed them down in front of them. There hadn't been much point in putting them on in the first place. It was only for the sake of tradition.

Kole took his off slowly and was the last to place his mask down, doing so more forcefully than the others so the ceramic made a grating noise against the stone table that set Donovan's teeth on edge.

Everyone was staring at his face. His broken nose had been well set and would heal nicely, but he had made no attempt to hide the damage and the bruise that spread across his cheek and eye.

"Did your whore of a sweetheart not take kindly to you, Kole?" Cornell mocked. Any resulting laugh was caught in the throat of the perpetrator when Kole turned a deadly gaze on Cornell.

"I have called this meeting today and I think it has been long overdue," Kole said tightly, looking at each of them and staring the longest at Donovan. "My *sweetheart* has become an uncontrollable nuisance to this group and the time has come to demand something be done."

"The time is convenient to his Lordship now, is it?" Velna spat. "Where were your balls when she was killing Lowell, Haydon and Kenneth? Now that she has caused *you* some personal offence, you turn to us to do something about it!"

Kole's joints clicked as he tightened the fingers on his hand, as if he imagined Velna's throat to be between them.

"Damn it woman, is this not what you wanted?" Kole snapped. "Can I not be excused for showing a little caution when a lack thereof clearly got our comrades killed?"

He indicated with his hand towards the three empty seats around the table. Velna opened her mouth to say something before her sister put a careful hand on her knee. Only Donovan noticed the action and was surprised when Velna sat back in her chair and took a few calming breaths.

"Can we please have a meeting that doesn't involve you two tongue fucking each other?" Maverick said.

"Like he would ever be that fortunate," Velna retorted.

Kole looked close to igniting and Donovan thought it about time to step in.

"What exactly do you propose we do, Kole?"

"I propose you stop playing the father and do something for once, Dux Ducis."

Donovan laughed at Kole's accusation. "Playing the father has kept me alive, unlike the others who chose to reveal themselves to Bronwen. You yourself had a hand in protecting her from one of our own to save face with the Lady – playing the valiant fiancé."

"The fool attacked me!" Kole started but Donovan spoke over him.

"From Kenneth's death, we know Bronwen has help that is beyond us and until we understand that, then we should watch and wait. I have done my part in sacrificing her and our Dominus has chosen to return Bronwen to this world, what makes you so sure she can be killed?"

"She can die," Mara said. A calm voice amongst the animosity.

"*Mara,*" her sister hissed.

"They should know what we know."

"You had best tell us, you two," Kyran said in his best attempt at being relevant in the meeting.

"Put your dick away, boy, no one is impressed," Maverick said, putting a quick end to his son's dominance. Mara looked at Kyran pityingly as he hung his head. Even Velna would not have spoken to her like that.

"The spies Velna and I have in place indicated that Bronwen's bodyguard, Adam Whyms, a spy of your own I think, Kole, was more interested in her than just platonic."

"Platonic?" Maverick questioned.

"It means he wants to have sex with her," Cornell explained. "Don't you read, you moron."

Lindy laughed in a high pitch shrill and Maverick jumped up out of his chair so that it fell over behind him.

"I don't need books to cave your fucking skull in you pompous..."

"Enough," Donovan cut in with a roll of his eyes. The

dynamics of the group had always been strenuous which was one of the reasons it was necessary to have a strong leader. "Sit down, Maverick."

The man did so with stiff acceptance of authority and the smirks of the others slowly faded.

"Continue, Mara," Donovan said, though his stomach churned at what she might say. Her words had made him consider all instances he had seen Adam and Bronwen together. He had never liked the man Kole had insisted on, and now that he thought about it, his looks and body language towards Bronwen had always given him an uneasy feeling in his stomach.

Rape had never been something that appealed to Donovan and he didn't think he would ever get that desperate for something he could pay for. He had fantasized about whether he would have forced himself on his wife, had she been unwilling to have him, but it was difficult to imagine when she had been more willing than him on numerous occasions. He gathered it was more to do with asserting power anyway and he had never been lacking that. He didn't need to rape a defenceless woman to prove himself a man.

"Our sources told us that Adam was looking for chloral hydrate, a new medical drug used to sedate patients – knock people out," Mara added, looking directly at Maverick who clenched his jaw. "We suspected he wanted to use it on Bronwen for... obvious reasons and Velna placed herself in his path and sold him our own cocktail of medicines. Enough to kill everyone at this table in one dose."

"It would have been excruciating," Velna said with obvious delight and Donovan struggled not to keep the disgust from his expression. He had seen what their concoctions of potions could do first hand when they were hunting a difficult group of future demons and had always imagined the women stood around a cauldron like haggard

469

witches from one of Shakespeare's plays.

"So, he must have failed," Cornell said.

"He succeeded," Velna countered, taking over from where Mara left off. "He came into the brothel a few days later and told me he had managed to inject her. He was raving at me that he had killed the bitch, said that she began foaming at the mouth and hadn't been able to breathe. Even a small drop of that stuff would have killed her and she got the whole dose. Trust me, it worked, but she hasn't stayed dead."

The group were quiet as they digested these words. Donovan had wondered why Adam had disappeared so suddenly from service and he was both pleased and disturbed that he hadn't succeeded in raping his daughter. He wasn't sure if her dramatic death was any better, but it wasn't the first time Bronwen had been killed and he saw in the eyes of the others that it would not be the last time either.

"So, you are saying she cannot die?" Kyran asked, confused.

"She can die," Mara said. "But it is temporary."

Maverick slammed his fist down on the table. "This is bullshit! How can we be rid of her if she doesn't fucking die!"

"Maybe you were mistaken, Velna?" Donovan asked, but the thought of a daughter immune to death made even him feel anxious - like a recurring nightmare.

"There is only one way to find out," Kole said. He had been unusually quiet up until then, letting the group come to its own conclusions, ready to fan the fire of disquiet when needed.

"No," Donovan said, surprising even himself. "We wait and watch, as we always have, or risk more of us dying in the process."

"Not if we do it right. It was not difficult to get her the

first time."

"And you think she will fall for that again?"

"Why don't you tell me, Donovan? Seeing as you know her so well?"

The conversation was getting heated between them as the men stared at each other in open aggression.

"Listen to me, Kole..."

"No!" Kole slammed his fist down on the table. "You listen, Donovan. I have carried you so far and I will do so no longer. I told you there would be a consequence for protecting that pathetic daughter of yours. I should have fucked her when I had the chance and perhaps that would have loosened the uptight little cunt!"

"How dare you speak to me like this!" Donovan boomed.

"How dare I? Ha! Did you have this little control over your wife? No wonder she died just to leave you!"

"At least I had her in the first place. Only just now I sent Bronwen away with Thomas Nasta and she was more than eager to go with him alone."

Kole growled and stood up as he pulled a dagger from under his cloak. Lindy gasped and even Velna looked concerned as Kole held it towards Donovan.

The Dux Ducis didn't even flinch. He didn't fear death and he certainly didn't fear Kole. He was weaker than Donovan if he needed a threat to assert himself. Donovan lifted his chin to the man and Kole's angry scowl turned to a grin of satisfaction as he turned back to the table and held his hand over it.

"Kole?" Denny questioned in a panicked voice.

Kole ignored him and breathed in as he pulled the knife over his palm in a swift movement. Everything seemed to happen at once.

"No!" Cornell yelled.

"Shit! Don't do this, Kole," Maverick said in a frightened voice.

Kyran sat forwards in his chair. Mara made to stand but her sister held her back. Denny made a frightened whimpering sound and Lindy was shaking her head.

Kole hadn't stopped staring at Donovan, who was the only one who hadn't shown any emotion at the display, almost daring Kole to do it as he held his hand over the table in a clenched fist, pooling blood from between his fingertips.

"Nothing to say to me now, Lord Wintre?" Kole sneered. "Or are you remember what happened the last time you interrupted a ritual?"

Donovan's eyes widened. How did he know about that? How did he know he had stopped whatever ritual his wife had been trying to perform the night she had killed Bronwen and had made his deal? He had no time to find out.

"I call for Lacessere," Kole announced as he slapped his hand down, splashing his face with his own blood that had made a puddle on the table. A line of it had slithered away to the edge where Donovan sat and the only sound that broke the dead silence was the drip of Kole's blood falling into Donovan's lap.

IX

"Good evening, your Grace," Bronwen said, removing her gloves as she stepped up to the door of the house and turned back to Thanatos. "I have had a most pleasant day."

"As have I, my Lady," Thanatos replied. He hooked Kharon's reins over his saddle and walked up a few paces to Bronwen. He stayed a few steps below so she was still higher than him.

"I would like to call on you again, if I may."

"I would like that," Bronwen said genuinely.

Thanatos took another step up. "Truly?"

"Yes," Bronwen said, but she was a little uncertain now, from the way he looked at her.

He took yet another step and was in front of her.

"Come with me, Bronwen," Thanatos whispered so sweetly that she almost felt herself reach out to him, mind and soul. Her body rocked towards him and pulled back again. She took a step away.

"Be with me. I can open your eyes." He held a hand out to her. Offering himself and all the powers he had to give. "When did you last let your heart decide?"

A shiver when up Bronwen's spine. Only *his* words could ever make her feel like that. Like the earth was tumbling beneath her and nothing was right. And the reason he could do this was because *he* was not right.

He had put on a show for her, seduced her, opened her to him and the possibilities he held. He was a distraction from the truth of her life and the more he pulled on her, the more she wanted to leave with him.

Bronwen slowly reached her hand forward, seemingly of its own accord. It hovered delicately over his. Thanatos did not move while she did this, his hand didn't shift an inch. It was her choice to make in this moment.

Bronwen left her hand there as she stared back into his eyes. They were an impossible colour. The deepest blue with hints of auburn and crimson that seemed to swirl within like an icy fire. She wondered if she was the only one who could see them for what they truly were, or if those too were changed for the benefit of appearance.

Bronwen pulled her hand away and held it to her chest, panting slightly.

Thanatos's face darkened beyond a comprehensible emotion. His hand made a move to reach for her...

"My Lady," Mr Durward's strained voice came from behind her. She tore her eyes away from Thanatos. "I am afraid I have received some terrible news from Guildford."

He held a letter out to her addressed to the house. Bronwen stared at it, a sick feeling in her stomach.

"What is it, James?" she asked, too scared to take the letter for herself.

He swallowed. "I am afraid Mrs Emry was in an accident. Her carriage lost a wheel in the woods and she went for help. Her horse must have been injured from the crash and threw Mrs Emry from it."

"But... she is alright?" Bronwen said though she knew from the look in his eyes what he was about to say.

"I am afraid not, my Lady. She... did not make it."

"I do not understand."

474

Mr Durward swallowed again and lowered his hand which was still holding the letter out to her.

Bronwen stepped towards him, panicking now.

"James, tell me you are lying. Tell me this is some jest. Tell me Lord Guild sent the letter to hurt me."

Durward couldn't look her in the eyes and she spun around to stare at Thanatos who was still there, now looking deeply concerned for her.

She took a step towards him, her eyes pleading and her voice small. "Tell me it is not so. Tell me Josette is still alive."

Thanatos met her eyes where James could not but he did it out of kindness. She needed to know the truth.

"Josette is no longer in the Realm of the living, Bronwen. I am sorry. I did not know until now."

"How... why could you not... you must have..." Bronwen was unable to form a question.

"I do not feel every passing. Her soul does not speak to me as your does and she did not go to the Half-point."

Bronwen turned back to James. If he had thought what they had said was strange, he did not show it.

"Where is Azubuike? I want to speak with him."

"He went to look for you when he heard the news."

"He left the house?"

The pit in Bronwen's tightened and twisted. She had warned Azu not to leave and stay out of sight until she knew what Kole had planned. She had wanted to ask her father for help that day when Thanatos had shown up.

She turned back to him again, wanting to be angry but knowing she needed his help.

"Daemonium, et opus vestrum," she pleaded quietly. He met her eyes. "Help me, please?"

He nodded and mounted Kharon, his hurt from her rejection forgotten at the desperation in her eyes.

"This way," Thanatos said, pulling Bronwen up onto the

horse with him.

Kharon began to run through the trees at a heady speed. Bronwen had to close her eyes tightly as the wind made them water and the fast-moving scenery made her disorientated. She begged for Azu to be alright and for Josette to turn up at her door alive and well and only opened her eyes when Kharon came to a stop.

They were in the woods which had become too dense for a horse. Bronwen heard men laughing close by and jumped down before Thanatos could help her. She sprinted uphill in the direction of the sound.

"Damn this dress!" she cursed as she tripped again on a tree stump. Thanatos helped her up without a word as they ran a short way uphill together. She had no idea where she was, only knew she had to reach her friend.

A gap in the trees revealed a clearing with a single large oak tree in the centre. Bronwen spotted Azu immediately and fell into a sprint towards him.

An arm came out to stop her.

"Wait," Thanatos said. "You have time to think about this before you charge in."

As if to confirm, the lead man with a dagger in his hand addressed the other men; busy tying a noose around Azubuike's neck.

"Do not drop him," he said. "We want this to end slowly."

"Adam," Bronwen breathed. The men in the clearing were too far away to hear and had their backs to her but she knew it was him and recognised his dark coat and slick hair, even pulled up and tied back.

"What is there to consider?" Bronwen asked Thanatos frantically who still had his arm across her path.

"They have weapons." Thanatos pointed out the pistols and daggers in holsters on their belts.

Two of the men yanked on the rope attached to Azu and hoisted him up using the branch of the tree. He made a gargled noise as the noose tightened and the muscles in his neck bulged with the strain.

"And I cannot die," Bronwen argued. How long could a man hang for before he died? Even one as strong as Azubuike?

"It will take time for you to return and Azu does not have that time," Thanatos said. "I have given you gifts, Bronwen. Think of another way."

Bronwen had to begrudgingly admit he was right and turned to look at the scene again. The men had finished hauling Azubuike up towards the canopy of leaves and tied the rope off. Azu was slowly changing colour as the men watched with sick satisfaction.

If only Bronwen could break the rope somehow? She didn't have a knife to throw and doubted that would have any affect anyway. Bronwen concentrated hard on the rope. She had produced a knife from thin air when Kole had threatened her. Surely, she could break a rope using whatever magic Thanatos had given her?

There was a stillness around her and Bronwen didn't think that simply wishing for something to happen strongly enough would work. And Azu, the closest friend she had ever had would die.

He was her anchor, her protector, her friend. He couldn't die, she needed him and if he lived through this, she would tell him about Thanatos and everything that had been going on in her new and strange life.

The stillness turned to a frozen warmth and her body felt like a wind was rushing through her rather than around and over.

A wild crack pulled Bronwen back to the present and her eyes widened in shock as she watched the entire tree, almost in slow motion, rip itself from its roots and collapse to the grassy carpet.

The rope strangling Azu swung him outwards and under

the canopy of the tree as it fell, covering Azubuike and two of the men in a smothering of leaves and branches.

"Shit!" Bronwen exclaimed, cursing in a rare moment. She could still feel her anger within her and decided to use it.

"Not exactly what I meant," Thanatos said, a hint of amused awe in his voice. "He is still alive at least."

Bronwen ran into the clearing before Thanatos had a chance to stop her again.

Adam was cursing in bewilderment when Bronwen tackled him to the ground with all her small amount of weight. There was a brief moment when she didn't think he would fall, then his legs gave way and he collapsed onto his face.

Bronwen clumsily picked up the short blade he had dropped and held it against his neck as she used her knee between his shoulders to hold him down, as Azu had taught her.

"Do not move," she ordered in her most threatening voice and looked up to assess her surroundings.

Two men stood stunned at the tree's abrupt and unnatural fall and the appearance of this strange woman wielding a knife.

Another three men stood beside the tree, one seemingly unconscious with only his arm visible from under the brush, another bald man was still fighting his way out of the encasing branches and a blonde thug appeared to be searching for Azu from the edge of the mass.

"Stand down! Or I will slit his throat!" Bronwen yelled. The man underneath her spat the dirt from his mouth.

"Bronwen?" Adam said in shock, trying to turn to see her face. She pushed him harder into the ground.

"Do not speak you evil bastard," Bronwen hissed, becoming used to the taste of curse words.

Adam laughed. "It is you."

"Do you want me to cut your tongue out?" she threatened,

but it sounded weak even to her.

"I found the nigger!" the blonde man pulled a semi-conscious Azubuike from the leaves; using the rope that was still tight around his neck.

He looked badly beaten with a swollen lip and purple eye. He was covered in cuts from the fall and his arms and legs were tied together. He tried to focus on Bronwen with his one good eye.

"Azu," Bronwen breathed, glad to see him alive.

"Him!" Adam growled. "You came for *him*!"

He bucked his body and Bronwen struggled to keep him down. He gained enough space to pull his pistol out of his holster and point it at Azu.

"No!" Bronwen yelled and grabbed for the gun as Adam cocked it and closed one eye to aim.

She grasped it just as he pulled the trigger and the both looked up to see if the bullet had found its mark.

Azu's eyes were wide as he fell towards the floor. But it was only from the deadweight of the blonde man still holding onto the rope around his neck. Killed in an impossible shot to the head.

Bronwen sighed in relief and Adam wasted no time; rolling over and grabbing for the knife. Bronwen toppled off him and tried to claw at Adam's face. He grabbed at her wrists and easily won the dagger back.

She thought he would kill her then but instead he lurched forwards, his only goal to kill Azubuike who was busy untying his legs and removing his noose.

Bronwen grabbed Adam's ankle desperately. He stumbled and lost the knife again as he caught himself.

Bronwen lunged for it, holding it with both hands so it was pointing skywards just as Adam rolled over onto it.

The blade imbedded itself into his back; though Bronwen could not comprehend how she had managed it.

Adam yelled out in pain and grabbed Bronwen by the hair

as she weakly kicked him, trying to hit something soft.

The other men were pointing their pistol at the two of them, waiting for a gap to fire without hitting Adam. One man became too anxious and fired the bullet into the dirt next to Bronwen's head as Adam pinned her to the floor.

"Idiots!" Adam puffed as he struggled with her. "Get *him!*"

Everyone had been ignoring Azu in the confusion. He had gotten free of all but the ropes around his hands and pulled the pistol from the belt of the dead man beside him.

Azu fired as they moved towards him. His target had been stood close enough for his aim to be true and the man fell to the floor with a hole in his chest.

"You filthy bastard!" the remaining man yelled and pointed his gun at Azu who tried to move out of the way.

The man's aim was not as good but his bullet did graze Azu's leg. He cried out in pain and fell to one knee.

The gunman turned the pistol around and held it like a club as he advanced towards the limping Azu who scrambled for the dagger in the dead man's coat.

Adam yelled out as Bronwen bit deep into his arm like a wild woman. He yanked himself free from her teeth and Bronwen was able to roll out from under him. She spat some of his blood out and he again ignored her and started for Azu.

Bronwen screeched and pulled down on the knife that was still stuck in Adam's shoulder.

He howled and swung his fist at her, striking her for the first time.

Bronwen was dazed by the blow and stumbled to the floor.

Adam pulled the knife out of his back with a grunt and headed straight for Azu; the two men already circling him, decreasing the distance between them.

Bronwen shook herself and staggered forwards only to tumble over one of the fallen men, his chest oozing blood and his eyes unblinking.

His gun was still clutched in his fingers and Bronwen prized it off him.

She tried to stop her hands shaking as she cocked the trigger and pointed it at Adam's back.

He was only a step away from Azu now and she knew he could use the knives he owned. She closed her eyes and fired.

When she opened them, she had only managed to graze Adam's earlobe which bled onto his shoulder. Adam bellowed and swore and turned to face her, a hand to his ear in pain.

His eyes were murderous now, no hint of his announced love remained as he advanced on her.

Bronwen dropped the gun and backed away as he pulled on the chain hanging from his waistcoat. Attached to each end was a heavy weight.

It had not been the weapon that Bronwen had been expecting but as Adam held one of the weights and began to spin the other, so fast that it made a whirring sound through the air, Bronwen knew it would hurt if it hit her or topple her if he wrapped it around her legs.

Thankfully he didn't get the chance to use it, so intent on Bronwen that he did not see Azubuike come from behind him and stab past his sleeveless shirt and coat deep into his armpit.

Adam spat out blood, letting go of the chain and weight which went flying off towards Bronwen. She managed to avoid being hit and watched as Adam crumpled to the floor.

"Azu!" Bronwen yelled. He had forgotten the other two men.

Azu span around and hit the first one square in the jaw before he had a chance to use the butt of his gun to club Azu.

The second man with the bald head hesitated while his mate held his bleeding nose. Not one of them noticed the third man - the forgotten one who had finally awoken from his unconscious state under the tree. He had dragged himself out only to find his friends dead around the clearing. He pulled out his knife and moved behind Bronwen silently.

Azu easily disarmed the bald man and punched him in the stomach, doubling him over. He was about to stab him when he heard Bronwen's outcry.

He kneed the man in the face and turned in horror to see Bronwen cough blood onto her dress. Her body jerked as the long knife was removed from her chest.

The man who had stabbed her seemed to come out of his rage. He dropped the knife to the floor and backed away towards his friends.

"Bronwen," Azu choked.

Bronwen opened her mouth to say something but ended up falling forwards. Azu caught her and fell to the floor with her. His fight with the men forgotten.

"Get out of here," one of them said, grabbing the other two as they ran away towards the trees. "They'll kill him anyway when they find him like this."

Azu rocked Bronwen in his arms, shaking his head, tears came down his face freely as he sobbed.

She wanted to reach out and comfort him and tell him it would be alright, she would return, but her body wouldn't let her move and the pain made it hard to think. The taste of blood in her mouth kept her silent and she could feel herself leaving; familiar to the sensation now.

There was little use in holding on. The men had been right, the authorities would have Azubuike killed if they found him. Bronwen needed to get back as soon as possible, so she let go of life and faded.

X

"Back so soon?" Thanatos said, waving his hand to release her from the chains. Bronwen dropped to the misty floor heavily.

"Is he..."

"Not yet," Thanatos answered her question. "But he will be when they find him with the body of Lady Bronwen, bathed in the blood of white men."

"Send me back, quickly." Thanatos raised an eyebrow at her demand. "Please Thanatos, there is little time."

"And I have little patience for bringing you back to the living. You have had more than enough of my help."

Bronwen looked at him incredulously, rubbing at her painful wrists he made no move to ease.

"But our bargain..." she tried, but Thanatos held up his hand to stop her argument.

"My gift did not say I will continue to send you back should you die from stupidity or carelessness. I have known you for a good few months now, my Lady, and so far, you have been attacked by a tailor, groped by a piano teacher, attacked by men in a forest, murdered by your so-called bodyguard, gotten caught up in a brawl, been beaten by your loving fiancé, fallen from a castle ruin and now you have been killed by a gang of thugs. You take my power to bring you back for granted. You take *me* for granted with little knowledge of the cost." He stalked away from her and she followed at his heels. "If you cannot return yourself, then it will just give me more time in your company."

"A company I shall make unpleasant if you do not let me save Azu!"

Thanatos turned back to Bronwen as the darkness melted and they were in the warm red and blue corridor of his residence.

"So, the viper has a bite, does she?" Bronwen took a step back from the devilish glint in his eyes. "I have asked very little from you in return for my help. So, how far are you willing to go to save your friend?"

Thanatos moved towards Bronwen, his body steering her so he pressed her against the wall. He reached out and placed a hand on her waist, the other beside her head as it rested against the wall.

"Not that...," she said, her voice small again.

"Then you do not care enough," Thanatos whispered.

Bronwen was in turmoil. It was only her virginity. Was that such a high price to pay? Not for the life of a friend it wasn't.

"Will you save him then? Will you keep your word?" Bronwen said, turning her head so her neck was exposed to him. She felt his breath on her skin and felt him run a finger across her shoulder and down towards her breasts. She shivered.

"I told you, I will have you willingly, not begrudgingly." Thanatos pushed away from Bronwen and stalked up the corridor. "Your body is not all I want from you."

Bronwen put her face in her hands a moment, trying to control the tumult of her body. But she wasn't done trying yet and followed him down the flame-lit tunnels of his house.

"What then? I have no more to give you." Before Bronwen

had a chance to beg anymore, Thanatos turned on his heel to face her again.

"One month of the year you can have for yourself. The other eleven are mine to spend with you. Our bargain stands, but it is now to win your one month of freedom. Or all twelve become mine."

"Eleven months is too long," Bronwen despaired. There was no point in the deal if most of it would have to be spent with him anyway. "Two months I will spend with you."

"Two months is too little," Thanatos countered. He stalked through a set of large and decorative double doors, opening both wide without touching them.

"Three then!" Bronwen bargained, just as the doors closed on her. She tried the handle but found it locked - the latch mocking her with its futile clicking.

"Eight..." Thanatos's voice echoed down the empty corridors.

"Four!" she called into the air, resting her back against the door. Her hands still gripping both handles.

"Six. And that is being more than generous."

Bronwen closed her eyes briefly. Half a year. It was a high price to pay, but she knew no way to get back to the living. Thanatos's deals were her only hope of getting out and saving Azu's life. But hers would be an eternity of seeing the demon that tormented her. For six months of the year. She had seen both the good side to him and the bad. She had no guarantee of which she would get during the six.

"He is running out of time, my Lady Bronwen and this is my final offer."

Bronwen gritted her teeth and spun to the door, willing it open she twisted the handles again and was granted access. She stalked into the room but found nothing but empty pillars of stone, cold and dull in colour, the wisps of mist around them made them appear as if they were breathing and Thanatos was nowhere to be seen.

"Six months that are of my choosing each year," Bronwen said, her voice calling back to her in the echoic chamber. "And you must send me back to the living whenever I choose. No more deals, no matter how many times I die. You will send me back every time until this is done."

The door closed behind her and she turned to find it had disappeared entirely. A tickle on the back of her neck made her shiver.

"Deal..." Thanatos's voice whispered in her ear and she felt his warm touch on her waist before he kissed her neck with slow precision and she closed her eyes. Then the kiss deepened and Bronwen felt the sharpness of teeth, at first not unpleasant, but then it radiated outwards into all fibres of her being and the hand on her waist was too tight, fingers digging into her flesh. She thought he might tear into her skin.

Bronwen coughed the left-over blood from her mouth. She felt stiff but that was all and she was glad the knife had been removed before she had died. She tried not to scream in pain as her soul returned to its body.

"Bronwen!" Azu cried out.

Bronwen looked up and found him sat a little way away from her, his knees up to his chest and his cheeks wet from tears.

"Azu," Bronwen smiled. "You are alright." She moved towards him on the floor but he scrambled back away from her and she stopped.

"But you was dead!" Azu exclaimed wildly. "I checked! You was dead!"

"There is something I need to tell you," Bronwen said, bracing herself for his reaction. "I... have been dead before, but I can come back. There is this deal I have..."

"What you talking about?!" Azu said frantically. "This isn't right. This is wrong. No one comes back from being dead."

"Please, let me explain," Bronwen pleaded and held a hand out to him. Azu flinched away and Bronwen felt hot tears threaten to fall.

"What is you? A demon?"

"No," Bronwen answered, but was not completely sure herself. "I was murdered. Sacrificed to the Lord of the Under-realm. That man who was at the ball, Thomas Nasta, he rules the Under-realm and sent me back here to..."

She struggled with the words, "...to find my killers. If I am killed I will come back, I do not need to eat, I do not sleep and there are other things I find that I can do..." Bronwen trailed off, now not sure if she was trying to convince him of her humanity or her damnation. By the look in his eyes, he had already decided which as he processed her words.

Azu had seen it for himself. Seen her die and come back to life again. Bronwen wasn't sure how she would take such news either, but the way he was looking at her made Bronwen panic, she was beyond fearful that he would not understand.

She knew he was a religious man. He attended church with Josette every Sunday. Thinking of Josette made Bronwen even more frantic and her tears released themselves. Loneliness was far less bearable than death.

"Please, Azu," Bronwen tried to reach for him again. "I saved you. Does that not matter?"

"You have been possessed." He grimaced and pulled away from her, rubbing his head with his hands. He was terrified by what he had seen. "You made a deal with the Devil."

"No, Azu. I am not a demon. I am not a witch. Just please, let me explain." Bronwen moved again and Azu stared at her chest where blood spread out from a wound that had killed her.

"Malaika," he spat her nickname acerbically as he stood up away from her in one swift movement. Bronwen allowed him a moment as he took in his surroundings, as if waiting for the other bodies to rise as well and kill him.

He remembered all the horror stories the men in the village had told him as he grew up. He had been taught from a young age about the evil the Devil could do. And to find they had been true.

"How am I to save a thing that does not die?" Azu said finally.

"Please," Bronwen begged. "Just talk to me."

"You're not natural. You're not human." Azu looked down at her. For a moment, he looked conflicted at the tears in her eyes. They had become good friends, he cared for her immensely, but he did not know her anymore. Bronwen had died a moment ago and this new creature terrified him. The incarnation of all the things he had feared in the night. But she looked so sorrowful.

Then, Azu's gaze drifted to the blood on Bronwen's tattered dress again and he found his resolve and turned his back on her.

"Do not leave me..." Bronwen's voice was barely a whisper, almost a sob. She sounded as scared as he was.

Azu paused long enough to reply, before walking from her, leaving her alone in the clearing, cluttered with dead bodies.

"I won't serve demons."

EPILOGUE

The wine-coloured dress Bronwen wore pooled out around her in a perfect circle. She knelt in the dim blue hue of the Under-realm. Thanatos stood watching her, waiting to see what she was doing here.

"I came to thank you," Bronwen said softly. She knew he was there with her, could sense him.

Thanatos took his time to reply. He enjoyed seeing her here, in his home. Her hair was so soft as it fell freely down her back. Her shoulders were exposed and he wanted to feel her skin against his. He never wanted her to leave this place.

"Thank me?"

Bronwen bowed her head and shifted her weight on her knees, the world around her brightened mildly. Thanatos moved closer.

"For what you did, for Azubuike." Bronwen turned her head slightly when he moved so Thanatos could see the line of her jaw and her elegant neck. "And for me."

"If you were to thank me for every deed I do in your honour, our conversations would become very dull indeed."

Bronwen smiled and rubbed her wrists. Thanatos noticed the action. He was about to wave away the chains when he realised she was not confined - as he had first met her all those years ago. Had the Halfpoint accepted her presence again?

When he had felt her soul then, he knew she was meant for him. He had decided he had to have her. So, he sent her back. Nothing grew in the Under-realm, so for twenty-five years he had returned her to the living, to grow and develop into a woman. A woman he needed.

"How did you get here?" Thanatos asked.

"I jumped."

"You killed yourself? Why?"

"To come here. To find you," Bronwen replied. Thanatos stood just a little way behind her now.

"Open your eyes, Bronwen," Thanatos whispered next to her ear. He had moved behind her and placed his hands on her shoulders. She allowed them to remain there. The air felt cooler than before.

Bronwen did as she was bid and gaped at the change around her. Everything was white and there were flakes of snow falling past her eyes. She giggled like an innocent child and turned to face Thanatos who had also changed. He wore a shirt almost as white as the haze of the horizon. His trousers were loose grey and his feet were bare.

"Do you prefer it this way?" Thanatos asked, her haunting brown and blue eyes stood out more in this landscape.

"Very much so."

Her dress was still a brilliant deep burgundy. She held it out and caught a few flakes of snow in the dips of the fabric.

"Why are you here, Bronwen?"

She shuddered at the way he said her name.

"I needed to show you my gratitude," Bronwen replied. She looked at him and it almost hurt how angelic she appeared. It made her harder to resist. Harder to ignore the way her clothes moved over her skin. He stepped closer to her. Wanting to comfort her and smooth the frown on her face. Josette was dead, Azu had left her, Kole was not the man he appeared to be and her father had never been present in her life anyway.

"And how exactly do you wish to do that?" Thanatos smiled and Bronwen's breath caught in her throat. His eyes roamed her body appreciatively and he needed her.

"I have made my decision." Bronwen balled her hands into fists of determination. Thanatos glanced at them then back to her face. Bronwen took a deep breath and relaxed her fingers. Thanatos held his breath.

"I have not the fortitude for what you have tasked me. What I have tasked myself."

Thanatos raised an eyebrow and tried not to imagine how it would feel to bury himself inside her. To feel her around him. To feel her pleasure pulsing with his and to have her look at him with heated eyes and say his name in ecstasy.

"Through dangers untold and hardships..."

"Stop!"

Thanatos shivered and took a step back. There was something wrong here. She should not be saying things like this. Not so soon.

"I am in agony when I am not here," Bronwen continued. "When I am not with you..."

She closed her eyes as she reached behind for the fastenings of her dress and undid each hook, slowly and deliberately.

When she was done, she allowed the fabric to fall to the floor around her bare feet and bare body.

"Bronwen..."

She shivered at Thanatos's voice. Each snowflake was a chaste kiss on her fair skin.

"I choose not to return. I have done all I can do. So, I choose to remain here." Bronwen kept her hands loose at her sides. Thanatos wanted those hands to touch him. He wanted to pin those hands above her head and let her dig her nails in while he brought her to climax. "And, if I am to remain with you, then I see no further reason to deny what we both want. What we both need."

Thanatos closed his eyes. There was something not right here, but he was struggling not to embrace it. He moved close behind her and could smell her sweet scent. Jasmine, and the wild earthy aroma of the forest - of life.

"Say it." Thanatos laid a finger on her naked shoulder and ran it across her neck and down her spine. Bronwen shivered again and tipped her head to the side. He kissed her, tasted her skin and that sweet soul of hers.

"Habes meum..."

Thanatos sat up, breathing heavily. He was in his study, alone. He had awoken from a sleep and looked down at his groin to see the effects it had had on him. It was a dream and his encounter with Bronwen had been an illusion of the mind.

Thanatos shuddered at the memory. He had no need for such chimera. He had not dreamt in centuries. He had not slept in centuries. Not since...

No, it cannot be...

Not here. Not now...

She cannot be roaming the earth again...

NEQUE IN
FINEM.

{Never the end}

CHERRY STONES

*A preview from book two in the dead
tempted series*

PROLOGUE

She twirled her curly hair through her
fingers as she stared through the night at the gentle glow of
the city; illuminating the bare treetops as if it were ablaze.

It had rained not too long ago. The ground reeked of it
and the river was high in its banks and fast-flowing under
the bridge the woman stood on.

Despite the lack of moon, she could clearly make out the
fluffy mess of plant life scattered across the stones of the
bridge, appearing to blow in the breeze to the hum of birds,
the scampering of rodents and the chirping of crickets.

The woman smiled, flicked her hair over her shoulder and
stepped to the centre of the bridge, cobbles cold on her bare
feet. Her curls fell past her waist and darkness made it even
harder to tell its true colour. Was it red like fire, gold like
the sun, orange like the dawn or crimson like blood?

The woman's appearance was made all the more striking
by her attire. It was plain and tightly fitting like a silken shift
and was pure white with gold embroidery around the hem.
The thin material and the slit up one side that exposed her
leg was scandalous for the time, but the woman did not

know that and the cold did not bother her.

She stopped in the centre of the bridge and could hear the erotic heartbeat of the men that waited for her underneath.

It was intoxicating.

She briefly considered letting them have her willingly but discarded the idea when they scrambled out from under the bridge; like trolls asking for penance before she be let passed.

Though she was partial to a messy traveller, these dishevelled creatures, half-starved with madness in their eyes, were somewhat unappealing to the attractive woman. And she had more interesting things to do.

"Out alone are ya?" one of them slurred, blocking her path with a second man. "Don't ya know you gotta pay the toll to pass?"

So, they were trolls then. She turned when she heard a growl behind her and saw a third man stood holding three large dogs at bay, conveniently one for each man. They looked terribly underfed and their fur was matted and infested, but they were still powerful creatures.

"I am afraid I have no gold to offer you," the woman said in a light voice, totally unperturbed by her situation.

"Money won't keep us warm tonight but your mouth around my cock might help a bit."

The woman raised an eyebrow. "Well, it sounds like male tastes have changed very little since I have been away."

"What you talking about?" the first man demanded - the leader of the pack.

The woman just smiled at him and the men began to look a little unnerved by her reaction.

"You a nutter or something?" the leader said.

"Not in this life," the woman replied. "I would quite like to pass. Perhaps once you have bathed, I would be willing to negotiate as I would not like to get my dress dirty before I reach my destination."

"I'll make you dirty, be sure of that," the lead man took a step forward with a salacious grin.

"I don't know if I want'a be doing no loony," the second man said, looking dubious as his leader continued to advance.

"What's it matter?" the man replied, putting his knife away and undoing his belt. "A whore's a whore."

The woman said nothing, she just kept smiling as she leant back on the wall of the bridge, her blue eyes alight.

"If she tries anything, let 'er 'ave the dogs."

As the man grabbed for her, she spun gracefully out of the way and brought her knee up into his groin. When he crumpled forwards, she used his momentum to slam his head into the stone of the bridge and then pushed him over the edge and into the river.

The woman listened to his sputtering and cursing when he came up for air, trying to swim for the bank as he was taken away by the fast-flowing water.

"I did say he must bathe first," she explained to the other men, stunned and angry.

"You bitch!" the man holding the dogs said, the animals becoming more agitated from their master's mood. He let them go and allowed them to run headlong towards the woman. She remained calm as the hounds came closer and when they reached her, they stopped and sat down at her feet, panting and wagging their tails.

"You poor creatures," she said and bent down to stroke the animals gently.

"What are you doing you fucking mongrels!" the man yelled at his disobedient pets. "Attack or I will beat you bloody and throw you in the river!"

The woman shook her head. If only he knew how much of a mongrel he was. How history had diluted his blood even more than these sorry canines.

She lifted the dogs' faces to look into her eyes.

"You best do as your master tells you, my loves."

The dogs stood up again as the woman straightened, growling low so their bodies vibrated. Then, one ran straight for the man who had held them. He didn't look concerned until the beast snarled and jumped onto the man's arm, sinking its teeth in, refusing to let go even as the man tried to shake him off, screaming in agony.

"The fuck?" the last man said, wisely backing away. The woman turned towards him then glanced at the dogs who were gazing up at her in adoration. One nod from her and the two of them ran off together.

The man began to flee but he was no match for the dogs' speed and one soon had his ankle in its mouth. The third dog ran around the bridge, straight for the lead man who had just dragged himself out of the water. He sensibly jumped back in after seeing what had happened to his friends and began to swim away.

The woman sighed and stroked a bit of moss that was growing from the cracks of the stone bridge, listening to the men yell as they retreated, the dogs hounding them all the way.

Some things never changed. Men were still asserting their dominance over women; sex being their favourite method.

One of the dogs had returned to her, his tail between his legs. She studied it for any sign of harm and it began coughing, its hackles raised and a strange gurgling coming from its chest.

The woman watched with interest as a slimy green snake slithered from the dog's mouth onto the bridge. Once it was free the dog hopped away, whining quietly.

The snake reared up, showing its red underside and spat at the woman who shook her head at it.

"A serpent? How biblical of you," she said, bored.

The snake folded back on itself and turned to ice, then shattered into crystal shards that crushed beneath the feet of the man who replaced it.

"And the three dogs were not?" the man said in an equally amused voice. The two smiled at each other before the man's features turned to angry suspicion.

"What are you doing here?" he demanded in a voice that any normal person would have answered immediately.

"I sensed a disturbance in the..."

"Don't do that," the man snapped. The woman grinned wider when she noticed the shudder he tried to hide.

"But you used to love that game."

The man said nothing which was answer enough for the woman whose eyes glittered at the possibilities of what could have made him so defensive. She could see it already in the way he stood in the centre of the bridge, his shoulders wide and arms by his sides, blocking her path to the city.

"It has been a long time since when last you made such a connection, Ha..."

"It is Thanatos here."

"Is it so?" the woman said pushing herself away from the wall and circling Thanatos, appraising his new look. He changed himself so often that she imagined even he could not remember how he looked before he became master of the Under-realm.

"And how should I fashion myself in this land? Eve? Sariel? Eris, perhaps?" she grinned at Thanatos who narrowed his eyes. "Corinna, I think. I have not yet worn the name. It suits me, does it not?"

"You were never a maiden," Thanatos scoffed.

"And who do I have to thank for that?" Corinna accused but her tone was still jovial as she leant against the wall, casually sliding her leg out of the slit in her dress.

"What are you doing here?" Thanatos demanded again, losing his patience.

"I came to see you of course," Corinna said sweetly. "Are you not pleased to see me? Thanatos?"

"Why now, *Corinna*?" he demanded.

She leant back over the wall, smelled the air, felt the cold breeze over her skin, listened to a distant bell toll the third hour. Time. All the earth ever had was time.

"One of my own was killed," Corinna said, sounding sad for the first time. "She called to me before she passed to your Realm and returned what magics she had borrowed. There is something amiss here. Something you are trying to hide and I intend to discover it."

"What care have I for one of your Lamia?"

"Den ntrépesai pou tous les étsi?" {How dare you say such a thing?}

Corinna put a hand to her heart in mock offence, though she was not angry. Thanatos knew that insulting Corinna's precious witches was very likely to enrage the woman and Corinna knew he was only doing it to distract her.

She grinned. "You have something here. Something you are hiding. I want to know what it is. And, I want to play."

Corinna started to walk across the bridge, the city in her sights. It had been so long since she had set foot on the earth amongst the humans Thanatos minded. It would be fun seeing how things had changed and what had remained the same.

Thanatos held a hand out to block her path. She looked at him, his handsome face, changed once again to suit the time he was in. There was obvious disapproval in his eyes and irritation and something else, concern? Fear perhaps? It surprised Corinna to see it there and angered Thanatos when he realised what she saw.

There would be fun to have here indeed.

"Do not think to cross me, Corinna."

"I would not dare," she said sweetly.

Corinna stroked the wall as she glided away from Thanatos. He allowed her to leave and once she was gone, he noticed new growth on the bridge wall where she had touched it. Little white flowers had sprouted there with the occasional red petal.

Corinna's presence here would complicate things with Bronwen, but perhaps Thanatos could use it to his advantage somehow?

He remembered how the snow looked kissing Bronwen's soft skin in his dream. But that was all it was. A distant dream, caused by Corinna and her irritating blend of power. He could have fought it, of course, he was far more powerful than she. But when unprepared for her arrival, Corinna had been known to make his life hell.

Thanatos grimaced and the foliage frosted over and died. He knew it had been likely that Corinna would come to nose around his business and delight in involving herself in his affairs but he had hoped to be more progressed in his courtship of Bronwen when that happened.

He needed more time. He needed to lead Corinna astray. Keep her attention for a while. At least until he had repaired what damaged he may have done to his relationship with Bronwen when he had forced her into another deal. A deal to save her friend who had ultimately abandoned her.

Another problem to solve.

He felt as though he was putting out fires when really, he wanted to start them.

Also by RMRayne

THE DEAD TEMPTED SERIES
Pomegranate Seeds
Cherry Stones
Apple Core

ARAMAN

You can find more from RMRayne on her website
www.rmrayne.co.uk

Made in the USA
Monee, IL
18 January 2023

25514008R00291